Then I'll Come Back To You

by

Larry Evans

Double 9 BOOKS

Then I'll Come Back To You

by Larry Evans

ISBN: 978-93-73403-59-5

Published by

DOUBLE 9 BOOKS
2/13-B, Ansari Road
Daryaganj, New Delhi – 110002
info@double9books.com
www.double9books.com
Tel. 011-40042856

ABOUT THE AUTHOR

Larry Edward Evans was an American novelist and playwright whose work captured the spirit of early 20th-century storytelling through both print and stage. Known for his compelling narratives and emotionally resonant characters, Evans authored several novels and stories that were widely adapted for silent films. His best-known works include Then I'll Come Back to You and Once to Every Man, the latter of which was adapted as The Fighting Heart in 1925. Many of his stories, such as The Painted Lady, found new life on screen, being reinterpreted multiple times under different titles, including When a Man Sees Red, The Painted Lady, and Pursued. Evans' story Conahan was transformed into the film The Silent Lie, later reissued as Camille of the Yukon. His presence in the literary world extended to respected publications like Metropolitan Magazine, where he was listed among its notable contributors during World War I. A number of his film adaptations were scripted by celebrated screenwriters like Frances Marion. Evans died in May 1925 from tuberculosis, leaving behind a body of work marked by romance, moral struggle, and a sensitivity to human emotion.

CONTENTS

TO

The Memory of
My Mother

CHAPTER I
I DON'T MIND IF I DO!

That year no rain had fallen for a score of days in the hill country. The valley road that wound upward and still upward from the town of Morrison ran a ribbon of puffy yellow dust between sun-baked, brown-sodded dunes; ran north and north, a tortuous series of loops on loops, to lose itself at last in the cooler promise of the first bulwark of the mountains. They looked cooler, the distant wooded hills; for all the shimmering heat waves that danced and eddied in the gaps and glanced, shaft-like, from the brittle needles of the pines which sentineled the ridges, they hinted at depths to which the sun's rays could not penetrate; they hinted at chasms padded with moss, shadowed and dim beneath chapel arches of spruce and hemlock, even chilly with the spray of spring-fed brooks that brawled in miniature rocky canyons. And they made the gasping heat of the valley a little more unendurable by very contrast.

Since early afternoon Caleb Hunter had been sitting almost immobile in the shade of the trellis which flanked the deep verandas of his huge white, thick-pillared house on the hill above the river. It was reminiscent of another locality—the old Hunter place on the valley road. When Caleb Hunter's father had come north, back when his loyalty to a flag and his pity for a gaunt and lonely figure in the White House had been stronger than bonds of blood, he had left its counterpart down on the Tennessee. Afterward, with one empty sleeve pinned across his breast, he had directed with the other hand the placing of the columns. And finally, when he had had to leave this home in turn, along with its high, white painted walls and glossy green shutters, he had passed down to his son his inborn love of the warmth, his innocent delight in indolence—and an unsurpassed judgment of mint. The mint bed still lay where he had located it, to the west of the house, moist and fragrant in the shadow.

Caleb Hunter had been drowsing contentedly since early afternoon, his chin on his chest and the bowl of his pipe drooping down over his comfortably bulging, unbuttoned waistcoat. The lazy day was in his blood and even the whine of the sawmills on the river-bank, a mile or more to the south, tempered as it was by the distance to the drone of a surly bumble-bee, still vaguely annoyed him. Tiny dots of men in flannel shirts of brilliant hue, flashing from time to time out across the log-choked space between the booms, caught his eye whenever he lifted his head, during the passage of a green-sprayed glass from the veranda rail to his lips, and almost reminded him of the unnatural altitude of the mercury. He, without being analytical about it, would have preferred it without the industry and the noise, even softened as both were by the distance.

Morrison had changed since Caleb Hunter's father topped with the white-columned house that hill above the river. In those days it had been little more than a sleepy, if conservatively prosperous and self-sufficient, community, without industry of any sort, or, it might be added, ambition or seeming need of one. The Basin where the river widened and ran currentless a mile or two from bank to bank, in Caleb's father's time for weeks and weeks on end often had showed no more signs of activity than a dawdling fisherman or two who angled now and then and smoked incessantly. And now even the low-lying foothills in which the elder Hunter had tried to see from homesick eyes a resemblance to the outguard of his own Cumberlands were no longer given over to pasturage. They had taken on an entirely different aspect.

The northern streets of the town were still dotted with the homes of those families who had been content with just the shade and the silence and the sheen of the river, and an ample though inaugmented income. But the outside world, ignoring the lack of an invitation too long in the coming, had in the last year or so grown in to meet it more than half way. From the Hunter verandas a half-dozen red-roofed, brown-shingled bungalows, half camps and half castles, were visible across the land stretches where the cattle had grazed before. And just beyond Caleb Hunter's own high box hedge, Dexter Allison's enormous stucco and timber "summer lodge" sprawled amid a round dozen acres of green lawn and landscape gardening, its front to the river.

To Dexter Allison's blame or credit—the nature of the verdict depending entirely upon whether it was rendered by the older or the newer generation—was laid the transformation of Morrison, the town proper. Caleb Hunter had known Allison at college, where the latter had been prominent both because of the brilliance of his wardrobe and the reputed size of his father's steadily accumulating resources. Since that time seven-figure fortunes such as the younger Allison had inherited, had become too general to be any longer spectacular. But Dexter Allison's garments had always retained their insistent note. Hunter himself had sold Allison the ground upon which the stucco house stood; he had heartily agreed that it was an ideal spot for a loafing place—and the fishing was good, too! Now whenever Caleb thought of those first conferences which had preceded the sale, and recalled Allison's accentuation of the natural beauties of the spot, Caleb allowed himself to smile.

The fishing was still far above reproach, a little further back country—and Dexter Allison owned the sawmills that droned in the valley. His men drove his timber down from the hills in the north; his men piled the yellow planks upon his flat cars which ran in over his spur line that had crept up from the south. His hundreds and hundreds of rivermen already trod the sawdust-padded streets of the newer Morrison that had sprung into being beyond the bend; they swarmed in on the drives, a hard-faced, hard-shouldered horde, picturesque, proficient and profane. They brought with them color and care-free prodigality and a capacity for abandonment to pleasure that ran the whole gamut of emotions, from raucous-roared chanties to sudden, swift encounters which were as silent as they were deadly. And they spent their money without stopping to count it.

The younger generation of the older Morrison was quick to point out the virtues of this vice. And after a time, when the older generation found that the rivermen preferred their own section of the town, ignoring as though they had never existed the staid and sleepy residential streets above, they heaved a sigh of partial relief and tried to forget their proximity.

Little more than a year had been required for that transformation. The boards of some of the newer shacks down river were still damp with pitch. And twice during that period Dexter Allison had come into the hills to take up a transitory abode in the stucco house which had been quite six months in the building:—once, two years before, when he had disappeared into the mountains upon a prolonged fishing trip, to return fishless but with an astonishing mass of pencilled data and contour maps; and the second time for an even longer stay, a year ago when the mill was being erected.

Since then the stucco and timber place had been closed, with no one but a doddering old caretaker and a gardener or two about the premises, until early that last hot August week. On Monday Caleb Hunter had noticed that the blinds had been thrown open to the air; on Wednesday, from his point of vantage upon the porch, he had watched a rather astounding load of trunks careen in at the driveway, piloted by a mill teamster who had for two seasons held the record for a double-team load of logs and was making the most of that opportunity to prove his skill. And the next morning the tumult raised by a group of children racing over the shorn lawns had awakened him; he had descended to be hailed by Dexter Allison's own booming bass from behind the intervening high box hedge.

It was the hottest day of the hottest fortnight that the hill country had known in years. The very temperature gave color to Allison's statement that the heat had driven them north from the shore—him and his wife and Barbara, their daughter of ten, and the half-dozen or more guests whose trunks, coming on the next day, made an even more imposing sight than had Allison's own. And yet as he sat there in the shadow, methodically pulling upon his pipe, Caleb Hunter smiled from time to time, reminiscently. He last of all would have been the one to admit that the owner of the big stucco place and the mills, and—yes, of the newer Morrison itself—had not given a good account of the talents and tens of talents which had been passed down to him. But the use of so much evasion, where no evasion at all seemed necessary, rather puzzled as well as amused Caleb; and yet, after all, this merely branded him as old-fashioned, so far as the newer business methods were concerned which were crowding into Morrison. Allison's way of going about a thing made him think of the old valley road that wound north in its series of loops on loops; and yet, reflecting upon that parallel, he had to admit to himself, too, that the road achieved final heights which, in a straightaway route across country would have necessitated more than a few wearisome and heart-breaking grades.

The comparison pleased Caleb. He was nodding his head over it as he buried his nose in the mint-sprayed glass again, when a haze of dust to the north caught his vagrant attention. Quite apparently it was raised by a foot-traveler, and the latter were not frequent upon that road, especially foot-travelers who came from that direction. Trivial as it was, it piqued his interest, and he lay back and followed it from lazily half-closed eyes. It topped a rise and disappeared—the dust cloud—and reappeared in turn, but not until it had advanced to within a scant hundred yards of him could he make out the figure which raised it. And then, after one sharp glance, with a quick intake of breath, he rose and went a trifle hastily out across his own lawn toward the iron picket fence that bordered the roadside. He went almost hurriedly to intercept the boy who came marching over the brow of the last low hill.

Caleb Hunter, particularly in the last year or so, had seen many a strange and brilliant costume pass along that wilderness highway, but as he hung over the front gate he remembered that none of them had ever before drawn him from his deep chair in the shadow. For him none of them had ever approached in sensationalism the quite unbelievable garb of the boy who came steadily on and on—who came steadily nearer and nearer.

With a little closer view of him the watching man understood the reason for the dense cloud of dust above the lone pedestrian. For when the boy raised his feet with each stride, the man-sized, hob-nailed boots which encased them failed to lift in turn. Indeed, the toes did clear the ground, but the heels, slipping away from the lean ankles, dragged in the follow-through. And the boy's other garments, save for his flannel shirt and flapping felt hat, were of a size in keeping with the boots.

His trousers had once been white cotton drill, but the whiteness had long before given up the unequal struggle against grime and grease and subsided to a less conspicuous, less perishable grey. They had been cut off just below the knees and, unhemmed, hung flapping with every step he took above a stretch of white-socked, spindly shanks. But it was the coat he wore which held Caleb spellbound. It was of a style popularly known as a swallowtail, faced with satin as to lapels and once gracefully rounded to a long, bisected skirt in the rear. The satin facings were gone and the original color of the fabric, too, had faded to a shiny, bottle-green. But the long skirts—at least all that was left of them—still flapped bravely, as did the trousers. For they, like the nether garments, had been cut off, with more regard for haste than accuracy, so that the back of the coat cleared the ground by a good foot and a half. The sleeves, rolled back from two slender, browned wrists, were cuffed with a six-inch stretch of striped, soiled lining.

For a time Caleb had been at a loss to make out the object which the boy carried upon one shoulder, balanced above a blanket tight-rolled and tied with string. Not until the grotesque little figure was within a dozen paces of him did he recognize it, and then, at the same moment that he caught a glimpse of an old and rusted revolver strapped to the boy's narrow waist, he realized what it was. The boy was toting a double-springed steel trap, big enough it seemed to take all four feet of any bear that ever walked—and it was beautifully dull with oil!

Caleb stood and stared, mouth agape. A moment or two earlier he had had to fight off an almost uncontrollable desire to roar with laughter, but that mood had passed somehow as the boy came nearer. For the latter was not even aware of his presence there behind the iron fence; he was walking with his head up, thin face thrust forward like that of a young and overly eager setter with the bird in plain sight. The world of hunger in that strained and staring visage helped Caleb to master his mirth, and when, at a tentative cough from him, the small figure halted dead in his tracks and wheeled, even the vestige of a smile left the wide-waisted watcher's lips. Then Caleb had his first full view of the boy's features.

There were wide, deep shadows beneath the grey eyes, doubly noticeable because of the heavy fringe of the lashes that swept above them; there was a pallid, bluish circle around the thin and tight-set lips. And the lean cheeks were very, very pale, both with the heat of the sun and a fatigue now close to exhaustion. But the eyes themselves, as they met Caleb's, were alight with a fire which afterward, when he had had more time to ponder it, made him remember the pictured eyes of the children of the Crusades. They fairly burned into his own, and they checked the first half-jocular words of greeting which had been trembling upon his lips. His voice was only grave and kindly when he began to speak.

"You—you look a trifle tired, young man," he said then. "Are you—going far?"

The boy touched his lips delicately with the point of his tongue. His gravity more than matched that of his questioner.

"Air—air thet the—city?"

The words were soft of accent and a little drawling; there was an accompanying gesture of one thumb thrown backward over a thin shoulder. But Caleb had to smile a little at the breathless note in the query.

"The city?" he echoed, a little puzzled. "The city! Well, now—I—" and he chuckled a bit.

The boy caught him up swiftly, almost sharply.

"Thet's—ain't thet Morrison?" he demanded.

And then Caleb had a glimmer of comprehension. He nodded.

"Yes," he answered quietly. "That's the city. That's Morrison down there."

The shoulders of the ancient coat lifted and fell with a visible sigh as the strange little figure turned again, head keenly forward, to gaze hungrily down at the town in the valley. And Caleb translated that long-drawn breath correctly; without stopping to reason it out, he knew that it meant fulfillment of a dream most marvelous in anticipation, but even more wonderful in its coming true. Words would have failed where that single breath sufficed. The man remained quiet until the boy finally turned back to him, eased the heavy trap to his other shoulder and wet his lips once more.

"I thought it war," he murmured, and a thread of awe wove through the words. "I thought it est nachelly *hed* to be! Haow—haow many houses would you reckon they might be daown—daown in thet there holler?"

The owner of the white-columned house gave the question its meed of reflection.

"Well, I—I'd say quite a few hundred, at least."

The odd little figure bobbed his head.

"Thet's what Old Tom always sed," he muttered, more to himself than to his hearer. "An'—an' I guess I ain't never rightly believed him till naow." And then: "Is—is New Yor-rk any bigger?" he asked.

The man at the picket fence smiled again, but the smile was without offense.

"Well, yes," he answered. "Yes, considerably bigger, I should judge. Twice as large, at least, and maybe more than that."

The boy did not answer. He just faced about to stare once more. And then the miracle came to pass. Around a far bend in Dexter Allison's single spur track there came careening an ashmatic switch engine with a half-dozen empty flats in tow. With a brave puffing and blowing of leaky cylinder heads, it rattled across an open space between piles of timber in the mill-yard and disappeared with a shrill toot of warning for unseen workmen upon the tracks ahead. The boy froze to granite-like immobility as it flashed into view. Long after it had passed from sight he stood like a bit of a fantastic figure cut from stone. Then a tremor shook him from head to foot, and when it came slowly about Caleb saw that his small face was even whiter than it had been before beneath its coat of tan and powdery dust.

He swallowed hard, and tried to speak—and had to swallow again before the words would come.

"Gawd—I—may—die!" ho broke out falteringly then. "There goes a injine! A steam injine—wan't it?"

Long afterward, when he had realized that the boy's life was to bring again and again a repetition of that sublime moment of realization—a moment of fulfillment unspoiled by surfeit or sophistication or a blunted capacity to marvel, which Caleb had seen grow old and stale even in the children he knew, he wondered and wished that he might have known it himself, once at least. Years of waiting, starved years of anticipation, he felt after all must have been a very little price to pay for that great, blinding, gasping moment. But at the time, amazed at the boy's white face, amazed at the hushed fervor in the words he forgot,—he spoke before he thought.

"But haven't you ever seen an engine before?" he exclaimed.

As soon as the question had left his lips he would have given much to have had it back again; but at that it failed to have the effect which he feared too late to check. Instead of coloring with hurt and shame, instead of subterfuge or evasion, the boy simply lifted his eyes levelly to Caleb's face.

"I ain't never seed nuthin'," he stated patiently. "I ain't never seed more'n three houses together in a clearin' before. I—I ain't never been outen the timber—till today. But I aim to see more, naow—before I git done!"

The man experienced a peculiar sensation. The boy's low, passionlessly vehement statement somehow made him feel that it wasn't a boy to whom he was talking, but a little and grave old man. And suddenly the desire seized him to hear more of that low, direct voice; the impulse came to him and Caleb, whose whole life had been as free from erratic snap-judgments as his broad face was of craft, found joy in acting upon it forthwith, before it had time to cool.

"The view is excellent from my veranda," he waved a hand behind him. "And—you look a little warm and tired. If your business is not of too pressing a nature—have you—" he broke off, amazed at his helpless formality in the matter—"have you come far?"

And he wondered immediately how the boy would receive that suggestion that he hesitate, there with the "city" in front of him, a fairy-tale to be explored. And again he was allowed to catch a glimpse of age-old spirit—a glimpse of a man-sized self-discipline—beneath the childish exterior.

The boy hesitated a moment, but it was his uncertainty as to just what Caleb's invitation had offered, and not the lure of the town which made him pause. He took one step forward.

"I been comin' since last Friday," he explained. "I been comin' daown river for three days naow—and I been comin' fast!"

Again that measuring, level glance.

"An' I ain't got no business—yit," he went on. "Thet's what I aim to locate, after I've hed a chance to look around a trifle. But I am tired a little, an' so if you mean thet you're askin' me to stop for a minit—if you mean thet you're askin' me that—why, then … then, I guess I don't mind if I do!"

"That's what I mean," said Caleb.

And the little figure preceded him across his soft, cropped lawn.

CHAPTER II
THE LOGICAL CUSTODIAN

Caleb Hunter had never married, and even now, at the age of forty and odd, in particularly mellow moments he was liable to confess that, while matrimony no doubt offered a far wider field for both general excitement and variety, as far as he himself was concerned, he felt that his bachelor condition had points of excellence too obvious to be treated with contumely. Perhaps the fact that Sarah Hunter, four years his senior, had kept so well oiled the cogs of the domestic machinery of the white place on the hill that their churnings had never been evidenced may have been in part an answer to his contentment.

For Sarah Hunter, too, had never married. To the townspeople who had never dared to try to storm the wall of her apparent frigidity, or been able quite to understand her aloof austerity, she was little more than a weekly occurence as dependable as the rising and setting of the sun itself. Every Sunday morning a rare vision of stately dignity for all her tininess, assisted by Caleb, she descended from the Hunter equipage to enter the portals of the Morrison Baptist church. After the service she reappeared and, having complimented the minister upon the sagacity of his discourse, again assisted by Caleb, she mounted to the rear seat of the surrey and rolled back up the hill.

That was as much as the townspeople ever saw of "Cal Hunter's maiden sister" unless there happened to be a prolonged siege of sickness in the village or a worse accident than usual. Then she came and camped on the scene until the crisis was over, soft-voiced, soft-fingered and serenely sure of herself. Sarah had never married, and even though she had in the long interval which, year by year, had brought to Caleb a more placid rotundity grown slender and slenderer still, and flat-chested and sharp-angled in face and figure, Caleb knew that underneath it all there had been no shrinkage in her soul—knew that there were no bleak expanses in her heart, or edges to her pity.

They often joked each other about their state of single blessedness, did Caleb and his sister. Often, hard upon his easy boast of satisfaction with things as they were, she would quote the fable of the fox and the high-hanging grapes, only to be taunted a moment later with her own celibacy.

But the taunt and the fable had long been stingless. For Sarah Hunter knew that one end of Caleb's heavy gold watch chain still carried a bit of a gold coin, worn smooth and thin from years of handling; she knew that the single word across its back, even though it had long ago been effaced so far as other eyes were concerned, was still there for him to see. And Caleb, rummaging one day for some lost article or other, in a pigeonhole in Sarah's desk in which he had no license to look, had come across a picture of a tall and black-haired lad, brave in white trousers and an amazing waistcoat. Caleb remembered having been told that he had died for another with that same smile which the picture had preserved—the tall and jaunty youngster. And so their comprehension was mutual. They understood, did Caleb and his sister.

But sure as he was of Sarah's fundamental kindness, Caleb experienced a twinge of guilty uncertainty that August afternoon as he closed the iron gate behind the grotesque little figure which had already started across his lawn. For the moment he had forgotten that the sun was low in the west; he had overlooked the fact that it was customary for the Hunter establishment to sup early during the warm summer months. But when he turned to find Sarah watching, stiff and uncompromising, from the doorway, he remembered with painful certainty her attitude toward his propensity to pick up any stray that might catch him in a moment of too pronounced mellowness—stray human or feline or lost yellow dog.

Sarah's gaze, however, was not for her brother at that moment. Her eyes were fixed unswervingly upon the figure in the once-white drill trousers and bobbed swallow-tail coat and shuffling boots. She was staring from wide and, Caleb noted, rather horror-stricken eyes at the huge steel trap above the blanket pack. But the boy who must have received her glance full in his face had not faltered a step in his advance. He went forward until he stood at the foot of the low steps which mounted to the veranda; and there he stopped, looking up at her, and removed his battered hat. Caleb ranged awkwardly up alongside him and looked up at her in turn. He, searching desperately for a neat and cleverly casual opening speech, could not know that beneath her forbidding manner a peal of soft laughter was struggling for utterance; could not know that, at that moment, she was telling herself that, of the two, Caleb was far the younger.

At last he cleared his throat, oratorically, and then she promptly interrupted him.

"Supper is served, Cal," she drawled in her gentle, almost lisping voice.

Caleb received the statement as if it were an astounding bit of hitherto undreamed-of news.

"Comin', Sarah!" he chirped briskly. "Comin' this blessed minute!"

And then, with an attempt at disingenuousness:

"I—I've a friend here, Sarah, whom I'd like to—er—present to you! This is my sister, Miss Hunter," he announced to the silent boy, "and this young man, Sarah, this young man is—er—ah—Mr.—"

"I'm Steve," said the boy, mildly. "I'm just Stephen O'Mara!"

"Certainly!" gasped Caleb. "Quite so—quite so! Sarah, this is just Steve."

The frail little woman with her quaint dignity of another decade failed to move; she did not unbend so much as the fraction of an inch. But hard upon the heels of Caleb's last words the boy went forward unhesitatingly. Hat in the hand that balanced his big steel trap, he stopped in front of her and offered one brown paw.

"Haow dye do, Miss Hunter," he saluted her, gravely. And with a slow smile that discovered for her a row of white and even teeth: "Haow dye do? I—I reckon you're the first—dressed-up lady I ever did git to know!"

The calm statement took what little breath there had been left in Caleb's lungs; it left Sarah breathless, too. But after an infinitesimal moment of waiting she held out her own delicate fingers and took the outstretched hand.

"Haow dye do, Steve?" she answered, and Caleb was at a loss to interpret the suppressed quality of her voice. "And I—some day I am sure it will be a great pleasure to remember that I was the—first!"

Then she faced her brother.

"Will you—will your friend, Mr.—Steve—remain for supper, Cal?" she asked.

And Caleb, quick to see an opening, made the most of this one.

"Stay for supper," he repeated her question, and he laughed. "Stay—for—supper! Well, I should hope he would. Why—why, he's going to stop for the night!"

From the vantage place there at the top of the steps Sarah stood and surveyed her brother's wide and guileless face for a second. Then her lips began to twitch.

"Very clever, Cal," she told him. "Quite clever—for you!"

And she nodded and withdrew to see that the table was laid for three.

Caleb, chuckling, watched her go; then with a nod to the boy, he started to follow her in. But Steve paused at the threshold, and when the man stopped and looked back to ascertain the cause of his delay he found that the boy was depositing the bear trap upon the porch floor—found him tugging to free the rusty old revolver from his belt.

"I'll leave Samanthy here," the one called Steve stated, and Caleb understood that he meant the trap. "An' I reckon I'd better not lug my weapon into the house, neither, hed I? She might—" He nodded in the direction of Sarah's disappearance—"Old Tom says womin folks that's gentle born air kind-a skittish about havin' shootin' irons araound the place. And I don't reckon it's the part of men folks to pester 'em."

Caleb didn't know just what to say, so he merely nodded approval. Again he had been made to feel that it was not a boy but some little old man who was explaining to him. Silently he led the way upstairs, and after he had seen the blanket pack deposited in one corner of Sarah's beloved guest-room, after he had seen the rusty coat peeled off as a preface to removing the dust accumulation of the long hot day from hands and face, an inspiration came to him. While the boy was washing, utterly lost to everything but that none-too-simple task, he went out of the room on a still-hunt of his own, and came back presently with the thing for which he had gone searching. He found the boy wrestling a little desperately with a mop of wavy chestnut hair which only grew the more hopeless with every stroke of the brush.

"Never mind that." Caleb met the misapprehension in the boy's eyes. "Never mind that! And I—I've taken the liberty of digging out this old canvas shooting coat. It's one I got for Sarah—for my sister—but, as you say, women folks are mighty skittish about anything that has to do with a gun. She never would go even so far as to try it on, but if you don't mind— That coat of yours must be a trifle hot for this weather, I should say."

Steve reached out a hand that trembled a little and took the coat. He took it and stared at it with that same strained and hungry look which he had bestowed a half hour before upon the "City."

"Do you mean," he asked, and his lips remained parted breathlessly upon the question, "do you mean—this yere's for me?"

Caleb thought of the "injine"—the "*steam* injine."

"I mean just that, if you'll have it," he replied. The boy slipped his little body into the garment and wheeled to survey himself in a mirror. In comparison with the dismembered swallowtail it was the purple of a Solomon. There was a cartridge web across its front, with loops, and after he had looked long and long at his reflection, the boy thrust both his thumbs into the belt it made.

Then: "Them's fer ketridges," he announced solemnly.

He scowled judiciously and nodded.

And, "I'll hev to git me some, the first thing in the mornin'," he said.

That was his only remark then, and yet Caleb felt amply repaid. Later he had more to say, but for the time being he merely followed Caleb back downstairs, walking very stiff and straight except when, with every few steps, he leaned over the better to see the looped webbing across his middle.

And at table that evening the man came to know another trait in the odd little stranger's odd makeup which, coupled with those which he had already mentally tabulated for future private contemplation, set him to wondering more than a little.

With the appearance of the first dish upon the table that night the boy was very frankly nonplussed at the array of implements upon each side of his plate, placed there for him to manipulate. He scarcely knew one from the other, and the separate uses for each not at all. But the way in which he met the problem made Caleb lift his eyes and meet Sarah's inscrutable glance with something akin to triumph. For there was no awkwardness in the boy's procedure, no flushing embarrassment, no shame-facedness nor painfully self-conscious attempt to cover his ignorance. Instead, he sat and waited—sat and watched openly until Miss Sarah had herself selected knife or fork, as the case might be—and then, turning back to those beside his own place, frowning intently, he made painstaking selection therefrom. Nor did he once make a mistake. And Caleb, after he had begun to mark a growing softness in the color of his sister's thin cheeks, ventured to draw into conversation their small guest.

The boy talked freely and openly, always with his wide eyes upon the face of his questioner, always in the grave and slightly drawling idioms of the woods. Again he confided that he had never before been out of the timber; he explained that "Old Tom's" untimely taking-off a fortnight back had been alone responsible for this pilgrimage. And that opened the way for a question which Caleb had been eager to ask him.

"I suppose this—this 'Old Tom' was some kin of yours?" he observed.

The boy shook his head.

"No," he answered, "no, I ain't never hed no kin. I ain't never hed nobody—father ner mother, neither!"

Caleb saw Sarah start a little and bite her thin lips. But the bird-like movement of surprise was lost upon the speaker.

"I ain't never hed nobody," he re-averred, and Caleb, straining to catch a note of self-pity or plea for sympathy in the words, realized that the boy didn't even know what the one or the other was. "I ain't never hed nobody but Old Tom. And he was—he wasn't nuthin' but what he called my—my"—the sentence was broken while he paused to get the phrase correctly—"he was what he called my 'logical custodian.'"

Guiltily Caleb knew that his next question would savor of indelicacy, but he had to ask it just the same.

"Still, I suppose his—his taking-off must have been something in the nature of a blow to you?" he suggested.

The boy pursed his lips.

"Wall, no," he exclaimed at last, nonchalantly. "No-o-o! I can't say's it was. We'd both been expectin' it, I reckon. Old Tom, he often sed he knew that some day he'd go and git just blind, stavin' drunk enough to try an' swim the upper rapids—and two weeks ago he done so!"

And the rest of the words were quite casual.

"I kind-a reckon he'd hev made it, at that," he offered his opinion, "if they'd hev been a trifle more water. But the rocks was too close to the surface fer comfortable swimmin'. The Jenkinses found him down in the slack water, Sunday noon or thereabouts, and they sed he'd never be no deader, not even if he'd a-died in a reg'lar bed, with a doctor helpin' him along."

Caleb threw his sister one lugubriously helpless glance. Sarah had choked, apparently upon a crumb of bread, and was coughing, stranglingly. And Caleb made to change the drift of the conversation, but he was not quick enough.

"I ain't never been much of a hand for licker," Steve finished naively. "Old Tom sed he never could understand it in me, neither, but he reckoned it was lucky in a way fer both of us. He sed he'd whale the life outen me if he ever caught me even smellin' of a cork; and as fer him—well, it come in handy for him, havin' a sober hand round the shack when he wan't quite hisself!"

This time when Caleb lifted his eyes he met a startled gleam behind Sarah's half dropped lashes. She was peering steadily into the boy's lean, untroubled face. Caleb voiced the query which he knew must be behind her quiet intentness.

"You said your name was O'Mara, I believe. I suppose that was—ah—Old Tom's last name, too?"

Steve laughed; he laughed frankly for the first time since he had halted, hours before, outside in the dusty road.

"Why, Old Tom had a dozen different names in the last few years," he replied. "He had a new one every time he went outen the woods fer a trip. But he always sed he mostly favored Brown or Jones or Smith, they bein' quiet and common and not too hard to remember. He just changed names whenever he got tired of his old one, Old Tom did. But he always did say, too, that if he'd hed as good a one as O'Mara, he'd a kept it—and kept it proud."

At the conclusion of that statement it was Miss Sarah's gaze which went searching across the table for her brother's eyes. But the boy just ran on and on, totally oblivious to their glances.

He told them of his lonely days in the woods shack, when Old Tom went down river and was three or four weeks in returning; he dwelt upon blissful days in the spring when he had been allowed to play a man's part in the small drives which he and Old Tom and the "Jenkinses" began, and which Old Tom and the Jenkinses alone saw through to market in Morrison. He touched lightly and inconsequentially upon certain days when Old Tom would hang for hours over an old tin box filled with soiled and ink-smeared memoranda, periods which were always followed by days of moody silence and a week or more of "lessons" in a tattered and thumbed reader which the woodsman had brought up-river—lessons as painful and laborious to Old Tom as they were delightful to the starved mentality of the pupil. And Old Tom, the boy explained, was pretty likely to be "lickered up fer quite a spell" after such a session which invariably began with an exploration of the battered tin box.

The boy told Caleb of days and nights on the trail—boasted unconsciously of Old Tom's super-cunning with trap and deadfall, and even poison bait. And that brought him to the beautifully oiled bear trap which he had left outside the door.

"I brung Samanthy along with me," he stated. "I brung her just because somehow I kind-a thought mebby Old Tom'd be glad if I did. Next to me he always sed he set a heap o' store on thet ole critter. He sed Samanthy was as near to hevin' a woman around the house as anything he knew on—she hed a voice like a steel trap, and when she got her teeth sot in a argument she never did let up. I brung her along with me, and the gun he give me, but I didn't take nuthin' else."

Caleb waited there until he knew that the boy had finished.

"You never bothered about that old tin box?" he inquired casually.

The boy shook his head again.

"Old Tom, whenever he went away for a spell, always sed I wan't to meddle with it," he explained. "This time I reckoned his goin' was just about the same thing, only he won't be comin' back, so I—I just locked the box up in the cubberd and hitched the staple into the door and come down myself."

By the time that meal was finished the boy's eyes were so heavy-lidded that, fight as he would, they still persisted in drooping till the long lashes curled over his cheeks. And in spite of Caleb's remonstrance it was Sarah who saw him upstairs and into the huge guest-room with its four-poster and high-boy and spindle-backed chairs.

When she came back downstairs her eyes were shining more than a little and the flush upon her cheeks was undeniably rose. Her brother, from his seat before the unlighted fireplace, puffed methodically upon his pipe and barely lifted his head at her coming. He was deep in meditation. She stood looking at him for a time from the foot of the stairway.

"He's asleep," she began finally in a very little voice. "He fell asleep almost before his cheek touched the pillow."

Caleb made no answer. He nodded but his eyes were vacant with thoughts of his own.

"Cal," she went on, "did you give him that old coat of mine?"

Caleb nodded again—an affirmative.

"Well, the last thing he asked before he slept was that I deliver a message to you. 'Tell him thanks for me,' he said. 'Tell him I clean forgot it til now!' And as for me, Cal—why—why, 'he'd git me anuther, anytime I took the notion thet I wanted one!'"

And still Caleb nodded. The room was quiet for a long time.

"Sarah," he murmured at last.

"Yes, Cal," she answered.

"Has that boy's—yarn—set you to thinking a little?"

"It was very interesting and unusual," she admitted. Then she rose and crossed over to his chair and perched herself, with odd, elfish, girlish grace upon its arm.

"Do you mean Old Tom's tin box?" she asked gently.

And he nodded.

"Yes, in part—yes," he said. "But not just that alone, either. I mean everything, Sarah. The way he handles himself; the way he looks one in the face when he is talking. The—the—now what are you grinning over?"

She stroked his sparse hair.

"Cal, you old romancer, you. Who'd ever suspect it in a man of your age and—and avoirdupois!"

"Avoirdupois!" he snorted. "Can't a man continue to have ideas now and then, even if he does become a—a trifle plump. And that boy—why, Sarah I tell you—!"

And then his sister put one hand over his lips.

"I know, Cal," she interrupted placidly. "I know! You're going to tell me, once more, your pet theory that there's many a boy in that backwoods who might paint a great canvas, or model a deathless bronze—or—or lead a lost cause, if he could only be found and provided with the chance. It sounds—it sounds very big and grand and romantic, Cal, but has it ever occurred to you that anyone big enough for things like those would find the way himself?"

Immediately, jerkily, Caleb started to straighten up. Argumentatively—and then she checked him.

"Oh, I know you don't believe it and I—I don't think I do myself, Cal. A man has to know what opportunity is before he can go out and hunt up his own big chance. I just said it for the sake of argument, Cal. I—I'm like Samanthy—ole Samanthy, you know! I'm a woman, and when I git my teeth sot in a argumint I never do let up. Have your dreams, you—you boy! And in the meantime, if you have any plans, tell me, please, what are you going to do with him in the morning?"

Caleb Hunter bobbed his head, vehemently. Rapidly he related to her the episode of the switch engine in Dexter Allison's millyards.

"And I believe what I believe," he insisted, doggedly. "And tomorrow I aim to give that boy a ride in one of Allison's 'steam injine' cabs, if it's all I do!"

"I thought so," said Miss Sarah.

For a time she sat there upon his arm chair. Neither spoke, nor felt the need for words. Just before she rose to go upstairs, she broke that quiet.

"He has an odd, strange, half-wild beauty," she mused aloud. "A beauty that is quite unusual, I should say, in children of his—his station. His hair is silken and, oh so thick! And his eyes and square chin with that little cleft. And his nose—his nose, I should say, might be said to denote estheticism—and—a—a—ah—"

Caleb Hunter threw back his head at the telltale little quaver in the voice and found Sarah Hunter smiling down at him, whimsically.

"Get all the amusement out of it that you can," he invited her. "And—and trust a woman to take note of such points as you have mentioned!"

From the stairs she gave him one backward glance.

"Forgive me, Cal," she hogged. "I meant it all—truly! Even the estheticism, which I only included to tease you. And if you don't want to trust to a woman's judgment on such points as I have mentioned, I would suggest that you peep in on him when you retire, and—and confirm them for yourself."

Hours later Caleb acted upon her suggestion. Every characteristic which Sarah had mentioned he found and noted in that half-lighted moment or two while he stood at the bedside.

And he noted more than just that. Sarah's old canvas hunting coat was folded into a small bundle and lay, guarded by one outflung, loose-fingered brown hand, beside the sleeping boy's face on the pillow.

Caleb went to bed with a half dozen wild notions whirling in his head, and a strange something tugging at his heart.

CHAPTER III
THREE QUARTERS AND SIX EIGHTHS

Saturday morning dawned as hot and dry and windless as had been the other days of the week which had preceded it. Caleb Hunter, rising from an uneasy night, blamed his sleeplessness upon the weather. It was fully an hour before his usual, not-too-early hour of rising, when he slowly descended the wide stairway; and yet he was but little surprised to find the boy already there before him, seated upon the top step of the verandah, when he strolled outside.

The little stranger with the grave voice, who had introduced himself as Stephen O'Mara, had not heard Caleb's step and the latter stood for a time in the doorway, contemplating the small, square-set shoulders in the canvas coat which had been his sister Sarah's, and the small, shapely head above them.

Throughout the night while he lay awake pondering the fantastic possibilities which the boy's story had stirred him into half believing, Caleb had had gradually lengthening moments of doubt in which he admitted to himself that his sister was right in her chafing analysis of him, her brother. Before morning came he had told himself a dozen times that he was nothing more than a sentimental old romancer, who saw in every beggar a worthy spirit bewitched by Destiny, and a Circumstance-enchanted fairy-prince in every ragamuffin who chanced to have big eyes. Merely because they had so persistently denied him sleep—those thoughts of Old Tom and his cherished tin box and the boy's own unmistakable poise and surety of self which even the shuffling boots and ragged clothes had only made the more impressive—merely because they persisted in endless procession through his brain, while he rolled and tossed and re-arranged the pillow, he had grown more and more peevishly eager to discount and discredit them, during the darkness. But when morning came, and he rose and went into the big guest room to find it empty, he experienced a moment of panicky disappointment; suddenly anxious for another opportunity to verify all that which, in the hours of sleepless pro's and con's, had become figment-like and whimsical, he wondered if the boy really could have gone without even waiting to bid them good-bye. He could not make that abrupt sort of a leave-taking harmonize with the rest of the youngster's actions—and then he caught a glimpse of him, motionless there on the verandah steps.

The boy did not hear Caleb's coming that morning. His head was tilted forward in that keen attitude of straining intentness which to the man had already become eloquently characteristic of his hungry spirit. And for a time Caleb withheld his greeting; instead of speaking he stood and studied him, and while he studied it all came back again, until the illusion, if such it were, was far more vivid, far more compelling than it had been the night before. Caleb told himself that to look only meant the discovery of new and compelling "points" both in feature and body, new and surprising suggestions of inbred fineness totally at variance with the unhemmed white drill trousers and uncouth shoes. And then, while he was nodding to himself, he realized that the boy was not looking down into the town in the valley.

Chin in palm, elbow upon knee, Steve was gazing fixedly in the direction of Dexter Allison's stucco and timber "summer lodge," and although Caleb could not have known it, there had been no need for his silence, for the boy's rapt preoccupation was sound-proof. Caleb heard voices coming from behind the shrubbery and just as he, a little perplexed, turned to follow the direction of that fascinated gaze, Allison himself squeezed through a narrow aperture in the box hedge and hailed him jovially from the far edge of the lawn. And Caleb Hunter's brows drew together in a bit of a frown when a slender figure in kilted black velvet and bright-buckled low shoes, hatless and with thick, gleaming hair bobbed short in a style strange to Morrison in those days, flashed through behind him. For Caleb heard the short gasp which came from the boy's lips, even before the little girl had paused in her darting advance, on tip-toe like a hovering butterfly, to wave a slim hand at him.

Caleb heard the boy's breath suck in between tight teeth; heard it quiver unsteadily as she appeared on swift feet—and Caleb understood what had been holding so closely his attention. He understood absolutely and yet, strange as the mood was, at that moment he couldn't help but feel, too, somehow a little sorry for the boy—he couldn't help but think— His eyes went from Steve's forward thrust head, from the hair shaggy and unkempt for all its fineness and thickness and wavy softness, across to that dainty vision which, poised in her absurdly short skirt like a point of flame, was already gazing back at the boy upon the steps in open and undisguised amaze.

All of that characteristic which had been most pronounced in Dexter Allison, the latter had passed down to this slender girl who was his daughter, Barbara. No matter how vivid Allison's raiment had been, Caleb remembered that even when Dexter was a stripling at school, it had always seemed more a part of the man himself, than just protection for his body. Caleb had never given it a serious thought up to that moment, but now it came back to him with added cumulative force. He recollected that he had often wondered at the child's unconscious adaptation of mood to the clothes she happened to be wearing; he recalled how he had seen her demure and distant in misty, pastel-tinted party frocks or quaintly, infantilely dignified in soberer Sunday morning garb. But that Saturday morning he realized what the woman was to be like, when the hem of the velvet skirt no longer hung high above spindly black legs and the bobbed hair had been allowed to grow and grow, far below the tiny ears which it now barely covered.

To Caleb who, without knowing it, from sheer sympathy was viewing her through the untaught eyes of the boy at his feet, she was no longer a mere slip of a girl-child, dark-eyed, bewildering of mood and pulsingly alive. Caleb caught his first illuminating glimpse of the woman she was to be—of the dainty grace and more than usual beauty which was there in the promise of the years. And he who was fond of insisting to his sister Sarah, that there was many a boy back in those hills who, with his chance, might some day achieve greatness, suddenly realized how long and weary the road would be for just such a one as the fascinated little figure on the steps, before he could begin to approach that level which, to a society that Caleb understood, was typified by this exquisite, elfin figure, Dexter Allison's daughter.

He was no snob—Caleb Hunter—and yet the little girl's bearing at that moment doubly accented for him the gulf which lay between her and the hills-boy, by name Steve. For though she did pause to stare at his white drill trousers and unbelievable man-sized boots with frankly childish astonishment, the next instant she had recovered herself and without another glance preceded her father across the grass. Quite as though Steve had not been there at all she passed him, to hesitate demurely at Caleb's side.

"Good morning, Uncle Cal," she greeted him.

And then, quite suddenly, Caleb didn't feel so very sorry after all for his little visitor. He stopped pitying him. Steve's eyes had not wavered once from the little girl's face, from the time she appeared in the hedge gap until she mounted the steps, utterly oblivious to his nearness; but when she brushed against his elbow, the boy rose and stood, hat in hand, gravely quiet, gravely possessed, and silently sure of himself.

Even after he had answered Barbara Allison's greeting and turned with his grown-up, ponderous courtesy to present the boy to her, only to be left with the words hanging upon tongue-tip by her instant disappearance inside in search of Sarah, Caleb caught no hint of the thoughts behind those impassive and steady eyes. And yet he knew that Steve had risen in order that he might bow as he had the night before, when Caleb introduced him to his sister.

Dexter Allison, coming up in less airy fashion across the lawn, surprised Caleb with his mouth still open.

"Well?" said Dexter Allison—and Caleb recovered himself.

"Well?" he countered; and then they both laughed softly and shook hands. It was their unvaried formula of greeting, whether they had not seen each other for twenty-four hours or twenty-four months.

And while they were shaking hands the boy turned quietly and re-seated himself upon the top step. But Allison gave him more notice than had his daughter Barbara. He stood with his pudgy hands in his pockets, gazing at the averted face, unconcealed and growing amusement in the scrutiny, until Caleb, not yet aware of the boy's woods-taught habit of seeing while seeming not to see, was simultaneously annoyed at Allison's fatuous grin, and glad of the fact that Steve apparently was looking the other way. After a time Allison raised quizzical eyes to Caleb's face.

"Wel-l-l?" he intoned, and with a little reluctance as reasonless as it was unnoticed, Caleb answered the inferred question.

"This—this is a little friend of mine, Dexter," he said, "down from the hills. He's in to have a look at the city which you have been so instrumental in arousing to its present state of teeming activity. This is Stephen O'Mara. Steve—this is Mr. Allison, Steve!"

Then the boy turned and again rose to his feet, and at that moment Caleb could have hugged him for his deliberation. The boy inclined his head; he bowed, without a word. And it was Dexter Allison who first offered a hand.

"Glad to make your acquaintance, Stephen," the latter exclaimed with quite violent good humor. "And how are you?"

Steve took the hand and closed his brown fingers hard upon the puffy white ones. For an instant he stood, his eyes, grave and inscrutable, full upon Allison's smaller ones. "I'm tol-lable," he drawled soberly. "And—haow be you—yourself?"

Allison gasped, stood with mouth agape, and then burst into one of his rather too-frequent, too-hearty laughs.

"Well, I'm—" he began his favorite phrase of ejaculation, and then stopped to look down again into the small face before him. "Well, I'm—" and he stopped to chuckle. Then he turned back to Caleb.

"I suppose, Cal, you know what this early morning call presages?" he suggested.

Caleb recalled himself with an effort from a contemplation of the sudden, prideful something which had warmed him while Steve was shaking hands. He smiled, mechanically.

"I suppose it's the usual raid upon the commissary," he answered.

Allison mounted heavily to the verandah.

"Right!" he exclaimed. "Right! You'll notice that Barbara has already gone on ahead. She's the skirmish line—scouts—videttes—whatever you please to call 'em. There's no-one up yet—none of the family—over to our place. We are hungry, Cal. I hope this is waffle morning?"

Caleb smiled at him, less impersonality in the mirth. It was a regular custom, this truancy of Barbara Allison and her father—one of the little human foibles which Caleb often told himself accounted, in part at least, for his real liking of the man.

"Waffles it is," he said, and he turned toward the boy.

"Would you mind finding Miss Sarah, Steve?" he asked. "Will you tell her, please, that we are to be subjected to another neighborly imposition?"

After the boy had disappeared Caleb followed the larger man to a chair. And this time it was Caleb who met Allison's silence with a challenging, "Well?"

"Where did you get him, Cal?" Allison demanded. "Where *did* you get him? Those shoes, and those trousers—pants, I guess is the word, eh? And say, how that little beggar did squeeze my hand! Look here!"

He held one soft hand up for inspection. There were faint red welts still visible across the finger joints.

"Friend of yours, did you say?"

Without stopping to think about it, Caleb was not so keen to enlarge upon the boy's obvious "points" as he had been with Sarah. He omitted to mention his thoughts of the night before, and he omitted any reference to Old Tom, except for the most hazy explanation that the boy had no immediate kin. But with an increasing eagerness he dilated upon the small foot traveler's first view of the "city," his breathless reception of Allison's own switch engine, and his avowed intention to "look around a trifle," before he located something to do.

"I thought I'd take him down this morning and get McLean to give him a ride in the cab of one of those sheet-iron steam relics of yours," he finished.

If Caleb had expected his unadorned recitation of the boy's appearance to make any impression upon his hearer he would have been disappointed. But, without any confessed reason for so doing, Caleb had aimed rather at the opposite effect. And Allison turned from it with a large, matter-of-fact indifference, to rise and bow to Sarah Hunter, who appeared that moment in the doorway.

"Surely—surely," he echoed Caleb's suggestion. "Take him down and give him a ride! McLean'll be glad of the chance to show someone his pet buzz-saws and things. I'll walk down with you, myself, after breakfast. I may be away for a day or two, and I want to leave directions for changes to be incorporated while I'm gone."

At the table that morning Caleb noted that there was no hesitation in Steve's selection from the silver beside his plate, no waiting to follow in the lead of Sarah Hunter's choice. He noticed, too, that the boy's eyes did not once lift to those of Barbara Allison, opposite him. And while the little girl from time to time joined in the conversation, he not once opened his mouth to speak, until they were almost ready to rise from their places.

Allison had been growling genially at the lack of water and the prolonged drouth which was burning the pasturage to a crisp and juiceless brown.

"If that everlasting sun would only stop shining for a while," he said, "if it'd only rain a bit, I'd like to take a trip back north, a-fishing, before it gets too late in the season."

"You mean you'd like a fishing trip as an excuse to go back north, don't you, Dexter?" Caleb badgered him.

Allison was smiling blandly, for Caleb's joke over his round-about methods was an old, old joke, when Stephen O'Mara spoke.

"It's goin' to rain," said the boy.

Allison turned toward him, his eyes again quizzical.

"I suppose so," he admitted. "In the general course of things it'll come, no doubt, but—"

The boy interrupted him, shaking his head.

"It's goin' to come before mornin'," he stated inflectionlessly, "and it's comin' to stay fer a spell, too!"

And Allison did not try to hide his broad grin of amusement.

"You think so, do you, sonny?" he dismissed the matter not unkindly. "Well, at that, your guess when it comes to the weather, is about as good as the next man's."

Once more the boy shook his head.

"I ain't guessin'," he finished unabashed. "Ner I ain't thinkin' it will. It'll jest be rainin', come sun-up, and it'll be good for 'til Wednesday, fer sure!"

Caleb, watching the boy's face, was on the point of offering to wager two bits with Allison that the prophecy held good, but Sarah's well-known attitude toward the vice of gambling checked him in the rash offer. Besides, he wondered how he could make sound anything but foolish an offer to back the certainty of a weather forecast which was based upon nothing but the unassuming and quiet finality of the prophet.

Barbara Allison insisted upon joining the excursion down to the mill that morning; she developed a sudden and unshakable resolve to be one of the party, and after his remonstrances had finally brought stormy tears to her eyes, Allison surrendered in perplexity to her whim.

"All right, then," he gave in. "If you want to come as much as all that, but—but you—now run along, then, with Stephen."

On the way down the hill he voiced his perplexity to Caleb.

"When it comes to dealing with men," he said, "I pride myself upon being able to go back, rather incisively, to first motives. But the other sex is beyond me! She's always turned up her dainty nose at the noise and dirt before, and—and now she's ready to cry because I suggest that she wait with Miss Sarah until we return!"

Caleb's eyes rested upon the oddly matched little couple ahead in the road. The boy was carrying his battered hat in his hand, but Barbara walked with small head up, without a single glance for her escort. Caleb, noting that Steve's head was forward-thrust, knew that his eyes must be fastened hungrily upon the town in the valley; and he understood the reason for the disdainful tilt of the little girl's chin. For even at the age of ten Barbara Allison was not accustomed to inattention. Caleb smiled, rather covertly for him.

"I never knew but one woman whose motives were absolutely transparent," he mused. "And she—she was the most uninteresting, unsuccessful female person I ever did know."

As Allison had promised they found McLean, the white-haired mill superintendent, only too eager at the prospect of an audience for one of his voluble tours of the premises. But when Caleb had explained the main errand upon which they had come, after a long, keen scrutiny of the boy's face, the burly river-man led the way, without a word, to a wheezing old two-wheeler in the piling yard.

"So you'll be wantin' to take a spin in one av me ingines, is it?" he asked then. And, after a moment: "An' do you think you'll be able to hang on, whin she gets to r-rollin'?"

Steve's eyes were like bits of polished steel, so bright they were. It was a struggle for him to take them, even for a moment, from the engine before him.

"I cal'late I kin," he quavered.

"Well, thin, we'll see." McLean looked up and winked at the engineer in the diminutive cab. "It's car-reful you'll be, Misther engineer," he cautioned, "an' watch your steerin' on the cur-rves!"

He leaned over to lift the boy to the running-board, but Steve, with one foot upraised, hung back. He faced toward Caleb and, without a glance in the girl's direction, said:

"Mebby she—mebby she'd like to go, too?"

Barbara Allison, chin lifted a little higher, half wheeled and slipped her hand within that of her father.

"Thank you, but I don't care to," she refused.

Steve caught the little toss of her head from the corner of his eye, and his face went pink. Without another word he clambered up beside the driver and the engine rolled out of the yard and went clanking down the uneven, crooked track, leaving a dissolving trail of steam behind. When it returned the little face at the cab window was tense and somewhat pale beneath its tan, but the hand upon the throttle beside the engineer's lay steady as a little pine knot.

"Well, an' what do you think av her?" McLean demanded with an assumption of anxiety as the boy dropped to the ground.

Steve turned and patted the footboard with a proprietary hand. As grave of mien as his questioner he bobbed his head.

"She—she certainly kin git up and step," he volunteered. And then, cocking his head judiciously: "I'll hev to be a-gittin' me one of them fer myself, some day!"

McLean chuckled—he chuckled in deep delight within his white whiskers—and led the way to the mills. But once there the amusement in his eyes rapidly deepened to amazement, for there were few steps in the processes upon which the boy could not talk as fluently and technically as did the mill boss himself. And he knew timber; knew it with the same infallibility which had, even in McLean, always seemed to border upon the uncanny.

It was Allison himself who first called attention to an unsawed log which was being discarded.

"That looks like too good a stick to be wasted, doesn't it, McLean?" he asked.

Before McLean could answer the boy spat gravely into a pile of sawdust, his piping voice rising above the shrill scream of the saws.

"She's holler," he stated succintly. "Dry rotten above the stub!"

And when Allison raised his brows, interrogatively, McLean dropped one hand upon the boy's shoulder, a bit of pride in the gesture.

"Holler she is," he agreed, and he added: "An' I'll be afther knowin' where to find a riverman av the old school, I'm thinkin', some day whin the need arises!"

A man came hunting for McLean at that moment with news that the tram which carried the logs up from the basin to the saws needed his attention. They followed him out, Steve hard at his heels, and Barbara Allison, lips pouted, tight to her father's side. After a brief examination of the trouble McLean gave a half dozen hurried orders; then turned to the boy beside him and jerked one thumb over his shoulder.

"Run down to the smithy shop, lad," he directed, "an' tell the smith that I'll be wantin' a strip av str-rap iron, two feet in lingth, av quarter inch stuff—and three-quarters av an inch wide."

The boy was off like a deer and back again in a twinkling, empty-handed, but with an astounding bit of news.

"The blacksmith says he ain't got no—no iron three-quarters of an inch wide," he said, and the words were broken by his panting breaths. "But he says he's got plenty that's six-eighths. Shall I—shall I git some o' that?"

He waited the word, poised to go.

McLean had been kneeling upon the saw-dust strewn ground. Now he rose and stood, feet apart, gazing down into that face, afire with eagerness, uplifted to his. Quiet endured for a long time, and then, at a chuckle from Allison, Steve wheeled—he wheeled just in time to see Barbara Allison's brows arch and her lips curl in a queer little smile. And suddenly Allison burst into a loud guffaw.

Caleb had never seen a change so swift as that which came over the boy's face. The eager light faded from the gray eyes, until they were purple where they had been gray before. And Caleb had never seen a face grow so white—so white and set and dangerous. Stephen O'Mara's head drooped, he turned and wavered away a step or two. Allison stopped laughing, abruptly. Then McLean spoke.

"'Twas funny, mebby," he muttered. "But it was not so damned funny, aither! An' I—I'll be goin' down now to teach that smith to kape his funny jokes till afther hours."

He started toward the shop, and stopped again.

"It's all right, buddy," he said. "'Tis nothing that you need feel badly about, for 'twas I who made the mistake. I should have sint you out to estimate whether our spruce would cut two million feet or less, an' you'd have come as close as mor-rtal man could, I'll wager. 'Twas a trivial thing, lad. What's a little matter av figures between min av the river, eh? We'll leave that to the capitalists who laugh at our dinseness, me bhoy!"

With that shot at his employer McLean strode off, fuming.

Steve hung back beside Caleb on the return trip up the hill. Not once did he speak, and Caleb, aware of his thinned lips and the bleak whiteness of his face, did not know what to say himself. He only knew that he, too, felt unreasonably bitter against Allison for his burst of mirth. Not until they had left Barbara and her father at their own gate and were crossing the Hunter lawn did Caleb attempt any remark whatsoever.

"I—you musn't feel badly just because you didn't know that three-quarters and six-eighths were the same, Steve," awkwardly he tried to comfort him. "I guess there was a time when Allison, in spite of all his tutors, didn't know it himself, if the truth's old."

Then Caleb learned that Steve had not even heard Allison's burst of laughter. He whirled—the boy—and his eyes blazed, hurt, shamed, bitter, into Caleb's kindly ones. He shook with the very vehemence of the words that came through twitching lips.

"*She* didn't hev no call to smile like that at me," he flung out. "If I'd ever hed a chance to learn that they wa'n't no difference between them figgers, and *hedn't* knowed, she could'a smiled. But I—I ain't hed my chance—yit!"

He swung around and stumbled blindly up the steps and groped his way upstairs.

Caleb stood there for a long time, motionless, and the one thought uppermost in his mind was that Steve, like Allison, was scarcely woman-wise. A low muttering behind him finally recalled him to himself, and when he turned he saw that here were thunder-heads piling up in the southwest. One long finger of black cloud was already poked up over the horizon. He remembered the boy's prophecy of the breakfast table; remembered what McLean had said in scorn of trivial things, and he went upstairs to urge Steve to remain and join them in their fishing trip on Monday—the trip north which Allison had proposed, if it rained.

He found the boy stretched, face down, upon the bed, a rigid figure of misery. Out of his deep desire to heal his hurt he even promised him the use of a most precious rod; he promised to teach him to cast a fly, come Monday!

And when the boy finally nodded his head in mute assent, he left him alone for a while—alone with his bruised spirit that was bigger than the spare little body which housed it.

CHAPTER IV
I'LL TELL HER YOU'RE A BAPTIST

It rained that night. The storm which hung for hours, a threatening bank of black in the south, finally tore north at sundown, to break with vicious fury. And again Caleb spent a sleepless night, this time alone before the fireplace, but the thoughts which kept him awake failed to grow fantastic and romantically absurd with prolonged contemplation, as they had the night before.

Never until that day had he considered his oft-repeated theory that there was many a boy in those back-woods who, with a chance, might go far, as anything but an idealistic truth, in the abstract. The realization that a chance had come to test it, in the concrete, stunned him at first.

Dispassionately he summed up all the boy's characteristics that night and reviewed them, one by one: His poise and utter lack of self-consciousness, his fearless directness and faith in himself, in all that he said or did; and they came through the mental assay without fault or flaw.

He had already decided that he must go up-river and explore the old tin box which had been left there, locked in the "cubberd," but he was a little proud to make his decision before he learned all that it might, or might not, reveal; he was proud to believe that he knew a thorough-bred, without a pedigree for confirmation. And when Sunday morning dawned and the floodlike downpour had subsided to a gray and steady rainfall, even Caleb, none too weatherwise, knew that it had come to "stay fer a spell." He knew that the boy who had come marching down the valley road, two days before, was going to stay, too, if it lay within his power to persuade him.

Steve was most taciturn at the table the following morning; his moody silence puzzled even Sarah Hunter. But when the latter, whose Sunday schedule no storm could alter, came home from church and found Caleb and the boy immersed in a mass of flies and leaders, and lines which had been skeined to dry, her thorough disapproval loosed the boy's tongue. She stood in the doorway surveying with a frown their preoccupied industry.

"It seems to me, Cal," she commented, "that even if *you* haven't any regard for the Sabbath, you might do better than lead those younger than yourself into doing things which might better be left for days which were meant for such things."

She swished upstairs before Caleb had a chance to answer. But minutes after she had gone Steve looked up from a line he was spooling.

"She ain't particularly pleased, I take it," he remarked.

"Not particularly," Caleb chuckled. "It's funny, too, because I do most of this sort of work on Sunday. You'd think she'd become resigned to it, but she doesn't."

The boy thought deeply for a while.

"Didn't—didn't the 'Postles cast their nets on Sunday?" he asked presently.

Up shot Caleb's head.

"Huh-h-h?" he gasped.

"I sed—didn't the 'Postles cast their nets on Sunday?" Steve repeated. "Seems to me they did, but I can't just rec'lict now what chapter it was in."

Caleb pulled his face into a semblance of sobriety.

"Seems to me they did," he agreed, a little weakly, "now that you mention it. I don't just recollect where it occurred, either, at the moment, but we'll have to look it up, because, as a case of precedent, it'll be a clincher for Sarah."

He chuckled for a full hour over the thought before he forgot it. The boy, however, upon whom Sarah's disapproval had made a more lasting impression, recalled it to him later.

Allison joined them Monday morning at daybreak. All day they drove through the seeping rain—drove north in Caleb's buckboard, to turn off finally upon a woods trail that ran into the east, along the lesser branch of the river. During the ride Steve's bearing toward the third member of the party was too plain to escape notice, for he never looked at nor directed a word to Allison unless it was in reply to a direct question, and then his answers were almost monosyllabic. But Allison, who, as usual, gave his undivided attention to the country through which they were passing, in attitude toward the boy was even more remarkable.

Once when they had halted at noon he pointed out a hillside of pine, black beneath the rain, close-clustered and of mastlike straightness.

"There's a wonderful stand of pine, Cal," he remarked. "I'd venture to say that it would cut at least two million feet."

Instantly, although the remark was addressed to him, Caleb knew that it was Stephen's comment for which Allison was angling. And hard upon his casual statement the boy's head came sharply around.

"She'll run nigh double that," he swallowed the bait. "She'll run double—and mebby a trifle more."

Nor did Allison even smile now.

"What makes you think so?" he asked.

Again there came the boy's pat answer.

"I ain't thinkin'," he said. "It's jest there! They're close set—them trees—and they're clear, clean to the tops. There ain't a stump there that won't run near ten standard."

Allison squinted and finally nodded his head.

"Maybe," he agreed, "maybe."

But later Caleb saw him enter some figures in his small, black-bound notebook.

That night the episode was repeated with a bit of variation. They had set up their tent and made camp, a little before nightfall. Far below them, hidden by the trees, the east branch cut a threadlike gash through the center of a valley broad enough and round enough to have been a veritable amphitheater of the gods. The whole great hollow was clothed with evergreen, a sea of dripping tops in the semi-gloom, and Allison, when he had set aside his plate and lighted his pipe, lifted a hand in a gesture which embraced it all.

"If you weren't so lazy-brained, Cal," he said, "that sight would stir in you something more than a mere appreciation of what you call the 'sublimity of sheer immensity.' For the man who can look ahead ten or a dozen years there is an undreamed of fortune right here in this alley."

Caleb yawned.

"No doubt," he agreed. "But I didn't coin that phrase for immense fortunes. I guess I'm old-fashioned enough to like it a whole lot better just as it is."

Then he became suddenly aware of the tense earnestness with which Stephen O'Mara was listening. And when Allison, thinking aloud, mused that the cost of driving the timber down the shallow stream to the far-off mills would be, perhaps, prohibitive, words fairly leaped to the boy's lips.

"But they—they won't be drivin' that timber by floods, when they git to tacklin' these here valleys," he exclaimed. "Old Tom ses when they really git to lumberin' these mountains they'll skid it daown to the railroad tracks and yank it out by steam!"

That sober statement in the piping voice had a strange effect upon Allison. He leaned forward, a sort of guarded astonishment in his attitude, to peer at the childish face in the fire-glow. Then he seemed to remember that it was just a bit of a woods-waif who had spoken. But Caleb, who was lazy-brained in some matters, sensed that Steve had put into words Allison's own unspoken thought, just as Allison at that moment voiced the question which he was about to utter himself.

"I suppose it was this—this Old Tom who taught you all these things you know about timber?" he said, curious.

Steve pondered the question.

"Wal-l-l, yes," he answered at last. "Old Tom learned me some, but—but most of it I kind of feel as if I always knowed."

The boy was fast asleep, curled up beneath the blankets, when Caleb finally broached, that night, the matter which had kept him awake the entire night before. And when he had finished Allison sat quiet for a long time before he offered any reply.

"You mean—" he began, at length.

"I just mean that I'm going to give him his chance," Caleb cut in. His voice was hushed, but vehement. "Why, man, think what he has this minute, to start with! A brain as clear as a diamond, absolutely fresh, absolutely unspoiled or fagged with the nonsensical fol-de-rol which makes up the bulk of the usual boy's education of his age, and a working knowledge, for instance, of this north country which most men might envy. Why, the possibilities are limitless!"

Allison puffed his pipe in silence.

"No doubt you're right," he admitted. "In ten years, with a technical education to back up his practical knowledge, he might prove priceless to someone who had need of such a specialist. Always assuming, of course, that he developed according to promise. But the possibilities are limitless, too, in the other directions, aren't they?"

"Meaning?" invited Caleb.

"Well, you don't know any too much concerning his antecedents, do you?" Allison suggested. "And still—"

"I don't have to," Caleb interrupted, "not after one look at him!"

"—And still, if you catch a boy young enough," Allison finished serenely, "you can make a fairly presentable gentleman out of almost any material, with time enough and money enough to teach him what to do."

"You can," Caleb came back, "but no matter how much money you spend, you can't make the sort of a gentleman out of him, that knows without being taught, what *not* to do! They—they have to be born to that, Dexter."

And there they let it drop. But the next morning, when they were alone upon the brook, Caleb, after several false starts managed to re-open the subject with the boy himself.

"Has it ever occurred to you, Steve," he asked, "that all these things you know about the woods might be valuable, some day, to—to men who pay well for such knowledge?"

Steve paid no apparent heed to the question until he had landed a trout which he had hooked a moment before. It was a heavy fish—and Caleb had promised to teach him how to handle that fly-rod! Then he looked up.

"Once Old Tom sed they'd be payin' me more'n he ever earned in his lifetime, jest to go a-raound and tell 'em how much good lumber they was in standin' trees. Is that—is that what you mean?"

"Partly—partly, but not entirely, either," Caleb went on. "You said last night that when they got to lumbering these mountains, they'd be taking it out by steam. When they do they'll want men who know the woods—but they'll have to know how to bridge rivers and cross swamps, too, won't they?"

The boy promptly forgot his fishing. Knee-deep in the stream he faced squarely around toward Caleb, and from that glowing countenance the man knew that he had only repeated something which, long before, had already fired the boy's imagination.

"They's places where I kin git 'em to learn me them things, ain't they?" he demanded.

"Yes," said Caleb. "There are places. And you—you were thinking of going to school?"

"Thinkin' of it?" echoed Steve. "I always been thinkin' of it. Why, thet's all I come outen the timber fer!"

"But you said you meant to locate something to do," the man argued, nonplussed, "after you had looked around a trifle."

Steve's eyes dropped toward the white drill trousers and big boots, the latter half-hidden from sight by the swirling water.

"I got to earn money first," he explained patiently. "I—I jest couldn't git to go to school—in these here clothes!"

"Oh!" murmured Caleb. "Oh!" And then, recovering himself: "That'll take a long time," he ventured.

The boy smiled, strangely—the first smile of man's sophistication which Caleb had seen upon his face.

"I've always hed to wait a long time fer everything I've wanted," he answered, "but I always git it, just the same, if I only want it hard enough."

["I've always hed to wait a long time for everything I've wanted," the boy answered, "but I always get it, just the same, if I only want it hard enough."]

Caleb cleared his throat, self-consciously.

"Still," he argued again, "it would waste some very valuable years. Now—now what do you think of staying with me, and—and starting in this fall?"

The boy's lips fell apart while he stood and gaped up into Caleb's slightly red face.

"You mean," he breathed, "you mean—jest live—with you?"

"That was my idea," said Caleb.

And then, slowly, the boy's head dropped again, as it had when he bowed to gaze at his uncouth, begrimed clothes. The man thought that he caught the inference of that moment of silence.

"We can fix up the matter of clothes later," he made haste to forestall any objection in that direction. "That doesn't amount to anything, anyway."

The clear eyes lifted again, steady and wide and very, very grave.

"I always knowed it was comin'," said Stephen O'Mara. "I always knowed it was a-comin'—this chance—even when I didn't know *haow* it would come. Ner I wa'n't thinkin' about my clothes. I reckon I kin learn jest as fast in these as in any. I was jest thinkin' about Miss Sarah. She—she might not like it, hevin' two men folks a-raound the house, under foot."

It was Caleb's turn to stand, agape.

"Miss Sarah?" he faltered, astonished—and then he remembered. He laughed, unsteadily, with relief. For an instant he had been inexplicably afraid that the boy was going to refuse his offer.

"Why, you musn't mind what Sarah said yesterday," he rushed on. "She—she—well, she's a Baptist, Steve, and you know what that means."

He leaned forward a little, his voice quite stealthily confidential.

"But I can fix that all right," he promised. "I can surely fix that. For I'll tell her—I'll tell her you're a Baptist, too! Will you—will you stay?"

And after a time solemnly Steve nodded. Later, when alone, Caleb chuckled mountainously over his reply.

"Thet's—thet's what I cal'late I be," he said.

CHAPTER V
THEN I'LL COME BACK TO YOU

On the drive home Wednesday Caleb rehearsed a half score of speeches with which he might apprise his sister Sarah of the step he had taken; but when the time came for him to employ one of them, he forgot the entire lot and had to resort to a bald and stammered statement of the facts, which sounded more like a confession of guilt than anything else. It had grown colder with the storm and directly after a hastily swallowed supper, with many indignant glances for her brother, Sarah had bundled the boy off upstairs to bed, for he had come in out of the rain as sleekly wet as a water-rat, and blue-fingered and blue-lipped from cold. So it happened that they were alone before the fireplace when Caleb made known his decision.

"I've never done much of anything for anybody but myself, you know, Sarah," Caleb hesitatingly tried to account for his conduct. "And this seems to me to be as big an opportunity as I'll ever have. You—you like the boy, don't you, so far as you have become acquainted with him?"

While he was explaining Caleb wished that his sister would look him in the face, once at least. It was hard to know what she was thinking when she sat like that, staring into the fire. He waited, not without grave misgivings, for her reply.

"Yes, I like him," she assented, after a while.

"You do think that he might amount to something?" Caleb insisted.

"I feel almost sure of it," his sister admitted.

There didn't seem much ground to be gained along that tack, so Caleb gave up trying to apologize for what he had done.

"Of course it—it comes as a surprise to you," he murmured. "It is pretty sudden—but I don't think that either of us will ever regret it."

And then Sarah faced 'round toward her brother. Her eyes were unaccountably wet, but there was laughter on her lips.

"A surprise—a—a somewhat sudden!" she faltered. "Why, I knew you were going to do it that first day when you came sidling up to the veranda behind him. I was certain of it, even then. And if you hadn't decided to, why, I'd made up my mind that I'd do it myself, if you ever came back from that endless fishing-trip!"

And there, as Caleb put it later to Allison, were three days of perfectly good diplomatic preparation gone all to waste. For it was Sarah who monopolized the conversation that evening. She ran on and on, from one plan to another, eager, half-breathless, and more wildly prophetic than the man had dared to be, until the realization gradually dawned in her brother's brain that great as had been his desire to keep the boy there in the white place on the hill, it had been dwarflike beside her woman-hunger. It astonished him, when he mentioned the subject of clothes, to find how far she had outstripped him in actual deed.

"I've been rummaging through some of the old chests upstairs, too," she caught up his suggestion. "To-day I explored for hours and found some of the things you used to wear which look as though they hadn't been worn at all. I laid some of them out for him to put on when he gets up in the morning. And, Cal, who'd ever believe now that a plump behemoth like you ever could have worn such—such dainty and cunning things!"

The inferred description should have prepared Caleb, but at the moment he failed to remember that it was some forty years since the garb she mentioned had been in vogue. Instead he blushed uncomfortably at the gurgle in her throat. And so, the next morning, when a little figure in velvet jacket and pantaloons—velvet of the same jet hue in which Barbara Allison had first appeared to the boy a day or two before—stopped at the head of the long stairway, the moment was robbed of not one whit of its sensationalism.

Caleb remembered then; and it did seem inconceivable that he could ever have worn that costume, for the boy in the black velvet might have stepped bodily from the pages of sheerest romance. There were red-topped boots upon the slim feet which the day before had been encased in Old Tom's cast-off brogans; these were ruffed cuffs of sheerest white linen at brown and sinewy wrists, and burnished silver buttons down the front of the jacket for the silken corded clasps which fastened it across his small chest—silver buttons to match upon the quaintly short sleeves.

Stephen O'Mara hesitated just the fraction of a moment before he started methodically down the stairs. And immediately Caleb's amazement at the thought that those clothes had once been worn by him gave way to a newer wonder. For the boy, in spite of the fact that his small face above the pleated collar was burning hot with consciousness of self, wore them in a fashion unforgettable. Then Caleb realized how great an effort it must be costing the boy to make that slow descent in the face of his goggle-eyed stare, and with the most casual of good mornings he led the way to the table.

There was something in Sarah's fluttering delight over the boy's appearance that morning which awoke an almost hysterical impulse in her brother. For he knew, as completely as though he had heard it from the boy's own lips, that nothing in the world but the knowledge that "Miss Sarah" wished it would have carried Steve through the ordeal of his first appearance. They had a word together—Sarah and Caleb—after breakfast.

"Did you ever see anything like him, Cal?" she demanded of her brother. "Did you! Oh, I never dared hope he would look like that!"

Caleb pulled reflectively at his lower lip.

"I never did," he admitted. And then, offhandedly: "What—did he say anything, last night, when you told him to wear those things, this morning."

"Why, no," Miss Sarah laughed a little. "No. But he—Cal, he just sat and looked at me, oh, so soberly, for the longest time. He made me think somehow of a puppy that knows he's going to be scrubbed and—and dreads it exceedingly. It's because of those dreadful things he's been wearing, don't you suppose so?"

"No doubt of it," her brother said. "No doubt! And now I'm going over to invite Dexter Allison to come and take a look at him. I was telling him only yesterday that a gentleman had to be a gentleman born."

When Caleb came back, an hour later, with Allison at his heels, he searched the house through without finding the boy. In his perplexity he appealed to Sarah, who followed him to the front door.

"Where's Stephen?" he asked.

Sarah nodded to Allison.

"Why, I waited a half-hour, Cal," she said, "and then, when I thought you wouldn't be back for a while, I sent him downtown—I sent him to the village—"

Caleb seemed fairly to shrink.

"You sent him down to the village?" he echoed. "Did he—did he change his clothes?"

"For some eggs," Sarah rounded out the sentence.

"And of course he didn't!" Suddenly her brother's face alarmed her. "Cal," she exclaimed, "I haven't done anything I shouldn't have done, have I?"

Caleb turned a wry face toward Allison.

"In—that—outfit!" he groaned. "Down to the village, and it's a lumber town! He's gone, and if he doesn't have to fight his way back then I—"

Sarah's alarm changed to fear instantly. She stepped out upon the porch.

"I never thought of that," she whispered. "But you don't really think—"

In her agitation she turned to Allison for contradiction. But Allison, after placing a chair for her, drew one up for himself and, with an expansive smile of anticipation upon his face, propped his feet upon the rail.

"I think," he assured her, with no comfort in the assurance, "that this will be well worth watching through to the finish!"

They sat and waited and in due course of time the boy returned. As he appeared at the gate Sarah, with a strange choking sound in her throat, half rose and then dropped weakly back into her chair. And even to Allison, who had fondly looked forward to the worst, the little suit with the pretty ruffed cuffs was an unbelievable wreck. The coat had been ripped from hem to collar and dangled loose upon either side as the boy advanced toward them; the knees of the trousers were split till the bare skin showed through beneath, and those portions of the fabric which were not encrusted with dirt were liberally o'er-spread with egg.

After one stricken glance at the spectacle Sarah tottered to her feet and retreated none too steadily into the house. But it wasn't the condition of the boy's clothes which held Caleb's gaze. He was watching his face. For as Steve marched across the lawn the dangerous whiteness of the boy's countenance half frightened the man. His lips were a thin streak across a jaw tight clamped and flecked with blood in one corner. And his eyes had the wide-open fixity of a sleep-walker. Steve had reached the top of the steps in his mechanical approach before Caleb spoke. And even then, when he turned, he seemed only half to see the two men who were waiting his coming.

"Well?" faltered Caleb.

The boy stopped short and slowly turned his head. Both men heard that breath, short and harsh, in the moment of silence.

"Just what does this mean?" Caleb attempted again. "Where have you been?"

He hardly recognized the boy's voice.

"I been daown to the city," Steve slurred the words. "I been daown to git Miss Sarah a dozen eggs—and I run into trouble—daown there—a-gittin' 'em!"

"I—I should assume that you had," murmured Caleb. "But you've brought the eggs back with you, or most of them, I see, even though they aren't in particularly edible condition."

That was as long as Allison could endure it; he burst into a fit of laughter which lasted until he was moaning for breath. And Steve, teeth set, waited without moving until the noisy outburst was over.

"You'd better go upstairs and get into your old clothes," Caleb advised him then. "And I'll get you something less—less dangerous to wear before night."

But the boy stood rigid still.

"Will you," he asked, "will you give me another quarter now?"

Allison looked up quickly from wiping his eyes.

"A quarter," echoed Caleb slowly, even while he reached into his pocket and handed the coin to the boy. "Now what do you—Here, where are you going now?"

Steve had turned and was marching down the steps. He paused a minute to explain, however.

"Why, I'm goin' back daown to the city," he grated out. "I'm goin' back after Miss Sarah's eggs!"

And he went and when he returned the creases in the paper bag which held his purchase were as fresh as when it had left the grocer's counter.

"Well I'm—I'm damned!" Allison murmured, after the boy had entered the house. "I *am* damned! You'll have to bring that youngster over, Cal, and introduce him to the children."

Caleb couldn't help it.

"I told you so!" he said.

That was only a beginning. The next fortnight was filled with more new experiences than either Caleb or his sister would have believed could be crammed into twenty times that duration. And Caleb spent most of his waking hours boasting to the tolerant Allison of new and quite astonishing traits which he found in the boy.

Acting upon Dexter's suggestion the man took Steve across the very next day and presented him to the children who were guests in the big stucco and timber house: Little, shy, transparent-skinned Mary Graves and Garret Devereau and Archibald Wickersham—the Right Honorable Archie. But from the very first, Steve's lack of enthusiasm for their company impressed itself upon Caleb. As a matter of fact, the boy did cross over and join in their games the first day or two, but it was only after Caleb himself had suggested it. And more often than not he would be back again, before an hour had passed, to sit silent and moody, chin in hand, upon the steps, gazing north at the hills. It puzzled Caleb mightily; he laid it to homesickness at the beginning.

Toward Barbara Allison, throughout those days, Steve's bearing was that of frank and undisguised wonder and worship. Whatever they did, no matter what they played at, his eyes rarely left the little girl's bobbed head. For any feat which he performed he invariably turned to her for approbation. And in return for that worship Barbara's treatment of him was truly feminine. He out-ran the other boys as a deer might outrun an ox; he out-leaped them without putting himself to an effort, but he won scant attention or visible admiration from the dark-eyed Barbara. She was far more likely to turn from his hungry eyes to compliment the Honorable Archie upon his clumsy performance with a sweetness that left Steve biting his lips in lack of understanding. More than once it made even Caleb grit his teeth—the little girl's disdainfully tilted chin—and when Steve's reluctance to leave his own yard became an unmistakable thing, he spoke to Sarah about it.

"Maybe I'm prejudiced, blindly," he growled, "but I do believe that there is nothing in the world to equal the absolute and refined cruelty of a woman-child of ten—unless it is that of a woman of twenty or thirty, and on up the scale—when she first finds out that a man cares enough for her so that she can really hurt him! If that Barbara was a boy I'd catch her and switch her—Allison or no Allison!"

At any other time Sarah would have defended her own sex with much asperity; instead, there was something oddly wistful in her answer.

"If it were only the way she treats him," she mused, "I wouldn't mind so much." The sudden outraged glint in her eyes startled Caleb. "That isn't the reason he doesn't want to play with them. They have been laughing at him, Cal; they have all been making fun of him, openly—mocking his speech and—and manners! All of them, that is, save Garry Devereau."

Caleb's face hardened.

"Did he tell you that?" he demanded, surprised.

"Oh, no," Sarah exclaimed. "And you musn't mention it to him. I just gathered it from something he let drop the other day. You know, Cal, he hardly knows one figure from the other, but his reading is truly marvelous. He can read as fluently, as expressively, as you or I can; and one day, after he had been reading aloud for me, I asked him why he didn't talk as—as he read. He didn't know what I meant at first, but he understood the minute I tried to explain.

"'Do you mean I ought to talk in book language?' he asked.

"I told him that was my meaning, and after a time his blessed little face began to go red.

"'Do—do they,' and he nodded over yonder, Cal, 'do they all talk—like books?'

"So you see! And he's been trying ever since to correct his quaint idioms and funny contractions, but it'll take a long time to correct a mental process which is habit with him." Sarah's face grew resentful. "I wish we'd never let him go over there, in the first place. We should have known! For there isn't a look or a whispered comment, which he doesn't catch. And, Cal, I doubt if even I have fathomed the depths of his sensitiveness."

"We'll stop his going," Caleb stated flatly. "We'll keep him away from them." And under his breath he added something which Sarah had never heard him say in her presence.

But it needed no word of Caleb's to keep Steve at home. Without some suggestion to urge him, the latter showed no inclination to leave his own yard; and yet he would sit, too, for hours upon the top step of the veranda, staring in the direction of the stucco lodge and listening to the voices behind the high hedge. More and more often Garry Devereau came over and joined him instead, and together the pair made almost daily trips down to the mills. A quick intimacy had grown up between the two boys—an intimacy which seemed all the stranger to Caleb because of the very contrast between them.

Garret Devereau was two years older in actual age and a half dozen in the matter of knowledge. Already, while still in knickerbockers, he was beginning to show how entirely he was the son of his father. For the older Devereau had grown up from a handsome, dark-skinned, reticent boy into a moody and cynical skeptic who, at the age of thirty, had put the muzzle of his own revolver against his temple and pulled the trigger, because as he phrased it, "he was tired of the game." The skepticism was already there in Garry Devereau's slow smile. And Caleb often felt that the boy's black eyes were looking through and beyond, rather than at him. The bond of mutual understanding which seemed to exist between him and Steve puzzled Caleb; but he was glad of it, for all that. It kept the boy from being left entirely alone.

Later, when he had had weeks and months to ponder it, the outcome of it all seemed only logical to Caleb Hunter. It seemed to him then that he should have foreseen it from the very first. But as it was, when the denouement of which neither he nor Sarah had dreamed did come, it broke with a suddenness that was cataclysmic to both of them.

From the beginning Steve had evinced an insatiable appetite for books; he started in to devour everything upon which he could lay his hands, and the Hunter library was lined with well-stocked cases. But it was the history volumes which drew him most; with a fat tome upon his knees he would sit for hours in a corner upon the floor, his eyes glued to the pages. And one day, two weeks after the occurrence of the eggs, he came to Sarah with a shy question, a book in one hand. After she had caught the drift of his query, Sarah took the volume and found that he had been reading of the fabulous deeds of King Arthur and his Knights of the Round Table. His breathless interest in the subject thrilled and warmed the tiny woman, for more than once she had asserted to her brother that his very bearing was that of a small and sturdy knight of old, and she explained and elaborated upon the printed text far more appealingly than she had had any idea was in her power.

Steve went back to his reading after she had finished, but ever and again that morning his eyes, blank with preoccupation, wandered from the type; ever and again his ears seemed to be straining to catch the echo of childish trebles from the yard beyond the hedge. And after dinner Caleb was astonished when the boy explained, a little awkwardly, that he was going over to Allison's grounds for a while. Allison himself passed Steve in the hedge gap and, with a word of greeting, stopped to shake hands with him gravely. So it came about that they were sitting together, Dexter and Caleb, smoking in silence, when Barbara Allison's first wild scream came shrilling to their ears. They waited, staring at each other until the riotous clamor which rose set them to running across the lawn. But the scene which met Caleb's eyes when he burst through the shrubbery froze him into immobility.

There was a seething pack of children around two writhing figures upon the ground; they were all shrieking in soprano panic—all save Garry Devereau. He, standing a little to one side, was smiling his queer, crooked, handsome smile, while Stephen O'Mara mauled the Honorable Archibald Wickersham with true riverman thoroughness, which meant the infliction of the greatest possible damage in the least possible time. An inscrutable sort of contempt curled his lips when Barbara Allison frantically begged him to rescue the small Britisher from the storm of fists—a man's contempt for another man who does not take his punishment in silence. For the howls of the Honorable Archie were louder and more piercing than the loudest of the hysterical little girls who were watching.

Caleb felt as a man feels who tries to run in a nightmare and cannot make his feet obey the commands of his brain. It was only when Barbara Allison dropped desperately to her knees beside the huddle of arms and legs and straining bodies and began to beat with tight-clenched little hands upon Steve's tousled head, that the power of action returned to him. He fairly leaped forward then, scattering the circle before his weighty rush and, leaning over to get a firm grip upon his collar, jerked Steve upright with one mighty heave. That effort raised the Honorable Archie to his feet, also, for Steve was clamped to his antagonist, or victim, with a bulldog grip.

It grew very quiet when Caleb whirled the boy around and stood peering sternly down into his battle-streaked features. Allison strode quietly up in that moment.

"Well?" Caleb didn't know just how to begin, but his voice was cold. "Well, young man, can you explain just what this means?"

The Honorable Archie limped away a pace or two and, whimpering, fell to rearranging his crumpled raiment—fell to dabbling at a bruised and swollen nose. When he found that there was blood upon his handkerchief he howled again, but the rest of the children waited, appalled, for Steve's answer.

Had the boy burst into bitter expletive at that instant Caleb would not have been so surprised as he was at Steve's reception of his question. The latter looked up, just pushed his long hair back from his forehead with one quick hand; and then smiled, very, very slowly.

"Nuthin'—nuthin' much," he qualified the statement. "Only we was goin' to play King Arthur and the Knights of the Round Table! He wanted to be her knight"—an uncomplimentary thumb indicated the Honorable Archie—"and—and so did I." This time his eyes went to Barbara, who was listening, her teeth sunk in her lip. "He wanted to be her knight—an'—an' he ain't got no call to be, because in case of trouble, or anything, he couldn't purtect her! He couldn't fight good enough to take good keer o' her, because I kin fight better. I—I just licked him to prove it!"

And there the matter-of-fact explanation halted.

Caleb never knew just what he had meant to do when he first dragged the boy away from his shrieking rival. But while he stood there, looking down into that glowing face, he realized that he had walked into a situation bigger than any with which he was prepared to cope. Already it had become veritable comedy to the broadly grinning Allison—but it seemed symbolic to Caleb. He sensed how close it lay to tragedy itself; he found himself arguing kindly, in place of the rebuke which he had thought to deliver.

"But in the days when knighthood was in flower, Steve," he explained ponderously, "the—the fair ladies always chose their own knights, didn't they?"

But the question had an entirely unexpected effect upon the boy. For, instead of wiping the smile from the small and wistfully earnest face, it only softened it. Shyly Steve fell to kicking the turf with the toe of his new boot; then his head came up and, flaming red, he squared his shoulders and faced Barbara full. The move was unmistakable—he was just waiting for her to name him the knight of her choice. And, instead, the little girl, her eyes twin shafts of searing scorn, curled her lips at him and fairly spat out the words in her shaking rage.

"You—you—*my* knight?" she half whispered, "*You*!" And she turned her back and went, solicitously, toward Archie and his rumpled clothes.

Even Allison stopped smiling, even Devereau forgot his curious amusement, at the livid change which came over Steve's face with that answer which she flung at him. The boy fell away a step before her fierce little visage; he crooked one arm, over the cheek where her fists had beaten the skin pink a moment before. And then her meaning struck him like a blow between the eyes.

Shoulders slumped forward, head hanging low, he wheeled on heel and started for the gap in the hedge. Caleb could not move, nor did Allison, whose wits were quick enough in most things. But Garry Devereau followed and overtook his friend. He did not speak to him; he merely dropped one hand upon his drooping shoulders. And yet the men, had they talked for an hour, could not have conveyed all that there was in that second of contact. For it proved electrical in its effect. Steve whirled again and came marching back, head up now—back to the group which had not moved. Straight up to Barbara he went and faced her once again.

"I wa'n't good enough to be your knight, was I?" he accused her in a hushed and vibrant voice. "I—I don't know enough, ner I can't talk good enough, to be your knight. I ain't good enough fer you! But I'm a-goin' to be—do you hear? I'm a-goin' to be—an' when I am … when I am … then I'll come back to you!"

This time, rigid as a lance, he disappeared from sight. Caleb stood staring at the ground. Allison stood and stared at the horizon.

And when Barbara finally started, white of face and silent, toward the stucco house, Caleb, too, turned and followed his boy home. It was the first time in his memory that he and Dexter Allison had parted in anger, and at that moment Caleb believed that he hated the man and all that was his!

Steve had gone straight to his room, but one glimpse of his bloodless face had told Sarah too much and too little. After her brother had explained she would not let him go upstairs to the boy.

"It will be better to leave him alone for a while," she said. "It has been coming for days, this thing. I think I knew it would come—but how could we have stopped it, Cal? And you won't believe me, but it's because Barbara Allison cares more for our boy's little finger than she could for a hundred Archie Wickershams that she—she said what she did. Women do those things, and even I, who am a woman, can't tell you why!"

Steve did not come downstairs for supper that night, and when he failed to appear at the breakfast hour, both Caleb and Sarah mounted to his room, fear in their hearts. The bed had not been slept in; the sheets were not even disarranged, but there was a scrap of paper pinned to one pillow-slip. It wasn't written in "book language"—that short message—for it was not his brain, but his heart, which had phrased it:

> I'm a-comin' back—I'm comin' back to you, someday when they won't be no need fer you to be ashamed fer me. I'm takin' my new clothes with me because I knowed you would a-wanted me to—and the shoes, too. I'm askin' you to take keer of Ole Samanthy til I come fer her—and Miss Sarah ain't got no call to worry, fer I could always take keer o' myself.

It was signed "Stephen O'Mara."

Sarah's face went white when she had read it through. Her knees weakened under her and she had to sit down.

"Why, Cal—why, Cal, he's—he's gone," she quavered.

And Caleb nodded down into her stricken face.

"Yes—he—he's gone," he breathed.

Sarah swallowed hard. Then two bright tears crept out from under her eyelids and went coursing down her cheeks. She rose and groped her way to her own room.

Caleb found Barbara Allison waiting in the living-room when he, still numb from the shock, went back downstairs. She came up to him and stood a moment, twisting the fingers of one hand within those of the other.

"I want to see Stephen, please, Uncle Cal," she faltered.

Caleb drew a deep and unsteady breath.

"Steve isn't here, Barbara," he said as gently as he could.

The child didn't understand.

"Father sent me over to apologize," she explained slowly. "I'm to tell him that I'm sorry. But I—I want to tell him, too, that if I couldn't have him for my knight—I—I wouldn't ever have any knight at all!"

Caleb felt a tightening at his throat which made speech difficult.

"But Steve has gone away," he managed to gulp.

A shadow came into the big dark eyes lifted to his.

"He'll be back for breakfast, won't he?" she asked, hopefully.

"I'm afraid not, Barbara. I'm afraid now that he may never come back—again."

She didn't understand what he meant at first, so Caleb tried to explain. But when his voice broke and trailed off into a husky whisper there was no further need of explanation. She ran then and threw herself in a passion of tears upon a window-seat in the corner. Caleb found his chair. And after a time he felt a small hand touch his sleeve; he felt a wet cheek pressed tight to his own.

"Oh, don't you feel so badly, too, Uncle Cal," Barbara sobbed. "Please—please! Because he *is* coming back! He told me he would—he told me he would, himself!"

CHAPTER VI
MY MAN O'MARA

For a week and more Caleb Hunter scoured the surrounding country. He whipped over the hills in every direction, half hopeful that he might overtake the boy who had gone in the night. But none of the farmers on the outlying roads had seen pass their way a little foot traveler such as he described, and after a time even that small hope died.

When Dexter Allison came over the next day, his face far more perturbed than Caleb had ever before seen it by the news which Barbara, in tears, had carried to him, Caleb found that his anger had somehow oozed away during the night. Allison's concern was too genuine to be feigned; and Caleb learned too, that morning, that beneath his neighbor's amusement at the boy there had always been a strain of admiration for his sturdy gravity and more than a bit of wonder at his uncanny knowledge of things which were as sealed books to Dexter.

Together the two men searched for Steve, driving in silence through the country, until they both realized that the search was useless. And at last one day in early fall, Caleb started alone upon his errand into that stretch of timber to the north which the boy himself had vaguely designated as "up-river."

He spent a week in the saddle before he located the cabin of the "Jenkinses" in an isolated clearing upon the main branch of the river. If the journey could have been made cross-country, straight through the wilderness itself, it would have been no more than a ten-mile ride from that cabin to the same huge valley at the headwaters of the east branch, where he and Dexter and the boy had camped only a few days before. But it was a two days' journey around the backbone of that ridge alone, by trail. And even then, when he did locate the "Jenkinses," it took hours of quiet argument before Caleb could convince those shy and suspicious people that his errand was an honest one. Eventually they did come to believe him; they led him, a-foot, another half mile up the timber-fringed stream, to a log cabin set back in the balsams upon a needle carpeted knoll. And they stood and stared in stolid wonder at this portly man in riding breeches and leather puttees, when he finally emerged from that small shack, "Old Tom's" tin box under his arm, and, with lips working strangely, pinned the door shut behind him.

Caleb left in the limp fingers of the head of the Jenkins' household a yellow-tinted note of a denomination which they had not even known existed; he left them half-doubting its genuineness, until later when there came an opportunity to spend it. And Sarah was waiting at the door of the white place on the hill when Caleb wheeled into the yard at dusk, two days later.

"You've found him!" she exclaimed as she glimpsed his face when he entered the hall.

Caleb shook his head, his heart aching at the hunger in her question.

"No, I haven't found *him*, Sarah," he said gently enough. "But I—I've found out *who he is*!"

They forgot their supper that night. With heads close together they hung for hours over the ink-smeared sheaf of papers which the tin box yielded up. Most of them were covered with a cramped and misspelled handwriting which they knew must be that of the one whom Steve had called "Old Tom." Some of them were hard to decipher, but their import was very, very clear.

There was one picture—a miniature of a girl, eager of face and wavy of hair. Her relationship to the boy was unmistakable. Sarah found that and wept over it silently, and while she wept Caleb sifted out the remaining loose sheets and came upon a bundle of tax receipts. These puzzled him for a moment, until, at the very bottom of the box he found a folded and legal-looking document. He opened that and then he understood—he understood just how every penny had been spent which Old Tom had been able to earn. After the swiftest of examinations, Caleb refolded the paper and slipped it into his own pocket, without showing it to Sarah at all. Just at that instant he was not sure why he meant to keep its existence to himself, but even then, back in his brain, the reason was there. At length he turned to his sister.

"It's not hard to understand now, is it?" he said. "It's pretty plain now why he had to go. And we, Sarah—we who were going to 'make something of him'—why, we should have known absolutely, without this evidence. They laughed at him; they made fun of him—and there isn't any better blood than flows in that boy's veins! He was Stephen O'Mara's son, and no more brilliant barrister than O'Mara ever addressed a jury of a prisoner's peers and—and broke their very hearts with the simplicity of his pleading."

Sarah folded her thin hands over the woman's picture.

"I like his mother's face," she murmured, faintly. "And I'm jealous of her, Cal! You don't have to remind me of the rest of it, either, for I recall it all. She died, and he—he went all to pieces. They said, at his death, that he was destitute. And when he did follow her—across—they hunted everywhere, didn't they, and never found the boy? Didn't some of the newspapers argue that a servant—a gardener—had stolen him?"

Caleb nodded his head.

"Most of them ridiculed the suggestion, but it was true, just the same. That servant was Old Tom. And the only defense he makes is just one line or so in—in this." Caleb dropped a hand upon the half legible pages. "He says that he wasn't going to let civilization make of the boy's life the wreck which he, poor, queer, honest soul, thought it had made of his father's. And do you know, Sarah, do you know, I can't help but believe that this over-zealous thing which the law would have prosecuted was the best thing he could have done? I'll take these things, now, and lock them in the safe for the boy, until he—until he comes back home!"

But Sarah Hunter kept the picture of Stephen O'Mara's mother separate from the rest; she took it upstairs with her when she went, white and tired-faced, to bed. And it was Sarah's faith which outlasted the years which followed. She never weakened in her belief that some day the boy would come back—she and one other whose faith in his last boyish promise, phrased in bitterness, also endured. For during the next five years there was not a summer which brought Allison into the hills but what the first question of his daughter Barbara, motherless now herself, was of Steve.

"Has—has Stephen come back?" she asked invariably.

At first the query was marked by nothing more than a child's naïve eagerness; and later, when it was brought up in a casual, by-the-way fashion, it was, nevertheless, tinged with hope. Five years lengthened into ten, and still Steve did not come. But whenever Barbara asked that question Caleb remembered, as though it had happened only yesterday, that morning when she first appeared to the boy.

He wondered sometimes what Steve's reception of her would be now—if he did come back! The thought supplied many idle hours with food for speculation for Barbara Allison, year by year, had grown into that slender, dark-eyed creature of more than usual beauty whom Caleb had seen, as through the boy's own eyes, in the promise of the years. Caleb had long before given up all hope, but he wondered just the same. And then there came a morning when he didn't have to wonder any more. There came a morning when that self-same scene was staged again by Chance—staged with Caleb for an audience. There came a morning when Stephen O'Mara did return.

More than a few times in those intervening years the Hunter home had been closed. Sarah Hunter developed an uneasy restlessness which would have worried her brother had it not been for the light of wistful expectancy which never left her eyes. She developed what her brother termed a habit of "seeing America first and last, and in the interval between." But he, beneath his jocularity, was glad enough to accompany her upon those rambling journeys which, without itinerary, led them from coast to coast and he never smiled—at least not so that she might see him—even though he was certain that she, in her simplicity of spirit, was really looking for the boy.

All winter and throughout the summer, too, the Hunter place had been closed, until that day in late October. It had been a warm week—a week of such unseasonable humidity for the hills that Caleb, rising somewhat before his usual hour, had blamed his sleeplessness, as usual, upon the weather. He was glad to be home again that morning; he had been so lonely away from home that he was warmed unaccountably by the thought that Allison was in the hills, too. And he was sure of that fact, for the night before, when their train pulled into the station which occupied the spot where Allison's mill-yards had stood before, the bright brass work upon the private car of the owner of the stucco place next his own had been unmistakable.

Caleb was even wondering if Barbara would be with her father on this trip. Barbara had, he knew, been two years on the continent, "finishing," Allison called it, always with a wry face and a gesture toward his wallet pocket. He was wondering, as he came down the stairs, if she would ask him again if—if ... and then, at the sight of a seated figure outside on the top step of the veranda, he pulled up sharp in the doorway.

Caleb didn't have to wonder any longer!

The attitude of that figure before him was so like the picture which time had been unable to erase—so absolutely identical in everything save garb and size alone—that the man, recoiling a little, dragged one hand across his forehead as though he doubted his own eyes. But when he looked again it was still there, sitting chin in palm, small head under a rather weather-beaten felt hat thrust slightly forward, gazing fixedly toward the stucco house beyond the shrubbery. And before Caleb could move, before he was more than half aware of the painful pulse in his throat, it all happened again, just as it had happened years and years before.

Caleb heard voices in the adjoining grounds, and as he half turned in that direction Allison's bulky form, vivid in a far more vivid plaid, appeared in the hedge gap. While Caleb stared another figure flashed through ahead of him, laughter upon her lips, and paused a-tip-toe, to wave a hand in greeting. And instantly, as they had a dozen years before, Barbara Allison's eyes swung in instant scrutiny of the one who was seated at Caleb's feet. She hesitated, and recovered herself. But when, with quite dignified deliberation, she finally came forward to pass that motionless figure upon the steps, every pulse in her body was beating consciousness of his nearness. And yet, at that, when she paused at Caleb's side and bobbed her head with a characteristic impetuosity which she had never lost she seemed completely oblivious to the presence of anyone save Caleb and herself.

"Good morning, Uncle Cal," she murmured, very demurely.

Then the man upon the steps moved; he rose and turned and swept his rather weather-beaten hat from his head. His hair was still wavy, still chestnut in the shadows. And Caleb, though he could not force a word from his tightened throat, marveled how tall the boy had grown—how paradoxically broad of shoulder and slender of body he seemed to be.

It was a man's face which was lifted to his, tanned and wrinkled a little at the corners of the eyes by much exposure to sun and wind. But the eyes themselves hadn't changed a bit. They were still the same steady and unwavering gray. A smile crept into them, a smile crept across the even lips, and for all the change there was in that slow mirth it might have been the little figure of other days—the boy in the white drill trousers and uncouth boots—who was smiling up at Caleb.

Standing there in his blue flannel shirt and corduroy trousers, clasped tight to knee by high brown boots below them, Stephen O'Mara held out a sinewy brown hand. His voice was a little unsteady, but the mimicry of his own drawling speech of former years held an echo of boyhood—a twanging, boyish echo—which dragged at Caleb's very heartstrings.

"Haow—haow d'ye do, Uncle Cal?" he quavered.

Barbara had turned and started indoors in search of Miss Sarah. Now she halted, her slim back toward the two men at the veranda's edge, and stood motionless at the sound of that voice. When, little by little, she faced around at last, it was fairly to feel those grave gray eyes resting upon her own face. The blood of a sudden came storming up into Barbara's cheeks. And Caleb, even if he did not know what all of the girl's emotions were at that moment, knew that he knew one of them at least. Caleb had just learned himself what it was to see a ghost.

Dexter Allison, coming up less airily across the lawn, surprised his daughter poised with one hand outstretched, red lips half open. Ho found her staring, velvet eyed and pink of face, at a tall figure in blue flannel and corduroy, and although he had never seen him in all the months that the latter had been in his employ, Allison knew this must be the one in whose keeping lay, directly or indirectly, the success or failure of the biggest thing he had ever attempted in this north country—the man to whom he always referred, whenever he boasted of his exploits, as "my man O'Mara."

Beyond that point, however, Allison's immediate recognition did not go. The past interested him but little, except as a matter for precedent or a record of past performances. But memory fairly clamored in the girl's ears that morning. There was not one tiniest detail of the strangely intense, sturdily confident little hill-boy's bearing but what came back to her at that moment. She remembered them all, and seconds later, when Steve's fingers had closed over her own outstretched hand, she realized that she was staring at him in a childishly concentrated effort to read again in the man's gaze the undisguised worship and wonder which had always followed her from the eyes of the boy who had fought to be her knight. And she realized suddenly that he had sensed the effort behind her eager scrutiny, even though his own eyes remained whimsically unreadable.

"I always told them that you would come back," she murmured then. "Just as you—you said you would."

The remark was barely loud enough for even Steve to hear, but hard upon its utterance she caught her breath in anger at herself for her own senseless confusion, which had led her into saying the one thing she least of all had wanted to voice. Even an inane remark concerning the weather would have been better than that girlish naiveté which she felt seemed to force upon him, too, a recollection of the very letter of a promise which had, no doubt, long since become in his mind nothing but a quaint episode not untinged with absurdity.

She realized that her hand still lay in his; she grew hotly conscious of her father's rather perplexed survey of the tableau. And in that instant when Allison's first words reached her burning ears, even before Steve could reply to her greeting, she wrung free her fingers with an abruptness which, when she remembered it afterward, only added to her fury at her absurd confusion.

"Hum-m-m," puffed Allison. "Hum-m-m!" He spoke directly to Stephen O'Mara, who half turned his head at the first heavily facetious syllable. "So you did get my message, eh? I rather thought that it wouldn't reach you, up-river, until to-day." An ample smile embraced the tall figure in riverman's garb and his own daughter's crimson countenance—a most meaningful smile of roguery. "Well, from what I've heard," he stated, "and what I've ... seen, I should say that you are my man, O'Mara. Mr. Elliott himself has informed me that your quite spectacular success in one or two vital campaigns has been entirely due to the fact that you are an—er—opportunist! I agree with Mr. Elliott, absolutely—that is, if my first premise is correct."

And his laughter rumbled softly.

Barbara's face had cooled a little in that moment since Steve's eyes had left her face. Now she forgot her confusion—forgot to be annoyed, even at her father's clumsy banter.

"*Your* man, O'Mara!" she exclaimed indignantly. "*Your* man! Why, he—he's *my*—" and that was as far as she went.

Her voice thinned into nothingness, but words were not necessary to tell either Caleb or Steve that she had been about to assert a prior claim which dated back years and years.

The man whose smile was still that of the boy turned slowly back to Barbara. His quiet mirth, which crinkled the corners of his eyelids, seemed totally detached and impersonal; and yet it hinted, too, at an intimate enjoyment of the situation which they alone could appreciate. Steve merely held out his hand again and took her slim fingers within his own.

"I have always insisted to Mr. Elliott," he said, "that the solution of all the difficulties, which he chooses to view as gloriously romantic tilts with Destiny, depends one-half upon luck, and the other half on being on the ground personally, when the—affair—starts." He half faced toward Allison. "I am O'Mara," he finished very briefly, "your man, O'Mara—if you happen to be the East Coast Development and Timber Company?"

There was at most no more than the barest suggestion of it in Steve's crisp question, but Caleb sensed immediately that Allison's placid appropriation of the blue flannel-shirted one as his own particular property was not a mutually accepted status. Dexter, however, failed, or chose, to read nothing in the drawling question.

"I'm it," he agreed, jovially. "That is—I and two or three others, including Mr. Elliott, our esteemed president."

He mounted the steps heavily and stood contemplating the small hand still within the larger, browner one.

"The introductions seem to have outstripped me," he remarked, "but—er—any objection to shaking hands with me, too, Mr. O'Mara?"

Stephen laughed aloud. Allison's attempted lugubrity was really funny. From the door Barbara echoed his laughter in bubbling, throaty amusement at it all.

"Poor, blind papa!" she chanted mockingly, and disappeared on swift feet.

Allison scowled after her.

"Not so blind as some—the unprincipled jade!" he retorted. "But that's another thing I've heard about you, Mr. O'Mara, if you will pardon a garrulous old gossip's personalities. They tell me that you aren't particularly—susceptible?"

And then the bantering tone was dropped entirely. In the rest of Allison's greeting was all that Caleb found most lovable in the man's whole make-up—his proneness to accept men as men, for what they had done or might do, in a man's world.

"I've heard much of you, Mr. O'Mara; I've looked forward to this meeting," he said, as he shook hands. "Now I want to tell you that I am proud to know you. And so you didn't get my message, after all?"

The handclasp left Allison staring ruefully at his reddened fingers. Steve shook his head.

"I had to come down river, yesterday," he explained. "Your telegram found me here, and I waited over until this morning, as you suggested."

"Surely ... surely! I see ... I see!" Allison emphasized his comprehension. "Not that it was anything of vital importance. I just wanted a short conference with you, yourself, that was all. Elliott's own reports on the work are so tinged with his eternal optimism, so colored by what you aptly termed his romantic zest for the game, that I wanted your own opinion concerning the possibility of the East Coast Company finishing that railroad in time to fulfil their contracts. No hurry about it; but that's my house over yonder. You were just one place too far north to find me."

He turned to face Caleb. There was a flood of questions upon the latter's lips. Caleb wanted to seize the boy by the shoulder, and spin him around toward the light and stare and stare into his face; but he waited because he found much that was hugely diverting in Dexter's bland ignorance, which had even accepted Steve's presence there as a case of misdirection.

"I suppose you know what this early morning call presages, Cal?" Allison challenged.

Before Caleb could reply Steve knew what the answer was to be. The request found him already at the door, grinning broadly.

"Would you—would you mind finding Miss Sarah, Steve?" Caleb asked. "Will you tell her, please, that we are to be subjected to another—neighborly imposition!"

Steve's going left Allison frowning a little.

"We've played this farce through a hundred times, Cal," he murmured, "and it wasn't according to formula—that last remark of yours. But, do you know, just for a minute it sort of reminded me of something—something that seems to have happened before, and I can't recall just what."

He shook his head and led the way to a chair.

"It wasn't our nonsense that affected me, either," he finished. "I believe it was O'Mara himself who ... but I didn't know that you were acquainted with him, Cal. Have you known him long?"

"Um-m-m—yes!" Caleb weighed his reply. "Quite some time, I think I might say."

He shook with scarcely suppressed laughter, but Allison ignored his senseless mirth.

"I'd like to claim that boy as my own discovery," he avowed, "but I can't—not without fear of successful contradiction on Elliott's part. And in point of service it isn't fair to call him a boy, either, though I suppose both of us are old enough to be his father. He's Elliott's find. Elliott suggested him as the one man for this job, when I consolidated with the Ainnesley crowd and they took up the contract to move the Reserve timber from Thirty-Mile and the valleys above. Elliott knew of him, but I've been looking up his record pretty closely, since he took hold in earnest.

"He's in his twenties, as near as I can make out, but he's come through on one of two jobs that might well make an old campaigner envious. He took a fortune in hard woods out of San Domingo for a Berlin concern; he was the only man on the St. Sebastian River job who said the construction was too light. He said it wouldn't stand when the ice began to move in the spring—and it didn't! Oh, he knows his business! But it wasn't his successes which caught Elliott's eye. It's the way he has failed a couple of times, fighting right back to the last ditch—and fighting and fighting!—when all the rest had quit, that made me anxious to get a look at him. Perhaps there are older men who can outfigure him on loads and stresses, but as a field general he stands alone. He can handle men. And, when it comes to meeting conditions just as they arise, Elliott says he's a wonder—he can outguess dear old Mother Nature herself!"

There was grave appreciation in Allison's voice—honest appreciation of a man who had himself achieved, for another man's achievement. And yet Caleb, in spite of the proud pumping of his heart, in spite of his desire to murmur, "But I told you so, Dexter, years ago," still found room to wonder at a thin strain of speculation which seemed to underrun the speaker's words. In his reiteration of O'Mara's qualities Allison seemed almost to be assuring himself that infallibility was not a human attribute. And his next remark only served to heighten that suggestion.

"That's why the East Coast Co. brought him up here to build their bit of road," he went on slowly. "They've got to move that Reserve Company timber. They have a contract that'll break 'em—break us—if we fall down. And do you know, Cal, I—I can't help but believe that the thing is beyond the pale of possibility. I believed it six months ago, when Elliott and Ainnesley and the rest of them were so keen for it, and I believe it still, even though I have seen Elliott's engineer and know what he has already accomplished. That track'll never go through on schedule—and that's why I'm up here for the winter. It's going to be a hot little race against time, with some millions for a purse. It'll break the East Coast Co. if he fails, and"—his voice became oddly intense—"and I tell you again that it—can't—be—done!"

Then Allison became aware of Caleb's mild astonishment at his vehemence.

"An amateur's opinion, of course, Cal," he laughed, "which is strictly *entre nous*. But, win or lose, this man O'Mara will be a valuable man to have around after the thing is decided."

"You said that he reminded you of something," Caleb began rather heavily. "It recalled something to me, too. I wonder if you remember a little fishing trip that we took, some ten or twelve years ago, Dexter, up into the hills? It was to the headwaters of the cast branch, somewhere in the neighborhood of the Reserve Company's holdings, I should say."

"Why, yes," the other answered, off-handedly. "Why, yes, now that you mention it, I do remember. May I ask your reason for speaking of it?"

"No reason in particular," Caleb hesitated. "Only this O'Mara reminded me of something, too—something that you said, that night at the camp-fire."

"Well?"

Allison's monosyllable was coolly noncommittal.

"Can you remember what it was?" Caleb asked, positively uncomfortable now.

"I think I remarked that there was a fortune for some man in that valley, if he was far-sighted enough. Was that it?"

Then Caleb understood the challenge in his friend's voice. He thought he understood. The names of the stockholders of the Reserve Company were all strange to Caleb save one. The Honorable Archibald Wickersham, who was said to represent huge foreign interests, he had known as a boy. And Caleb had seen Dexter indescribably sore, before this, from having overlooked, as he termed it himself, "a sure thing bet." He laughed, more like his placid self again.

"Bless you, no!" he exclaimed. "What have I ever done to make you believe that a mere commercial estimate would remain with me this long? It—it was something that you said concerning the making of a gentleman. I just wondered if you were of your early way of thinking. I wondered if you would consider that—that—"

Allison lay back in his chair and breathed deeply, slowly—and Miss Sarah appeared that moment in the doorway, pinker of cheek and more tremulous of lip than her brother had ever seen her before. She dropped Allison an old-fashioned curtsy, which was an exceedingly frivolous performance for Sarah.

"Breakfast is served, Cal," she fairly chortled, "and there are two very hungry children inside."

CHAPTER VII
HARRIGAN, THAT'S ME!

Never before had the air of that long, paneled room been so surcharged with half-suppressed hilarity. At first her father merely scowled at Barbara's intermittent little gurgles, which refused to stay entirely pent-up; he frowned at her seemingly inane interruptions of the technical discussion into which he had immediately plunged with the East Coast Company's engineer, until he could no longer ignore the smile which pulled at the lips of the latter, too, at every fresh attempt of the girl to swing the conversation into an utterly irrelevant channel. He looked around the table then and caught the gleam in Caleb's eyes; he took note of Miss Sarah's illuminated face, and gave way to a burst of querulousness not all simulation.

"*What* is the joke?" he demanded in a voice that set them all to rocking in their chairs. "Let me in on it—let me laugh, too—if there is anything worth laughing at. Cal, you're growing old—old and feeble-witted!"

He turned sternly to his daughter, but the darkly glowing eyes which she lifted to his absolutely silenced him for an instant. Twin devils of mischief fairly danced in their shimmering, liquid depths. The girl's face, even to him who had long before grown overfamiliar with its beauty, was a wonderfully lovely thing. Allison sat and stared at her for a moment, blankly, and when he went on his voice had become less testy.

"And you," he growled, "you have interrupted me a dozen times already, always with some nonsense of which I can make neither rime nor reason. Now, if you don't mind, I'd like to get Mr. O'Mara's reason for establishing his headquarters at Thirty-Mile, instead of directing the work from Morrison, which would seem to be far more convenient."

Barbara bobbed her head, meekly. Her giggle, however, was shameless.

"But Mr. O'Mara has been trying to tell you," she defended in a suffocated small voice, "that it's because the work at this end is not so difficult. There are several miles of swamp work, I think he said, and a bridge or something, which promises trouble. I—I am sorry if I interrupted. I only wanted to ask Mr. O'Mara a question myself—a—a very unimportant question, I'm afraid!"

Allison had had experience with his daughter's seeming meekness. Moreover, the working of Caleb's and Sarah's faces baffled him. He waited, fuming.

"Just before you and Uncle Cal came in we—we were talking about the weather," the girl struggled on. "Mr. O'Mara predicted it would rain soon and I just wanted to ask him what made him think so."

"Yes?" Allison temporized.

It was very quiet for a moment. Steve sat, a little red of face himself, gazing across into the girl's starry eyes.

"Go ahead!" she prompted him with a gasp.

Then his lips began to curl until a smile overspread his face and half-closed his eyes. He leaned back and raised obediently a quaintly solemn, quaintly boyish treble.

"I wa'n't guessin'," he averred soberly, "ner I wa'n't thinkin' it will. It'll jest be rainin', come sunup, and it'll be good fer till Wednesday, for sure!"

At the beginning of that quavering statement Dexter Allison's lips fell apart. They remained open long after Steve had finished. Once he started to rise, and then dropped back into his chair, dumfounded. There was no doubt concerning the success of his daughter's query. At last he got to his feet and padded around the table. With a hand on either of the boy's shoulders, he turned that browned face up to his own.

"You," he murmured, weakly. "You! And Elliott said that you could outguess dear old Mother Nature herself! Well, I—I'm damned!"

They talked no more business at table that morning, and Allison found scant opportunity to make himself heard at all. Even the reticence which seemed a part of Steve's grave face and big body was swept aside before the tumult of questions that tumbled from Barbara's lips, promptly to be supplemented by Caleb whenever her breath gave out.

"And to think that you didn't recognize him, even when you met him face to face," she rallied her father. "It was dense enough of me not to have known instantly who it must be, the first day you began your endless reiteration of 'my man, O'Mara.' I, at least, should have known, because—because"—she faltered a little—"well, they always do, in books!"

It raised another storm of laughter—that faltering, ingenuous reason of hers—and Barbara hastened to explain that the phrase was a relic of her own childhood, which she had once coined in extenuation of conduct to which her mother had objected. She still employed it, she explained, in particularly irresponsible moments.

It was minutes before Allison could wedge in a single remark, longer than that before he stopped frowning to himself in a fashion which made Caleb remember that moment of inexplicable vehemence, outside on the veranda. They had retrogressed as far as the "injine"—the "steam injine"—when Allison finally made himself heard.

"What I can't remember is just why you left us so suddenly. I know it was some sort of a rumpus, with Barbara in it—there's always a woman, of course—but I can't recall—"

He paused to ponder—paused and became aware immediately of Barbara's swift silence and Steve's hint of self-consciousness. Then it all returned to him with a rush. He had his turn.

"Oh, but I do remember," he drawled. "Why, of course—*of course*! It was a matter of knight-errantry and ladies fair! But who was it whose choice conflicted with your own?"

He cocked his head on one side, mock thoughtful; then he fell to pounding his knee and roared with laughter.

"Archie Wickersham!" he shouted. "Archie Wickersham—oh, Lord! I never really appreciated that *mêlée* until this minute. And you promised that you'd be back, didn't you, and—well, b'gad, here you are! And now don't suffer any longer, Barbara, though I must state that this is the first time I ever knew you to search so diligently beneath the table for renewed composure. I am not going to expound Mr. O'Mara's reasons for going, any more than I could dilate upon those which have brought him back. But please shake hands again—Steve. And, if I may be pardoned the idiom, allow me to assure you that it was some battle!"

If it did nothing else, Allison's ponderous raillery served one end. It removed any sentimental awkwardness which might have attached to the episode, and yet the girl rather resented its being so completely reduced to terms of farce-comedy. When the men rose, after breakfast, to go down into the town, she, too, declared her intention of accompanying them, as though it were the expected thing. She crossed the lawn at Steve's side, ahead of her father and Caleb, with Miss Sarah watching from the door. Both men walked for a time in silence, their eyes upon the slender figure in short skirt and woolly sweater beside the taller one in blue flannel before them. And, as usual, Allison was the first to speak.

"Now I know what you meant when you referred to that trip up the west branch, Cal," he said. "And you were right. It does take stuff to make that sort of a gentleman. Isn't there anything more to tell me? I am truly interested, Cal."

So Caleb told him then of "Old Tom's" tin box. And while he was explaining the man and girl ahead, all in one breath, skipped back to that day-before-yesterday now many years gone. There was a quality of camaraderie in the girl's half-parted lips and eager impulsiveness of tongue that morning that was entirely boyish. Her very unconsciousness of self intensified and emphasized it for the man whose steady gaze rarely left her warm face. And more than once she caught herself watching for his slow smile to spread and crinkle the corners of his eyelids; once or twice, in a little lull, she found time to wonder at that new and quite frivolous mood of hers. But when Steve finally asked for Devereau—Garry Devereau, who had followed him to the hedge-gap that day and laid one hand upon his bowed, shamed shoulder—the light went from Barbara's eyes. And Stephen O'Mara, who did not understand at first the quick hurt which entered them, stopped smiling, too.

"I liked him," Steve said simply. "I've always remembered and liked him. Thinking of him and—and—has often kept me from being too lonely nights when I was lonely enough."

That statement concerning his friend contained the first personal note which had come from his lips. Barbara did not answer immediately, and Steve thought that she was phrasing her own reply. He could not know that she wanted a moment in which to contemplate the little hint of diffidence in his voice and to wonder at herself for not having wondered before if he had not, many, many times, been very lonely indeed.

"Do you remember a little girl who was at our place the summer you were here?" she asked finally. "A pale, red-lipped, very shy little thing named Mary Graves?"

Stephen nodded.

"And do you remember how, even then, Garry seemed to care for her? He was always supercilious with the rest of us; he tormented us or ignored us entirely, but never her."

Again the inclination of the head.

"Well, he grew up just that way," Barbara went on, thoughtfully. "One never could tell what was behind his indifference or—or flippancies. He mocked at things ... customs and courses of action, which we have come to accept and ... and recognize. But he was always gentle with her, and kind, and—oh, I think reverend is the right word! Now, knowing Garry as I do—as you will, when you see him again—the phrase may seem a strange one to apply to him. And yet it describes best his bearing toward Mary Graves, two years ago."

She was walking more slowly now, without knowing it.

"I doubt if Garry ever revered anything on earth, or above it, except just little, white, shy Mary Graves, who never grew much bigger than she was when you knew her. I don't know whether you know it—of course you don't!—but his father cared that way for a woman, cared just as utterly. And everybody thought this match was an assured thing; they even wondered at it a little, she was so ... so mouselike, and Garry so brilliant and hard and—I don't like the word sophisticated. It seemed to me that Garry's wisdom was not a thing which he had acquired himself. It seemed more the accumulated wisdom of ages and ages which was his just by—by instinct.

"He cared for her that way, Mr. O'Mara, and she married another man, almost without a word of explanation to him. Nobody ever cited Garry as a shining example, but he—that man whom Mary Graves married—had an unspeakable record! Her family made the match—the newspapers call it a union of America's fairest youth and powerful millions, don't they? Well, he had them—and she married him. And Garret Devereau dropped out of the world for a long time.

"It was a year before he came back. People had already begun to talk about the way his father had gone before him—he shot himself, Mr. O'Mara, when he became tired of waiting for Garry's mother to return—and when Garry reappeared they talked more. I never knew before that a change so terrible could take place in anyone so much a man as I know Garry to be. It's not just his face and his rather dreadful silence. It's not the fact alone that he drinks too much, and shows it, pitifully. It's—oh, it's the pity that a brain so keen could so deliberately commit suicide.

"They've begun to drop him, Mr. O'Mara, and you know what that means. But I'll always care for him deeply. That's why I have asked him up this fall. Don't you think you could come down again, Friday, if you have to go back into the woods before then? I'm going to have a party for some week-end guests—a masque dance. Garry needs his friends now, more than he ever did, and—and when you meet him will you—will you, please, not let him see that you notice how much he has changed?"

Barbara put one hand upon his elbow, and again in that moment of contact the directness of her appeal made Steve think of a slim and clear-eyed boy. He realized that she cared for Garrett Devereau only as he cared himself with fine and lasting appreciation for the finenesses of him whom they had known together. Steve nodded his comprehension, and made no answer to her invitation to him, then. But they found conversation somehow less easy after that. It was not until they had traversed the streets of the lower village—long lanes of red and blue and saffron-fronted saloon-hotels and rivermen's lodging-houses—and reached the newer, huger mills down-river that the girl regained in part her former vivacity.

Morrison had grown, inconceivably, in those elapsed years. A railroad station and freight-yard occupied the ground which had been occupied by the former mills; a single track road stretched arrow-straight into the south to a junction with the trunk line, which swung westward twenty odd miles below. And even the very atmosphere of that lower portion of the town was different. The men still swarmed in on the drives, brilliant dots of color against the neutral background of the dusty wide streets. Their capacity for abandonment to pleasure, their prodigality, was as great as ever, but the old-time picturesque simplicity of it all seemed lacking—the simplicity which had once mitigated much that would have been otherwise only brutish. The dingily gaudy saloon fronts, like drabs in blowsy finery, struck a too sophisticated, sinister note—which, after all, only sums up completely the change which had taken place. Even the vices of the older Morrison, in being systematized, had become infinitely more complicated, too. It was no longer a river village. Morrison was a city now.

Once, when a squatly huge, red-headed, red-shirted riverman with a week's red stubble upon his cheeks, lurched out of a doorway ahead of them and stood snarling malevolently at O'Mara, the girl shrank against her companion and clutched his arm. The red-shirted one fell to singing after they had passed. A maudlin rendition of "Harrigan, That's Me," followed them long after they had rounded a corner. Steve looked down and smiled casually into Barbara's wide and startled eyes.

"That's a river-boss," he explained, "enjoying what he considers a roaring good time. His name is Harrigan. He works on the Reserve Company's cut, which we are to move in the spring, and whenever he has had a trifle more than enough he always sings that song. He's willing to fight, too, to prove that it was written especially for him!"

The girl continued to gaze up at him. His short laugh failed entirely to clear her face of apprehension.

"He's not exactly a friend of yours, is he?" she said.

"Well, not exactly," Steve admitted. "Not when he is in that frame of mind!"

"Nor in any other," the girl persisted, and she glanced down at her hand, still lying upon the blue-flannel sleeve. "Did you know that your arm grew as hard as iron for an instant? I never knew that anyone's arm could grow as hard as that. And is that the way you always prepare to receive your—friends?"

Steve colored a little.

"Perhaps I'm overcautious," he replied. "But it has to be hard. It constitutes what one of my men, Joe Morgan, calls 'accident insurance.'"

Then her face lighted up again. The delighted bob of her head with which she greeted that name astonished the man.

"Do you—why, you must have heard of Joe," he exclaimed.

Mischief danced again in the dark eyes.

"Joe Morgan," she laughed. "'Fat Joe,' isn't it? And of course I have heard of him. You don't realize it, but I know more about this East Coast work and—and the men who are doing it, than I had any idea myself. Why, I'll wager that you never knew, yourself, that he once wrote in to the officials insisting that the entry of his name on the files be changed from 'Joe Morgan, cook,' to 'Joseph Morgan, assistant to Chief O'Mara'!"

Steve's chuckle of appreciation was answer enough.

"I didn't know," he admitted, "but it's like him. And it was no more than reasonable, either—that request—even if it is funny. He has been cook for me; but he's been doctor and nurse and countless other things in as many crises. He's the most trustworthy and capable adviser, too, that any man ever had."

She scanned his face closely at the timbre of those words. Then, with face averted, "Didn't he embroider you a—a sofa-cushion, too, once?" she inquired, quite demurely.

Steve grew very red.

"Who told you that?" he blurted, and Barbara giggled again.

"Mr. Ainnesley, I think. Then it is true? I—I never believed it before."

Watching the blood creep up beneath his tanned skin, she told herself that she did like more than a little the way his eyelids crinkled when he grinned.

"We were in San Domingo that year," he explained none too composedly. "It was near Christmas, and Joe wouldn't consider any of the native wares as a gift. So he—he worked it himself in—in yellow worsted on a red background. I have it still, displayed in a conspicuous place in the shack up-river. But now I'll wager that you can't guess what the motto is across its front. He told me that he didn't care for it particularly himself, but it was the only one he could find. You can't guess, but you are permitted to try."

And he gasped when she threw back her head and burst into her gurgling, throaty laugh.

"'What is home without a father?'" she sing-songed. And when they were both sober-faced again she added:

"I want to know him, please! Can't I meet him, Mr. O'Mara?"

Side by side they turned in at the millyard, between towering piles of aromatic raw planks. Behind them Caleb and Allison had lost still more ground while the latter paused to speak a peremptory word in the ear of a mildly intoxicated, red-headed riverman who was pouring forth his whole soul in the refrain of "Harrigan, That's Me!" And almost immediately, in answer to Barbara's question, Steve pointed across to a short, plump figure in conversation with McLean, the mill superintendent. Even at that distance his broad face gleamed from the closeness of a recent shave; even at that distance it was quickly apparent to the girl that his garb was as near a replica of O'Mara's own clothes as his lack of height and extra weight would permit.

"Will you bring him?" she asked eagerly. "Will he come?"

But the question was unnecessary. Joe Morgan—Fat Joe to the river-front and the construction squad—was already hustling in their direction, even before Steve, with that slow smile tugging at his lips, had finished assuring her that it was never necessary to summon Joe into the presence of an attractive member of the opposite sex. He came without being called. Barbara had a closer and closer view of him, until he stopped at last directly in front of them and bowed. She wanted to laugh at that wide face—at the grandiloquent flourish with which he removed his hat—and would have had she not recalled the grave respect with which the man beside her had referred to him a moment before. His eyes were palest blue, his nose a smooth pink mound in an expanse of pink, pink cheeks. She noted that his teeth were as white and even as those of O'Mara himself. Fat Joe bowed again.

"Morning, Chief," he saluted, in that thin and reedy tenor which none but fat men have.

Then Barbara laughed.

Steve managed the presentation with extreme punctility and left them. When he returned, almost an hour later, he heard them both laughing long before he came into view, and on the way back up the hill the girl detailed for him much of her conversation with Fat Joe.

"Hereafter I shall be more dignified when in your presence," she informed him in as deep a bass as she could summon. "I had no idea how great and important a man was escorting me when I came down this hill! But Mr. Morgan has enlightened me."

With that she discovered that she could still tease him, almost as easily as she had teased the sturdy small boy of the uncouth shoes and napping trousers.

"Joe is necessarily prejudiced in his opinion," he argued, "and therefore shouldn't be taken too seriously."

"He told me that you had one regrettable characteristic, however," the girl went on. "He lamented your strength at the ancient and honorable pastime of stud-poker! And he also bewails your taste in literature. Why, he tells me that you are indicted to Dickens and Dumas—he didn't pronounce it that way, either—and even fall back upon Shakespeare, in dark and dour hours. No, I am positive that Mr. Morgan docs not approve of such fiction. He confided to me that he finds more entertainment, of a winter's night, in perusing a Sears-Roebuck or a Montgomery-Ward catalogue. And—and do you know what I admitted to him? No? Well, I told him that some of the happiest moments of my life had been spent in just such fashion. I've always thought they were fascinating!"

She badgered him on the way back up the hill that morning, but when they paused for a moment at the edge of the close-cropped lawn which rolled back to the stucco and timber house facing the river, she abandoned her facetiousness.

"Why should there be any—any element of personal danger in this work you are doing, Mr. O'Mara?" she asked. "And did I do wrong in mentioning to Mr. Morgan how that man came out of that—place, and glared so at you?"

His rejoinder should have been very reassuring.

"So Joe has been hinting at that mystery stuff again, has he? After listening to him one is almost compelled to believe that I run daily a veritable gauntlet of nameless perils."

Barbara stood, small fists buried in her sweater pockets, studying his smile of amusement.

"I shouldn't like to believe so," her voice was faintly diffident. "And you—you haven't accepted my invitation for Friday. May I expect you? I didn't tell you, but Archie—Archibald Wickersham—will be there, as well as Garry. So—so you won't be entirely unacquainted."

And then, at those words, his face changed. All in one fleet second, in spite of the whole morning's quick intimacy of mood and the spirit of companionship which to her had seemed a delightfully new yet time-tried thing, Barbara found that she could not read an inch behind those grave gray eyes. She found his quiet countenance as unreadable as that of the utmost stranger might have been. And while she waited, not entirely certain how displeased she was at his deliberation, a blackest of black horses soared splendidly over a fence to the north and came cantering down the road. The rider, a tall, bare-headed girl, lifted her crop in salute as she caught sight of them.

"My friend, Miriam Burrell," the girl murmured in explanation to Steve, and something had gone from her voice and left it conventionally impersonal. "She's riding Ragtime, and isn't he a beauty—almost as much a beauty as she is herself?"

The horse came on, to be reined up at last directly in front of the two at the roadside. Stephen O'Mara met for a moment the level, measuring glance of its rider, before Miriam Burrell turned to Barbara.

"I've enjoyed exceedingly our morning canter, Bobs," her alto voice drawled.

Then, before Barbara could reply, she threw one booted leg from the stirrup and dismounted. With the reins looped over her elbow she faced the man in blue flannel and corduroy, a tall, lithe figure with coppery red hair and whitest skin and doubly vivid lips.

"You're Stephen O'Mara," she said, and the calmly direct statement might have been overbrusk had it not been for the modulation of her low voice. "You're Stephen O'Mara, for a thousand!"

And she held out a gauntleted hand, the clasp of which corroborated the suggestion of wirelike strength in that lithely straight body.

Barbara Allison had never been able to analyze her preference for Miriam Burrell. Even the girl's undeniable beauty of face had often puzzled her, for, taken each feature by itself, it was far more striking than beautiful. There was no color in her pale skin; her red mouth, if anything, was a trifle too wide, and her wide-set eyes were tip-tilted in an almost Oriental slant. Her utter lack of hypocrisy, her unsparing arraignment of fundamental motives—her own and those of all with whom she came in contact—often resulted in calmly direct comments which were stunningly disastrous to casual conversation. For Miriam Burrell told the truth to others, which was unusual enough to puzzle more than a few; she did not lie to herself, and that was an enigma to almost all. It resulted, of course, in a reputation for "unconventionalism."

There was scarcely a day passed but that her coldly dispassionate dissection of this or that foible of their own set, did not startle or sometimes distress Barbara Allison; hardly a day but that her cool voice, which could be as tempered as edged steel, did not cut through the veneer of some custom or other and expose the crooked grain beneath. Barbara did not know just why she cared so deeply for Miriam Burrell—we scarcely ever realize that such a regard can be based only upon the deepest of deep-founded faith—

but at that moment, while she and Steve were shaking hands so soberly, she felt very little, very much ignored; felt as though she did not share at all the understanding in their eyes.

"I've just asked Mr. O'Mara to come to my dance, Miriam," she said, "and how did you know him, pray? I've asked him, but he is unflatteringly long in accepting."

"Know him?" she echoed. "Know him! Oh, Mr. O'Mara and I have met before. I think just before the fall of the Roman Empire, wasn't it, Mr. O'Mara? Weren't they dragging me in at the wheel of a chariot one afternoon, when you were dealing out a gold piece to each of your legionaries?"

She laughed, dryly, and Barbara felt smaller and more forlorn and lonelier still.

"No doubt Mr. O'Mara hasn't time to be flattering, Bobs," she commented. "But you will have time to come Friday, for a little while, won't you?" she asked.

Steve glanced down at the hand which still felt the pressure of her buckskin clad fingers.

"I have to work—day and night—some weeks when things break badly," he told her simply. "If I can"—and he turned to Barbara—"if I can, I want to come."

Miriam nodded her head with brisk finality.

"If you can," she agreed. "Barbara, no doubt, has been telling you about Garret Devereau, hasn't she? Yes—come if you can. I have heard, Mr. O'Mara, that you have once or twice fought your way out of the dark, when everybody else had lost hope. I want an opportunity to talk with—a specialist in such campaigns!"

Stephen O'Mara had read a meaning in the words of that contained, often abrupt, straightly tall girl of which Barbara Allison had not even dreamed. He stood watching them when they turned up the driveway, the horse Ragtime muzzling the woolly white sweater and following like a dog. But he wasn't thinking of Miriam Burrell or of Garry Devereau, while he waited for Caleb and Dexter Allison to come up with him. He was wondering about Archie Wickersham—the Honorable Archie—thinking about that funny brawl of years before, which had not been so funny after all—wondering if—

It was past twelve that night when Miriam Burrell's door was pushed softly open by a slim white figure which hesitated on the threshold; but the night-light was still burning upon the table. Barbara stood for a moment, staring at her friend, who was sitting bolt upright in bed.

"Then you aren't asleep," she faltered. "Are you—reading?"

The older girl turned and gazed, half blankly, at the dark-eyed face in that mist of loosened hair.

"Yes," she drawled, for all that her hands and hunched-up knees were bookless. "Yes, I'm reading. I'm having a little squint at this puzzle-scroll they call Life."

She made a peremptory gesture and Barbara crept in beside her.

"I—may I turn off the light?" she asked.

Miriam snapped the button.

"I couldn't sleep," Barbara began presently, in a quaintly small voice. "And I—I wanted—Miriam, I've acted so like an unschooled, half-grown girl to-day that it has perplexed and worried me! From the moment when I first recognized him and became so—tangled up—I've just chattered and chattered. You don't think I'm utterly frivolous and unstable, do you?"

"Haven't you always been famed for your poise?" came back the uncompromising voice she knew so well.

"Are you—you aren't laughing at me, are you?" she hesitated. "Because I don't think I am in the mood to be laughed at. And I have poise. I am not a child. But looking back now, I can't quite account for all my—shall I call it cordiality? Don't you believe, Miriam, that it was because I wanted to make up, a little, for the way I treated him when he was a boy?"

"Maybe!" agreed Miriam, unenthusiastically.

"Because I did treat him abominably," went on the drowsy voice. "And, do you know, all day, even when we seemed so—such good friends, I still felt as though he was on guard against any repetition of such a slight. I wouldn't want him to feel that way, but it was there just the same, even in the way he received the invitation to my party. It was on the tip of my tongue to tell him that there are men who—who'd almost charter a liner to come—if I'd invite them. It would have sounded conceited, but I wanted to *jolt* him! And he just said he'd come if he could!"

"He has his work," Miriam answered, and into her voice crept that wearied, indescribably hard note which the younger girl couldn't understand. "He has to work, and a lot of those others would be a lot more worth asking, if they had to work, too. I wish every man had to—work—hard; had to work until body and brain were numb with it!" Her voice slurred and she recovered it. "I don't know whether he remembers or not. Probably not! You've just had a unique experience for one of our kind, that's all. You've met a man!"

Barbara raised herself upon one elbow.

"You don't mean to infer, do you, Miriam," she reproved, "that Archie Wickersham or my other friends, or—or Garry, aren't men?"

"Males!" snapped the other girl. "Just males! But"—and she seemed to be arguing with herself—"but Garry might have been, though—he might have been!"

Barbara lay awake a long time, pondering.

"It's odd," she murmured once, "but we did seem so—so congenial. I can't remember when my brain has been so quick to catch a thought or supplement one. Have you ever wondered, Miriam, why we—we can't seem to marry one who brings out the best in us, like that?"

"Can't? You mean, dear child, that we don't! Some of us because the 'best that is in us' is far, far too decently unexciting for daily diet. And some of us—oh, just because we haven't the sand and backbone, I guess!"

But Barbara was too nearly asleep to catch the bitterness of that reply. Just once again, before she slept, she asked a question.

"Should I have told Mr. O'Mara that my engagement to Archibald Wickersham was to be announced at the party?" she murmured.

"Why should you have?" Miriam crisply wanted to know.

"Oh, I don't know," she mused. "Only I thought he might be interested. You don't seem to realize that we are—very old friends!"

And long after Barbara was sound asleep, her face buried in the palm of one hand, Miriam Burrell lay stiffly awake. Once she smiled a little, for such perplexities which, of themselves, must work out inevitably. When dawn came it found her still struggling stubbornly with her own, for which it seemed there could be no solution now.

CHAPTER VIII
GREETINGS, SIR GALLAHAD!

It was late that night when Steve climbed into the rig which was waiting with Pat Joe at the reins and they turned north into the hills. For he had remained with Caleb and Miss Sarah long after the logs in the fireplace had crumbled away to a flaky ash, discussing that ink-smeared record which Caleb himself had ridden to find, ten years before, in the shack up-river. And the latter was surprised at learning how much of it was no longer news.

"Yes, I know," Steve told them, after Caleb had finished relating, with quite ponderous pride, many things which he ascertained concerning the Stephen O'Mara who had gone before. "I know! Four or five years ago, when I found out that it was—customary for one to be certain as to such things, I started to look it up myself. And when I found out from the records that a boy by that name had disappeared—perhaps been stolen by an old servant—I remembered instantly, of course, the box over which Old Tom used to hang, hour after hour. I came back into the woods looking for it that summer and found it gone and nothing left of the Jenkins' cabin but a pile of charred logs. On my way out I stopped here—somehow I thought that maybe you might have it—but the house was closed. And no one seemed to know where you had gone or when you would return."

Caleb nodded, and his eyes turned to Sarah.

"We were sleuthing, Steve," he explained as soberly as he was able. "We were ranging from border to border and coast to coast, looking for you." He stopped to scan the browned face closely for an instant. "But couldn't you have written—or—or tried again? We've been waiting—boy!"

Steve's face colored a little.

"I did try, twice after that," he stated, hesitatingly, "but I didn't have much surplus cash for travel in those days, or—or clothes, either. I'm afraid I wasn't too prepossessing an object, on any of those visits, after I had tramped in overland. The house was closed both times I came. And then I did write once—that was from San Domingo—the third year after I left college. I was so lonesome down there that I had to write, I think. But there—wasn't any reply, so I sort of thought perhaps—"

He halted lamely, but his meaning was plain enough. Caleb faced about abruptly, his face sternly accusing.

"Do you mean to hint that you ever dared believe we didn't want—" and there Sarah stopped him with an capable nod of her head. "We didn't get that letter, Steve," he finished. "If we only had we—we would have been less lonely waiting, too."

Steve sat and stared down at his heavy boots.

"I should have known that," he faltered. "I should have known that there were too many presidents on that island, both coming and going, for the mails to be infallible. But I wasn't just sure—"

Miss Sarah cut in then and took the conversation serenely in hand.

"We have something else of yours, Stephen," she said in her soft, almost lisping voice, "something which Caleb brought back with him which he has neglected to mention."

She left them for a moment, and when she came back downstairs with the picture of the girl with the steady mouth and eyes her brother breathed with less difficulty than he had during her absence. For a second or so he had almost believed that she might have run across that bunch of loose tax receipts and the folded, legal-looking document which he had tucked away in his own iron box. Stephen O'Mara sat and looked long and long at his mother's picture. When he finally raised his head again Miss Sarah's eyes were misty, too.

"This is one of the things for which I can never thank you enough," he murmured. "I can only tell you that I didn't know—I didn't understand—"

Miss Sarah took the gilt-framed picture from his hand. She did not need his disconnectedly self-conscious explanation to understand.

"Voluble, verbal gratitude is not an uncommon thing," she answered. "I am going to ask far more than that of you. I've kept her picture always on my table, Stephen, ever since we found it; and I should miss it greatly if I were not to see it often. Do you mind leaving it here, in your room upstairs? I am going to ask that of you, and if you don't mind doing so, then I—I would suggest, too, that you might kiss the—the first 'dressed up lady you ever did git to know,' who must bid you good-night now."

The boyish hesitation with which he saluted Miss Sarah's faded pink cheek was far more delicately flattering than all the effusion in the world could ever have been. After she had left them alone Steve turned and gazed at Caleb, wonder in his face.

"I've never forgotten the way she shook hands with me, that day," he said slowly. "I wondered then if there could be other women with voices just as kind. And I—I'm wondering now."

Caleb smiled.

"I've often speculated on that myself, Steve," he remarked. "And I don't know. I don't know! Sarah is pretty human—even for a Baptist, eh?"

They both laughed over that rainy day which the words recalled; they sat and talked and smoked, but no matter what trend the conversation took, Caleb failed to mention the document or the tax receipts which he had found ten years before in Old Tom's tin box. Even if he had not been entirely certain of it that first day when he had neglected to show them to Sarah, he knew now just what reason underlay his secrecy. Like Old Tom, he felt that his action was in a way more or less extenuated by circumstance. And still mindful of Dexter Allison's odd moment or two of guarded antagonism that very morning, he gradually led the conversation around to more recent things.

"I suppose you have had your conference with Mr. Allison, Steve?" he suggested in a matter-of-fact way.

Instantly at that question all the boyishness left the other's face. He looked away and looked back again, very deliberately.

"No more than a word," he answered. "He asked me to come down again, toward the end of the week, if I could get away. He said no doubt I would want to spend all the time I could to-day with you and Miss Sarah."

"Of course," Caleb exclaimed, "of course! I see. Is it—is it unethical if I ask, privately, your opinion of this job which the East Coast Company has on its hands? Do you believe they can swing it in time to fulfill all their obligations?"

Again there followed a moment's pause while Steve's eyes roved thoughtfully around the room.

"Mr. Elliott wouldn't have risked every cent he has," he finally replied, "unless I had assured him that it wasn't so very much more than a man-sized gamble. Nor Mr. Ainnesley, either, I think. So that puts it up to me pretty squarely, doesn't it? We'll have to win through—because we have to, now!"

"Quite so!" murmured Caleb again.

He studied a long time over his next words, and it was a very vivid vision of a rigid little figure in a wrecked black velvet suit—a vision of a bleak-faced boy with bruised lips who had insisted upon going back downtown for Miss Sarah's eggs—which eventually overbore his distaste for anything that might savor of disloyalty to a friend.

"Of course there could arise unforeseen circumstances," he ventured. "Unforeseen interference which, unless one guarded against it, might defeat every effort."

The room seemed very, very quiet.

"Of course," came the calm answer at last; and Caleb could not see Steve's face behind the cupped hands at his pipe bowl, "of course—unless one more or less guarded against it."

And there, just as calmly, they dropped it. The topic was not discussed again that night, unless a bit of news which Fat Joe Morgan himself delivered might be construed as somehow relative. Fat Joe had been driving for an hour, silent some of the time, but for the most part devoted to a whole-hearted rendition of "Home, Sweet Home," in his thin and bell-like tenor, when he broke off in the middle of a stanza to chuckle.

"Say, Chief," he exclaimed, "I've got news for you that'll just fill you plumb full of happiness and good cheer. I hired another hand to-day who'll be a distinct addition to our gang up-river. Just to while away the dark hours I'll let you guess for a while who he is. I'll let you guess from here to Last Oak, above the cypress bend at the rapids. One, two, three—and the contest is on!"

The man beside Fat Joe stirred and opened his eyes. Fat Joe couldn't see it, for it was too dark, but Steve frowned somewhat at the levity which had interrupted him. He had just been thinking about the tight grip of a slender hand which had fallen upon his arm that afternoon when a red-headed riverman lurched drunkenly from a doorway ahead. Joe's words were exactly coincident with that thought and the answer came mechanically.

"Harrigan," grunted Steve.

And in the darkness Fat Joe sighed mournfully.

"Bull's-eye," he whimpered, "and there goes the whole evenin's entertainment! Why didn't you cast around, sort of fruitless for a while, and prolong the excitement? But you're right. Harrigan, that's him! He'd just met up with that fat party who owns the plaster palace on the hill—just met up with him, down the road a piece, and Allison had fired him for keeps, he said. He asked me if we didn't have room for a nice steady hand, so I hired him. And I'll leave it to you if it ain't Harrigan's feet that's mostly unsteady, at that. He seemed awful cheerful for a man who'd just been allowed to resign, but who was I to entertain dark doubts? I hired him; I thought you might like the touch of color his hair'll lend to the landscape.

It'll be comfortin', too, havin' him around where we can have a look at him any time we take the notion. Don't you think so?"

Steve's grunted reply was hardly intelligible, but it seemed to satisfy Fat Joe. The latter had long before learned to read the signs; he knew when his best efforts were only wasted words, and once more he gave his attention to the jogging horses and his neglected melody.

Caleb Hunter, wondering after Steve had gone just how much he might have seemed to insinuate, regretted that he had spoken at all. Recollection of Allison's bluff cordiality with O'Mara only made him the more ashamed of his suspicion, and yet the next morning at table he attempted, covertly, to sound Sarah for an opinion, too. She invariably solved his perplexities or relegated them to the limbo of gentle ridicule.

"Just why should he want this East Coast job to fail?" he puzzled aloud. "He's in it, along with Elliott and Ainnesley, even if he isn't in so deep. That is, of course, assuming that he does want it to fail."

The preoccupied gleam in Miss Sarah's eyes promised a reply that might be worth considering, but when it came Caleb found trouble in assimilating it.

"They did look so well together," she murmured absently. "He's so much broader—and a whole head taller, too!"

It didn't seem to be exactly a relevant answer, but Caleb nodded patiently.

"Taller, yes," he admitted judiciously. "But he isn't half so big around."

Sarah sat, fork poised, and gazed at him.

"Not half so big as who?" she neglected her sentence structure.

"Why—Dexter!" said Caleb. "Isn't that what we were talking about?"

"Maybe you were," Miss Sarah sniffed. "But I was not discussing Dexter's height or girth either. I was referring to his daughter and—and our boy, Stephen. I was going to ask you if you thought she could be entirely disinterested in him. I don't believe any woman forgets a man who has ever thought enough of her to fight for her."

"I suppose not," agreed Caleb humbly.

"And I was wondering, if that argument ever came up again—I'm wondering if Archibald Wickersham wouldn't come out second best, just as he did before?"

Then her brother understood. He threw back his head and laughed until Sarah's face registered a trace of vexation.

"Sarah," he saluted her, "I'm a mere babe in arms when it comes to finesse, in comparison with you. But since you have introduced the subject I might remark that there are two individuals to be considered. Maybe she might be—interested—as you so delicately phrase it. But the boy—well, he's had one mighty pointed lesson, you know."

But there was no mirth in Sarah's eyes. She was most serious.

"That's the very thing which perplexes me," she confessed. "I was going to ask you about that. For it was hurt pride that sent him away and he hasn't forgotten the hurt, even yet. He was going to tell us, last night when I stopped him, that he hadn't written again because he wasn't certain that we wanted to hear; and he was painfully conscious of how childish it would sound in words, too. Some men quit when they are whipped once, but don't some of them refuse to recognize that they've ever been whipped at all, Cal? And then, she told me that she had asked him to her party, Friday night. If he comes I think I'll be better able to tell just what—"

"He won't!" cut in Caleb flatly, and when she taxed him for it he proceeded to elaborate at considerable length the reason for his certainty. His argument was rather tight and so, just because of that, woman-fashion she believed the contrary.

All day Friday she watched the hills' road. Not until the orchestra in the lodge beyond the hedge had begun tunelessly to strum their instruments, to insure their later tunefulness, did she reluctantly abandon her position at the window. But then, from his chair at the fire, Caleb noticed how wistfully disappointed her face was.

It turned much colder with nightfall; a wind sharp with the tang of autumn was blowing in off the river when Barbara, muffled from throat to ankle in a sapphire fur-edged wrap, slipped in at the door, having stolen away ostensibly to display to them her costume. It was after the hour of ten, but the girl lingered a little after she had executed that mission; she stopped again in the door, indecisively worrying her lip with small teeth, when she finally turned to depart.

"We are very sorry that Mr. O'Mara could not come," she hesitated. "I had promised both Garry and Archie Wickersham that he would be down."

The older woman nodded and accepted the statement for what it was—a question which the girl's eyes failed to conceal.

"We haven't heard from him since he went back into camp," she answered. "He, no doubt, has been unable to get away."

Barbara turned without replying and passed out, less airily than she had entered. But Miss Sarah's eyes were no longer disappointed as she again took her place at a window. And a second later, when she had drawn back suddenly into the room with a muffled exclamation, her brother was astonished at her beaming face. A moment earlier he would have sworn that it was only wistful, but before she went upstairs, exclaiming still further at the lateness of the hour, it began to look more than a little like veritable triumph to him.

Barbara Allison recrossed the lawn very slowly that night; she retraced her steps with head bent, the fall of her slippered feet muffled by the carpet of thick, unfrosted grass. Vaguely troubled, vaguely disturbed at herself for her inability to analyze that strange mood which, twice in the last few nights, had sent her with aching throat and wet cheeks into Miriam's room, she was within arm's length of the dark figure in the hedge gap through which she had just come, before she was aware of its presence. Stephen O'Mara, weatherbeaten hat in hand, was standing there in her path, peering steadily at the stucco and timber lodge alight from end to end like a huge and sprawling glow-worm.

Even in that first moment when she stopped and caught her breath, audibly, from sheer surprise, the girl sensed the indecision in the attitude of the man before her. But she could not know that it was not a thing of the moment—that irresolution; could not know that throughout the week Steve had periodically abused himself for his inability to settle the question once and for all, and leave his brain free for more important things. Just as often as he told himself that he would not go, he had found himself reopening the mental discussion, and yet—and strangely enough—it was not the recollection of Barbara's repeated invitations, or even her distress over Garry Devereau, who had been ceaselessly in his thoughts ever since she had spoken of him, which finally achieved the decision. An insistent desire again to meet the Honorable Archibald Wickersham in the end led him to request Fat Joe to hook up the team, that day at noon, for the long drive down river. With Steve himself handling the reins, they had rolled the thirty miles at a speed which might have mildly surprised Fat Joe had he not been accustomed to putting two and two together to make six or eight or more. And Fat Joe's thin tenor was just drifting faintly off down the hill—a mournful rendition of "Home, Sweet Home"—when the girl stepped noiselessly forward and put a hand, feather-light, upon the man's arm.

Again she felt the swift tensing of the flesh beneath; she fell back a step before the startling abruptness with which Steve whirled. She even threw up one small hand, as if to shield her face. And then, the cloak falling open at her throat, a slender, swaying figure in blue and shimmering white, she stood and flung a little laugh at him—a laugh a little unsteady, a bit tinged with mockery, and as untroubled as the spirit of youth itself.

"Is that the way you always prepare to greet your friends?" she asked.

The man just stood and stared at her—stared much as if he mistrusted his own ears and eyes.

"Not all my friends," his slow voice drawled at last, but even the words were tinged with doubt. "Not all my friends," he said.

And again he was conscious first of her slimness, her smallness. He was aware of the insistent, impish suggestion of boyishness in tilted head and poised body, before the rays that wavered over his shoulder from the windows behind him disclosed the misty gladness of welcome in her eyes, splashed now with points of light not so very unlike the blurred star-points in the infinitely deep, purplish pool of the sky above them. Silently the man reached out and found the hand which had lain for a moment upon his arm.

"So you are—you," he murmured, when his fingers touched hers. "I wasn't—just sure."

The girl bobbed her head—her quaint and childishly impetuous affirmative. She looked down at the hand holding her own, contemplating her small white fingers curled up now into a warm, round fist, and wondering at the completeness with which it was swallowed by his big palm.

Suddenly unable to think quite clearly, she wondered at the new pulse in her throat, which beat and beat until it seemed not easy even to speak.

"Then it—must be you, too," she faltered. "I wasn't sure, either, even when I knew it must be. I'd begun to believe that you hadn't forgotten—that you didn't care to.... Will you please say that you forgive me—please—for something over which I have been sorrier than you can know?"

It was not more than a wisp of sound—that request. The words were stumbling, and very earnest, and not very hard to understand. Silence came again, broken only by the treble strains of violins beyond. Once, in that quiet, his eyes strayed to the small and round, and yellow object which she carried in the crook of one arm—a tiny papier-mâché pumpkin strapped to two fuzzy mice in patent leather harness—but the pumpkin coach and tiny animals were not necessary to translate her costume to him.

His eyes came back and clung to the velvety face of that slim Cinderella in bits of transparent slippers and shimmering, star-edged white, until even in spite of the gloom the girl recognized the change which had come creeping over his face. She saw it surge up in his eyes—the old undisguised wonder of the boy of ten years before, for which, until that instant, she had looked in vain—but it was a man's wonder of woman now, utter and absolute and all-enveloping. She caught her breath then; she touched her lips with a dainty tongue as though they had gone dry of a sudden. Involuntarily she stepped toward him, that single pace which she had fallen away. And above the tumult of her own senses she heard herself trying to laugh and realized how unsteady the effort was.

"Then you do forgive me?" she breathed. "Do I—pass inspection? Do you like me—in my masquerade?"

Steve answered her last question first and, lips parted, she listened, conscious of nothing save the words he was speaking.

"There was never need of a fairy-godmother for you," he told her, his voice grave. "There was never need of a transforming miracle; you have been that, always, yourself. And you are not permitted to ask forgiveness from me, nor pardon. Men do not admit that there can be need of that, where they have worshiped, as long as I have worshiped you. You knew I was coming.... I've been coming ten years now. But you can never know, either, how long ten years can be."

The words were blurred as a far-off echo in her ears. She started to speak, but all that she would have said caught in her throat and hurt her, and only her unsteady breath came from parted lips. Her head drooped forward again, while the small fist twisted and searched and found and clasped tight one finger of the hand that held it. She realized that his free arm was lifted toward her. As she started forward, her ankles became entangled in the soft pile of satin at her feet, and she stopped to free them—and started forward again. But when, at her inarticulate effort at speech, he bent his head to her swiftly upflung face, her whole slender body tightened at the rough contact of blue flannel against her cheek. Almost before they held her she struggled madly from the circle of his arms. White of face, white of lip, she broke away from him and darted through the gap in the hedge, only to shrink back against him in panic the next instant before the black shape upon a blacker horse, between her and the lights.

He was gazing in their direction—the man upon the horse. He was laughing softly. And when he thrust back the black cowl that hid his face and began to speak, Stephen O'Mara recognized that terribly pale, terribly drawn face. Garry Devereau rocked a little in the saddle and waved a gracefully unsteady hand.

"Blessings, my children!" he called to the two in the shadow, and his tongue was not thick, but only wavering. "My felicitations! And e'en though I know not your identity, still I may sense your fond confusion. And yet—why blush, dear unknowns? 'Tis in the air to-night. Even I myself have yielded to spirit of frivolity. Two hours ago I appeared masked in these dingy vestments as Love's Young Dream; but with me the mood has passed. Fellow romancers, you have witnessed a metamorphosis; you are now gazing upon the Wrath of God, about to thunder forth upon a coal black charger. I merely paused to bid you haste inside, lest you miss the crux of the evening. When I withdrew the Honorable Archie was already searching, with bravely concealed distraction, for the fair daughter of the house. The hour has struck—it's masks off—masks off, from eyes and hearts!"

["Blessings, my children!" he called to the two in the shadow. "My felicitations! And e'en though I know not your identity, still I may sense your fond confusion."]

He laughed again, a low and ugly chuckle. Sparks flew from Ragtime's hoofs when he touched the sleek flanks with his heels and the splendid animal quivered and bunched hard thigh muscles and spurned the gravel. White face whiter still against the background of his somber vestments, debonaire and drunkenly insecure in the saddle, Garret Devereau tore out into the main road and thundered off into the night.

Barbara Allison stood a long time motionless, her back to the motionless man so near her. She stood and stared, pale as had been that black-robed horseman, straight ahead of her. Then a tremor shook her. Mechanically she started forward, but at the first step Steve's hand reached out and found her arm and drew her back to him. She faced about, and waited.

"Is that—true?" he asked her, quietly.

She made no move to answer.

"Is that true?" his low and gentle voice commanded this time. "You still mean to—marry—him?"

She recovered her voice then. All her confusion and stunned realization was swallowed up by that tide of fiercely unreasoning, deadly resentment which his very gentleness evoked. There was nothing girlish in his reply—nothing boyish in that high-held chin and stiffened body. A hard note marred her utterance, a perfection of insolence edged with scorn, which Steve's world did not know. She wanted but one thing in that moment; she knew but one impulse—a mad desire to cut and tear and rend savagely his gravely possessed kindliness.

"What I have done to-night I can never hope to explain," she told him. "I can only hope that some day I may cease to despise myself as utterly as you have taught me to, at this minute. And since you choose to regard it now as your right to ask that question, I'll answer it for you. I do not *mean* to marry him. I shall be proud to be his wife!"

The light that streamed over her shoulder fell full upon his face. She saw the blood pour up, staining throat and cheek and brow, and then ebb away. She gave him time to answer, but he did not speak; and suddenly she knew what scene of another day he was remembering. Her eyes dropped to her imprisoned hand.

"You are—detaining me," she said.

He released her immediately, and yet she did not move. And while she waited he turned and stooped and turned to her again. She stood like stone while he wrapped her fur-edged sapphire cloak about her and fastened it close beneath her uptilted chin. He waited, bare of head, in the hedge gap until she had crossed the lawn to the house that lay a sprawling glow-worm in the darkness. A tumult of voices leaped out to him when she opened the door—a lilting crash of syncopated melody. And then it was quiet again.

After a glimpse of his chief's eyes that night, Fat Joe essayed not so much as one facetious protest against turning the fagged team homeward with scarcely any rest at all. And hour after hour he drove in silence, checking himself apologetically once or twice when he forgot himself long enough to burst into the opening strains of his inevitable ballad. He remained as quiet as that too quiet man beside him, until Steve himself opened his lips.

"It's a—lonesome night," mused the latter at length.

Fat Joe could not have endured it much longer. His pent-up spirit leaped fervidly forth in reply.

"Lonesome!" he ejaculated. "Man, it's lonesomer'n hell! Hear that damn wind sighin' in the branches, as your poets say. Hear her moan! And look at them clouds edgin' in on the moon like they was thugs a-packin' blackjacks and waitin' for an openin' to whale in. Lonesome? Say, it gives me chills, a night like this. It don't seem to have no heart, somehow, nor mercy nor nuthin', does it? It's all wrong! It ain't dark enough, and it ain't light enough; it's too quiet, and the wind makes too much noise. It keeps whisperin' over your shoulder, tauntin' yuh with somethin' you can't understand. No, sir, this kind of a night ain't popular with me, at, all, at all!... Say, Steve, how do you pronounce C-e-c-i-l-e?"

Steve pronounced it for him, dully inattentive, but the flood-gates of speech were opened for Joe.

"That's the way I would of handled it myself," he averred, "but I wanted to be certain sure. It ain't exactly genteel to call a lady out of her name, any way you look at it. And not that I've reached that state of exceedin' intimacy, as you might say, either. I just aim to be prepared, that's all."

He fell to whistling after that, and almost immediately his thin tenor was rolling ahead of them, through the black alley between the pines, to continue in soulful reiteration until the construction camp clearing loomed up ahead. And there, twice within a hundred yards, with the long bunk houses already visible, the weird hoot of an owl fluted through the darkness. At its third repetition Fat Joe's song hushed; he cocked his head on one side to listen, and shot a glance at Steve, but he knew that the latter had not heard. And when that night-bird's call rose again, clear and measured and louder than before, Fat Joe tightened the reins above the fagged team; he shot forward suddenly and laid the whip across their tired flanks as they cleared the last breastwork of trees.

Steve's head was jerked backward by the abruptness of their first plunge; and then he saw what Fat Joe had seen a second before. High up on the hillside there was a light glowing from the windows of the shack which served the chief engineer of the East Coast job as office and domicile, too. While Fat Joe laid on the whip a man came hurtling past the outflung door, sprang to his feet and, running low to the ground, disappeared into the blackness of the brush. Joe swung the horses up in a galloping curve and with one catlike leap, incredibly light for a man of his chunky build, was down from the seat and crashing through the bushes on the trail of that fugitive whose noisy flight had already become a faint crackle in the distance.

Flame poured from Fat Joe's revolver. Two whiplike reports shattered the night quiet before Stephen O'Mara moved. Then he lifted himself heavily from the seat. Something nuzzled his shoulder while he stood listening to the diminishing tumult of the pursuit; and even before he turned he knew what it was. He paused a moment to stroke the soft nose of the black horse standing there with reins a-trail. It was Ragtime, wet with lather and caked with dust. But even then he was not prepared for the sight which met him when he entered the shack. Seconds must have passed while he stood staring from the threshold, for Fat Joe came puffing back from his fruitless chase in time to see him bend and lift a black-robed, lifelessly limp body from the floor and stagger with it toward a bunk. Fat Joe's steady flow of profanity, oddly, double vicious in his thin, complaining voice, was checked short. He, too, stood and stared from the doorway—stood and lifted his nose and sniffed.

"Seems to be our night for callers," he remarked with bad mildness; "and, say, this one's got a peach of a load, ain't he?"

Then Garry Devereau's head rolled over, ghastly loose and slack, and the plump one caught sight of a ragged gash in the senseless man's temple.

"So-o, that's it?" he droned, and his complaining voice was deadly again. "So that's it! But he wasn't so far gone that he couldn't put up a tidy little battle, was he? Funny about that, too, but I could always do my best little jobs of man-handling when I was about half-over myself."

His pale eyes swept the floor; he pounced forward and recovered a sheaf of blue-prints from a corner.

"This, I take it," he muttered, "was what they was arguing about when we busted in. Steve, them's our bridge estimates—and there wa'n't no copies of 'em, either. It wouldn't take us more than two weeks to replace 'em neither—not more'n two precious, priceless weeks. I'm only hopin' now that when our other caller, who seems to want them more than we do, calls again, I'll be here myself to entertain him, with tea or somethin'. I'd plumb hate to seem so inhospitable as not to be home, twice hand-runnin', to visitors."

Fat Joe's round face was congested with murderous rage before he had finished, but Steve seemed hardly to have heard him at all. He had finally straightened out that sickeningly slack figure upon his own bunk. He was listening now to his heart, and at a jerk of his head Fat Joe joined him at the bedside. The latter's thick fingers were as delicate, as competent, as a skilled physician's might have been. He, too, listened and peeled back the unconscious man's eyelids. He shook his head, dubiously.

"Maybe that was a tidy little battle, while it lasted," he stated, "but it ain't deuce high alongside this fight we've got on our hands right now. For he's just as near over as I'd care to see a man, unless it was someone I'd a little prefer dead! It ain't that scratch on the head that's got him slippin', either." Joe paused and turned to address Garry Devereau's still white face itself. "You sat in an' backed my game like a gentleman born," he said, "and now I'm a-goin' to play yourn, blue chips and white and yello'. But this is goin' to be your last celebration, friend of mine, even if we do win through, or you'll be holdin' your next one where the company ain't so select and the climate nuthin' to compare with ourn!"

And while he talked he worked, for it was Fat Joe who gave the orders that night. He called for ammonia, for brandy, for a half-dozen drugs from the camp hospital chest; and each of them Steve brought in an automatic fashion that finally penetrated even Fat Joe's professional pleasure in the struggle.

"Friend of yourn?" he asked in an interval while they rested.

"A friend," Steve repeated with a tightening of his jaws, and Joe knew what that tone meant.

After that they fought on in silence, side by side—sometimes waiting, sometimes fighting, both of them, to hold that horribly racked man upon the bed. He fought them with every pound of strength in his emaciated body. He moaned up at them, screamed at them, cursed them frothingly, and Fat Joe hung on and cursed him back—cursed him and promised him profanely that he would not let him die. Steve's face was gray, sweat was pouring from Fat Joe's scarlet face when the life-tide ebbed lowest and there came a sudden cessation in that stream of babbled madness, Garry Devereau lay so quiet that an oath jerked huskily from Fat Joe's lips; but when he had listened at the motionless chest he lifted his head and smiled, seraphically.

"There, by God," he stated in his high, complaining tenor, "there, by God! And if I ain't created a vacancy in the angel chorus aloft, then I'm a liar!"

And his explosive diagnosis proved to be as correct as it was utterly unprofane in spirit. Before day broke there came an hour when Garry Devereau lifted himself upon one elbow and opened his eyes to stare half wildly, but very sanely, about the room. His gaze flitted wonderingly from wall to wall before it rested, fearfully fixed, upon Steve's brown face. Instantly he looked away, flinchingly, and met Fat Joe's voluminous grin—and looked back again, cunningly cautious. Finally he reached out a timid, blue-veined, pitifully unsteady hand and plucked at Steve's blue flannel sleeve. And his words were an echo of those which Stephen O'Mara had heard before that night from other lips.

"Then you—are you," he framed the words laboriously. "I wasn't sure—even when I knew it must be."

And Garry Devereau tried to smile—his slow smile of sophistry.

"Greetings, Sir Galahad!" he faltered. "And how are you, Steve—and who might your—fat friend be?"

CHAPTER IX
A MATTER OF ORNITHOLOGY

Of all the fragmentary pictures which those crowded twelve hours left registered upon Stephen O'Mara's brain, none proved more enduring than did the change which Garry Devereau's first haltingly weak but very sane greeting wrought in the expression on Fat Joe's pink visage that morning. The banter in Garry's labored words was so characteristic of the mocking spirit of the man who had come back the same inexplicably intimate friend which the boy had been, that it left Steve's dry throat speechless for the moment. The visible effect upon Fat Joe was even more positive.

Almost before he had finished his facetious query as to the identity of the one who had dragged him through that bad night Gary fell asleep; he slipped off into slumber, the very calmness of which guaranteed that the crisis had passed. But the lugubrious astonishment which the question had evoked consumed more time in fading from Joe's face. The latter's jaw had sagged open; he dragged a sleeve across his damp forehead while he stood and gazed in a sort of dumb dismay down at those pale and handsome features. Then he chuckled suddenly; his whole squat body shook with comprehensive mirth.

"Now what do you think of that!" he gurgled in admiration. "What do you think of that? A-hangin' on all night, alive once in a while, maybe, but the best you could say for him the rest of the time was a hope that he wasn't dead. And now coming at us with the airy persiflage, the first regular breath he's drawed. Fat! It was me he meant to indicate, wasn't it? He was joshin' me! Say, Steve, ain't he the merry little joker? *Me—fat*! Now that's real funny—I'll leave it to you if it ain't."

Fat Joe leaned over and drew a blanket a little higher across the sleeping man's shoulder, while Steve continued silently to study Garry's face. Even in unconsciousness a faintly crooked smile of skepticism still clung to the lips.

"It was like him," Steve remarked at last, very soberly. "Somehow, the minute he began to speak I knew it was exactly the sort of thing I expected him to say. The probability of death is a much more amusing prospect to some men, Joe, than the perplexity of living."

Fat Joe flashed a swift, half-puzzled glance at his chief's face; he started to ask a question, then scowled and checked himself and turned instead to kindle a fire in the stove of the lean-to kitchen of the cabin. But a half-hour later he was still murmuring the last phrase over to himself, perplexedly, when Steve came leading the horse Ragtime up to the open door. Saddled and with reins a-trail, the animal had been wandering throughout the night about the upper end of the construction camp clearing. At the sound of hoofbeats outside Fat Joe left the stove and the half-cooked breakfast he had set himself to prepare. From the doorway he stared through narrowed lids.

For the moment Joe had half forgotten those night birds whose mournful hooting along the trail, a few hours back, had first stirred him to alert suspicion. While he was struggling with Garry Devereau's faltering heart he had had scant leisure to devote to the problem of the other man's identity—that shadowy figure which had come plunging out of the cabin door and gone crashing off into the brush, a noisy but invisible target for his revolver. Now recognition and a light of partial understanding rose and intermingled in his eyes.

"So that's the way one of 'em come," he murmured. "I was wondering some. Last night I didn't notice the horse, being a mite too hurried to give ample attention to details, as it were. But ain't—ain't this one of Allison's horses?"

Steve straightened from an examination of a deep scratch in one of Ragtime's knees and stood, back to the door, slowly stroking the soft black nose. Just as well as though it had been voiced he caught the unphrased inference in the plump one's query. After a time he shook his head, absently, in negation.

"No, Joe," he answered heavily. "He is from Allison's stables, but we have him to thank, just the same, along with Garry, for our blue-prints and estimates. It was Mr. Devereau whom he brought up here last night, and in fairly good time I should judge, too, from the pace at which they set out. Garry turned him into the hill-road, and he must have stuck to it blindly until he struck our fork." And, after a longer pause: "The horse is Miss Allison's own property," he added quietly.

Joe pursed his lips. Instantly, at the mention of the girl's name, he felt himself better equipped to understand both the lack of immediate action and the seeming preoccupied indifference of his superior which, in the face of the night's developments, would have been otherwise utterly unaccountable that morning.

There had been more than one instance of gross neglect and misinterpreted orders, particularly in the last week or so, that might have resulted disastrously if luck had not been with them; but Fat Joe had been unable to convince the chief engineer of the East Coast Company that their repetition was in any way a thing of sinister import. Steve had merely smiled at his dogged belief in a veiled campaign of opposition, blaming the minor catastrophes upon blundering incompetence which they could hope to combat by unflagging vigilance alone. And now, when the finding of the roll of estimates upon the floor and the blood clotted crease in Garry Devereau's forehead made further argument superfluous, his listlessness would have left Fat Joe alarmed had it not been for a recollection of the light he had glimpsed in Steve's eyes at the beginning of their sudden and unexplained return to camp the night before, and his brooding silence on the road. At the mention of Barbara Allison's name it all recurred to Joe in nicely balanced and comforting sequence. Fat Joe confessed shamelessly to a romantic soul. And it helped him now to choose his own course of action, even though he had, for once, misread the other's mood.

For if Steve had not forgotten the picture which Garry Devereau had made, robed and cowled and areel in the saddle, any more than he could ever hope to forget the slim, shimmering figure who had shrunk back against him in panic, there in the shadow of the hedge, both pictures had momentarily given way to an even more vivid memory. He was thinking of Miriam Burrell's face and her last words to him: "I have heard, Mr. O'Mara, that you have once or twice fought your way out of the dark, when everybody else had lost hope. I want an opportunity to talk with—a specialist in such campaigns!"

The probable nearness of him who had gone bounding away empty-handed from the lighted shack was of far less moment than the possible identity of the one who had furnished the inspiration of that night raid. And to Steve the need of assuring that tall girl with the vivid lips and coppery hair of Garry Devereau's safety bulked quite as important as did the advisability of seeking immediately an informal interview with Dexter Allison, such as the latter himself had so genially suggested.

But Fat Joe, squinting at his chief's broad back, misread the signs that morning. From where he stood in the doorway he could see the men of the upper camp already swarming out over the works, some of them mere dots across the expanse of swamp-land. The rhythmic beat of pile-drivers thudded in his ears; raucous echoes of shouted orders floated up from the nearest gang-bosses, and punctuating it all came the intermittent boom of dynamite explosions from far north in the deep cut alongside the river edge.

The construction camp had been nearly two hours awake; the race against a well-nigh impossible time limit which would brook neither mistake nor miscalculation had been picked up automatically at daybreak, where it had hesitated at nightfall the day before. While he stared down at this activity, a realization of the months of bitter toil which stood between them and ultimate, uncertain success, crept over Fat Joe. Little by little his features took on that look of hard and dangerous setness which always seemed so doubly threatening upon his placidly round countenance. And as casually as he was able he elected to go upon that errand of which his chief must have lost sight, in a dulled and moody contemplation of an entirely different matter.

"Maybe," Joe suggested vaguely, "maybe I'll just ask you to watch these things on the stove a while, Steve. I've got the fire to drawin' and some coffee set on, because I knew we'd need 'em before that cook-boy got his eyes open wide enough to see his way up here. It ain't exactly a fancy repast, neither, so it won't tax your culinary skill none to tend it. I—there's something I'd like to look into a little—something I sort of lost sight of while we were soothing our mutual friend in yonder. But I'll be back in a minute. I'll just run down and see if everybody's onto his job."

Hard on the heels of that explanation he started rapidly down the long bare slope and Steve watched his departure without comment. While Joe was gone he tethered the black horse at the door frame, found a nose-bag and methodically presented the grateful beast with his breakfast. And when Fat Joe returned he had finished preparing the meal which the former had begun; in absent-minded inattention that resulted in more than one perilously close call, with one hand he was placing brimming cups of blistering hot coffee beside the plates of food and condensed milk-cans upon the table, while he leafed slowly through the sheaf of blue-prints with the other, satisfying himself that they were untampered with. Fat Joe shook his head mournfully over this last exhibition and dropped into a chair.

They ate in silence that morning—a silence so heavy that the faint breathing of Garry in the bunk beyond them sounded almost stentorian at times. More than once Joe's gaze went to that colorless face; just as often it searched Steve's gravely unreadable countenance, and it was Fat Joe who first found the silence no longer endurable.

"What," he ventured to interrupt the other's brooding, "what is it, Steve, you call one of them little, gangling, bow-spectacled guys that fools his waking hours away studyin' the customs and morals and suchlike of birds and things?"

Almost immediately Steve's face grew less blank at that bland question, and although his eyes failed to shift from the invisible point beyond Joe at which he was staring, his lips did curl a little. He had long before learned to play up, solemnly, to those unprefaced and disingenuous leads.

"Ornithologist?" he inquired soberly. "Ornithologist—if that is what you mean."

Joe nodded briskly.

"That's it!" he exclaimed. "I knew it was ornery something-or-other, and—and that makes it fit the case all the prettier, now don't it? Because in the last half-hour or so, since I left you here to tend to the cookin', I've been studying the birds somewhat myself. And having been a little successful, so to speak, I'm ornerier'n even before I commenced." He stopped to swallow half the steaming coffee in his cup, and if when he began again his voice had hardened perceptibly, it was nevertheless still elaborately guileless. "Steve," he said, "have *you* ever stopped to consider real close and earnest any of the peculiarities of our feathered friends? Say—well, say owls, for instance?"

Then Steve ceased to smile. He thought a moment, but his reply remained tuned to the other's artless key.

"Why, yes," he drawled. "Yes, and no. As for the latter, however, I will admit that I have always believed their reputation for—er—wisdom to be a greatly overestimated thing."

Widely Fat Joe grinned his pleasure. His chief's eyes were no longer vague nor blank.

"Which just bears out my own personal research in the field," he stated. "Not that I'm saying I've been real thorough in the matter, because I ain't had the time. But what I've done I accomplished because I just naturally dote on that kind of thing." His eye flitted carelessly toward a window. "I happened to run into Harrigan, too, this morning," he murmured.

As disinterestedly as had Joe, Steve now drained his coffee cup and waited.

"He was down to the cook shanty," Fat Joe rambled on. "It's an hour since he'd ought to have been out there with the powder squad in the north cut, and when I asks him if he was feelin' indisposed this morning he says no, but the supply teams was going out and one of the drivers had told him that I was sending him along to help with the loadin'. He had such a nice, frank, open-faced way of lying that I couldn't bring myself to correct him. I just let it stand that way and told him such was the arrangement." Joe saw swift satisfaction play across Steve's face. "And—and then, after that, him and me—why, we just drifted off into a real interestin' and scientific discussion about them birds I been mentionin' to you. We—somehow we got to discoursing about owls.

"I told him I'd never noticed 'em to hoot so close together and persistent as they did last night, down along the trail, and wondered if by any chance he'd heard 'em, too. And he said he had. He's a nice smooth talker, Harrigan is, when he ain't too sober and not too drunk. Oh, yes, he'd heard 'em, being wakeful, he explained, what with worrying all night whether we'd ever get this line of steel laid before our contract run out on us! Now wasn't that interestin'—wasn't it, especially coming from him? Neatly put and self-possessed, I call it. He was worried because he's dreadful superstitions. [Transcriber's note: superstitious?] He claims when them birds gets to hedgin' in on each other's solos like they did last night it's a sign of bad luck or an accident for somebody, sure. That give me an opening to ask him if the accident hadn't happened already, him having a bandage around his head not much different from this one our friend here is wearing. But he couldn't see it that way. A scratch he called it—just a scratch from a twig."

The room was very quiet for a breath. That thin note had crept into Fat Joe's tenor voice—thin and chill and menacing. And there as abruptly as he had assumed it, he flung aside his mask of disingenuous irrelevance. Fat Joe wheeled, put both elbows upon the table edge and leaned forward heavily. It was much as though he were setting himself to shoulder by sheer weight through the discouraging wall of indifference behind which the other was apparently withdrawing once more.

"But as for me," his high voice rang a little, "but as for me—well, I always did pride myself that I could shoot some, whether it was by daylight or dark!"

And the only result which that statement achieved was an answering, meditative nod. Fat Joe subsided. All that he could say had been said, and they finished breakfast as they had begun it, in absolute silence. But when Steve, with a word, halted him in the doorway as Joe was on the point of returning to the work in the valley, the latter turned to find the slow smile which he knew so well hovering upon the younger man's lips. He fairly gulped in his sudden relief.

"Joe," Stephen O'Mara began, and the words were suspiciously unsteady for those of a man who was bearing up bravely under a hidden sorrow, "Joe, you've missed your calling, I'm afraid. As a naturalist you might have scored an instant and sensational success, in spite of the fact that you are neither bow-spectacled nor—er—gangling, as no doubt Mr. Devereau's reference to you has this morning made plain."

He stopped to touch a match to the dry grains of tobacco which he had been tamping into the bowl of his pipe; he swung slowly around toward the inert figure on the bunk. When he spoke again the thread of raillery was gone from his voice.

"He'll sleep the day through, I think," he said, "and the night, perhaps. But I'd advise you to look in on him now and then, just the same. He did us a good turn last night. It's the second good turn he's done for me, Joe. And now perhaps the chance has come to even up the score a little. You would know, wouldn't you, Joe, just how many drinks to prescribe for a man who has been as—as ill as Garry has?"

Fat Joe's face commenced to shine, and at that he was only beginning to understand.

"Ain't I the doctor?" he demanded aggrievedly. "You don't have to go no deeper into technicalities with me. And I told you last night, anyway, didn't I, that it would have to be his last little celebration, unless he was figurin' on a longer journey than he's ever took before. Well, I've handled so many cases just like his that there ain't even a little enjoyable novelty in 'em any more for me."

Steve received the statement with another nod.

"That's it," he mused. "That's it exactly. It would have to be his last, unless he is figuring on a longer journey than he has ever taken before."

He crossed and leaned over the thin and motionless form of his friend. He laid one hand gently upon the sleeping man's shoulder.

"He did that for me once, Joe," he spoke quietly. "He dropped his hand on my shoulder like that, and I never forgot the weight of it. You watch him, Joe—watch him closely for a while, because—because, you see, a man does stray along once in so often who's so badly bewildered and trail weary, so tired of trying and—and hurt in soul, that the thought of such a journey as you speak of begins to seem the shortest route after all to an end of thoughts which even alcohol can't wipe out. You take care of him, and if he wakes before I get back, explain to him a little just how he came here, and thank him a lot for what he did. Ask him to wait until I come back from Morrison, will you?"

For a moment Joe just stood and blinked, dumfounded.

"Huh!" he blurted at last. "Huh! So that's what you been hintin' at all the time, is it? I didn't just get you right until now. But, do you know, it did seem to me once or twice while we were working over him—once or twice when the goin' was pretty bad—that his spirit wasn't heaving real hearty into the traces. And, say, ain't that a poor idea for a guy to get into his head? Now ain't it?" And then, as the purport of the rest of Steve's words struck home: "Do you mean you are going to Morrison to have a—"

Steve recrossed to the door and began to unfasten the feed-bag from Ragtime's nose.

"And now about this ornithological problem, Joe," he cut in with a blandness that outdid Joe's best effort. "About owls in particular! Your research work was illuminating; in view of its casual nature it was unbelievably helpful. But personally I feel that a thorough sifting of the matter requires slightly different methods. One should endeavor to get at the thing in its embryonic state, as—as it were. Don't you think so? If one could locate the place of incubation, the—er—nest from which these night birds of yours first stretched their wings, it might prove really worth while—no? And—and at the same time I'll just return Miss Allison's horse to her, too, this morning."

He leaned over to lengthen a stirrup; stopped again to light his pipe.

"Watch things," he called, as he swung to the saddle and put Ragtime to the slope. "Watch things!" His voice drifted up from below, clear and eager, and alive with mirth. "And drive 'em, Joe—drive 'em—drive 'em from daylight till dark!"

From the threshold Fat Joe watched him until horse and rider disappeared beyond the line of timber; with broad face aglow he stood, head cocked upon one side.

Then, "He was figurin'," he muttered in blithe delight, "he was a-figurin' to himself, all the time I thought he was thinking about her! I guess my own mind has lately got to dwelling too insistent on trivial things, for a laboring man.... He's taking her back her horse—real broke up and sorrowful like over the prospect of seein' her again so soon, too, now wasn't he? And me—me sympathizin' with *him*! Sometimes, Joe, your lack of penetration is plumb aggravatin' to me. You talk a lot, but you don't say much! You got to learn to listen."

He stepped forward, remembered and turned back into the cabin. There was womanish solicitude in the scrutiny he bent upon Garry Devereau's crookedly smiling face.

"You and me was ordained to be friends," he declared oratorically, "because anybody that Steve O'Mara calls friend is good enough for me. And so I'll just naturally have to persuade you to put off indefinitely this idea of a prolonged excursion, won't I—convince you maybe of the unnumbered delights of our own earthly suburb, as it were. And fat, eh? You think I'm fat, do you? Well, that's a matter we'll have to thrash out when you come to—that and one other which ain't going to be half so amusin' nor congenial while under consideration. About the best I can promise you for both of them arguments is that you ain't got a chance to win either. I got my orders to take care of you."

He tiptoed to the door and went with his oddly light and cat-footed tread down the hill. Just once more he paused, halfway between the headquarters of the East Coast Company's chief engineer and the thudding pile-drivers at the edge of the swamp.

"It won't be so lonesome, having him for company," he told himself. "It'll be a new mind to delve into,—that is, if he'll only listen a little to reason, when he wakes up. And I wonder if he takes kindly to a little friendly game. I wonder, now—I wonder!"

CHAPTER X
NOT A CHANCE IN THE WORLD

Barbara Allison's presence upon the dusty hill-road that morning was more than the result of a merely casual whim, even though, when she turned her mount north into that mountain highway a scant two hours before, the choice had been made without actual thought for the route which she was selecting. And yet, conscious or instinctive, the choice had brought her the things for which both brain and spirit were ahunger that morning: A silence so profound that the vague, crackling wood noises which disturbed it from time to time were not noises at all, but only a part of its very being; a solitude so breathlessly big and sweeping that she must needs throw out both slim arms finally in a childishly eager effort to embrace a tithe of it—and a chance to be alone!

The night before, as soon as she had re-entered hurriedly the glowing lodge asprawl upon the hill, the impulse had first come to her—a swift and almost blind desire to turn and escape, if only for a little while, from the roomful of chatter and laughter and bright-eyed badinage loosed upon her immediately after the unmasking, by Dexter Allison's perfectly cadenced announcement of his daughter's engagement. All in a breath the huge room had become stiflingly oppressive; the gaiety unbearable. And at the end of the first half-hour following her truancy she might have yielded to the impulse, pleading the first flimsy excuse which would have purchased an opportunity to reconstruct that hysterically mad minute or two with him whom she had just left a little before in the hedge-gap, had not Miriam Burrell, at the very moment of decision, stung her into realization of what meaning such an act might convey to other less generous minds.

That tall and lithe-bodied and abrupt-tongued friend of hers, colorless cheeks even paler against the black background, of her Mongolian costume, still had eyes for the change which had come over the younger girl, in spite of the terror which had been congealing her own heart since the moment of unmasking. Her vivid lips were still able to smile, stiffly, when she finally drew Barbara into a corner and under cover of her lacquered fan mockingly pinched a little color into her wan cheeks. But that strange girl failed to realize how much of scorn for a thing she labeled her own cowardice, she put into her words that night.

"Please remember, dear child," she whispered, "that you are on exhibition as the ingenuously happy bride-to-be. If you are going to play the game this way, like the rest of them, why not be a good sport and play it for all there is in it? One owes it to one's partner, you know, not to reveal entirely the weakness of the hand that's just been dealt. You should smile—at least a little!"

Barbara, brain already hopelessly entangled, wheeled in astonishment at the almost viciously satirical suggestion, refusing even while her face flamed to believe that she had caught correctly the impossibly cynical, unbelievably unkind insinuation of this girl who was her closest friend. But Miriam's eyes silenced the demand for an explanation, which had risen with an hitherto unknown coldness to her lips. Instead Barbara reached out impetuously and took the girl's icy wrist in both her own hands.

"Miriam, child, what is it?" she breathed. "What is the matter, dear? You're ill—you're cold as death!"

And at that the lash of scornful intolerance for all things hypocritical, the flick of which Barbara had never known before, was gone from Miriam's tongue. She moistened her lips and tried to speak, and had to try again before her voice would come.

"Have you—seen Garry?" she asked huskily. "Do you know where he went?"

The hopelessness of the query made possible but one interpretation of all that lay behind it, and yet Barbara, who had not so much as guessed at it until now, refused the thought as too fantastic for credence. Again a wave of conscious color stained her face.

"Do you mean since—since—" Her lips refused to phrase it, but Miriam finished it for her.

"Since he went swinging out into the dark on Ragtime." She, too, strained at the sentence, but for an entirely different reason. "I was looking for him, but I was too late. Bobs, all evening his eyes have been mad—his mood insane! I heard just his last word or two to you and—Mr. O'Mara, out there on the lawn. His father, you know—but you don't think.... Barbara, I'm frightened—I'm so terribly frightened!"

It ended in a little moan of fear. And now, astounded past all belief, Barbara understood. But before she could speak the seeming need of woman reassurance, no matter how illogical, was gone. Amazingly, all in an instant, the living dread disappeared from Miriam's face; she stiffened and threw back her head with that short laugh which contained so little of mirth, so much that was hard to translate. And the Honorable Archibald

Wickersham, appearing the same instant at Barbara's elbow, frowned at its note of derision.

"I've just been warning Barbara," the tall girl was already drawling with consummate impudence, "that the record of past performances are all against your finishing the distance without coming a cropper in these international matrimonial hurdles. Just what is your opinion, Archibald?"

Wickersham had never liked Miriam Burrell. Now he smiled a trifle wryly into her insolently uptilted face, without attempting to answer the question. And during the next dance with Barbara he unburdened himself, rather positively for him, of his distaste for her. The pronounced frown, however, remained even longer upon his countenance.

But that one moment had served where everything else might have failed. For the rest of the evening Barbara was again a creature of moods so frothy, so evanescent that she swept aside even Wickersham's habit of precision. And if the spur that brightened her eyes and quickened her laughter was, after all, nothing more nor less than a hot contempt for herself—for the stolen moment in the hedge-gap and the inexplicable impulse upon which she had all but acted following it—her merriment was none the less a palpitant thing.

And yet afterward, alone in her room, when the last treble note had died away and she had dismissed Cecile, her sleepy-eyed maid, the sense of oppression had returned redoubled. She did not want to sleep; she was glad of her wide-eyed wakefulness, but in the darkness walls and ceiling and floor seemed fairly to close in upon her and hedge in soul and brain as well as body. It was the first time the girl had ever known the need—the driving desire—to be alone out of doors, where there was nothing but sky and skyline to bound her thoughts. And at last, when her restlessness became no longer bearable, while the remainder of the house still slept behind drawn curtains, she rose and slipped into boots and breeches and riding coat, and descended to order a not too wide-awake groom to saddle a horse. And in the very middle of his sensational report of Ragtime's empty stall she swung to the saddle and turned toward the north.

She rode hard at first. She put the small roan mare between her knees to a pounding gallop, pulling to a walk only after the rushing air had whipped back into her cheeks a part at least of the glow which the sleepless night had robbed from them. And if the tang of the trees and the solitude and the warmth of the sun did their work slowly, they nevertheless did it well. Little by little her tense body relaxed; the line of her lips softened. Almost before she realized it that morning, she had relegated her anxiety over Garry Devereau and her astonishment at the confession which she had beheld in Miriam's eyes to a rather hazy background, and turned to those very thoughts against which she had fought so fiercely throughout the night.

She drifted into a surprisingly unanalytical and most femininely inquisitive wonder concerning a tall figure in blue flannel and corduroy. She suddenly found herself pondering the very incidents which, a few hours before, had set her small fists to clenching in a tide of incomprehensible resentment—against herself or him she could not for the life of her tell.

Mile after mile, the roan mare placidly choosing the pace, she rode with one leg dangling over the pummel of the saddle, everything else forgotten in that preoccupied endeavor to review each moment she had shared with him. Again she felt his arm harden threateningly under her startled clasp as a red-headed and very drunk river-man lurched out of a doorway ahead of them; with breath softly audible between arched lips she tried to recall the gentleness of his hands when he was refastening her cloak beneath her rigidly upflung chin. And when the higher morning sun found her far beyond the rolling pasture land, miles in the heavy timber, she had dismounted, there where the highest loop in the road commanded its breath-taking sweep of country, and was sitting cross-legged upon the trunk of a fallen tree at the road edge. Frowning a little over the vexing uncertainty of details, Barbara was wondering just what their next meeting would be like; she had just finished picturing his man's discomfort and self-consciousness and lack of ease and, with a soberness so childish it would have dumbfounded her had she given it thought, was nodding approvingly over a contemplation of her own kind cordiality, when that very blue-shirted figure itself rounded a near corner in the narrow lane between the trees. Stephen O'Mara, in the flesh, appeared before her, astride Ragtime and leading her roan, which, contentedly cropping the bush tops, had disappeared a full quarter of an hour before.

The girl gasped at the suddenness of his coming; she half started to rise before she remembered the instability of her perch, and then crouched even lower than before when she saw that he was not yet aware of her nearness. It was not at all like the encounter which she had so ably managed in her imagination an instant before, and somehow that graciously kind greeting of hers was lost completely through the perversity of an utterly different mood. She waited, eyes gleefully bright, until he was almost opposite her before she coughed, ever so faintly. Then she tilted her nose aloft in enchanting mimicry of his lean and forward-thrust face.

"We never speak," she confided dolefully to the empty air in front of her, "we never speak as we pass by." He whirled. So swiftly that it took her breath he was out of the saddle and across the road, and standing knee-deep in the undergrowth beside her. Only his profile had been visible to her at first. Now the white line of his jaw and the light in the eyes that searched her face chilled her, even while they sent the blood singing in every vein. Only a few hours before she had seen that same cold fear in Miriam Burrell's eyes; and yet not the same, either, for hers had been a panic of lost hope, and the gleam in the man's eyes was already only partly dread of disaster and partly a great and unmistakable glow of thankfulness. Barbara remembered then, with a twinge of guilt, that she could have forgotten it so completely, the black-robed figure that had gone thundering off on the same mount which Stephen O'Mara was riding now. She half lifted both hands to him, apprehensively.

"You aren't going to tell me, are you," she asked, "that anything dreadful has happened to Garry?"

Dumbly, but most reassuringly, Steve shook his head. From the top of her hatless, wind-tossed, brown-crowned head to the tips of the absurdly small boots tucked up beneath her, he scanned her slim body. Barbara realized that he was trying to speak and finding the effort hard. Slowly he removed his hat and passed one hand across his forehead.

"Man," he ejaculated fervidly to himself, "but that's the longest hundred yards you've ever traveled, on foot or a-horseback!" And abruptly, accusingly, to her: "Do you know that I've been months and years and ages rounding that bend to—to find you a little crumpled-up heap in the road?"

After all, her unaccountably high spirits may have been only the natural reaction from the hours of depression through which she had lately passed. But whatever the reason behind it, Barbara's levity was a totally spontaneous, deliciously colored thing. She sat and tilted her head at him in audacious provocation; she assumed as chastened an expression as she could in the face of her very real relief at the news of Garry's safety.

"I'm sorry," she murmured humbly. "I'm sorry to—disappoint you. But, you see, I didn't know—"

She laughed at him. Her lips curled, petal-like, in a gurgling peal of enjoyment at his shame-faced grin.

"I found your horse rolling," he explained, and his gravity was dogged in the face of her brightness. "How I knew it was yours I don't know, but I did just the same. I thought she had thrown you; I'd already made up my mind, if there was one scratch on your body, to take that mare's head between my hands and break her neck! You see, I believed I knew already just what it would mean to me if anything ever happened to you. But it's a lot different imagining the world without you—and—and facing the actual possibility of it. Was I—fairly tragic?"

And now it was his turn to laugh over her pink-faced disconcernment. Most decidedly it was not the sort of an encounter which she had been contemplating a moment earlier. There was no discomfort in that big, loose-limbed body. She had imagined him as just a little moody and sad-eyed, at least. And now she realized that she had never seen the latter so easy to read as they were at that minute. Gray as the shadowed silver thread of the river far below in the valley, they glowed with a great gladness for her safety, and far, far more than just that. The alarming cheerfulness of his gaze was too confusing to sustain.

"Of course you've found Garry," she hastened to swing the conversation to a less personal quarter. "Is he—will you tell me about it, please?"

One small, gauntleted hand made an almost imperceptible gesture toward the unoccupied space beside her on the fallen tree. But he chose the ground at her feet. And after he had disposed his long length to his liking he answered her hurried question—answered it with an amiably lazy deliberation that promised a sure return to a topic of his own choosing, in his own good time.

"No," he stated, and there was something lugubrious in the baldness of the statement. "He found me. And it was the biggest stroke of luck that he did. I grow more and more lucky this morning, wouldn't you say so?"

The question was quite innocently direct. No, decidedly he was not discomfited—not ill at ease at all! Apparently he found it much easier to look at her than at any of the points of interest in the landscape toward which her glances persisted in flitting. While he marveled, without any manifestations of sorrow whatever, at the curve of her throat and the satin texture of that cheek turned toward him, he told her drawlingly all there was to tell of the night before. And after a time Barbara forgot her warm face and the too plain message there in his eyes, in her growing excitement over that recitation. When he stopped her first question instinctively pounced upon the one detail he had purposely withheld.

"But you must have an inkling as to the man's identity," she cried. "Why, you've got to find that out, before he does more harm next time. Haven't you a suspicion, even?"

One foot swung free; she leaned forward in her eagerness, a slender and entirely boyish figure in diminutive breeches and boots and straight-lined coat. And the man laughed aloud up into her flushed face, softly and not quite steadily at her hostile indignation, her intuitive feminine curiosity, and most of all, most unsteadily, at his wonder of her, herself.

"Why, yes," he admitted. "Both Joe and I do believe we know who it was, but we aren't sure because we don't understand yet what that man's motive might be. I'd tell you, only I don't like to accuse anybody until there is cause for it. But that's what brought me down here this morning—that and because I wanted to tell Miss Burrell that Garry is safe, and will continue to be from now on, I hope. Those were two of my reasons for coming, at least. I had a more important one than either, but—"

Barbara did not wait for him to tell her what it was. She was staring at him in unfeigned surprise.

"To tell Miriam?" she echoed. "Do you—you can't mean that you knew she cared for Garry?"

"Didn't you?"

The girl shook her head.

"Never, until just a little while ago! I—do you know, in the last few days I've begun to realize how much more you—other people—observe than I do. I've begun to wonder if I haven't been very blindly self-sufficient. For I never dreamed of such a thing, until something happened after I left you last night." Her voice faltered, but her eyes clung resolutely to his. "She came to me and asked me if I knew where he had gone. She had seen him ride away, too, Mr. O'Mara. And I learned it then, just from the terror in her face. But I didn't know until later how much she cared.

"She came into my room this morning, and that, although you can't know it, was more than odd in itself, because I have always been the one to carry my woes to her. It must have been between four and five, for I had counted a clock striking four; and yet she was still dressed in her party costume. Have you guessed what she had been doing? Mr. O'Mara, she had been out looking for him! She had slipped out and been waiting because she was sure Ragtime would bolt and—and come back home, dragging him by a stirrup! Wasn't that a horrible thing to wait for, alone in the dark?"

With a little shudder the girl put her hands over her eyes, as if to shut out the picture.

"She wasn't hysterical, either. She was—just—ice! And wringing wet and blue with cold. Cool, proud, intolerant Miriam Burrell—and I'd never dreamed of her caring for anybody, until that minute. I sent her to bed and I think I hated Garry Devereau for an hour or two. Why, Mr. O'Mara, I'd never believed that a girl could care that much for any man!"

He stopped toying with a handful of dry twigs and let them slip away between his fingers. She saw his head come up; saw his eyes narrow. Then her own body stiffened as she realized what she had said. And yet it was, after all, only a part of something she had decided she must make clear to him, ever since he had surprised her there at the road edge; it was part of an explanation which, without quite knowing why, she felt was due to him. But she had not meant to employ that abrupt confession as a preface. That made it inconceivably harder, it seemed. And he, silent at her feet, stared out at the blue rim of the hills and gave her no assistance now—not so much as a smile. She sat a long time, nursing one slim knee between her palms.

"Mr. O'Mara," she appealed to him at last, "how might one reopen a—a rather difficult subject with—with a suddenly most difficult conversationalist?"

Without turning his head he made answer:

"I think Fat Joe's method is as good as any," he suggested. "Joe says the only way to reopen any argument is to take a running jump and land all spraddled out, right in the middle of it. He insists that such procedure leaves no doubt in the mind of anyone that the discussion is about to be resumed."

She laughed a little.

"Then shall we consider that I've taken—the—the jump, and landed?"

Just when she was wishing most that she could see his face he swung around toward her. Again his gravity was a totally gentle thing. It made her remember the self-possessed kindliness with which he had met her unreasoning rage the night before.

"You don't have to explain," he told her, "unless you are sure you want to. Sometimes, you see, I understand things without any special explanation. It's a trick one learns from living alone a lot with one's own thoughts. I told you, last night, that I wouldn't have you saying 'I'm sorry' to me. And now I'll tell you that nothing you can ever say, now, is going to stop me from—"

"I want to, please," she interrupted him vehemently. "I—have to! And I'm not going to make believe that I don't know what you are going to tell me—what you have been saying to me, all morning. But it can't do any good. Why, I'm just realizing that something which has been hurting me for hours was just—just sorrow for you. It can't do any good, oh, truly! But will you let me talk first, if I promise to listen afterward?"

He promised.

"Twice I've been bitterly unkind to you," she began again. "Once a long time ago—and—and once last night. And on both occasions you had just tried to tell me, indirectly at least, that you cared, hadn't you?"

"Indirectly?" he murmured. "Was I as obscure as that?" And then, whimsically: "Won't you call that explanation enough, and let me tell it to you again—so you can't misunderstand?"

"I've asked you to forgive me the first offense," she hurriedly denied his appeal. "And the second—Mr. O'Mara, last night Miriam said something to me, something that she wouldn't have said if she hadn't been half mad with fear. It was unkind, unfair, but it made me wonder if, perhaps, you might not be thinking the same thing, too. Years ago you told me I didn't think you good enough to—to be my knight. My outburst was only childish temper that day, but did you think last night that I still underrated you?"

Steve finally shook his head when she persisted in waiting for his answer.

"You just have to finish now," he warned her, however. "It was your own bargain. I'm not going to tell you one single bit of what I think of you until it comes my turn!"

She tried to laugh at his stubbornness, but she had trouble with this explanation, which grew more vexingly intricate and involved the further she went.

"Then we'll say you didn't," she continued. "I told you last night, less kindly than I might have, that I was engaged to Mr. Wickersham. And I've just confessed, too, that I didn't know a girl could care for any man as unutterably, as blindly and pridelessly, as Miriam cares for the man Garry is. That is the truth. For quite a long, long time it has been understood that I was to marry Mr. Wickersham. I have always admired him—found him above petty things. But, Mr. O'Mara, I have always been sure, for just as long a time, that the ability to care for anyone the—the way I think you believed last night I might care for you, was left out of me. And so it wasn't you who awoke my contempt, even though I did turn it against you. It was I, myself. It was I, and not you, who was not 'good enough'! For even if I am the kind of a girl who can't love anybody, very much, except, perhaps, herself, I should at least play fair. Isn't—isn't that so?"

Minute after minute passed while she sat plaiting the cloth tight-stretched over one knee. Lips softly aquiver, she waited, earnest, eager that he understand from her explanation that which she did not yet understand at all herself. Again she wished that he would turn; she wanted greatly to see whatever there might be behind his heavy silence.

"Isn't it?" she faltered timidly.

And yet, when his head did come around she found she couldn't face him.

"Is it my turn now?" he asked.

Her answer was barely audible.

"If—if you have to—have it. But I've told you how useless it is."

"Would you mind looking at me, just a minute?" said Steve.

The brown head drooped even lower over the restless fingers. It shook, ever so faintly.

"I'd rather not.... I'm listening!"

His laugh lilted recklessly in sheer joy at her refusal.

"Then I'll have to tell you," he stated, "that I'm smiling in spite of the hopelessness. I'm smiling, even though my throat is aching and my lips pretty dry.

"You've just finished trying to argue my man's case from your woman's point of view—one of the hardest, least satisfactory things that could be attempted, no doubt. And if it were possible, I know I'd be loving you right now even more than I did before, just because you've been so entirely unsuccessful at it. Maybe I could straighten out a point or two that must have been not quite clear to you; maybe—but I don't want to argue back at you now.

"You say my telling you all I must tell you can't help my case a little bit. All right—we'll let it stand like that, for the moment. And you say you are going to marry Mr. Wickersham. All right again—but better prophets than either of us have made mistakes before now! If he hadn't forced on me one condition which I would have liked to be different, I'd rather have had to mention no other man at all. This isn't the way I'd have chosen to tell you how much I care. I'd rather have told you, a little at a time, but there isn't time for that now. So maybe it'll sound crude to you. I've not rehearsed it with any other woman, you see. And if it does sound that way it won't help me much, either, will it? But you're going to believe what I say!

"You started back a dozen years or so, in order to make your explanation clear. I'm starting there myself, so I'll be sure you understand. You've been grieving because you hurt me—hurt me twice. Will you stop now, if I tell you that I wouldn't exchange those two—shall we call them wounds—for all the kindnesses of all the other women in the world? I did believe that you didn't think me good enough, that first time. That was why I was cut deeper than you'll ever know, because I knew it was only the truth. I admitted it—remember? I admitted it when I said I was coming back. Well, I'm back now—and I'm still not good enough, and not because I haven't tried to be, either. I'm just not admitting any man alive could be that. But I'm telling you, too, in the same breath, that the man who takes you will have to prove he's a whole lot better—before I stand aside!"

For the first time since he had begun the girl moved. Her head leaped back; she half lifted one hand in protest, but the very gladness in his face silenced her.

"My turn," he reminded her quizzically. "You made the bargain, you know. You've just finished a rather involved bit of reasoning concerning the way other women love, a lot of which I'll have to confess I didn't attend as closely as I should have. Perhaps that's because no man's method of caring has ever interested me a great deal, except my own.

"I loved you when you were a little bit of a girl—because I loved you! And I love you that way now. Your face was the first woman face I ever looked on—and—really—saw. And since that first morning it's been with me—been with me a lot of times when I didn't have anything else to look up to. I've been less hungry, for thought of you; less thirsty, when the road got pretty long at times. I—I worshiped you, do you hear? Why, I've prayed to you, dumbly, wordlessly, out of black bitterness, when it seemed that any other divinity must be too busy to give any heed to—to the ragged little tad I was. Now do you think I haven't known what it was, long before this, to go on when there wasn't any hope?"

He waited. Her breath came in a long and quivering gasp. And yet he did not realize that she was crying.

"I—I don't think that I want to—listen any more," she faltered.

His face went white at that—and then he was smiling again.

"I told you I'd have chosen to tell you differently," the drawling gentleness was unaltered, "but I'll have to finish this way now. There may not be many chances for me to speak, for I've come back to you almost too late. And I don't want to hurt you; why, I'm going to keep the laughter in your eyes and heart as long as you live. For I thought it would be a woman I'd find when I came back, and I've found you still all girl—all save in those moments when you've seemed half boy to me. And that is strange, too, isn't it—strange that I never knew how much I wanted you to be like that, until you taught me the wonder of it yourself? My—eyes are stinging. I don't talk quite plainly. My throat is too tight for easy speech. For it's just the old wonder of you, after all—just the same—reverence, isn't it? I'll never let you grow up now. You'll have to stay girl—Boy—all the rest of your life! I've learned to be fairly sure of myself, but I'm not asking to be sure of you yet. I'd never want to be too sure of you unless all the rest of my whole world had come tumbling down. And then—then I'd need to know always that I could stake my soul on your keeping faith. I'd want to know that I could reach out and find your hand searching for mine in the dark. Your face was the first, girl—it's been the only one. It'll be the last thing I'll see, the last moment there is sight in my eyes!"

His slow, infinitely gentle voice stopped. He sat head up, before her. And then her choking sob answered him through that blind silence. He was on his feet then; he started forward, and remembered again. And as if that slim-limbed, huddled little figure had been a boy indeed, he dropped one arm reassuringly over her bowed shoulders.

"Pity, Barbara?" he asked quietly. "Are you crying from pity? Because if it's that—it—it beats me!"

She shook her head vehemently.

"I'm not crying because of anything," she sniffed. "I'm just crying—that' all!"

One hand went searching through pocket after pocket; one elbow came up to shield her eyes. She slid from the tree-trunk and swayed unsteadily, and groped out and found his arm. And it was the boy he had just tried to comfort who curled both hands tightly around his flannel sleeve and hid a wet face against his shoulder.

"I—I'm sorry. I'm so terribly, terribly sorry. I shouldn't have let you start to tell me—I knew it all along. But I'm not pitying—big Stephen O'Mara; it—it was just little Steve who made me cry, I think." Again that long, sobbing breath. "Will you—will you—I can't find my handkerchief," she gasped.

Long after they had remounted and turned their horses toward the south Barbara rode with head bowed, slim shoulders turned toward the man beside her, a shield for her averted face. From time to time she dabbled furtively at her eyes with the big, crisp square of linen with which Steve had answered the wailed announcement of the loss of her own handkerchief. Once or twice she caught her breath, unsteadily. And yet in spite of the fact that the actual desire was furthest of all things from her heart at that instant, when she did finally grow curious at his long silence and turn to steal a sidelong glance at him, the utter gloom upon Steve's face awoke within her an irresistible impulse to mirth.

It was partly hysterical, partly the sudden realization that he was not the only one who had, that morning, found much in his companion which was insistently boyish. For until then she had not glimpsed this side of that grown-up spirit which, in the boy, had evinced more than once a confidence in self so serenely unshakable that it had bordered on doggedness at times.

In those days it had always irritated her, and set her small fists to clenching in a childish antagonism. More than once she had answered it with superior little, child-woman smiles which had sent him marching, white of face and lip, back through the hedge gap, never realizing herself that her own pique sprang from the belief that his promises of conquest dealt only with material things—splendidly visioned, most vaguely detailed conquests which set his eyes afire but seemed to hold no place for the feminine of her. She had never understood that he, with quite masculine bindness [Transcriber's note: blindness?], had taken for granted her comprehension that each and every conquest was to be solely a glorification of her, any more than she understood now why his black discouragement awakened in her a sudden warmth as different from her old perversity as the pulse in her throat was painful. And yet she couldn't stifle that impulse. She giggled aloud. And when he turned—when he wheeled and encountered her shining eyes, still wet and brimming above the screen of his own handkerchief, she sensed immediately that he was flushing as little, too-sensitive Steve had flushed years before, when she had laughed at him less kindly.

The girl was not conscious of it; she had no actual realization yet of how very deeply her unwilling readjustment of fundamental values had, in the last twenty-four hours, undermined her hitherto unquestioning acceptance of those inbred standards which, to all her world save Miriam Burrell, were creed and code of conduct. That morning she only knew she was unaccountably glad because there was no malice in her mirth; had she given it thought she would have insisted that, in her heart, there no longer lurked a ghost, ignoble or otherwise, of what had once been a childishly snobbish belief in her inherent superiority. And as suddenly as she had giggled she now laughed aloud at the expression she had surprised there on his face. Again, for an instant, the very spontaneity of her swift changing mood gave the situation into her hands.

"Please," she begged him mockingly, "please, I did have to laugh, a little. I had to! It just occurred to me, all in a breath, that perhaps there is another of us who—who hasn't entirely grown up. You looked so morbidly disheartened. And I know it won't sound logical, but all this time during which I supposed you were smiling upon my—my absurd tears with that benign surety of yours, it hurt—hurt like everything—just knowing that it was all so hopeless for you. But now that I have seen that you do understand, do we have to be so gloomy any longer? Are we going to be so tragic, every time we meet? They tell me it is an admission of unformed, unbalanced youth, Mr. O'Mara. And, whether that is so or not, I do know that it is a great strain upon my complexion."

Momentarily her effrontery had given the situation into her hands—but only momentarily. For even while she was speaking the corners of Steve's eyelids began to crinkle; before she had finished mocking at him in a voice that still caught unsteadily in her throat, it was her up-turned face which had grown pink under his gravely amused scrutiny.

"Was it as bad as that?" he asked. "I don't know that I mind the 'benign' part so very much, but as for my 'surety'—well, now I must set you right. I have seen men holding four aces sit with faces so sad and hopeless that they might have earned their fortunes as professional mourners, could their expressions have been rendered permanent. I've seen men with straight flushes bow their heads in sorrow over the cards they held. And I think the one beatific visage it has been my good luck to behold belonged to Fat Joe, one night when the rest of the table had raised his very feet out from under him. He sat and beamed; he radiated good cheer—now and then he chuckled with positively insulting self-confidence, while he was pushing forward all the chips he owned ... and he had two deuces and four spades to back it up!

"You'll find that most men play that way—most men, I mean, who play for big stakes and play to win. And so—but I've told you already that I'm going to put all my cards on the table, with you. You're going to know, always, the hand I hold. Why, I told you I wasn't sure, even a little bit. I've been smiling just to make it easy for you to understand that I know how to lose, if it has to come to that. And do you suppose I'd have let you weep into my handkerchief, if I'd been half way certain, even? Do you? Because I wouldn't. I have a pair of arms and two shoulders that have been reserved for that purpose—reserved, oh, for years and years."

Barbara had lifted the handkerchief again. The explanation which Steve had begun in half-assumed soberness ended in drawling, unmistakable gravity.

"Perhaps it wasn't a particularly good parallel to use," he went on, even more slowly, when she failed to answer. "I only wanted to make you see—to have you know—"

Her brown head flashed up then, radiantly eloquent of entire understanding.

"It was a very good parallel," she defended spiritedly. "I liked it immensely. I was thinking that some day when I get involved with Miriam in a particularly erudite discussion, I'd employ it myself. But just now the one point which interests me most is this. Did—did Fat Joe win?"

His single quick word that checked Ragtime brought her roan mount also to a standstill. Lightly Steve swung out and took both her gloved hands in a grip that made her draw back a little.

"If you weren't the *girl* to whom I'd just told my love," he stated, "I'd be telling you, right now, that I like you best of all the *men* I know!" He sat and looked at her. "And since I don't remember clearly whether I've said it already this morning, I'll chance repeating it. You're the one prettiest thing in all this world—and it's not an unhandsome world this morning, either."

For a moment longer her mood lasted while she surveyed him with dark-eyed audacity, head poised on one side in that attitude of wholly happy intimacy with which he had seen her many times greet Caleb Hunter.

"For a man who claims to be strictly an amateur," she murmured, "I can only reply—you do extremely well, sir!"

And then, as if her words had rung too cheaply flippant in her own ears, she took both hands impetuously from his. She started her horse abruptly. And it was yards before he overtook her, rods before she dropped back to a walk. Her face had become wistful in its earnestness.

"That was pretty, and sincere, and—and like you," she mused. "I wonder why my answer sounded not quite so innately fine? Do you suppose it was because I've already become accustomed to meeting flippancy with flippancy? For if that isn't the reason then how would you explain my—my persistent tendency toward frivolity with you? Because it exists, you know. Truly it does! If I yielded to the impulse that is always with me, I—I'd coquette with you, disgracefully. Doesn't that—even surprise you? Now you *are* laughing at me ... why, you weren't listening at all!"

His shamefacedness was an admission of guilt, but he shook his head in contradiction.

"Not at you," he corrected her. "I wasn't laughing very heartily, or very steadily, was I? And I'm trying to listen; I am trying to pay attention to everything you say. It just isn't an easy thing to do, that's all, when—when I'm looking at you, too. But I promised you that you were always going to be sure of me. Couldn't that be reason enough; can't we just say you'd sensed it, yourself, even without my telling you so?"

She bobbed her head, most anxious for his gravity now that she was not sure whether it was real or not.

"I knew that must be it," she argued seriously. "I thought it must be, anyway. I just feel safe with you. And yet I don't want you ever to believe, either, that I am deliberately playing. It's just—oh, in my heart I know that you haven't any more than those two deuces, and—and the deal is mine. Do you understand what I'm trying to say? They always say it in—in books, Mr. O'Mara. They always agree to be the 'best of friends,' and it reads so funny and flat. But that is exactly what I am trying to put into words. It couldn't be anything more, ever, and yet I want this friendship which is different from everything I've ever known before. I like you very, very much. Listen, and I'll make a confession, too! I used to watch and hope you'd come back, after I'd sent you home, heart-sick, years ago. Do you suppose we might say the—the 'best of friends' in real life, too, and not sound instantly absurd?"

"We might try it out," he suggested.

Then she was positive that his face was too stiffly sober, but she ignored it—ignored, too, the tinge of whimsicality in his voice.

"If I weren't so sorry for you I might not be so sure; but I am sorry. If you weren't so dismayingly cheerful about it, I wouldn't feel so badly. But I've begun to understand how very long you have been playing your cards and smiling over them, no matter what might be dealt you. And that is some improvement over the girl I've been, isn't it? For I've never had to struggle very hard for anything I've wanted. I want to be friends, but I'm not silly enough to think you won't tell me again that you—care. I want to be friends, but not at the price of your heart-ache and disappointment, and—why, I wonder, do I get all tangled up when I try to explain myself to you? It's just this: I'm not going to be unkind to little Steve any more, Mr. O'Mara, or—or big Steve, either. But I—I want to see you sometimes, too, and—and I just won't let myself cry any more this morning!"

Her voice had grown very small toward the end. It trailed off into a stifled but unmistakable sniff. And a moment later, when she ceased fumbling with the reins and glanced with resolute brightness up at him, the film of hot tears in his eyes brought her hands to her throat. But even then in the face of that light which she had never before glimpsed in any man's eyes for her, she was conscious of his use of her name—vaguely conscious of how different it sounded on his lips.

"Barbara," Steve faltered, "Barbara, you blessed child, you!" And there, dumbly, he shook his head over his stumbling utterance and tried to laugh to cover it. "Sorry? Sorry for me? Why, God bless you, girl, you refuse me whenever you want to—whenever you have to! I'm not asking you to help. And don't you suppose after last night I know how near to losing out I am? I understand. Why, you're going to get quite a few refusals ahead of me, no doubt, before—before I catch up with you! But don't you waste one bit of worry on me.

"It would be your telling me that you did care, and then telling me that you didn't, that would about break me. I have to keep on asking you; I have to keep on trying, but you can tell me 'no chance' whenever, in your heart, you believe it to be the truth, and I'll take it smiling. Just don't let it become mechanical, that's all I ask, will you? And—and if some day after I've gone, you suddenly begin to wish, even the tiniest bit, that you hadn't made the last refusal quite—quite so final, you needn't let that worry you, either. Because I'll be back! You can know that I'll come back, next day—next month—next year—thirty miles or three hundred—oh, just to see if my chances haven't improved any! That does make you smile, doesn't it? I reckon experienced match-makers would tell me that that isn't the way for me to talk if I'm going to win out. But it's the way I like best. I want you to know that there is one person you can be sure of, all the days of your life. I began a dozen years ago—I've only started loving the whiteness of you."

She rode with wide eyes fastened upon his now wholly smiling face; rode with lips parted, all else submerged in that wonder which quickened her breath. Once she leaned toward him as if to speak, and then shook her head at the inadequacy of the words. They topped the last rise in the dusty, winding road and raised the river basin and the town itself in that long period of silence. There, once more, she checked the roan mare.

"If women could care like that," she told him quietly. "If I believed that I could ever—" She shook her head with a sad little smile. "Since you have come home you've made me feel very insignificant and petty at times. You've made me wish I might have been as—as wonderful as you say I am to you. But I know, you see." She lifted one slim arm toward the newer Morrison stretched out along the river front. "Do you remember the first day you saw the village it used to be, that day when you first came down river?"

Steve knew what she was going to say. She read amused anticipation in his eyes and grew self-conscious at it.

"I thought yours was a perfectly good parallel," she asserted stoutly. "And you'll have to admit that you did believe it was wonderful then. Uncle Cal has told me how breathlessly you called it the 'city.' But is it as wonderful, now? Hasn't familiarity with real bigness dimmed its wonder a little?"

For the first time that day his attitude was frankly challenging.

"Maybe," he agreed, "maybe! And maybe I like it better than ever, for the others I've seen!" He frowned and shook his head. "I'm quite likely to stick to first conclusions," he finished, "and your inference is basically wrong. I do not need to look at other women to make me surer of the wonder of you. A man doesn't have to live in a desert all his life to know what thirst is, you know. And it's not bad—not bad as cities go!"

As they had begun the morning they now finished it, on a plane of thorough comradeship which years and years alone cannot achieve.

"Not bad," she echoed throatily. "Not bad, at all! It's marvelous too, how towns and people and—and things in general can improve, once they awake to their own importance in the scheme of things, isn't it?"

Quite on a mutual impulse they clasped hands and laughed into each other's eyes; quite unnecessarily it may have appeared to the small group on the veranda of the stucco and timber place halfway down the slope between them and town. And there on the crest of the hill, suddenly conscious of those eyes, the girl drew back as swiftly as she had swung toward him.

"What in the world will they think!" she breathed. "I've been gone since daybreak, without saying a word that I was going. And it must be noon by now. Come—no, don't hurry! It's too late to hurry now!"

Her chin came up; the line of her lips lost its soft fullness. It was his hot face which made her aware of how surely her imperiously quick orders had stung him. Then she was back, knee to knee, at his side.

"That wasn't fair," she said. "That was most unfair, to me. You didn't think, did you, that I—"

His interruption surprised her.

"If I shouldn't inquire," he asked, "will you please tell me so, and forget I asked the question? May I know when you—you and Mr. Wickersham are to be—"

Barbara's face went slowly crimson, flushed to the nape of her neck.

"It's not a certainty yet, the date," she answered kindly. "Just late in the spring, I think."

He nodded. Again she knew how wholly unreadable his eyes could be.

"Late in the spring," he repeated, so softly that he might have been talking to himself. "Late in the spring I'll have two time limits run out on me."

Wickersham himself was coming across the lawn to meet them when they drew rein at the head of the driveway. With a deliberation so proprietary that it set Barbara suddenly to gnawing her lip, he unbent his long legs and straightened from his place on the top step of the veranda; and even though the wicker chairs behind him were filled he stood forth quite alone, extremely tall and straight, perfectly poised and entirely immaculate. And without one outward sign of animosity to give it ground, that other man sitting loose-thighed upon Ragtime's back knew that he was wondering where she had been—why she had chosen to go alone. Without exhibiting a trace of it upon his long face, Wickersham still radiated a swift and chilling jealousy which, now that he saw it again, Stephen O'Mara knew had never been entirely absent from the face of the Archibald Wickersham he had known many years before. Just as Miriam Burrell, with a studied deliberation that matched that of the tall figure ahead of her, in turn detached herself from the throng and came down the steps, Barbara's eyes raised to Steve's. She did not stop to reason it; she couldn't have made it sound reasonable had she tried, but she did not want those two to meet again just then—those two whose boyhood quarrel had centered about herself.

"Won't you keep Ragtime until you come back to Uncle Cal's to-night?" she asked. "I've kept you loitering for hours and hours on the way. But it will save you a little time."

And this time Steve understood. He nodded in reply.

"Not a chance?" he asked her quietly. "Not a chance?"

She was wheeling the roan.

"Not a chance," she whispered. "Not a chance in the world! But we—Mr. Elliott promised to show us the works this afternoon," she added in the next breath. "Can you—do you suppose you can come?"

And then, as she turned the mare and went skimming up the drive toward the stable, she wondered why he laughed.

In his turn Steve set Ragtime's head toward the town in the valley. And therefore he did not see that Archibald Wickersham was left standing alone a moment in the middle of the lawn. But Miriam Burrell saw and understood the black rage that shadowed his face. Long before then she had penetrated to the layer of vanity beneath his air of boredom. More than once she had used that knowledge maliciously, to stir him. And she knew how unending could be his hatred for anyone who had ever made him appear ridiculous.

CHAPTER XI
I NEVER DID LIKE TO BE BEATEN

Stephen O'Mara found Hardwick Elliott lunching alone in the East Coast Company's main Morrison office, a big unpainted shack that stood half lost in a maze of high-piled ties, midway between the saw-mills at the river edge and the first snarled network of switches converging on one reddish streak of steel that lanced into the north. With moodily indifferent interest Elliott scarcely more than glanced up at the horseman's approach across the open plot of raw earth, hard-packed to a cement-like surface by the endless passage and repassage of countless hob-nailed, heavy-booted feet, but with that first glance his forehead began to smooth a little. His face had lost something of its hint of gauntness, even before his chief engineer had swung down from the saddle. Elliott had been exhibiting scant appetite for the cold food half buried in the pile of papers on his desk top; and though he smiled his characteristically courteous, mildly abstracted greeting when Steve loomed in the doorway, his attitude was still very patently that of a man who attempts to conceal his own perplexities lest they compound those of another whose perplexities are already more than enough. He rose and held out a finely tapered hand.

"Now, this is fine," he exclaimed. "This is really fine, Mr. O'Mara. Rather odd, too—coincidence and that sort of thing, I mean. Because I was just this instant wondering whether I had better send for you or wait until you just happened down river again."

In many ways the president of the East Coast Company reminded Steve of Caleb Hunter, even though there could be no two things more in contrast than the latter's calm and comfortable bigness and Elliott's thin and wiry and extremely nervous exterior. It was a similarity due entirely to the innate honesty of both men—such honesty as makes of every attempt at dissimulation an assured non-success. And Miss Sarah had never anticipated her brother's clumsiest finesse with greater ease than did Steve sense, that afternoon, the weight of worry behind his employer's first effort at jauntiness. He nodded, hopefully, it seemed.

"Something else gone wrong?" he asked. "Or are you going to tell me that McLean is still having trouble with that curve of his."

Elliott, too, shook his head, but his negative nod was less brisk, less hopeful.

"No," he replied. "No, we've got that laid, or at least practically so. It's not anything so satisfyingly material that I wanted to talk about. I wish it were, because—well, the fact is, now that you are here it appears I may have considerable trouble in making you believe that I'm not merely developing a most womanish case of nerves. Cold feet, I suppose, might not be far from correct, if we put it in the proper gender. No, it's not the work itself. You know the first few miles at this end afford pretty plain sailing. We figured on that: or we wouldn't stand any chance of finishing the job. And we are quite nicely ahead of our schedule, so far. But have you—I was wondering if you, by any chance, have noticed any signs of discontent in your own squad at Thirty Mile?"

Elliott eased himself back into his chair at the finish of the question. Repugnantly he jerked a thumb in silent invitation toward a plate of sandwiches. It indicated most clearly the state of his appetite—that gesture—and Steve could not help but smile a little as he refused.

"No more than the usual disturbances," he answered. "I have more or less trouble holding them—some of them—over the week-ends, of course. But then that's always to be expected. They aren't the sort of men that go to make up the general run of construction squads. One of my main reasons for wanting them was the fact that they were rivermen, hardened to swamping and white-water work and that kind of thing. In a pinch they're good for twenty-four hours a day, over stretches that would take the heart out of most gangs. I don't know of anything that can beat a lumber-jack on a squeeze job, once you get him to realize that he's up against long odds. It's this ten-hour-a-day thing and too much ready money every pay-day; it's a town too temptingly close that makes them a—a trifle temperamental, Mr. Elliott. Is that what you mean?"

Elliott pondered for a moment.

"That entirely duplicates what McLean said just a day or so ago." On any other lips Elliott's deliberate neatness of phrase might have sounded solemnly funny. "Thoroughly logical, of course,—thoroughly possible. And yet, somehow it doesn't fit the case. We've had the usual Monday morning vacancies, right along, as you know; but the delinquents always turned up before the five o'clock whistle blew, or at least reported Tuesday morning. But this is the end of the week and we're short right this minute very close to thirty men. They aren't coming back, Mr. O'Mara; on the contrary, they continue to dribble away, a few every day. And though they appear to do nothing but talk their time away in the saloons in the lower end of the town, they seem to have just as much money to spend, as they did when they were getting their time checks from us."

Steve leaned over and with nice deliberation selected a sandwich.

"What sort of talking?" he wanted to know, suddenly.

Again Elliott smiled in self-deprecation.

"That's just it," he exclaimed. "Their talk leads nowhere. I went down and attempted to find out what their grievance might be, but they close up like clams whenever I come within earshot. They stare at the ceiling, rub their chins, and laugh when there's nothing to laugh at. This morning, however, I finally convinced McLean that something was radically wrong. So he took one of them who had just decided to quit and pinned him up against the embankment—but you know McLean and his methods! He shoved his jaw up within an inch of the other's nose and invited him to talk, and—well, he found out enough to make him begin to worry, too. Somebody's been talking to them, Mr. O'Mara; somebody has put the fool notion into their heads that this strip of railroad will mean the end of all lumber operations in this country—the old-time river drives, of course. And some of them are beginning to believe—whoever was responsible for that statement.

"You know and I know how absurd it is. We know that this road will mean work for every riverman in this section, as often as he wants to work. But it isn't going to help us any if they can't see it that way. It isn't going to replace the men who quit. I've been deliberating one point. Don't you suppose we might import a regular squad of construction men now, before it's too late?"

"It's too late now," Steve told him, his words none the less final for all that they were absently quiet. "It was too late the day we began operations. And yesterday at this time I wouldn't have given much worry to this particular brand of trouble. They're an odd lot; they're the hardest working, hardest living crowd of big men that ever failed entirely to grow up." Steve stopped and looked down at the sandwich untouched in his hand, much as though he were surprised to find it there. "But since yesterday—since yesterday—who, did you say, was responsible for that statement, as you call it?"

"I didn't say." Elliott brushed away a persistent bluebottle fly, a lonesome survivor which the unseasonably warm day had reawakened. The insect's droning wings as it persisted again and again back to the sandwich plate made the only sound in that big, bare room. "And if I—if I had to guess—" The hand passed across his eyes now. "O'Mara, do you know how deeply Mr. Ainnesley and myself are involved in this prospect?"

After a long search the engineer of the East Coast Company had finally located his pipe.

"I don't believe I have ever given it much actual thought," he said. "I never viewed it as any of my affair. But I haven't forgotten the last time we talked the plans over, that you couldn't go into it to lose."

Punctiliously Elliott proffered a lighted match for the other's filled pipe; he lighted a long and thin and very black cigar for himself. Steve noted then for the first time that the man's hand was shaking a little.

"Of course," the latter answered quickly. "Of course—of course!" He seemed groping for a fresh beginning, then gave up suddenly all attempt at circuity and blurted it out much as though he had lived with the thought too long to endure it longer alone.

"I'm in up to my last dollar," he stated. "And Ainnesley—why, Ainnesley wouldn't have a roof over his head if we failed in our obligations! You must know as well as I do why the banking interests took our paper to those amounts which made it possible for us to drive the first spike."

When he failed to go on Steve understood that the last sentence had been a question.

"Mr. Allison, I suppose." His voice became utterly impersonal. "Without doubt you mean Mr. Allison?"

"They would have laughed at us," the older man came back instantly. "And what is more, they did! They wouldn't touch the proposition, until Allison came in with us. And then—but you know what Dexter Allison has done already in this country. I don't know what he started with. I do know that all that Ainnesley and I had scraped up between us looked like a shoe-string to him.

"We couldn't move until he, of his own accord, expressed his enthusiasm for the plan and asked for a share in the holdings. You know, perhaps, how he can laugh, too. Well, he laughed that way and confessed that we had just beaten him to it. He said it would tap a gold mine—this 'strip of steel,' as he called it. He even told us that he'd parallel our road with a competitor, jokingly to be sure, if we hadn't tied up the only available and practicable right of way.

"He came in. He opened up, merely through his own name and all there is behind it, loan possibilities for which we might have struggled uselessly the rest of our lives without his help. Between us Mr. Ainnesley and I just managed to hold the balance of stock control and—and that's how deep we are in, Mr. O'Mara."

Both men sat and smoked, each avoiding, elaborately, the other's eyes. After a long pause, Elliott cleared his throat, laboriously.

"This morning," he continued slowly, "this morning I am in receipt of a communication from Mr. Ainnesley himself, advising me that another right of way has been applied for, for a single track road here in the north. The gossip which chanced to come his way was rather obscure.

Little could be learned about the whole affair save that it was being put forward with a view to tapping the ore and timber lands all the way to and beyond the border. But as nearly as he could ascertain the southern terminus of such a road would seem to be about—about at the mouth of that valley southernmost in the Reserve Company's timber holdings. Rather a remarkable choice for a railroad terminus, Mr. O'Mara—wouldn't you say so?"

Steve leaned toward him.

"Do you mean that they've thrown out your earlier application for just such a grant?"

"That would be a rather harshly definite way of putting it," Elliott smiled wryly. "Ours is apparently just tabled—oh, tabled pending certain immaterial changes in the form! You asked me a moment ago—or did I offer to guess who might be responsible for the report which is costing us our men? I wonder if I need to tell you who controls this new northern route?"

"Maybe you've been telling me," Steve came back coolly. "You have already mentioned—"

"Wickersham!" Hardwick Elliott corrected. "Wickersham—that is, through allied interests which he represents or controls. O'Mara, I doubt if I would even insinuate this to anyone else; I haven't even intimated it to Ainnesley as yet. Wickersham is reputed to represent huge moneyed foreign interests. But have you ever stopped to wonder whether he might not represent big local interests as well?"

The tanned face opposite him was so gravely blank that Elliott once more laughed nervously, deprecatingly.

"Doubt of any man's loyalty such as that query would imply is not one of my characteristics. I would rather have left this thing unattempted than to have undertaken it in partnership with any man whom I felt I had to watch. But I just thought that I'd better put it all on the table for you to consider. I'd like to ask you—what do you think?"

The man in blue flannel and corduroy tapped the sodden heel from his pipe and loaded it afresh.

"Yesterday," he answered, "yesterday—Well I couldn't guarantee just what I might have thought, twenty-four hours back. But doesn't one fact remain unchanged still, no matter what we think? Suppose we admit that some one else does want this stretch of track we're laying? Suppose somebody is figuring on picking it up cheap, at a bankruptcy price, if we forfeit to the Reserve Company? You know yourself that you would never have begun it simply for the profit there will be in moving the Reserve logs and the millions on millions of feet of lumber both to the east and west, which can't be touched at anything but a prohibitive figure, without this road. We were going through to the border, too. And if some one else is betting that we don't; if some one else is betting that we can't yank a trainload of logs down to this end of the line, before the first of May, that doesn't alter our case any, does it? Even though we suspect that some man is playing us to lose, do we have to know exactly who he is?"

Slowly but very surely the older man's face began to smooth.

"Once or twice," he stated, "I've thought to anticipate you, perhaps because I have it on you a little, as they say, in the matter of years. I'm not going to attempt it any more. For I thought that this conversation would be at least a surprise to you. You sit there and take it very quietly, for a man who has been badly startled."

"Fat Joe has been preaching it for a month." Oddly enough, Stephen O'Mara chose that point at which to laugh, softly. "And I, for a month, have been ridiculing him. That's one of Fat Joe's pet diversions, you know. When all other excitement fails Joe invariably falls back upon an imagination too totally vivid to be wasted on technical things. I laughed at him, until last night. Do you—but of course you know Garry Devereau?" he finished.

"Knew his father," Elliott answered succinctly. "Know him well! Good blood—good brains—big hearts! Why?"

And then, for the second time that day, Steve related the salient points of that episode which had opened with the trio of owls along the trail and ended with the first gray streaks of returning day. During the recital the expressions which chased across Elliot's face were as varied as they were full of concern.

"Then I wasn't merely hysterical, was I?" he brooded after Steve had finished. "Who—who did you say you thought might be behind the man who would have had your plans, had it not been for Mr. Devereau?"

"I didn't say," replied Steve, and for the first time since his entrance there was mirth in the unison of their laughter.

"It all brings us back to the point from which we started," the younger man went on when they were grave again. "It's a plain enough issue, so far as we are concerned. We've got to be at the mouth of that lower valley by May. We're going to be! And as I see it, wasting time and energy in—shall we call it sleuthing, Mr. Elliott?—won't help us much. We thought that lack of time and the general nature of this country were going to be handicap enough. But now your money is in and I—I never did like to be beaten. Can't we let it stand like that, at least until some one else makes a plainer move? We know the cards we hold. If others care to sit in, perhaps we'll all come to a show-down, next spring at Thirty Mile. It'll be easy enough to explain just how we did it. Alibis based on veiled opposition wouldn't interest the Reserve people much, if we left their timber there to rot.... And I'm trying not to overlook any bets, Mr. Elliott."

Hastily the iron-gray man thrust his hat back from his forehead. He came to his feet and crossed and clapped one hand upon Steve's shoulder.

"Next May!" he barked. "O'Mara, I'm glad you came down this morning. I've been carrying a lot of those ideas around in my head until they had become nightmarish. But I'm through now. You won't hear me croak again. I staked what I had on you, months ago; I'd do it again this minute. What's the odds, after all, who it is that's playing us to lose. It's only the fact that somebody may be fighting us that needs to occupy our attention. I'm done worrying, do you hear? But what about those men who are quitting us? You are sure it would be unwise to import labor? It's cheaper, you know."

Steve, too, had risen.

"We'd have the prettiest kind of a scrap on our hands, the first day we tried to use them," he explained. "It would be dear enough before we got through. I guess I'd better run right out and have a talk with McLean. He knows these men even better than I do, and I'm almost one of them, you know. And I'll get a line on some of these delinquents who are crying calamity for the countryside. I'd better, because we'll need them. They simply haven't become thoroughly interested yet, that's all. It will take something to jolt them; something to set them on fire. And then—then just watch my plaid-shirted boys go! They'll eat up your sledge-swingers!"

Something of that promised fire was reflected now in Hardwick Elliott's eyes.

"By Gad," he exclaimed, "by Gad, if it wasn't for Ainnesley I'd say the thing was worth it, win or lose, just for the game itself. You go ahead and see McLean. I'll be out there later, myself. I promised Allison that I'd show the works to some of the young folks up there on the hill. His daughter—but I keep forgetting that you've known her longer than I have. There's quite a party of them. She announced her engagement to Mr. Wickersham last night, I believe. Heard that this morning—was too busy to go up last night myself. Maybe you'll find time to help me play the host."

Steve turned toward the door.

"So I heard," he replied, without facing around. "I'll try to be on hand."

He stood for another instant on the threshold.

"I'm going to ask you to see that my horse is fed and watered," he requested evenly. "And I reckon you'd better eat your own lunch, yourself."

But the man behind him had already anticipated that suggestion. Through a generous bite of sandwich he made answer.

"I'll see that he is taken care of," he called cheerfully. "See you later, Mr. O'Mara— Pshaw, the coffee's cold!"

CHAPTER XII
THAT WOODS-RAT

Between Dexter Allison's monopoly of his time and the persistence with which Miriam Burrell clung to Stephen O'Mara, Barbara Allison had opportunity for little more than a perfunctory word or two of greeting that afternoon, during the first hour or two that followed a jolting ride on the flat car which trundled them to the head of operations. Almost as soon as her feet touched the ground Miriam's eager survey singled out a tall figure at the edge of the farthest embankment; and in spite of the fact that he was at the moment in sober conversation with white-haired, white-bearded McLean, she crossed instantly to take possession of both Steve's arms and his undivided attention. Barbara, at Wickersham's side, glancing now and then in their direction, knew well what subject was engrossing them to the exclusion of all else. But Allison's acceptance of that arrangement as time passed grew less patient.

For a time he was content to stroll along with the rest—content with his facetious comments on Elliott's explanation of this matter or that. Yet whenever his eyes strayed toward Miriam and that other figure whom a week or two before he had designated as "my man, O'Mara," his jovialty faltered a little, his manner grew restive. After a time he, too, detached himself and sauntered in the direction of that wholly preoccupied pair.

"See here, my lady," he accosted the girl, who turned extremely bright eyes upon his approach. "This won't do at all. How do you suppose I am going to get a minute with Mr. O'Mara, here, if you persist in clinging to his elbow? You'll have to run along—you run over and listen, with the rest, to Elliott's heroic tale of this scarring of the face of nature. I've waited a good many days to talk business with Mr. O'Mara; I'm not going to lose him, now I've got him cornered."

Had Dexter Allison been less occupied with other thoughts, the face which Miriam Burrell turned toward him would have surprised him, if only because of the unusual color burning in her cheeks. At that he was vaguely aware that he had never before seen that quiet, self-contained girl so pulsingly happy. She stood and gazed at him a moment, then made him a low and mocking obeisance.

"Don't flatter yourself that I haven't noted your covetous glances," she flashed. "I've been talking very fast, because I knew this interruption was coming. But we've finished, thank you, so I'll leave you to—to bore him now!"

She turned back toward O'Mara. "And thank you," she murmured not very audibly. "Thank you, more than I ever thanked anybody before in my life. You've made me very, very happy."

No one could have missed the depth of real thankfulness in those last words. Even Allison stood astonished at it, mouth open, following her rapid withdrawal toward the group fifty yards away.

"Huh-h-h," he snorted. "Huh-h-h. A mighty strange girl!" And then, as abruptly as he had interrupted their low conversation, "Well, how does it go, Chief? How does it look to you, as far as you've gone?"

No man's good humor could be more infectious than was that of this big, noisily garbed man. Steve smiled and met his cordiality more than half way.

"Not too bad," he answered. "Not too bad." He swept the ground before them with a short gesture. "You aren't beginning to worry, too, are you?"

"Worry?" Allison's frown was barely perceptible. "Why should I? I never let anything worry me. Who is beginning to fret? You aren't, are you? You don't look—much disturbed."

"Not a particle!" Steve still smiled. "I never do either, unless that there is something worth while to make me. I just thought perhaps you might have contracted it from Mr. Elliott. He's been bothered, you see, by the way some of the men are acting. We're short a lot of labor this week."

The big man wheeled and squinted at the droves of men sweating under the unseasonably hot sun; he peered keenly at each clump of laborers, some of them scarcely distinguishable knots of humanity in the distance.

"Not very short," he stated comfortably. "I don't claim to be a wholly competent judge, but it looks to me as though they would be in one another's way if there were any more of them. What's wrong?"

The chief engineer's answer was drawling in its deliberation.

"I wish I knew," he replied. "I wish I could be positive. And there aren't too many of them; they are altogether too few. We're going to need them, and more, too, before we finish, Mr. Allison. Perhaps I'd better figure on—perhaps if they continue to quit on us, by twos and threes, as they have in the last week—I'll have to—"

His pause seemed almost an invitation that the other suggest a remedy; and whether it was or not Dexter Allison was quick to seize the opening. His suggested solution was heartily bluff.

"Import some more," he said. "When you've employed these men as long as I have—the type of man who has worked all his life on the river—you'll know as well as I do just how uncertain and unreliable they are. What you need is a gang that doesn't want to think for itself. This crowd has too much imagination for a grind like this."

Steve nodded very thoughtfully.

"If it is all imagination," he wondered. "But they're not merely discontented, you see, Mr. Allison. They—they are misleading themselves. They seem to think, from what I've gathered from McLean and a few with whom I have talked, that they are working themselves out of a job for good, when they help to build this strip of railroad. They think so—they have been convinced that such is the truth. Personally, however, I feel sure that between us, we can correct that impression."

Even though he was looking in the direction of a heavy smoke-cloud that had followed a sharp blast to the north of them, Steve felt the weight of Allison's questioning glance.

"We," he echoed. "Where do I figure in it?"

The younger man's upward glance was seemingly surprised.

"You? Why, you're a stockholder. It means as much to you as it does to Mr. Ainnesley and Mr. Elliott."

Allison interrupted him.

"Of course," he exclaimed. "Surely! I see! What I mean was how in the world can I make them understand that such a fool idea is all wrong? So far as this constructive work is concerned, I'm not an active member. I—I had that understood with Elliott when I went into this thing!"

"Of course," Steve in turn broke in. "I understand that. But they know you; they know that Morrison would be nothing more than a street of well-kept lawns and cow-pastures, if you hadn't seen its possibilities. And so I've already told some of them, Mr. Allison; I've gone even further, and given a lot of them my word that you'll guarantee, yourself, that this is the biggest thing for the good of this section that has yet happened."

The speaker smiled frankly into the bigger man's eyes.

"And that was all they needed, was it?" Allison queried, at length. "That fixed it, did it?"

"Absolutely!" Steve's cheeriness should have been infectious. "Absolutely, Mr. Allison. A lot of people have come to look on your word as law in this country, you know—a lot of them!"

"Hum-m-m," replied Allison. "Hum-m-m."

Both of them were quiet for a time. Steve's next remark brought Allison's head up sharply.

"I meant to bring some of my estimates and plans down with me, when I came," he told him. "You spoke of wanting to run over the whole proposition with me, you'll remember, the first day you arrived."

Allison nodded shortly.

"I remember."

"I'll bring them, next trip," Steve finished. "I came so near to losing them last night that I'm taking no chances until they're in duplicate. We can run over them later?"

Allison wheeled and gazed meditatingly toward the group who were slowly moving their way. His daughter Barbara, with Wickersham at her side, was in the lead.

"Any time," he agreed. "There's no particular hurry."

And then a moment later, just when she was beginning to wonder whether he was purposely avoiding her, Barbara was surprised at the calm ease with which Steve took her away from her tall escort. She had noticed that Wickersham and Steve had not touched hands when they first met, an hour or two before, nor even hinted at such a salute. But now, as earlier in the day when her dash toward the stables had left him standing rigid in the middle of the lawn, she failed to see the expression that settled upon Wickersham's long face. It was Dexter Allison this time who noticed it, and hours later, when he and Wickersham sat and faced each other in the downstairs room in the house on the hill, which served as Allison's office, he remembered and recognized it.

"You wanted to talk with me?" Wickersham inquired as he entered the room that evening.

Somehow Wickersham's unending politeness had always irritated Allison. That night his smoothly infectionless question nettled him.

"Your damned fool, Harrigan, bungled last night!" he blurted out. "He messed things up, beautifully. He not only failed, but he failed to get away without being seen. That's what comes of entrusting a job like that to a drunken sot."

Wickersham seated himself—sat and caressed a cigarette. Coolly he waited and blinked his eyelids.

"My man?" he murmured. "My man?"

"Ours then," Allison corrected sharply. "Ours." Then he seemed to recollect himself and his voice became less abrupt. "Listen. This afternoon I had a talk with O'Mara. That is, I started to have a talk with him, but—but he beat me to it. And in just about three minutes he told me that he'd caught Harrigan on the job—not mentioning any names, I don't mean—but he didn't need to, And he told me more than that. He as good as gave me to understand that he'd know where to place the blame, if there was any more interference with his men."

Wickersham crossed a long leg and blew a thin blue streamer of smoke.

"Yes?" he intoned bodilessly.

It brought a blaze to Allison's eyes—that nerveless monosyllable.

"That doesn't interest you, eh?" he snapped. "Doesn't interest you at all! Well, it does me. Three months ago I bought into this affair because I was as sure as any man could be that I'd collect a hundred per cent on my money, next spring. Elliott and Ainnesley? Pah!—Nice gentle old ladies, when it comes to a game like this. They're anachronists; they are honest business men, twenty years behind the times. You've heard of taking candy from children. Well, that's what it looked like then. But it doesn't look that way any longer. Talk with you? Yes, I did want to talk. I wanted to tell you that if you'd like to switch I'm willing, right now. I wanted to tell you that if you'd rather be a good little boy and get into line, I'm willing and more than willing. Because I can promise you, since I talked it over with O'Mara this afternoon, that we haven't any nice, dead-sure thing on our hands any longer.

"Oh, you can sit there and smile your cold-blooded smile! And if you think I'm experiencing pangs of conscience you're mistaken. All I have, I got from other men who—who weren't strong enough to hang on to it. There isn't any friendship in business—or if there is I never played it that way. I'm just telling you that now is our one opportunity, if we want to join hands and hurrah with the rest of them for the completion of this job by next May. We lose a railroad at a bargain, perhaps, but we've still got a mighty good right-of-way to the border, that will insure our welcome in the ranks. Maybe we lose and—and maybe—well, I never did like to be beaten! Nor do I say that such an argument will have any weight with you, but it's a chance to be on the dead level, for once. What do you say? Do we switch?"

Then Allison remembered the expression which had flitted over Wickersham's face when Stephen O'Mara coolly appropriated Barbara. But that expression had been a totally gentle thing beside the pale fury which now slowly overspread his features. Wickersham twisted the cigarette to fragments—flung them from him, and the very gesture was vicious.

"Switch," he snarled. And he leaned forward, face bloodless, and beat upon a chair arm. "Switch now!" He laughed shrilly. "Why, I'm going to beat that damned woods-rat in his matinée-idol costume so bad between now and next May that he'll be walking the roads for his next job. Switch? I'm going to brand him as the worst incompetent that ever dragged two poor fools down into pauperism. I'll see him broke. I'll wipe that damned smooth smile from his lips, by God, if I have to—"

Wickersham gasped; he came to his feet panting all in an instant with the rage that set his dry lips writhing. But at that point he, too, remembered himself. He swallowed and faced Allison, and the latter, sitting pop-eyed before his outbreak, gaped now at the change that came back over that twisted face. Wickersham smiled. Once more his bearing was the very essence of perfect poise and self-control.

"If you—if you are afraid—" he inferred. "If you—"

Allison's laugh was big and booming, for all that the astonishment had not yet left his eyes.

"Cold feet," he rumbled. "Cold feet! Me!" And suddenly his gust of mirthless laughter made petty the other's insolence. "Wickersham, I've broken better crooks than you'll ever be. A man has to have a big heart to be a big crook and you—and you—well, sometimes I wonder whether there wasn't some sort of an oversight in that line, when they put you together."

He couldn't have explained why the thought came to him at that moment any more than he understood his swiftly malicious impulse to use it; but all in a flash there came back to him a recollection of that day when he and Caleb had burst through the hedge to find the boy, Stephen O'Mara, pummeling a bigger prostrate boy who shrieked under the earnest thoroughness of that pummeling. Allison, too, rose to his feet.

"I only wanted to give you a chance," he stated dryly. "I reckon I can take care of myself. I always could. And you—well, you know as well as I do what sort of a scrap that—that woods-rat can put up, or you ought to. He gave you a sort of a demonstration, once, if I remember correctly. I stick! I never was overly squeamish. But don't fool yourself, Archie, don't fool yourself. If we light, we're fighting with a regular guy, your insinuation to the contrary. I merely wanted you to realize what I know now. We'll think we've been in a battle before we come to a finish!"

His hand was on the door knob when the door itself flashed open. Dexter Allison's daughter hesitated, surprised, on the threshold. Her eyes, brilliantly alight, leaped from her father's face to that of the man half toward her and back again.

"Oh," she exclaimed uncertainly, "I didn't know you were busy. I saw the light. I'd been over to Uncle Cal's, just for a minute. I wanted to tell you—good night!"

CHAPTER XIII
THIS LITERARY THING

It was dark, the night of that second day, when Stephen O'Mara came quietly up to the open door of his own lighted shack and stopped for a moment to gaze in at the two men whose faces were touched by the glow of the lamp on the table. There had been more than one moment in those forty-eight hours which had elapsed since he had lifted that black-robed, inert figure from the floor in which Steve had wondered whether Garry Devereau would even await his return to Thirty-Mile; more than once he had smiled whimsically to himself, during the trip back up-river, over the scene which he was certain would meet his eyes, had Garry chosen to wait.

But there were no poker chips in front of Fat Joe that night. Round face propped upon one hand, the latter was staring motionless at a thick pad of yellow paper flat before his eyes. And Garry himself was sitting with his back toward the light, staring as motionlessly into the cold fireplace. Merely from their attitudes, Steve knew that they had been a long time silent; he knew that Fat Joe would have been making conversation, no matter how desperately footless it might have been, had he been conscious of the quality of the other's moody quiet. And then, as he was himself about to go forward, barely in time to check the word of greeting on his lips, Joe lifted pensive eyes to the other's back. When Joe spoke his words were none too plain; he was gnawing a pencil tip in most evident perplexity.

"Say," he broke that heavy silence, "say, Garry, how do you spell reconciliation?"

Immediately the man outside in the dark decided not to announce himself just yet. And much of his own puzzlement was mirrored in the worn face which Garry turned toward his questioner.

"Reconciliation?" Garry repeated blankly. "What in thunder—"

"Of course I'd ought to be able to handle it," Joe cut in blandly apologetic. "I just dismember whether it goes with a 'c' or a 'k.'"

Garry tried not to grin; but outside in the dark Steve allowed his appreciation to spread and spread across his face.

"With a 'c,'" the man before the fireplace told him soberly. "Are you—what are you doing, Joe, making out reports?"

With much care Joe transcribed it upon the virgin sheet before him; with a painful precision that brought the tip of his tongue beyond one corner of his lips, he rounded out the letters to his complete satisfaction.

"No," his answer was mumbled in his abstraction. "No, I ain't writing a report. I'm—I'm just beginning my novel."

Steve heard Garry gasp; he saw a gleam of pleased anticipation flash into his eyes, and knew instantly at what degree of friendship those two had already arrived.

"Will you—will you please say that again, Joe?" Garry begged him, very earnestly. "I wasn't paying attention. I'm afraid I was thinking of something else too hard to hear you correctly."

Joe's smile as he looked up had in it all of that quality which at times made it almost seraphic. His answer seemed irrelevant at first.

"I wonder if you know that Cecile person who works down to that big plaster house at Morrison—Allison's place on the hill?" he inquired.

"Dexter Allison's?" Garry thought a moment. "Why, you must mean Miss Allison's little French maid, don't you, Joe? Yes, I know who she is, if she's the one. But what has she to do with it?"

Joe laid down his pencil and set himself to be frankly explanatory.

"Well, it's like this," he stated. "She and I, now—we've got more or less acquainted in the last week or two, so to speak. And that ain't bad progress when you figure out that she can't understand more'n a dozen or two of all the words I speak to her, and as for me—well, when she gets to talking back it just makes me dizzy, that's all. But we're pretty good friends, when you consider that handicap. The thing that really bothers me is that the only folks she seemed to have been real neighborly with, back in Paree—that's the way you say it, ain't it?—was mostly sculptors and painters and writers, and such lot. So that would let me out of the running, right at the start, you see.

"I figured I didn't class at all, at first, because about the best thing I can say for myself is that there ain't a man on the river who ever rode white water better. I'm mostly a lumber jack, coming or going, whichever way you take me, although I've punched cattle and placer mined for variety. But to-night—to-night since you been setting there quiet—I got to thinking, too. She's a real nice girl. We get along fine together. And I kind of think we would, anyhow, even if we could understand each other better. I got to thinking to-night that maybe I'd better not quit cold, just yet. Now—I can't sculp, and somehow I never was strong for them guys who sit straddle of a little chair and paint cows and posies and things on a strip of muslin hooked over a frame. But, say, I've seen lots of writers who didn't look a whole lot more intelligent than me! I—I just got to thinking, to-night, that I'd take a fall out of this literary thing!"

Steve always held it to his friend's credit that he did not laugh. Indeed, Garry's soberness at that moment was almost woebegone.

"I see, Joe," he answered. "Not a bad idea. May I ask what your story—your novel is to deal with?"

"Deal with? What do you mean?"

"Why, they always deal with some problem, Joe," Garry squared around. "They always attack the rottenness of the rich, or sob over the rottenness of the poor. They always expound the crime of divorce, or attack the error of matrimony. Now which of—"

"Then I ain't dealing with nothing," stated Joe. "What I'm figurin' on doing is a regular love story. I thought maybe I'd have a nice young chap who—who's building a railroad or something, fall in love with a real nice girl who's the daughter of a fat man who's a crook. I mean the fat man's the crook, not the daughter. And—and—"

"And then what?" asked Garry Devereau.

Fat Joe, unlike the man outside, did not notice that a new note, dangerously hard and wickedly edged with ridicule, had replaced the amusement in Garry's voice. He grew a little more enthusiastic.

"Well, that's as far as I've got, right up to now," he admitted with an explosive sigh. "But it looks like a good enough beginning, at that. All I got to do now is run 'em through three or four hundred pages, with him a-talkin' to her and her a-talkin' at him. All I got to do, accordin' to all the books I've ever read, is see that it don't all come too easy for him, and still turns out all right. I expect I'll run 'em into a clinch with another guy standin' around eatin' his heart out with jealousy. It'll serve him right; he's just that mean sort, you know. Oh, I'll just marry 'em, along toward the end of the last chapter, and that'll kind of close it up."

Stephen O'Mara had been watching Joe's face while the latter talked, and therefore he was no more prepared than was Joe himself for the burst of harsh laughter that came from Garry's lips. It seemed utterly illogical that all actual humor should so swiftly fade from that situation with the first really audible expression of mirth. Steve himself believed it was only simulated, until his eyes swung to Garry's face. But he knew then what thoughts had been with Garret Devereau, all evening, before he had come up unheard to the door.

"Why, you poor simple scholar of nature!" The wan-faced one's lips curled. "You're years behind your day! If you submitted such a screed to a publisher now, he'd think you'd written a history of archaic American types."

He stopped to sneer.

"Listen," he went on. "Listen, and I'll give you a plot, gratis, which, if you handle it right, will make you, overnight! Take your girl—a nice girl, to be sure, sweet and unsophisticated and—and childishly innocent, Joe, and—and well, you'll have to describe her, first, won't you? Let's dress her up, then—dress her up in an evening confection that leaves little to the imagination in front and—and ground for amazement in back. That's a fair starter. If you care to be analytical you can insist that the reason she dresses like that is—oh, just because she's so innocent that she doesn't know any better, eh!

"All right! That establishes her very well. And then we can do just what you planned to do with your dear lady. We'll run her through three or four hundred pages, but with just a trifling change or two. Every chapter or so I'd leave her, Joe, in a situation that ends with a gasp—no pause even for a caramel! Three or four hundred pages, and then, if you have to marry her off why, let's be honest about it—no? Marry her off to the sort of a chap whom you'd man-handle to a pulp, Joe, if he came near—say a sister of yours. A nice, white-skinned, red-lipped, sweet, innocent sort of a little girl, Joe—and—and that finish will keep her true to type!"

At the beginning Fat Joe had been all eager attention. His face became heavy with amazement long before Garry's hard voice was still.

"But—but that ain't the kind of a yarn I'm figurin' on," he argued, his high voice faint but dogged. "This ain't going to be any of that tabasco stuff. Nope, I like it better the way I've got it planned. It—it leaves a better taste in your mouth, too."

Again Garry laughed, to himself it seemed, this time.

"Have your own way," he muttered. "But if you're going to stick to it you'd better label it a romance! Because there's only one kind of a woman, Joe, in reality. Just the kind who's killed what used to be a demand for decent men."

And then, outside in the dark, Stephen O'Mara forgot how sick the other man had been. He was across the threshold in a single stride, and Fat Joe came lightly to his feet as he saw his chief's set face that night. It wiped, the smile from Garry's lips, too. Squarely in front of the latter Steve halted and spoke with monotonous lack of haste.

"You're going to tell me that you didn't mean that, Garry," he said quietly. "For I'm going to marry one of those women myself."

Garret Devereau's face had been white. It went whiter now. He too came squarely to his feet, his body stiff but very frail in the oversize garments from Steve's wardrobe which he was wearing. He stood and stared emptily into his friend's eyes until something close akin to dreary defiance rose and marked his numbed comprehension.

"What I said," he answered as quietly, "I'd alter for no man. My opinions are my own."

He turned and passed outside.

For longer than he realized Steve stood gazing down into the burnt-out fireplace, until another thought, swifter even than the impulse that had lifted him across the threshold and thrust him into speech which, already, he would have given much to recall, whirled him around again. There was a light in the near end of the storehouse building just above his own cabin, and as he hurried toward it he knew Fat Joe must have fitted it up for the third man's quarters. He knocked at the door, and when there came no response, unbidden he lifted the latch and entered.

Garry was sitting on the edge of his blanketed bunk—sitting with shoulders slumped forward and head bowed low. He did not look up, for he had not heard Steve's entrance. He was pondering over the cylinder of a heavy, blued revolver, spinning beneath his transparent fingers. But Steve's first inarticulate effort at speech brought his head around. Garry smiled up at him—a smile reminiscent of his rare smile of years before.

"I didn't mean anything, Steve," he said in a hushed voice. "I'm damned sorry I spoke as I did. You see—you see, I just didn't know it would hit you, that's all."

Again Steve swallowed. Dumbly he pointed at the gun.

"What are you doing with that?" he demanded hoarsely.

Garry's eyes dropped. He stared at the revolver in his hand in mild perplexity, much as though he, too, were surprised to find it there.

"Why, nothing—nothing. I often take a notion to—to look at it like this."

Then his face went crimson.

"You've heard the news, I see." He tried to hide the bitterness behind the words, but one lip corner twitched and quivered. "They posted you in advance, did they? But you did not believe I was as bad as that, did you? You didn't think, did you, Steve, that I—I'd go out leaving you to blame yourself even a little bit?"

His question was curiously wistful—wistful and as unsteady as the hand which now proffered that blunt-barreled, huge-bore gun.

"Here, you take it, if—if you'll sleep the sounder. And don't you worry over me. I'll see you in the morning, Steve."

CHAPTER XIV
A GIRL LIKE HER

Save for a short and casual "see you in the morning, Garry," Stephen O'Mara turned without a word that night and left the improvised sleeping-quarters in the storehouse shack. It was a man's leave-taking, short to abruptness, so badly stereotyped that it denied utterly any consciousness of threatened, reckless tragedy and cordially intimate only because in all man-to-man speech there is less and less of actual sincerity in a multiplicity of words. But he might have talked till daylight and still have failed to register the binding acceptance of Garry's promise, which his silence, unaided, achieved.

Soundlessly, unemotionally, Steve closed the door on that figure on the bunk edge which, suddenly slack of limb and shoulder, had averted its face. But then, there in the darkness, with the gun swinging heavily between loose fingers, he hesitated in his very first step back from the threshold. And twice, head bowed in indecision, he halted in his slow progress from that door to the lighted one of his own cabin which framed Fat Joe's immobile form—halted each time as though he would return—and each time went slowly forward again. Fat Joe's eyes barely flitted over Steve's face that night; they clung in a fixed, pale blue stare of fear to the weapon in his hand. And long after Steve had drawn up a chair next the one which Garry had vacated and fallen to filling his pipe, he stood, shifting from foot to foot in awkward, uncomfortable silence. He crossed after a time and slipped into the empty seat. His tongue was as haltingly guilty as his face was pink with shame when he began to speak.

"Steve," he stammered, "Say, Steve, I—I didn't know I was going to start anything like that when I begun talking my ideas of art and literature and such like. I didn't see where it was leading us to—not for a minute. Why, Steve, every blessed hour of the days and nights since you've been away, I've been dodgin' every topic of conversation I thought might hit him hard. I'm just several assorted kinds of fool—and you followed him that quick and quiet!" The apology was tinged with pride. "I just didn't think— But ain't he got a poor opinion of women folks, though? Was it—a close decision?"

Steve shook his head; he smiled and the returning surety in his face did much to clear Joe's features.

"No," Steve answered, "not very. Somehow I know already that I needn't have followed at all, so far as that contingency was concerned. And it was my fault, Joe, not yours. I should have told you exactly how such things stood in Garry's mind—would have, if I had had the time. His opinion of women isn't very high. And it's odd, too, isn't it, that both the very highest and very lowest of such opinions are always held by men who base them upon what they have been taught by one woman alone. Tell me, Joe, what's happened? How have you and Garry hit it off, since I went down river?... Trouble?"

The fat man's eager denial was still self-consciously defensive.

"Not a bit!" he stated. "Not one little wrangle, even. Of course I was expectin' it. I've watched 'em come around too many times not to know how they can cuss a man cold one minute, and then make him plumb ashamed of mankind in general, with beggin' and pleadin'. I just beat him to it the morning he woke up; I told him what he could have, and what he couldn't, and he took it calmly enough. He just set there, pretty blue and shaky, and not quite clear in his head, and smiled that slow grin of his that's hardly any smile at all.

"I don't mean that he didn't swear! O my—O my! It's nice, ain't it, to have the gift of ease and eloquence in speech? He made me feel sort of amateurish and inadequate—me! But he didn't beg. Not—one—peep—out—of—him! He told me what he thought of me just as polite and cool as could be and let it go at that. He said he guessed I was boss, for a while at least, and asked for chopped fine!" Fat Joe hesitated. His color grew higher again. "After what's just happened," he added, "I'm almost ashamed to mention it, but—but ain't this friend of yours one of them chaps they call 'thoroughbreds' in novels?"

Steve flashed a glance at that earnest face. For a moment he had forgotten the first glimpse he had caught of Joe that evening, bent double over the block of yellow paper—a glimpse which still seemed funny and yet not very funny either.

"He comes of a very old family," he replied. "Old as they are reckoned in this country." And his answer held a question.

Joe shook his head.

"That ain't quite what I mean. I've seen lots of the younger sons of them old families. I've run into them in Yokohoma and Buenos Ayres; I've met up with them along the Yukon and down on the Mexican border. They're scattered all around, out through the Panhandle, ridin' calico ponies, with jingly spurs and more than a bushel of doo-dads on the saddle. They all come from old families, and I suppose after all it was a blessing that they had that much in their favor. Because if most of them hadn't had a family tree to lean up against at times, they never could have kept their feet at all."

"No, that wasn't what I meant, Steve. I figured he was kind of a regular chap—the hero guy that's too hot proud to bat an eye, you know, even when he's—well, I just can't get it straight in words, but this is what I'm driving at. The first night after you had gone he was settin' right here where I'm settin' now, looking quiet into the fire. I didn't ask him what was on his mind, not because I've learned not to go trackin' across other men's mental preserves, but simply because I didn't even have to guess more than once. He's a nice lookin' boy, ain't he? Sort of fine cut and tight built, and clean and decent looking. I'd been thinkin' of that, too; thinkin' he didn't look like the others I've seen drop off so sudden it left me gasping. Nor like them who went over so screamin' mad it left my palms wet and clammy from hangin' on to myself while they were going. He looked different, settin' here and staring into the fire, and hell burning inside him, and saying nothing. I sort of got to figurin' over him about then—sort of begun to wonder, even before I hunted up a deck of cards.

"Oh, you can smile if you want to, but you'll have to admit, just the same, that it's helped you stay sane once or twice yourself, figurin' whether or not I had an ace in the hole. Lonesomeness like what we've both seen ain't so very different from what he was fightin' at that very moment—not if the thing you're lonesome for and the thing you're thirsty for are things you know you can't have.

"I invited him to set in for a bit of intellectual pastime; I had to invite him twice, but he smiled then and agreed just as though he was glad to. And then, careless and off-hand, I asked him would he care to name the stakes.

"He waited quite a while before he answered me. You know how quiet it can be here in the timber, Steve, when it starts out to be quiet. Well, I could just feel the silence right here in this room. And then he laughed! It wasn't hardly any sound at all he made, and yet it might have been a blast, it hit me that sudden. I don't like that kind of laughter.

"'Stakes?' he says after me, just as precise as could be. 'Why, surely! I should be happy to back my play, but I'm afraid that my present supply of cash would hardly stand a very heavy drain.'

"He didn't have to explain even that much. Right along I'd been certain enough that he didn't have a copper with him. I'd put his watch away where he couldn't find it and—and maybe swap it with one of the hands for a half a pint. But I let on to be thinkin' for a while, until I brightened up as if the idea just hit me.

"It wasn't exactly fair, I'll admit. It wasn't what either of us would call a straight play, but—but—oh, I'd been watching him, just as I've told you. I knew he would about pay his soul for the drink that was due him in fifteen or twenty minutes; he was eyein' the bottle on the shelf right that minute. But I'd never seen a man's face give the lie to his spirit, either, the way his did, if he was the kind that would quit cold.

"'Cash ain't no consideration with me,' I told him, generous enough. 'But, personally, I've reached that degree of excellence where I can't play the game just for the sake of the technique of it any more. It's a quarter to nine,' says I, 'and in just fifteen minutes you get your gill of Three Star. Now, how much—how much, figurin' on the present state of supply and demand—would you reckon that drink appeals to you, in dollars and cents, U. S. A.?"

"Steve, you know he wasn't too steady. His hands were shaking—oh, you've seen 'em, too. But there he sits and looks back across the table at me, monkeyin' with a stack of chips, and giving me smile for smile.

"'I wouldn't sell that drink,' he murmured, 'I wouldn't sell it for … well'—and he licked his lips that were dry as leather.

"That was enough! I knew as well as he did how much he wanted it, but I was kind of disappointed, too. I'd been hopin'—I thought maybe—Say, don't you just naturally hate to have your judgment of human nature miss the whole blamed target, just when you think you've scored a bulls-eye? I do. It hurts my self-confidence; makes me wonder if I ain't growin' careless of details. And then, right there, I found out how close I'd come, and shootin' off-hand at that, mind you! Right there he gave me my next lesson. The nice, gentle way he cussed me out, that morning, was the first. Maybe he'd read the disappointment in my face, because he laughed again, not quite so sudden this time.

"'I wouldn't sell that drink for any price,' he repeats. 'But when it resolves itself to a gamble, I suppose, Joe, no gentleman should refuse the issue. If I understand you correctly, if cash is no consideration, then suppose we say that one drink against the rest of the bottle, chip for chip and stack for stack. Your confidence is not entirely reassuring to me, and yet perhaps I should tell you beforehand that I've always thought I could play this game half way well myself.'"

Fat Joe rose and crossed to the table for a match.

"Now wasn't that meeting me half way?" he continued, when he was seated again. "Wasn't it neatly done? Why, for a moment I was most ashamed to go through with it. I wouldn't have, only he sat there, smilin' so easy and confident. But we played. We played until daylight came around. And accordin' to the way he scored it, just before we went down to the works in the morning, he didn't have a drink comin' to him for the next forty-eight hours! I play a real involved and scientific game, Steve—but that ain't what I'm drivin' at. When we'd got done—when we'd finished—I tried to make him take the glass that had been comin' to him at nine. And he needed it, don't doubt that. He needed it and could have had it, for I made it just as easy as anybody could.... Steve, he ain't had a drink since that first night. That was what I meant when I spoke about him being what they call a thoroughbred."

They sat for a time in silence after Joe had finished.

"Pride!" Stephen O'Mara exploded softly. "Pride! And Garry thinks his is dead; he thinks he has killed it himself. But it was there on his face to-night, too, laughing up at me, Joe, just as it did at you—laughing at me, all amused at itself, out of that crooked smile of his. And it'll never die. It'll live as long as he does!"

He looked down at the gun on his knee.

"That's all, Joe?"

Fat Joe cleared his throat.

"I—I gave him a job the next morning," lamely. "We seemed to be getting along together fine so I— Shucks, I was just afraid to have him go! That's the flat truth of it. And you told me to keep him, if I could. So I set him to checking up the stock in the storeroom and put him on keepin' time for the squad up here. He's drawin' eighteen a week, Steve. Was that all right? You were figurin' on keeping him here?"

And then Joe Morgan saw Steve's eyes light up. He saw a swift something flash out from within, which, once or twice before in the years of their friendship, had set his face to burning.

"Joe," Steve exclaimed, "you're right about that matter of family trees. I know a man right now who doesn't have to go back one minute in his pedigree to prove that he's a gentleman. I've left some tough propositions for you to solve, Joe. Lots of times, when I couldn't see the way out, I've put it up to you. If I merely say 'thanks, Joe,' and let it go at that, do you think it will do?"

"Suits me!" Joe's jauntiness was large. "And it goes double on the rebound. But how—how do you suppose any woman ever came to set a—boy like that to slipping? Or why didn't he sit down where it was quiet and figure it all out for himself? One bad guess don't make the whole world wrong. And say, wouldn't it be lucky, though, if he could meet a real nice girl about now?"

Steve leaned back and gave way to rare and subdued laughter. It was much as though he did not want the sound to penetrate to that dark end room in the shack beyond. And then he was quickly sober-faced again.

"I think he is going to, Joe. I think I may promise that he is likely to, very, very soon. And it will make a difference—a mighty big difference for Garry. For, if you don't mind my mentioning the matter again, in spite of the preachments of many of your novelists to the contrary, it's just about as Garry has argued it to be. Most men are just as fine—just as decent—as women demand they shall be."

He lifted the revolver and tossed it negligently across the room. It struck with a thud in the middle of his own bunk.

"Where did he get that six-shooter? It looks like one of yours?"

"It is," said Joe. "Nothing gaudy nor ornamental, but a right handy thing. And, there! That's another error I made, ain't it? I reckon it's going to be difficult for me to get used to the idea of any man being a dangerous enemy to himself. I gave it to him the first day he went to work."

Joe's eyes traveled across to the object under discussion.

"Harrigan came back before you did," his explanation seemed to veer to another quarter. "He was most punctual, I'd say, wouldn't you? He came in tuned up real melodious on the last load with Big Louie. He sung big-voiced that night; he's been talkin' big-voiced since, I'm led to understand." Again that mental shift. "Gun-play always did seem awful foolish to me—to talk about! When men start to advertisin' trouble to come, by word o' mouth, it never does worry me particularly. I just gave your friend the gun to keep around handy, if he should happen to need it. Did you know he could make the ace of spades look shopworn and weary at thirty paces with one of those toys? Well, he can."

Steve smiled.

"You're not totin' one of them yourself, yet, I see?" he remarked lazily.

Fat Joe spat in vast contempt. He clenched one pudgy hand and sat watching the knuckles pale, iron-hard, beneath the seeming softness.

"Are you?" he countered.

This time Steve's laughter was soundless.

"Scarcely! We're going to hear some of them yap lots louder than they do now, before the winter is over. But you might give that one back to Garry in the morning. And, as for the rest of it, I suppose we'll be quite likely to forget, won't we, Joe, that either of us has so much as seen or thought of a gun to-night?"

Both of them had risen. Joe puckered his lips.

"Forget it? How can we," he demanded, "when we don't even know anything to forget! Why, as I reckon it, we'll both get up in the morning and regard it as a dream just too foolish even to bother to relate."

Their eyes held for a moment, before Steve turned again toward the door. And perhaps his manner was a little too unconcerned that evening, a little too carefully careless, for almost before he had lifted the latch Fat Joe stepped forward, one quick, protesting step, and then stopped on second thought.

"You ain't goin'—" he began, and suffered that spoken protest also to remain uncompleted.

"It's not late," Steve's voice was thoughtful. "It's not late, but it's surely very quiet." He stood gazing out into the gloom. "Maybe I'd best run down and see what ails our soloist to-night. Somehow, the more I've thought about it, the more I've come to fear that he is temperamental, Joe—too temperamental, for such a wearing proposition as this one is likely to be. And you haven't slept much since I've been gone. Oh, that was easy, just from your eyes! So you'd better turn in. I'll just stroll down and let them know that I'm back home."

It is odd how much of finality there can be in the quietest of statements. Eyes narrowed, Joe stood in the middle of the floor and watched him depart without further objection. But the moment the blackness had swallowed him up he backed to the bunk, fumbled for the gun which Steve had tossed upon the blankets, and followed out into the dark.

Stephen O'Mara stood a long time outside the door of the men's bunkhouse that night, fingers upon the latch, before he made any move to enter. But neither a wish to eavesdrop nor a desire to frame, experimentally, the words he meant to speak was the reason behind that pause. It was in itself a new thing to find the long, low building lighted at that hour, even though, as he had himself put it to Joe an instant before, it was hours from being late. That night the almost absolute silence beyond the closed door was an even more unusual state of affairs. The voice of one man only was audible; the words he spoke indistinguishable altogether. But sudden bursts of laughter, punctuating the recital which he could not clearly follow, were indication enough to the man outside of what manner of tale was holding the ears of that roomful of rivermen. Stephen O'Mara, who had long ceased to wonder at the discovery in them, of new and impulsive finenesses which bordered close upon inherent nobility, knew fully as well how utterly and unspeakably gross could be the premeditated coarseness of those same men.

There was no movement to mark his entrance when he finally pressed the latch and swung the door open; not so much as a single glance to indicate that his presence was noted. Under the yellow light of flickering oil lamps the eyes of all those scores of gaudy-shirted figures lounging against the walls were fixed eagerly upon the face of him who held the middle of their stage—him who talked from where he half-lay, propped on one elbow, in his bunk at the end of the room. Harrigan, red-shirted, red-headed, was lounging at case, waiting for the last gurgle of appreciation to subside, before he gave them the close of the story—the last titbit, the savor of which already had set him noisily to licking his lips. And in the doorway Steve, rigid of a sudden, sensed what that climax was to be.

"—Her fi-an-say inside," the droningly indistinguishable words were very plain now, "her fi-an-say inside, consoomed with pr-ride and anticipation, tellin' all who had come to dance that she had pr-romised to be his, for-river more! And her, at that same minute outside with him—and both av thim...."

Harrigan did not hurry it in the telling. And if his portrayal of Archibald Wickersham was unmistakably deliberate, neither did he fail for want of sufficient detail, to make the other picture clear. Vilely he gave them the complete imagery of his vile brain.

A shout went up, a louder, hoarser outcry of applause which rocked the room. And then that rigid figure in the doorway had started forward. Between those lanes of suddenly silent men Steve passed in silence, to stand before him who had achieved his climax a breath before. And at his coming Harrigan slid from the bunk, started to reach within the blanket pack at the head of what had been his bed, and then thought better of such impulse. Bravado intermingled with blank surprise, he came haltingly to his feet. The voices of few men have been as unhurriedly deadly as was that of him who Harrigan that night.

"That was wise, Harrigan," Steve told him slowly—far too gently. "That was wise to let your knife lie safe within your pack. For if you'd touched it, I'd have killed you—as I ought to kill you now. But you're drunk, Harrigan! You were drunk a minute ago when you lied your lie.... You're soberer now. You're sober enough to start again and tell me you're a liar!"

They waited—the roomful of rivermen. Nothing stirred save the clouds of filmy blue smoke floating against the rafters—that and a bulky blot of shadow outside which shifted a little, noiselessly, just beyond the patch of light that streamed through the door. They waited, heavy-breathed, while Harrigan began to recover from the disconcertment into which O'Mara's coming had flung him. Slowly the former's lips twisted into a mocking leer; mockery rose and swam with the hatred in his inflamed eyes. He would have spoken, sparring for time, when Steve's hand leapt in and made of the joking effort only a rattle in his throat. Beneath the stiff red stubble the flesh was livid where those fingers had been, when he was able to draw breath again.

"'Twas only a bit av a joke," he gasped, and gulped and swallowed hard. "'Twas only a bit av a joke I was tellin' the bhoys, about seein' you an'—"

Steve's voice bit in and cut him short.

"Your turkey's ready, Harrigan!" He pointed at the pack toward which the other had groped and then thought better of the impulse. "You were going, of your own accord, I see. Well, I'm telling you to go, now! The door's open; I left it so for you, when I came in. And I'm telling you too, before you leave, that you'll do well not to come back. There's not room for both of us on this river any more, Harrigan!"

The riverman's eyes shifted. Furtively they flitted from face to face in those rows of faces at the walls. But whatever he thought or hoped to find—fleeting flash of support or encouragement—was hidden behind a common mask of astonishment as blank as had been his own. They were waiting for his answer; he knew they were waiting for that as he crossed to the door. And when he paused there, to turn in sudden savagery, he realized that his tardiness had robbed him of his chance. It was too late to talk back then.

"You're tellin' me," he rasped out, "and I was going—sur-re! But things ar-re not yet finished between you and me. For I'm pr-romisin' you that I'll be back; I'm pr-romisin' you I'll be wid ye again. I'll be wid ye again, come spring!"

He disappeared. And hard upon his going Steve wheeled and fronted those scores of silent men. His eyes leaped from point to point, as Harrigan's had craftily flitted. Briefly, crisply, he accompanied the sweeping survey with a voice that was loud enough for all of them to hear.

"Big Louie!... Fallon!... Shayne! This is your chance to say so, if you're going to be lonesome, now that your song-bird has flown. Speak up! I came down tonight just to hear you talk."

Nothing but an indistinguishable murmur answered him, a low growl that was neither argument nor evasion. For those hottest partisans, whose names had been called aloud, knew with Harrigan's going toward whom the chill finger had been pointed, even though Death had entered and stalked through their ranks and slipped back out at the door almost before they realised its nearness.

Rebellion was still a long way ahead for most of them. They had not yet had time to talk themselves to the pitch of open revolt. They had merely begun to listen to Harrigan whose disciples in dissatisfaction they were. And now, in his absence, they stirred uncomfortably under the gaze of him who remained; they dropped their heads and searched for matches. But Steve felt the weight of unspoken thoughts when he, too, faced back in the doorway. This time there was no naming of names; he embraced the whole room when he spoke.

"They tell me, boys," he said, "that there's talk among you of no more work on the river when we've put this railroad through. I've heard it said that some of you think you are cutting the ground out from under your feet with every shovelful of earth you lift. You ought to know better than that; you ought to know for yourselves that there'll be need for more men in these woods than there has ever been before. But if you don't; if you can't see it that way, why not come around and let me have a fair chance to talk things over with you, myself, before you decide to turn on this job? I want you to remember that a man who is a liar in one thing is mighty likely to talk loose-tongued, no matter what he preaches."

And there, without lifting his eyes from the floor, Big Louie cleared his throat and made answer.

"Maybe," he retorted. "Maybe. And maybe not so sure, either! I have listened to big words before now, me, that have put no food under my belt, no coat to my back."

Steve's smile was unruffled and kind. No matter what the hidden verdict of the rest of that room might be, he had known already that Big Louie was past saving. For there were not so many like him among those hills but what the type was instantly recognizable, wherever it was encountered. He had the frame of a giant—Big Louie—the splendid legacy of generations of men who had lived out of doors. But there was no depth in his seal-brown eyes which always seemed to brood; no decision in any move of his ponderous body. He had little chin; he had no name, save Big Louie which his size alone had sired. And Steve was very patient in making answer.

"If it's only food and shelter, and clothes for your back, Big Louie, you'll not have to worry. But I'm not promising either, mind, that there'll be easy money to blow on white whiskey. Were you expecting any?"

That brain which could cope with but one idea at a time was fertile ground for seed which such a one as Harrigan might sow. Big Louie failed to reply. He sat quiet, deep in thought when Stephen O'Mara closed the door noiselessly behind him.

It was minutes after Steve had gone back up the hill before Garry Devereau reached out a hand in the darkness and touched, experimentally, what had seemed to be only a shapeless black blotch at the edge of light, a rod or two from the door. And instantly at his touch the shadow was galvanized into life. It reared and plunged and enveloped the slighter man in a crushing embrace and bore him over backward. With the muzzle of a revolver chafing his ear Garry managed to worry his head high enough to free his mouth and nostrils from dirt.

"Get off me! Get off me, you fat romancer, you!" he whispered fiercely.

An explosive grunt of dismay answered him, before Fat Joe let him rise. In a thin and profane tenor he was bidden to explain his presence there.

"I couldn't sleep," Garry replied, his voice still peevish, "so I came out for a breath of air. I saw him start this way—saw you following him with that gun in your hand. I just slipped over, too, in case there might be doings. What's the row, Joe?"

Joe took him ungently by the elbow, turned him about and started him up the rise.

"An old grudge," he deigned an ungracious explanation. "It's years and years old. Steve licked him once. Once when they were boys the folks that live down next to Allison's dressed Steve up like a picture-book, the nearest I can make out, and sent him to town a-shoppin'. Harrigan, he—"

"I know! I remember!" Garry's eager whisper interrupted. "That is, I didn't know that Harrigan was one of the mob Steve whipped that day. But that wasn't what I meant. Who was the—the girl Harrigan was talking about, when Steve—when Steve—"

Joe's fingers tightened a little as the other evinced a tendency to lag.

"Hurry a bit, will you?" he urged complainingly.

"Show a little speed! I'm supposed to be up there asleep." And then, gruffly: "It was the Allison girl, of course."

In spite of the hand upon his elbow Garrett Devereau stopped short in his tracks.

"Barbara!" he stammered. "Barbara Allison? Joe, was that the girl he meant to-night, when he said he was going to 'marry one of those women himself?'"

Joe peered at him, trying to make out the expression upon his face.

"Why not?" he wanted to know. "Why not? Ain't he good enough for her?"

There came a pause—then Garry's stunned rejoinder.

"Good enough!" he repeated senselessly. "Good enough?" He laughed half wildly, as though he had suddenly hit upon a very funny thought indeed. "That man in love with a girl like her.... Good Lord!"

And Fat Joe, who had failed to understand, swore again beneath his breath because there was no time left in which to argue the matter. His face was still very red from his struggle for self-restraint, and his whole mental balance so disturbed that he forgot entirely to conceal the blued revolver dangling in one hand when he re-entered the cabin a moment later. The latter object ruined the effect of his insouciant rendition of "Home, Sweet Home."

"Thought you were going to retire, Joe?"

Steve was already undressed and crawling into bed. His question was slow-worded and a trifle stifled.

"I was," Joe assured him hastily. "I was. I just stepped out to see that everything was tight and tidy for the night, that's all."

Quizzical eyes contemplated the revolver now.

"Taken to carrying a weapon, after all, eh? Well, perhaps that's wisest. And blow out the light, will you, Joe? I'm tired. You'll have to undress in the dark."

Then Steve buried his face in his pillow. But sundry sounds, escaping, were unmistakably hysterical. Joe's mouth opened and closed, fishlike. He stood and stared down at his side, in beautifully eloquent profanity, if a stare can be both eloquent and profane.

"You need a nurse," he stated sulkily at last. He finished the light with a vicious blast. "You need a chaperon!"

But once again, just before he slept, Steve heard him mutter to himself, less injuredly, as he heaved over in his bunk.

"This has been a very busy evening," he opined.

CHAPTER XV
LAW AND LUMBER

Rain fell the following fortnight in a steady downpour that did not cease, even for an hour. Ragged, smokelike clouds hung over the valley at Thirty-Mile, dragged so low by their own weight that they not only hid the upper peaks but shrouded the lower ridges as well. They drove by in interminable files of grey, making sluiceways of every cut and drenching continually the men of the construction gang who, in spite of the chill of that downfall, still sweated at their labor. But both Steve and Fat Joe, for all that they caught each day a deeper note in the hoarse complaints of those same men—a note no less ominous than was that newer, hoarser one of the swollen river—nevertheless were duly thankful that the leaden sky had at least a tinsel lining. It might have snowed.

Each morning now as he stepped outside the shack Joe turned methodically toward the north, to cock his head and squint and sniff, questioningly. He was waiting for the first flurry which would herald those months of bitter whiteness to follow; and each morning his short nod was a brief of satisfaction at the continued height of the mercury. They made the most of that open fall, bad as was the weather. Without pause they toiled forward those wet days, or rather backward, for they had stopped, there at the edge of the river, in the work on that section of the rail-bed which, none too even-surfaced but almost arrow-straight, ran from the upper end of their valley to the very mouth of the Reserve Company's country.

A month earlier it had been Steve's plan to span that mile or so of swamp and bridge the river before the cold weather set in. Nor was his altered order of campaign due in any way to the storm which had raised the river and made of the alder-dotted stretch of flat bog-meadow an oozing, quaking morass. It no longer represented merely a positive not too alluring problem in engineering—that strip of swamp and open water. It had taken on a newer, strategic importance. And the change in Steve's plans, so far as the work at Thirty-Mile was concerned, was as much due to the news which Fat Joe brought home with him, one night toward the end of the next week, as it was the result of the interview which he had held with Hardwick Elliott himself.

Joe had been a whole day absent on the north end of the line. Alone he had been over every foot of that all but completed stretch which ended at the border of swampland, there at headquarters, troubling himself not at all over the unevenness of the roadbed, satisfied entirely with the surety he gained with every inspected mile, that a train-load of logs or a dozen train-loads, would stay on the rails when the rails were laid, and the day came to set wheels rolling. But the further report he brought back with him was far less reassuring.

"I wonder," Joe mused aloud that night, "I wonder, now, why any man who knows anything about handling timber should go to work bothering himself with skidways leadin' down to the river, when he knows, as well as Harrigan should know, that it ain't comin' out that way? It don't seem good sense nor logic to me, unless—"

He stopped there and left his own opinion unfinished. Since the evening Harrigan had stepped out of the main bunkhouse and disappeared, black rage in his face and a promise to return upon his lips, that lumberman's red head had been conspicuous only because it was absent from the landscape. So far Harrigan had failed to reappear and Fat Joe's method of apprising his chief of his return to the Reserve Company's pay-roll was distinctly characteristic. But Steve's reception of the news was little more than listless. He seemed to change the subject entirely.

"I don't see why it wouldn't be just as easy, or easier," he replied, "to cross here on pilings, practically the whole distance, as it would be to fill and bridge, too. And if we were to look at it in that light, then why wouldn't it be still easier to drive those piles, say next February or March, while the swamp is still crusted over and hard. It would afford us some sort of a footing to work on then, other than black ooze and lilypads. Wouldn't it seem so to you?"

Garry Devereau's agreement was quick with enthusiasm, but Fat Joe who was better schooled in those slow-syllabled discussions, barely nodded his head.

"We'd still have that track north of here to lay," he advised, "when we work in from the south with steel."

"Surely," Steve admitted. "Of course. But wouldn't that be a better bet than to stand to see our embankment and bridge—"

He broke off there, just as Joe had hesitated a moment before. The undercurrent of meaning for which the latter's ears were waiting came to the surface, however, when Steve began again.

"Suppose, Joe," he pursued lazily, "suppose you had contracted with a railroad—an infant road too young even to be named—to move for you more timber than either of us will ever own; contracted in apparent good faith, when all along in your heart you were certain that the railroad itself would never be able to fulfill its half of the bargain? Granting such a state of affairs, Joe, what do you suppose you would do?"

Garry was not quite certain that evening which was uppermost—the earnestness or quiet amusement which surely underlay that question. He only knew that both existed. But Fat Joe understood. As he had done many times before now he wrinkled his forehead and pondered.

"Maybe I'd hire me a red-headed river-dog," came his answer pat. "Maybe I'd hire me a bully-boy boss of white water, to build me some skidways to the nearest floodwater, so's I could teach the infant railroad you mention that business was business, contract or no contract."

"Of course you would!" Steve agreed instantly, and he might have been complimenting a first primer favorite so pleased was his tone. "Of course you would. I'm afraid that was too easy for you, wasn't it, Joe? But now suppose you were bent on proving to everybody, and particularly to those who had fathered it, what an unfortunate weakling this immature, unnamed child of constructive silence really was. In that event how do you figure you'd conduct yourself?"

Joe smiled oddly, a little balefully. It was magic-quick, that change in his expression—as swift as was the thought behind it.

"I'd have my logs all cut and ready to haul as an excuse, wouldn't I?" he inquired with simulated anxiety. "Could I tell folks, through the newspapers for instance, that I wasn't strong for letting my timber lie for the grubs to lunch on, if I had to square myself?"

"Quite naturally." Until then Steve's face had kept its preternatural gravity. He grinned ever so faintly now. "Very naturally you'd want to save your winter cut."

"Then I'd like to have 'em build a bridge somewheres along the river I aimed to drive—a bridge and a nice dirt embankment, all dressed up with rails and ties and things on top. I'm allowed to suppose I've got an awful long standin' score, ain't I, along with all this timber? Well, that's what I'd like to have 'em do, then. And when I opened her up, a few miles up river, and she began to roar; when that first head of water hit the bridge and the sticks begun to grind, I suppose I'd take up my position on the bank where I could watch real well. I'd light me a long, black cigar and murmur, sort of languid and sympathetic, 'There goes your railroad, gents!'"

Before the finish of that speech was reached Garry had begun to follow. When Joe drew down one corner of his mouth and puffed aloft an imaginary cloud of smoke by way of added vividness, his own laughter mingled with Steve's quieter appreciation. But his contribution to the conversation was not as complacent as Fat Joe's had been.

"Such a move in itself would be outside the letter of the contract," he expostulated. "Why, they wouldn't dare do anything; they wouldn't dare to begin driving the river before your time was up, much less do damage to your completed work. What excuse—what legal excuse—could they give, even though they were morally certain that you were bound to fail?"

Very slowly, almost pityingly, Joe turned toward him.

"Legal!" he droned. "Moral?" And then he laughed his clear tenor outburst which barely escaped being a giggle. "Dear child, judiciously speaking, law and lumber and morals and mill-feet don't mix. They don't mix at all, in this section of the country. If they wanted to bother their heads with an alibi, they could say it was top of flood, and they weren't eager to be hung up, just because a brass-buttoned conductor promised 'em a through express in the morning. They could say— But what good would explanations do us, huh, if they sent a half million logs sky-hootin' into our bridge? It wouldn't save our construction, would it?"

He wheeled back to Steve, his manner brisk.

"Do we leave that stretch open?" he asked. "Is that the way you have it figured?"

"I'm afraid we'd better," Steve said.

And from the very deliberation of that reply Garry Devereau realized how vital was the point which they had been weighing so irresponsibly.

That was as close as they came to anything resembling a discussion of the change which was growing more and more noticeable in the bearing of the men at Thirty-Mile. As far as all outward evidence was concerned, Steve seemed to ignore it utterly, to retreat oftener and oftener behind his habit of silence which even Fat Joe, after several unsuccessful, garrulous attempts, gave over trying to penetrate. And even Garry, who had greater respect for the other man's preoccupation because he felt that he understood it better, tried also to hide all evidence of the bitterness which it was re-awakening in him. Yet, at that, Garry's surmise was erroneous; his conclusion wide of the mark.

For it was not the hunger of his own heart; it was neither intolerance of restraint nor mental rebellion against the duties which were holding him so close up-river, that had caused the chief engineer of the East Coast work to withdraw so completely within himself, although, many times each day, his eyes did wander toward the south and Morrison. During that bleak period, as Garry had guessed, Steve's thoughts were often of Barbara, but they were not sombre thoughts. The very hardness of his life schooling had taught him too well how little of wisdom there is in fretting against the day of action, when that day cannot be hurried nor controlled. Steadfastedly he refused to let himself brood. If he could not go to her he would not, nevertheless, allow himself to dwell upon that impossibility. Instead his spirit ranged ahead to a hopeful, more or less indefinite and not too distant date when his absence might not seem to threaten too great a cost to those whose matters lay in his trust.

Garry's conclusion, borne of his own lesson in doubt, was wide of the mark. It was not heartache. The thoughts Steve had of her were his serenest thoughts, those days during which his body labored prodigiously and his brain groped for the solution of an affair that had not been his own, until he had chosen to make it so. It was the problem of Garrett Devereau which lay behind Stephen O'Mara's hours of gravity—that perplexing problem which Miriam Burrell, level of eye and brave of tongue, had brought to him for help. And in the end, as is usually the way, events of themselves finally gave Steve the opportunity to say all that he knew could not be introduced by him. Time showed the way just when he had reached the point of acknowledging that such an opportunity was beyond his own power to bring about.

He had had little chance for conversation with Garry in those days, except for a word or two over a hastily snatched breakfast, or perhaps at supper at night, and at night he was usually too tired to talk. But the other's growing restlessness had not escaped his notice. For a while Garry had seemed to accept his continuance there at camp as a matter of course, and for that very reason neither Fat Joe nor Steve had dignified the thought of his possible departure by so much as a single spoken word. Garry's own actions first began to indicate how incessantly he was debating that question within his own brain.

There came, times without number, an uneasy, far-focused look into his eyes; came hours on end when he would sit, every debonaire effort at lightness abandoned, staring moodily into the fire, motionless save for his nervous hands which never seemed to rest. Joe found it harder to entice him with the poker deck; oftener than not Steve had to repeat his question a second time, seeking to inveigle him into a discussion of what-not, before Garry even heard. And one night toward the end of the week the latter finally reached the point of voicing for their ears a decision which was old in anticipation to them. They were on the point of going to bed. Garry had risen, and then paused. He hesitated and crooked his arms and yawned, a trifle too carelessly that evening.

"Well, this finishes another day," he remarked, nor did he realize how soulful were the words. "And I cleaned up the last of the stock-room to-day, Joe. A swift but accurate workman, eh? I'll leave behind a record unblemished by oversight or sloth. And now—now it's about time, I suppose, I was going back to town."

It was out, nor could the yawn conceal his eagerness. His back was turned, but Steve knew what light was in his eyes. Steve's carelessness was a far neater thing than Garry's had been.

"What's your hurry?" he inquired easily. "Why rush away? And if you think your industry has betrayed you into idleness, you're reasoning poorly to-night. Want another job?"

Bantering indifference was the keynote of that reply. Mutually they had adopted it from the very first. It smacked of the free-masonry which always marked Steve's conversations with Fat Joe, were they earnest or frivolous beneath the surface. It is always recognizable in the speech of friends such as they, differentiated from actual indifference by an intimacy of inference between the lines which makes such discourse almost foreign to uninitiated ears. But Garry's answer was not in kind. Steve was caught so far off his guard by the question which came flinging back at him that he was glad Garry had not turned.

"What else is there I could do?"

No man save one who was very, very tired could have spoken in such a tone; no man except one who has tried himself in the highest of courts—his own opinion of himself—could have put such a degree of contempt into so simple a query.

"Why—why—" Steve faltered, and then he took command of his own wits again. "There's work enough, don't doubt that," he exclaimed, and laughed a little. "Joe, here, will be another week or ten days finishing with the fill up yonder; he'll do well if he manages it by then, and that too with every available hand we have. I don't want to rob him of a single man, if I can help it, but I've got to go ahead with the line to the south. To put it concretely, I'm in need of a rodman. Do you think you'd care to oblige?"

Again the hint of banter persisted, but Garry's jaw was tight when he faced suddenly around.

"I will!" he flashed back, hoarsely. "I will, if it's a man's job. But I'm done with filling a dinky pad with rows of figures, all day long. I'm finished with this damned tallying of cans of beans and soap and yards of rope! Do you understand? What *work* would I have to do?"

Out of the corners of his eyes Steve saw consternation o'erspread Fat Joe's face. His own was only amused.

"You'll have to swing an axe," he enumerated slowly, "and you'll have to lug a rod and tripod. You'll wade through bog and fight your way through underbrush. And then, for variety, swing an axe some more. If you've never learned yet what it is to be really tired, Garry; if you've never known what it is to go to bed wishing morning would never come, you'll find out what that's like, too."

As soon as it was spoken Steve recognized the slip. Watching Garry's eyes widen he knew that Garry had caught it also. For a moment a torrent of words trembled on the latter's lips. And then he swallowed and nodded shortly. The vague dreariness of his acceptance was fully as electrical as the threatened outburst might have been.

"I'll try it," he said, very simply. "I'll have a try at it, to-morrow."

And he pivoted on his heel and passed out.

Some minutes after he had gone Fat Joe, still a little dazed, rose softly and unostentatiously, crossed to a shelf shoulder-high on the wall and reached to remove a quart bottle of brandy which Steve, returning home soaked through and through, had brought out and left standing there. But Steve checked him in the very middle of that act.

"Let it stand, Joe," he directed. "Leave it where it is."

As slowly as he had reached for it Joe started to put the bottle back. The very briefness of that order should have been warning enough, but Joe found it impossible to keep to himself his disapproval.

"All right," he acquiesced, "only I can't help remindin' you, just the same, that when a horse is runnin' his heart out it's kind of superfluous to lay on the whip."

And then the whole accumulation of those days of silent perplexity, of indecision and fruitless mental forays, spilled over upon Fat Joe's entirely innocent head. Steve shot around and levelled a pre-emptory finger.

"Whip—hell!" he barked. "Put that bottle back!"

Joe's fingers came away as though the glass had blistered them.

"Lands' sakes!" he exclaimed; and in a voice that was chastened and meek when he had caught his breath: "Please, and it's back!"

Chronic ill-temper could hardly have persisted in the face of that reply, and Steve's had been but a mood. His first chuckle was in itself a plea for pardon. He supplemented it, aloud.

"I'm sorry, Joe—I'm worried. I've got a job on my hands that bothers me. It appears to be simple enough, until I get to planning how to tackle it, and then I can't make any headway at all. But there isn't anything to be gained in hiding that stuff; that's one of the things I need to know. It's better where it is."

Joe waved a hand in bland dismissal of the apology.

"My mistake," he averred, "though your harsh words have hurt me sore. I don't quite savvy it yet, but it's your affair, not mine. You're dealin' and bankin' the chips. And before now I've seen lots of well-meanin' bystanders get all mussed up from trying to horn into another man's pastime. At my age I'd ought to have knowed better!"

CHAPTER XVI
ACCIDENTS WILL HAPPEN

In itself that decision of Garry's to remain a little longer at Thirty-Mile was scarcely significant enough to be called sensational, and yet it proved to be the first of a series of events which, growing more and more sensational as they progressed, finally resulted in the hour for which Steve was biding his time.

Garry entered upon his new duties the following morning in a spirit anything but reassuring to his companion. Up to that time he had made his own industry the butt of much good-natured ridicule, viewing it apparently as a sort of vacation novelty amusing enough while the novelty lasted. But he went from task to task that next day in a methodical, dogged fashion that was farthest of all from amiability. Two or three times Steve, trying to spare him needless effort, attempting to show him how to favor blistered hands and aching back, met with rebuffs so curt that he learned to keep his advice to himself. He knew what end Garry was working to achieve; he would have allowed himself to smile over the thought that the other man would be tired enough, before night came, without trying to make that work any harder, only he did not dare venture that smile.

Times without number there were when Garry's monumental fit of sulks bordered close on the ridiculous, but the needed triviality which would have precipitated the whole fabric to a terra-firma of absurdity failed to materialize. He cursed the rain, cursed it with his fluent precision which already had earned Fat Joe's admiring comment. He complained, querulously, like a half-aged boy, over the treacherous footing which the flooded alder brakes afforded. And once when he had felled a tree and narrowly missed being pinned beneath it, in spite of Steve's quick leap that dragged him aside, he plunged into an incisive diatribe concerning the perversity of inanimate things—a short discussion in many-syllabled words which would have awakened Steve's admiration by its very brilliance, had he not already been fully concerned with the light of triumph which had flared and then died out in Garry's eyes when the hemlock only grazed him.

Now and again Steve saw his lips move and then crook in cynical amusement, and knew that Garry was talking to himself and finding such communion most absorbing. But he waited, outwardly patient at least, nor tried to hurry the issue. He knew the woods; he knew what the silence and solitude could do. For no man endures mutely the spell of the wilderness. He talks, or he goes mad. Put two men on a two-months trail and, be they the worst of enemies, they will still find a topic which each may approach. Trap them for a winter in a snow-buttressed valley where no other man can penetrate and they will have bared jealous secrets before spring sets them free to go again their roads of doubled hatred. And when dusk came—dusk and a fatigue which made it difficult to drag one foot after the other on the homeward journey—Garry had reached the point where he had to speak his thoughts aloud.

The woods were new to that paler, slighter man. He had to talk, but his beginning was circuitous. He had been gazing down at his rain-soaked length, grotesquely thin in the flapping garments borrowed from Steve's wardrobe, to look up at last and smile, wryly.

"I was just thinking," he began. "I was just thinking if they could only see me now—the crowd down at Morrison for instance. They used to gibe me. They called me the immaculate Garry, once. Aren't you a lot heavier than you look?"

Plodding along beside him Steve nodded as though the whole day had been common with just such conversation.

"No. Those clothes were built with an eye to largeness of movement which scarcely insured shape or draping, even upon me."

It was irrelevant, but it was a beginning. And the reference to the crowd at Morrison made Garry's next remark clear.

"Wouldn't it jolt them, if they could see me? I thought of it this morning when I was walking a log without so much as a waver. That phrase relative to walking a chalk-line is weak and inadequate, after a man has tried to work his way along a peeled hemlock. If anyone wants to measure sobriety by word of mouth, there's his standard. It involves the last degree in sure-footedness."

Again Steve bowed his head, but not so immediately this time. For already he realized that this was not to be the opportunity for which he was waiting. And the other man was quick to catch that uncertainty.

"The other evening—" he laughed unpleasantly—"that night when you came back to camp in time to hear of Joe's proposed novelistic effort, I think I mentioned it to you. I'm not sure. But whether I did or not, it was, no doubt, scarcely introduced in the spirit in which I should ask it now.... I suppose they have given you a fairly thorough report of my—career, since we were knights bold and ladies fair, haven't they?"

Without waiting for a reply he answered the question himself.

"Of course they have," he exclaimed, "because I recognized your fine hand in Joe's attitude toward me, the very minute I waked up, back a week or so ago, the morning after I'd done my Phil Sheridan stunt from Allison's to your shack. But do you mind telling me what your own opinion is?"

Stephen O'Mara knew they were not going to get far if they followed that lead. There was a challenge in Garry's voice which too closely resembled a snarl.

"Why—no." The pre-occupied note was uppermost in his answer. "I'd not mind at all."

But he offered no more than that.

"Nor the reason why you've been so insistent that I stay on up here?"

"Why not? I've not forgotten my manners, even though I've lived some months in the back-brush!"

No attempt at levity, however, could parry the other's deliberate insolence. Garry worked nearer to what had lain all day behind his bad silence.

"A man is wasting his time trying to reform another man," he vouchsafed, "if that other man has no desire for reformation."

"That is very, very true," Steve agreed with even gravity.

"Unless that man has the desire within himself, he need never waste his time even hoping to come back!"

"I'm forced to admit that there is no room for argument in that, either," said Steve. "Only it has to be more than a desire. It must have become determination."

He hesitated, and the whimsical note crept in and dulled the threatened edge of hardness in his voice.

"I know of a case in point, that happened right here in these woods. One of the finest sportsmen who ever hunted or fished over this country had a favorite guide—Long John LeClaire was his name. In fact, he never went into camp without him, for upward of a score of years, and he claimed there never was a better cook, between here and the border. But Long John had one bad failing. As long as one kept to the timber with him it was plain sailing, but strike a town and it meant a week's delay in sobering that guide up. Town and a spree were synonymous in Long John's mind; and after trying both mental and physical suasion the sportsman I mentioned finally hit upon another plan. He persuaded Long John to take the 'cure'; more than that, he put him on a train himself and saw him off. But there was nothing enthusiastic about John's departure. You see, way down deep in his heart, he was just a little afraid this proposed treatment would be successful.

"He went, but his going was reluctant. And then, a month later he came back again, and, oh, what a difference there was in his return! It took the conductor and two train-men to put him off at the station; they were considerably marked up in the operation. Once safely landed on the platform, however, Long John spread out his feet to steady his wavering body and waved a hand in hearty greeting to the crowd which had assembled to welcome him home. His hat was gone; he had a discolored eye, but the reluctance was gone from his carriage. And he made a speech which for expressive briefness surpasses anything I've ever heard, before or since:

"'There!' he declared his triumph. 'There! And now I guess I've showed 'em no sanatorium could ever cure me!'"

But Garry did not laugh. His smile was mirthlessly sardonic.

"Then why the devil have you tried to keep me up here?"

Any man might well have objected to the manner of that question; many men would have spoken too hastily, forgetting that there are worse ills than those of the body. But Steve was not ready to hit back yet. He was thinking of Miriam Burrell; he lied with skillful smoothness.

"I told you last night," he said. "I need men. And then, too, it's a long time since I've seen you. I've not made so many friends, you know, Garry."

Garrett Devereau would have stopped there, dripping as he was, in the middle of the timber, had not Steve held to his stride. And he must have caught a momentary glimpse of that self which he was exhibiting to his companion, for his next words were a little mollified.

"Perspective is an excellent thing," he murmured. "It's been said before, but I'm repeating it. It's not only illuminating in just the matter of view, but it unsettles one's sense of values, doesn't it? I mean the Bignesses and Smallnesses of things—and creatures. When I went away, or rather when you did, back I don't remember how many years, you were tugging at the bit to be up and at things. That used to perplex me, although you may not have known it; I never really caught your angle or viewpoint. But now that you are in the thick of it I'm puzzled to know whether you find it—well, sufficient in itself."

O'Mara laughed softly over his shoulder.

"Sufficient!" he echoed. "Wouldn't you, if you were fact [Transcriber's note: face?] to face every day with some problem or other that had you stumped? Wouldn't you, if you were playing a game that shifted so rapidly from point to point that it kept you dodging and ducking and swearing to hold your feet?"

Garry drew a deep breath.

"That's what I've been trying to establish in my own mind," he faltered. "I've been thinking perhaps—but, pah!" He spat out a fragment of laughter as though it were bitter to his tongue. "I tried one job—I tried once! I ought to know better than to wonder even, now. And if a man can see no reason for living his life, it's his to quit, if he wants to!"

And then Steve abandoned his air of tolerance; he changed his style of play. The contempt in his retort could not have been more measured, even had it been other than a premeditated thing.

"Quit is the right word," he came back coolly. "I wasn't quite sure until now. You asked me if the others had told me what sort of man you had become. And if silence is affirmation, you had your answer. You inquired concerning my own opinion and I withheld it. Whatever it was doesn't matter now. Maybe I was guilty of bad judgment, but you have set me right."

Each word was tipped with scorn. Again, with deliberate intent, Stephen O'Mara lied.

"And I tell you now that had I been sure you wanted that hemlock to get you, I'd have left you where you stood. The world is all cluttered up with fools, as it is."

It came so quickly that Garry was not immediately aware of the attack. He smiled, covertly.

"Accidents will happen," he feigned a protest.

Abruptly the taller man wheeled, lids a-droop.

"—Fools, and quitters, too," he supplemented, levelly. "Quitters and men who show a streak of yellow that doesn't assay even a little bit of pure gold. A minute ago I gave you one reason for my attempt to keep you here. But I made a bad mistake there, too. It's men I need!"

He couldn't have straightened the other any more quickly had he swung and slapped his face. Garrett Devereau went paper white. They reached the edge of the heavier timber and came out upon the soggy sod of the clearing in the hush which followed that wickedly barbed speech. Steve always stopped there, whenever he came back to the cabin alone. He liked to look up at Joe's light, waiting in the window. And now, a pace or two in the lead, Garry turned back and stared widely into Steve's cold eyes. It had taken heat lightning to clear that brain which had been all day befogged.

"That was frank, and altogether plain," he said. "Joe took it upon himself to hire me, during your absence—the figure mentioned was eighteen a week. Now, quite as frankly, I am admitting his lack of authority."

Dusk comes quickly in the woods; twilight is only the briefest of pauses between daylight and dark. In the half-light as he stood there it would have been very easy to have mistaken Garry Devereau for the man whose clothes he wore. And while they waited, strained and tense, facing each other, a lone sapling between them and the eastern fringe of the clearing swung frantically earthward as if stricken by an invisible hand, and then thrashed upright again. A fragment of green bark flew aloft. They heard the deflected bullet go whining away. Then the tardy bark of a rifle.

It was instant-quick, and yet little quicker than the expression that sped over Garry's features. He turned and faced the thicket from which the report had come; he lifted his chin and opened his arms and laughed aloud. The second time that day Steve reached out and jerked him viciously from his feet. This time the bullet missed the sapling. They felt the air shock of its passage.

There was nothing deliberate nor premeditated in the outburst which Steve loosed upon the man who had gone to his knees beneath the grip of his hands.

"You fool!" he grated. "You crazy-brained madman!"

Garry rose and made as if to dust his knees.

"Poor work," he criticised, easily. "Too hurried—the first shot. There should have been no excuse for a second."

With angry roughness Steve thrust him back into the deeper shadow.

"Wait here!" he commanded.

But Garry was only a step behind him when, a moment later, the former leaned over the spot where that invisible marksman had stood. There were deep imprints in the forest mold—an empty shell upon the leaves. And by that time Steve had regained his grave composure.

"Some idiot of a hunter," he ventured quietly, when he had straightened from a glance at those marks. "One of those enthusiasts who shoot in haste at any rustle in the brush, and investigate at leisure."

Momentarily the intimacy which had existed in other days between them was restored. Garry's answer held no more of antagonism than had Steve's calm comment. He tried to follow the tracks that led into the deeper timber. It was too dark to follow far.

"This is a hunter in a hurry, then," he remarked. "Too much of a hurry, even, to investigate."

"Hungry, and late for supper," suggested Steve. "And we'll be late, ourselves, unless we travel along."

He faced about and started straight across the clearing, and he maintained the lead in spite of Garry's effort to supplant him. Before they reached the door of the cabin reserve that amounted to actual coolness once more cloaked them both. Only once did either of them offer to speak.

"You might do well to vary your costume a little," Garry observed impersonally, "if your nimrod friend who hunts at dusk is going to persist in mistaking you for a deer."

He drank hard that night from the bottle which Fat Joe, in obedience to Steve's command, had left standing upon the shoulder-high shelf—drank first in a self-conscious fashion with a mumbled excuse to Joe that the rainfall had chilled him; then more and more openly, until he forgot that he had ever felt the need of an excuse. Not one of the three men had made a move to go to bed, and before midnight came around Garry's black fit of absorbtion had given way to another mood. Blithely he chafed Fat Joe one minute, blind to that one's sullen reception of his jocularity; the next moment he turned eyes that had long before lost their enmity in a glassier light of goodwill upon Steve, working over a drawing-board at the other end of the table, impatient yet elaborately approving of his industry. And when Steve finally laid aside his work, signifying with a sigh that he had finished, Garry rose and lifted a half-emptied glass and made him a rollicking toast.

"Here's to young Virtue's triumph, Steve," he chanted, "and damnation to the opposition! I may be leaving you—I'll be on my way back to town tomorrow at this time—but I'm leaving my moral support behind me."

Steve's reception of that flourish was in no way like what Fat Joe had expected. He smiled cordially—a little absently.

"Thanks, Garry," he said. "And I guess I'll be needing all the support I can find, both moral and otherwise, before spring comes. So you're not figuring on stopping off at Morrison? Planning on going straight through, eh?"

Garry made a gesture which was meant to embrace the whole chain of hills outside.

"Absolutely!" he emphasized. "This country is all right for those who were born to it—purple hills and purling brooks and silence brooding over all!—but it's too intense for your effete comrade. Too quiet—too easy to think! I'm going away from here just as fast as steam will haul me."

The other man stretched his arms and swung one foot negligently over the chair arm. His unqualified agreement brought sudden alarm to Joe's eyes.

"I suppose you're right," he drawled. "It does get on any man's nerves. Right this minute I'm as tired of it as I ever dare let myself get. I've sloughed around in the mud enough for one session."

Garry frowned, perplexed. His fast numbing brain refused to reconstruct clearly, and yet dimly he knew that this sentiment was not the one which he had heard a few hours before from Steve's lips.

"Too true," he was content to reply sadly. "Too true!"

"We've both earned a vacation." Steve's gentle smile never left his lips. "To-day I couldn't help but think that it was a shame to miss such perfect hunting weather as this. I wonder if I couldn't persuade you to postpone your going for just a day or two longer. I can show you some deer, Garry."

The frown upon the latter's forehead deepened with his effort at recollection. Then he brightened with happy satisfaction.

"Deer!" he chuckled, addressing himself to Joe. "Hunter took me for a deer, thinking I was Steve." He blinked, for the statement did not entirely please him. "Doesn't sound logical," he pondered, "but it's so. Fired twice and missed both shots. Poor work—very poor work indeed!"

Joe squared around, his perplexed scrutiny an accusation now. Steve had neglected to apprise him of that incident which had happened on the way home, and Joe had not heard the rifle reports. But O'Mara clung to the subject which he had introduced.

"That's the trouble with hunting right here in the front yard," he admitted. "There are too many gunners anxious to hear their rifles go off. We might swing over toward the west branch, though. As long as this rain holds on the leaves will be quiet as a carpet. You've never seen my own private shooting box, either, have you Garry?"

The questioned one tried hard to pay attention, but the attempt was no more than an indifferent success, for he was still grumbling to himself over that unknown marksman's lack of skill.

"Never knew you had one," he answered.

"My inheritance," laughed Steve. From his manner he might have been talking to a sober man. "And also the haunt of my boyhood days. It's the shack, you know, where I spent a good many years with Old Tom. It lies a half dozen miles through the woods from here. I've made it weather-tight and dry. I spend a day or so up there whenever I have a chance to get away. We're sure of a shot if we still-hunt over in that direction—sure of a tight roof and good beds, too. How does it appeal to you?"

Garry spilled over his glass and had to fill it again, with many apologies for his clumsiness, so ardent was his acceptance of the invitation. He rose and insisted upon shaking hands.

"A personally conducted tour," he stammered gayly.

"A pilgrimage to the nest from which young genius first spread its wings, personally conducted by my friend, Mr. O'Mara." But his moods were growing more and more uncertain and changeable, now. He bent a baleful glance upon Fat Joe. "Is this—person going to accompany us," offensively he wanted to know.

Steve shook his head.

"Joe'll have to stay here and hold things down until we return," he explained.

Garry resumed his seat.

"Then I'll go," he stated. The baleful light was slow in leaving his eyes. And, after a rambling, muttered something to himself: "Too officious ... wouldn't let me have but one drink every three hours ... better we left him alone. He might shoot somebody, too—looks as though he might shoot and investigate at leisure."

With that he turned once more to thoughts of him who, firing from ambush, had left a trail of hob-nails to voice mutely the haste of his retreat. It had a fascination for him; his mind went back to it automatically, the only idea apparently upon which he found it possible to center his faculties. Now and then he referred to it aloud, in jumbled and meaningless ejaculations. Both men knew that he did not know what he was saying, and yet his reference to Fat Joe had left a hint of pain in the latter's eyes. It was still there when Joe arose, an hour later, and jerked his head toward Garry's quarters.

"If you need me, sing out," he said. "There's whiskey locked in the medicine chest—and I'll be sleeping light."

The words meant nothing to Garry, but he noted Joe's departure. Steve saw that his eyes were fixed, his lips crusted with fever, when he too came to his feet in a supreme effort, and steadied himself by the back of his chair.

"I've been most thoughtless, Steve," he apologized charmingly. It was the spirit of the old Garry talking through the flesh of the Garry he had become. "I've been unpardonably selfish. You must be tired; you have worked hard to-day."

In turn he made as if to cross to the door. Steve drew him back.

"Joe's taken your bed," he explained. "He's been an hour asleep by now. We'll be getting away at daybreak, and he always did hate to be waked an instant before his hour, so you'll have to occupy his bunk."

It took Garry a minute or two to assimilate that.

"Surely," he agreed. "Daybreak." Then, drearily, with no knowledge of what he was saying: "I wish I could go to sleep—I wish it was daybreak, now!"

Yet he was almost sober again when Steve shook him awake at four the next morning, his first inquiry concerning the state of the weather proving that he recalled their plans of the night before. But his politeness had given way to a pallid stubbornness that would not budge an inch until he had had a drink and filled a pair of flasks with all that the fresh bottle from the medicine chest contained. He refused breakfast with sickened finality; declined even the coffee which Steve tried to press upon him. When the latter handed him Joe's rifle and a handful of extra shells, however, his eagerness to be away showed in his eyes.

Steve did not like that gleam any more than he understood it, and he did not understand it at all. It went around him—through him—much as though Garry was peering cunningly at a far-off, bodiless something which the other man could not see. And throughout the whole morning Steve was conscious of it whenever they met after skirting a swamp, or slipped noiselessly over a hardwood knoll, to rejoin each other. The day was half gone before Steve realized that it was the telltale sign of a brain no longer sober, even though Garry's body continued to maintain an incredible steadiness.

Long after it seemed that eyes such as his had become must needs be sightless the latter went on picking his way carefully over rough bits of going; when he had reached a condition where he no longer heard the word or two which, now and then, Steve addressed to him, he still flattened his body and crouched at the expected nearness of game. It became an uncanny exhibition of mechanics after a while—a sleep-walking sort of thing which wore upon Steve's nerves until he was more than once at the point of taking possession of Joe's repeater. And yet it was Garry who jumped a spike-horn buck, just before nightfall. It was he who fired twice before Steve's rifle reached his shoulder. But they found only blood on the leaves when they hastened forward.

"You hit him!" Steve leaned over to examine those crimson stains. "You must have found him with both shots, judging from the way he's bleeding. He's gone into that cedar swamp; he won't travel far, and I hate to let him crawl in there, wounded like that, to die."

Indecisively he paused, not sure just what to do. In that moment of quiet Garry lifted a flask to his lips and finding it empty let it slip heedlessly to the ground.

"Two shots," he muttered darkly. "Two, where one should have been enough."

That echo of the night before helped the other man to decide.

"This strip of dark timber runs straight west to the river—are you listening, Garry?" he asked. "Straight to the river—it's only a scant mile—

and you'll find the cabin on the rise of ground in a clump of balsams, three or four rods to the right. I'm going to take your gun—you look fagged out. You skirt around the edge of the bad going and I'll drive straight through. It may be only a scratch, after all, although it doesn't seem possible, with all this blood. I'll take your gun and, now, are you sure you can make it—sure you won't get turned around? It'll be dark in half an hour, you know."

Garry gave up his rifle without a sign of demur. His eyes were burning with some sort of feverish anticipation, but his answer was clear enough.

"I'll wait for you at the river," he said, and he started forthwith toward the west.

Steve watched him out of sight before he turned to take up, irresolutely, the trail that zig-zagged into the cedar brake. But once he had started he went ahead rapidly, jumping the wounded buck within five minutes and giving him no time to lie down again. And after he had covered a quarter of a mile Steve saw that it was much as he had told Garry it might be; it was a flesh wound that bled profusely and that was all. For the deer, holding to a direct line down the middle of the swamp, continued to travel strongly. Steve had all but reached the river-edge where they were to stop for the night, before he detected a stirring in the bushes ahead of him and his ear caught the crackle of a dry branch.

Instantly he forgot everything save the quarry he was running down; forgot Garry and the strange persistence with which the latter had gone back, after twelve hours, to quote himself word for word. With rifle poised he edged forward a step and halted; he stooped and laid Garry's gun at the foot of a tree and went on again. Once he made out a movement behind a nearer tangle and saw the branches shake before a heavy body that was forcing slowly through them. His own rifle came up; his finger was on the trigger when he thought better of it. Old Tom, more than a half-score of years before, had switched him well, not so very far from that very spot, because he had not made certain first of the target at which he was firing.

There was an open patch to the left. If the buck held to that quarter he would have to cross that clear. Rock-steady the muzzle came down and covered the first indistinct brown bulk which entered the notch of the sights. And then, with an oath, Steve let the gun slip to the ground at his feet and stood shaking, checks gone white. Garret Devereau, wearing an old tan canvas coat which he had unearthed in the cabin peered slyly around a bush which he had been stirring gently with one hand.

"Go ahead 'n' shoot," he ordered aggrievedly. "Hunter'sh alwaysh shoot at rush'le in the dark. Good joke on hunter'sh—good joke on my good frien', Misther O'Mara! Think'sh's got deer until he inves'gates at leisure. Best joke of all'sh on myself."

The muscles which all day had been a marvel of firmness beneath him gave way altogether. Without a sound he pitched forward upon his face. A second later Steve reached his side, but the horror had not faded from his own eyes after he had picked that prostrate figure up and carried it into the clay-clinked shack. His memory played him an odd trick during that moment. A vivid picture came back to him of the grave-faced boy he had been, struggling to steady Old Tom's helpless feet up that same rise.

Garry was limp and blue and pulseless when Steve stretched him out, inside. The second flask stood there where Garry had left it, upon a table, and while he was loosening the latter's clothing Steve shook it, experimentally, and found it empty. He swung it aloft and drove it through a window. The crash of shivered glass made the other stir. He opened his eyes and stared vacantly up into his friend's face.

"Steve," he moaned. "Steve, I'm cold!"

And that was the burden of the complaints which he lifted, time and again, throughout the first part of the night. Even after Steve had wrapped him in everything which the bare room afforded he still continued to whimper like a sick boy. But his body held strong. Just as, all day, it had been his brain which had shown the effects of the alcohol which he had consumed, so now, all night, it was his brain which suffered most. Again and again he called aloud a woman's name, in a voice which Stephen O'Mara had never before heard from his lips. In inconceivable tenderness he whispered it—the name of Mary Graves—only to cry aloud, "Steve—Steve," in accents of heartbreak the next.

Long before morning came his pulse was steady—a little jumpy but reassuringly rhythmic. But the sunlight was two hours old upon the floor before the silent watcher saw the white lids flutter and then part with a gaze that was once more sane. Garry's smile had always been mocking; it was shamed and wistful now. The clearness with which he remembered was a miraculous thing.

"You see, Steve," he faltered. "You see now, don't you, that I'm not worth trying to save? Oh, you've tried hard; I knew how hard you were trying! That's why I did—what I did. I'm no good; there's no use, friend of mine. Why don't you let me go?"

Steve groped and found the hand groping for his. He nodded his head, bruskly, to hide his eyes. But his voice was not brusk.

"I almost shot you, Garry," he said, and there was a husky echo of horror in the words. "In another minute I'd have killed you. Right now I don't know just what kept me from firing."

"And I meant you to," Garry murmured almost inaudibly, "I planned that you should—started to plan last night. I—I've been hating you for twelve hours—hating you because you were making me ashamed to do the thing I wanted to do most."

He tried to rise and fell back, slack. But his voice was stronger with sudden, swelling bitterness.

"It wasn't for myself, Steve," he cried. "It wasn't for what I might get out of it, or—or what it might bring me, I used to scoff at whatever others considered big and fine and clean, but I played it straight, just the same. I played it as well as I knew how—straighter than you'd believe. I thought it would make her happier, because I tried that hard. And she ... Steve, if I had been a woman—a woman like what I thought she was, little and clean and white—I couldn't have let a man like him so much as touch my little finger! And she—by God, she married him!"

The agonized voice broke there—the voice of a boy who had had to learn that it is woman and not women who is fastidious. Garry sat and swallowed, fighting for self-control. His eyes were numb, but Steve's had taken fire, for he knew that the hour for which he had been waiting had come at last.

"You've been trying to help me," Garry found his voice again, "you've been trying to throw me a line. And, for a day or two, I tried to catch it, Steve. But it isn't in me to try that hard, any more. Some men do things for what there is in it—the pecuniary reward, I mean; some men—you for instance—because their self respect won't let them stop, win or lose. But now and then there happens one who keeps on trying only because there is one other person, at least, who may be the gladder for his success. I don't expect you to understand; I know it will sound small and cowardly to you.... It's too lonesome living, Steve, when there's no one who cares whether you live or not!"

"That does not fit your case," Steve objected instantly, "when your danger or your safety keeps a woman watching, white-faced with terror through the night, for your return."

Garry propped himself upon one elbow, the better to see the speaker's countenance.

"My safety?" he repeated, blankly. "My return?" And then, wanly grateful: "You are not the sort of man who lies convincingly, Steve."

And then Stephen O'Mara let him have it—all the story which had lain so many days in his heart. There were times when Garry went even paler during the short recital; times when everything else was submerged by the incredulity that flooded his face. But before Steve had finished the last trace of doubt was gone. Before the end came Garry had bowed his head, this time in flushed, self-conscious wonder which transfigured him.

"Miriam Burrell!" he breathed. "Proud, intolerant—"

His head came up. The next instant he voiced the words which Steve most wanted to hear.

"You shouldn't have told me this," said he. "You had no right, unless—"

Steve laughed at him.

"God bless you, boy," he exclaimed. "I asked her if I might. Why, don't you understand that she meant to, herself, if I didn't? You see, she is—far, far braver than you are, Garry."

Garry lifted his hands and hid his face.

So quietly that his exit made no sound Steve slipped to his feet and passed outside. It had stopped raining; the hardwood ridges, touched by frost, were flaming streaks of color against the rainwashed evergreens, when he picked his way down to the river and found a dry stone for a seat. An hour and more he sat there, while his thoughts went back over the trail of the years—the trail which had led him from that cabin to a pair of violet eyes and lips that arched like a boy's.

Steve let his mind turn again, unreservedly, to his own problem that morning; he tried to face, sure-eyed, the road which still stretched ahead. He did not know that Garrett Devereau, the debonaire, the cynical, the world-weary and world-wise, had broken down and was sobbing noiselessly, as men sob, in the room which he had left—shaking with deep and terrible gasps that racked his very soul. But it was already daybreak; it was trail's-end now for Garry. It does make a difference if one knows that someone cares.

CHAPTER XVII
HONEY!

Upon their return to Thirty-Mile, two nights later, Joe's attitude of criticism was the first thing which piqued Steve's interest. There was something ludicrous in the former's voice as he sat and anathematized the food which the cook-boy brought to the table, even though he devoured hungrily all that his plate would hold. And because Joe was so obviously primed for a sensation that evening, out of sheer perversity Steve struggled to draw him into a discussion of a topic, which, just as obviously, had no appeal just then.

"What I hope to do," he confided gravely to Garry, "is to finish up at Morrison and make possible the transfer of some of those men up here. We are working only one shift now. With two I figure we could sail along a-fogging. How does that strike you, Joe?"

That was only one of his many attempts, but all of them, save for the inner laughter which they afforded; were totally without result. Joe's answers were monosyllabic—his attention wandering at best. To that particular question he nodded his head, spiritlessly.

"This butter ain't none too fresh," he growled sourly, "and I wonder if that cook-boy thinks we dote on ham every meal? I don't for one. It may be all right, if a man's plumb starving to death, but it don't lend no real elegance to a repast."

That gloomy complaint brought little more than a sparkle to Steve's eyes, but it made Garry lean forward in his place. Throughout the meal while the other two fenced in just such fashion he forgot his own food to listen, delighted anticipation in every feature. And when they had finished supper and pushed back their chairs, he stood grinning a little, watching Joe survey that littered room which served as office and sleeping-quarters for the chief engineer of the East Coast Company. Fat Joe's gaze swung from wall to wall, from littered corner to heaped-up chair. Then he shook his head in despair.

"It looks to me, Steve," he grunted, "as though you ain't never had no real training in tidiness, have you? There don't seem to be no system at all in the way you leave your things around. There's one boot over in that corner;

it's got a mate, I know, because I saw you take them off last night. I wouldn't be certain otherwise. And it's the same way with all your things. Just look at this room! A nice place to receive callers in, now ain't it?"

That was the first lead he tendered them, but Steve, rather than gratify him with a direct question, chose to go forward in the dark. He leaned over and followed his usual custom when he wanted to think. He tapped out his pipe.

"But I can always find everything," he defended, "that is, unless you have taken the trouble to put things away. Then it's a toss-up that something or other will never be found, until it turns up of its own accord. It's not so bad, Joe." He, too, swung to survey the room. "Not so bad! Just a little unsettled, that's all. Are we likely to have any callers, do you think, who would object to this layout?"

Joe snorted, but his eyes were mournful. He knew that there was nothing else to do but yield, a part at least.

"We ain't likely to," he murmured. "We're just naturally bound to have 'em. They're comin' in to-morrow, and I ask you again, ain't this a pleasing prospect to greet 'em?"

For all that he seemed to be staring ruefully down the room, he was watching for the surprise that darted across Steve's face. Momentarily the latter had forgotten his assumed air of placidity.

"To-morrow? Who?" And then Steve laughed. "Go ahead and tell us, Joe. I'm beat! I'll admit that I'm panting with curiosity."

Joe pulled up a chair and dropped into it. It appealed to him—this method—whenever he had the time to spare. His pink face was still innocent of guile.

"I don't mind the men-folks," he resumed. "That fat party, I mean, who wears the plaid suits, nor Caleb Hunter, either. Both of them are used to such truck as this. And I reckon it'll tickle the ladies, too. But I can see Honey sticking his nose in the air and sniffin', supercilious like, the first minute he gets his nose in the door. He ain't going to approve at all, at all—not any way you look at it."

"Honey!"

Both Steve and Garry ignored the rest of Joe's explanation to gasp that single word in concert.

"Who in the world do you mean by 'Honey'?"

"Who could I mean?" Joe demanded collectedly. "I didn't give him the name, did I? I mean that chap Wickersham who owns the timber north of us. Foreign, ain't he? Sure, I thought so? Well, every time I run across that man's path my heart swells with patriotism. I guess I'm just as glad to be born plain United States."

The first part of that statement was listened to closely enough by both men; the last sentence or two, for all that it was heartfelt and sincere, was lost upon them both. And Steve's mirth was even more hysterical than was that of Garry Devereau.

"Honey!" he panted. "Now isn't that a wonder? Joe, you're too good! You are altogether too good to be wasted on these timbered solitudes. Men pay two dollars a seat, Joe, to hear performers work who are rank amateurs in comparison with you."

The riverman's eyes grew belligerent.

"Funny, is it? So awful funny! Well, perhaps you think I can't read plain print yet, never havin' enjoyed a liberal education. But take a look for yourself."

He pulled up a pile of newspapers which had come in since their absence, sorted out one that was creased open, and handed it to Steve. It was an announcement of Barbara Allison's engagement to the Hon. Archibald Wickersham—that column to which Fat Joe had folded the sheet—a many-days-old announcement, now. But the smile did not even stiffen upon Steve's lips. The picture which accompanied it was a poor one, heavy-shadowed and smeared and lacking in detail, yet Barbara's face was unmistakable. The room became quiet. In that hush Garry realized that Joe's mistaken translation of the title had not been, as Joe had himself suggested, due to lack of knowledge, but to a desire to apprise his employer, delicately, of that which he believed was still news to him. And yet, from the easy way in which he read it, word for word, Garry was positive that all this which the New York daily blazoned forth with its customary mixture of snobbishness and vulgarity was no longer news to Steve. The latter's eyes lifted and dwelt long upon Fat Joe's face.

"So that's where you got it, was it, Joe?" he asked evenly. "You make it 'Honey,' do you? And when do they come in, Joe?"

"To-morrow night. One of the teamsters brought word this afternoon, just before you got back. Honey is going to have a look at his trees and things, the way I understand it. And the rest of them, I take it, want to look us over in our wild state. Where are we going to put them girls?"

Steve's answer was long in coming.

"Miss—Allison?" he wanted to know.

"—and her maid," Joe corrected promptly. "Her maid, Cecile. She's comin', too, and that tall, red-headed one. I don't remember her name?"

As studiously as he had done a moment before, Garry again avoided Steve's eyes.

"Miriam Burrell," the latter supplied the omission. "And that's fine, isn't it? How long are they going to stay, Joe?"

But Joe had finished with trifling.

"Where are we going to put them?" he insisted doggedly.

"Why, we have a couple of shelter tents somewhere in the duffle, haven't we? We might pitch those if—" he looked about, ruminatively—"if you think this is too squalid."

Joe turned appealingly to Garry, only to meet eyes flaring with deviltry.

"If you think that I'm going to give up my quarters for a troup of curious sight-seers, you're mistaken. If that's what you turned toward me for, don't allow yourself to dwell upon it another minute. I'm a laboring man and I have to have decent rest at nights.... Do you suppose Cecile would really mind a tent?"

And then Joe's face went red.

"Now ain't you the pair of rough jokers?" he whined. "Ain't you, though? But what's it going to be—this room or Garry's? The way I look at it we're elected to camp out ourselves. We're hardened sons of the wilderness, you know. That's what they always call us in print. But how am I going to get this place cleaned up?"

For another hour Joe argued it, and at last settled upon the store-house building as the likeliest for sleeping quarters for the feminine portion of the visitors.

"We have to eat in here, anyhow," he argued, "so I guess it's the best arrangement we can hit on. Honey won't be here much to meals, either. That'll be one nice thing about it. He'll be going north directly. And now—now I guess I'll go out and have a look at the pantry, even if it does make me feel sort of faint every time I think of the grub we've got on hand. Canned beans and boiled potatoes, and ham and bacon, to round out a banquet. Why couldn't a couple of mighty hunters like you bring home more than one little haunch of venison? Bacon and beans! Steve, you sure have been living mighty low-down on this job!"

He went out with a great show of haste, but returned almost immediately, forgot the urgency of matters in general in finding Garry idly shuffling a deck of cards. Throughout the evening Joe had exhibited an unwillingness to meet the third man's glances directly, but it was impossible for him to remain oblivious to the clicking of the chips. He balanced first on one foot and then on the other for a moment; then diffidently drew up a chair.

"Just a friendly hand or two, I suppose," he suggested, when the other made no move to begin. "Low limit and wide open, eh?"

Garry still toyed with the cards.

"I don't suppose you've ever forgotten the first game in which we indulged, have you, Joe?" he asked at length. Joe was not comfortable.

"Scarcely," he admitted. "Scarcely."

"Nor the—stakes?" pursued Garry.

"I—I seem to recall 'em, faintly."

Garry's peal of amusement was as rollicking as a boy's.

"So do I," he exclaimed. "And if I remember rightly you stated on that occasion that cash was no consideration with you. Does that still hold good?"

It was the first good look Joe had had at the other's face. The change he found in it seemed to perplex him more than a little.

"I take it that it does." Garry did not wait for his reply. "And now—what do you say to that same full bottle against a—a ninety-nine year blanket restriction, with me at the wrong end of the odds?"

Joe slitted his eyes.

"When they tuck a ninety-nine year clause into a franchise they mean it's forever, don't they?" he wanted to know.

"Forever, to all intents and purposes!" said Garry.

Joe's chest sank and rose in a long, long breath.

"It's no word to trifle with," he cautioned at last. "If you lose it'll be a considerable drouth."

"Cut!" invited Garry, and they started to play.

That other night Garry's stack of chips had lasted far longer than they did on this second occasion. A half hour later, when he rose to go to bed, his ninety-nine year promise of abstinence was piled symmetrically before Fat Joe. But his good-night was gay. For a time after his departure Joe eyed Steve, sidewise.

"Hum-m-m," he cleared his throat. "Hum-m-m! And I was expectin' you to turn up any hour of the last twenty-four with a request that I come and help bring home the remains. You must be quite a silver-tongued exhorter, aren't you, Steve?"

Stephen O'Mara was silent over the paper which Joe had handed him earlier in the evening, and the lack of any offer on his part to go into details did not trouble his questioner. Fat Joe sat and bobbed his head over what would never cease to be a miracle in his eyes.

"And he'll stick this time," he vented his wonder aloud. "He's surely going to stick!" Then he smiled widely. "And I reckon you'll have to admit that I handled the small part that come my way with ease and dispatch, when I tell you that he didn't catch so much as one lonesome pair, all the time I was dealing. I'm ashamed of myself. I haven't seen such a mean, crooked game of stud dealt since I come East!"

Garry was very quiet the next morning when he and Steve went back to their work; before noon came his uneasiness had become very apparent to the man whom he was assisting. But neither his silence nor his nervousness any longer worried Steve. Instead, the latter let himself smile over both those outward evidences of inward panic, whenever his thoughts were on Garry at all. For the latter's diffidence as the day aged became a flushed and warm-checked thing, until at four in the afternoon Steve could no longer withhold the suggestion for which wordlessly, Garry was asking.

"Joe was more than half right," he remarked, one eye to his level, "in spite of the fact that we refused to take him seriously. We can't let those people come in and find everything too hopelessly uncomfortable, so perhaps you'd better run ahead now, Garry, and see what he has accomplished. I don't want to leave this spot myself until I have some figures upon which I know I can rely. But you might run ahead, if you will. I'll be along later."

It was couched in the form of a request, but Garry's face flamed. He went, albeit a bit reluctantly. And he stopped more than a few times in his climb from the edge of the timber to the door of Steve's shack. But once he had passed over the threshold to find that unrecognizably trim room empty, his face grew heavy with disappointment; he was on the point of going back outside to scan the bowl of the valley when a tall, short-skirted figure, enveloped in a voluminous apron which Fat Joe in a moment of mistaken zeal had once provided for the cook-boy, flashed through the passage-way from the kitchen annex and barely missed catapulting into his arms. Miriam Burrell, pink-faced from the heat of the roaring wood-stove, and smudged with flour on forehead and cheek, lifted her apron and swung it like a flag of victory.

"I've found it," she sang triumphantly. "I've found out what was the matter! I'd just forgotten the baking-powder, that was all! Next time—"

Then she recognized him. With outstretched hands still clutching the edge of her apron, she stood, almond eyes widening, and scanned him from head to foot. Even Steve, who had been with him every moment, had noticed the hour to hour change that had been taking place in Garry's appearance. To the girl who had not seen him for weeks, that flushed, self-conscious man was a different Garry than she had ever known before. Hungrily her gaze went from open shirt to caked boots, from steady hands to clear eyes which made her own eyes shy. And then Miriam Burrell, cool and poised Miriam, did what many another maid in a checkered apron has done in similar situations. She lifted that stiff gingham to hide her unutterable happiness. But before he could speak she found her voice; nor was it very steady, at that.

"I thought you were that party of idlers come back," she hesitated. "How—how tanned you are becoming, Garry! I thought they—oh, I can't tell you how glad I am to see you so—so well. I'm making biscuits for supper—that is, I've just been practising until now. It seemed as though I'd forgotten something that was necessary to the recipe, because they were flatter after they were cooked than when I put them in the oven. And most marvelously heavy, too! But it was just the baking-powder, that was all. Do you—do you think you'd care to help?"

["Oh, I can't tell you how glad I am to see you—so well."]

Steve was very late in returning to camp that night. Throughout the rest of the afternoon he set himself a pace, knee-deep in slushy mud, which Garry could not have maintained. But when he paused there in the dark where he always stopped for a moment and a tumult of voices swept down to meet him, he forgot his fatigue. He had lifted his battered hat from his head, striving to distinguish a single note in all that treble of girlish laughter when, framed suddenly against the background of light within, he saw a slender silhouette take up its station in the doorframe. Barbara was still peering out across the darkness when he came up to her.

"We've been waiting dinner for you for almost an hour," she rebuked him, in place of what might have been a commonplace greeting. "We've been waiting in the face of Mr. Morgan's insistence that it was practically useless. He has been telling us that when a man here in the hills fails to turn up for a meal you never bother to look for him; you know that the worst has happened."

Over her head the first eyes that Steve encountered that evening were those of Archibald Wickersham. While shaking hands with the girl, he bowed in grave welcome to the tall figure in leather puttees and whipcord riding-breeches, and Wickersham, from the far side of the room, bowed back in equal gravity. Then Caleb Hunter grasped Steve's elbow and spun him around toward the light and peered at him accusingly. Barbara had not noticed until then how tired Steve looked.

"Before the others get to talking," said Caleb, "before the tide grows too strong for my weak voice, young man, I want to deliver a message. Miss Sarah wants it explicitly understood that unless you stop in to say hello on your next trip down, she herself will take the trail up here. And lest that ultimatum sound too little threatening, I might add that when Miss Sarah takes the trail she never travels with less than six trunks."

Caleb clung so tightly to his arm that it brought a tinge of color to Steve's cheeks. It was minutes before he could get away to change his wet clothes, and in that minute or two he could not help but contrast, grimly, his own mud-spattered attire with that of Archie Wickersham. The tired blue circles beneath his eyes wore even more noticeable when he returned, to be ushered with much ceremony by Fat Joe to the head of the table.

It was an utterly irresponsible gathering that leaned over the red tablecloth that night—an oddly assorted group which, from the very first, Joe realized was not at all to Wickersham's liking. Dexter Allison himself, fairly radiating good-will, sat at the foot of the table, with his son-in-law-to-be on one side and Barbara's little maid, Cecile, on the other. And between Cecile and Barbara, who sat opposite Garry and Miriam, Fat Joe leaned both elbows upon the table edge and monopolized the conversation. The seating arrangement was Joe's; it was his party. And the absolute inattention to detail, the large indifference to veracity which his discourse disclosed before that noisy supper was over, grew to be an astonishing thing. His nights of fancy left Steve aghast in more than one instance; they even forced a stiff smile to Wickersham's lips, and that is saying much for Joe's success as an entertainer, for in the bearing of those two men toward each other there had been evident from the first a chill antipathy which amounted, actually, to armed truce. And the color in Miriam's cheeks, whenever his gaze strayed to that side of the table, helped Steve to forget, temporarily, much that he found not pleasant to recall at all.

For Miriam's tongue was no less irresponsible than was Joe's. Her mood was so mercurial that she drew, time and again, the eyes of all at the table. She chattered with an abandon that scandalized Barbara; broke in and interrupted every argument with hoydenish trivialities, in one breath, to appeal to Garry the next for refutation. And Garry, the light-tongued and quick-witted, sat almost dumb of lip before her happy garrulity. But his eyes never left her; they spoke his thought aloud. The quick lift and droop of her eyelids, the brilliancy of her lips, made Miriam's face a living thing of happiness—made Barbara's silence seem even more profound. For the latter's withdrawal from the hilarity, dominated half the time by her father's booming bass, was nearly as complete as was that of Wickersham himself.

Just once, shortly before they withdrew for the night, Steve caught a gleam of mischief in the dark eyes she turned toward him. She rose the next moment and started slowly around the room, poking demurely into corners and closetted nooks. Every eye was following her when she finally found the thing for which she was searching. She drew a red felt, yellow-mottoed cushion from beneath the deer-hide covering a chair, and held it up so that all might read. "What Is Home Without a Father?" it ran, and when the joy that stormed through the room made it sure that the exhibition needed no interpreter, Fat Joe turned and hid his face. Miriam rose languidly and joined the other girl in an examination of his handiwork. Smooth face tinted by the firelight, copper hair almost dishevelled in its disarray, she was an exquisitely lovely thing. In her alto voice she expressed her opinion.

"It's an entirely new stitch to me, Bobs," she averred. "I don't think I have ever before seen just this method employed." And she turned to Stephen O'Mara. "Do you suppose, Mr. O'Mara," she asked, "that I might learn it from the one who did this work for you? It's rather"—and her head tilted to one side—"it's rather a pretty thing!"

Again they succumbed to mirth, and then Joe rose, bristling, and went forward much as a gamecock might step out to do battle. He took the cushion from the hands of the girls, who no longer had strength enough even to hold it.

"If you are aiming to do any sewing around this camp," he stated, "you can start in sewing on buttons. This kind of work is entirely too nerve-wearing for amateurs."

He carried the cushion across the room and placed it, not where it had been hidden by the deer-hide, but in colorful prominence against the back of the chair. Long after he had crossed with Steve and Garry to their tents he continued to explode with soft chuckles.

"I never did say," he defended himself, "that that sentiment was strictly appropriate. I always stated that it was the best I could. And as for my technique—well, either of you guys try it some time! You just take a needleful of that yellow worsted and start tracking across a couple of yards of red and pathless desert, and see where you come out. I know, because I've done it. I'm a pioneer. But if I ever tackle another job like that it's going to be a crazy-quilt!"

And Joe considered, in spite of the din which answered him, that his challenge was ample.

CHAPTER XVIII
I'M TELLING YOU GOOD-BYE

It was fully an hour after Fat Joe and Garry had rolled themselves up in their blankets when Steve, who had elected to sit up for one last pipe even though his body was aching with fatigue, heard behind him the approach of her footsteps. Outside at the top of the rise some fifty yards in front of the tents, he had seated himself on a log, chin buried in one palm and eyes vacantly steady before him; but even before he turned—before he rose slowly to his feet—he knew who was coming, knew and realized that she should not have come. Wrapped in a long heavy coat, face half-hidden by the upturned collar, bare of head, Barbara came quietly down to where he waited. And without word of greeting on the part of either of them, they sat down together, facing the silvered bowl of the valley.

Time passed before Barbara opened her lips for a long, quivering intake of breath.

"I never dreamed it could be so big," she murmured in awe. "And then to think that some day—within a few months in reality—engines will go screeching their signals across this very place. It doesn't seem possible; it seems almost a shame to spoil it, too."

Her earnestness was so unconsciously wistful that Steve could not help but smile at it a little, even though he had been telling himself, since the moment of her coming, that he must not let himself dwell just then upon that wistfulness which, for many hours, had been most apparent to him.

"I've felt that way about it often," he answered, almost dully. "I like it better myself, as it is. It does appear to be a long way ahead, doesn't it—that day of completion which you cover in the screech of the whistles? Only to-day, when we were scrambling about down there in the alders, it took nearly all the imagination I possessed to see two streaks of steel where there is nothing but thicket now. But as for the bigness of it"—he laughed deprecatingly—"it isn't so very big, you know. It's just a—a mean sort of proposition."

Barbara leaned forward, delicate chin resting upon interlocked fingers. She was not quite certain whether she had caught a thread of weariness in those words.

"To me," she said, "to me it is colossal! Why, I thought the work at Morrison seemed complicated and tangled enough, but there—there isn't even a beginning or an ending here. There's nothing but woods and water."

She pointed out across the valley toward a mound-like outline yellow under the moon; pointed into the north and asked another question.

"Is that part of the embankment?" she wanted to know. "Is that the direction in which Mr. Wickersham's timber lies?"

The man nodded.

"Just a few miles up through that notch," he told her. "That's the end of the rail-bed which we have been building along the river-edge."

Her next words made him start and then try to cover that moment with a readjustment of his long body.

"I'm going up there to-morrow. Mr. Wickersham has asked me to ride with him, in the morning." She waited a moment or two. "That—that's why I came out here to-night. We'll be going back to town the next day or two, and I wanted to have a chance to bid you good-bye, before I left Morrison for the winter."

He had known that she would not be likely to remain in the hills much longer. He had realized that each day which he checked off, always hopeful that the next might open the way for him to see her again, was steadily bringing nearer the date of her departure. But he had not let himself think that it would come so soon. There was no doubt this time about the heaviness of his voice.

"I see," he said. "I see."

There came another long silence. Rising out of it, Barbara's voice sounded very, very little.

"I've never known a sky in which the stars were so thick. They're—they're like a field of buttercups. And have you ever seen such an irrepressibly happy creature as Miriam was to-night. She was radiant—positively shameless! Did you know that Garry knows—"

"I told him, myself," said Steve, simply.

The girl faced around in her surprise.

"You?"

"Most certainly! Why not?" His voice was not quite so unenthusiastic now. "It's one of the few unmistakable opportunities I've ever had to make two people permanently as happy as Miriam was to-night. I'd feel guilty all my life if I didn't help all I could, knowing how happy I am going to be, myself!"

Thus did he work around, quite without abruptness, to a renewal of that discussion which she had thought to close, weeks before.

"Are you trying to infer that I am to be a part of that happiness?" she asked none too promisingly.

"You ought to know. I said 'all my life.'"

And there, suddenly, Barbara laughed.

"I suppose now they'll marry and live happily ever after!" she exclaimed with an attempt at airiness.

"Most certainly," asserted Steve, although her mirth puzzled him. "Why is it funny to you?"

"It isn't, but—yes it is too, now that it's no longer a thing one need worry about. That's always the trouble with emotions which are too intense. They're either very sad to contemplate, or very, very absurd. And they will persist in exchanging faces, to the confusion of the on-lookers. Garry was so dangerously in love with Mary Graves, you see!"

"He was in love with an idea," the man contradicted flatly. "He was in love with just that. And it is not safe for any man to live alone with an abstract conception of anything. He's bound, sooner or later, to lose his grip on tangible things if he does. He's likely to start destroying property to further the cause of labor, or liable to turn to shooting men who were born to jobs I'm certain some of them never wanted—kings and that sort, I mean—figuring on solving the social problems of men and women who must solve that problem themselves. Perfection is a fine thing to anticipate; expectations of it are dangerous. And women aren't made that way."

"No?" her voice slid coolly upward.

"No," he told her, and smiled with that serenity she had come to know so well. "Not even you, though I suppose I'd about annihilate anyone else if he ever hinted at it." He chose to be didactic in tone. "No, you're not perfect; you've too much intelligence for that. Why, right now you're fighting with your brain against the dictates of your heart, and if you were above mortal error in judgment you'd know that you are wasting your time."

The girl forgot entirely that she, too, had promised herself that their leave-taking should not cross the border of personalities. And with that lazy joy of her on his tongue she might not have been quite so quick to hold that she could love no man, had she stopped to give it thought. Her advance to the skirmish was most spirited.

"Your opinion has the merit of sincerity," she said, "although, looking back upon a—a certain day, I can't help but wonder whether you haven't been guilty of mouthing pretty nothings for my poor ears."

"That proves my point right now." He was imperturbable. "You're begging the question to gain—"

"You said—" she flashed, and then grew red.

"I said I'd let you ask no pardon of me. I said I'd let myself find no flaw in you. But how does that embarrass my present argument? Flawless perfection would be a mighty difficult thing to live with, day in and day out. Living with a woman who never made a mistake could have no appeal for me. She'd always be emphasizing my own shortcomings. You become consistent and you'll catch me yawning some day; grow logical and you'll almost scare me off! Why, you're a girl!"

Her laughter was like a bell on the still air.

"And you—you still sit there and insist that perfection has no attraction for you? When you've just described, without knowing it, the—the sort of a girl you think is perfect."

His lips curled in a way to quicken any woman's pulse.

"You have me beaten," he laughed. His eyes, dark as was the shadow upon his face, made her breath unsteady. "I would like to watch you play poker with Fat Joe. Your game would puzzle him more than a little. Yes, you've surely left me without a leg on which to hobble off, because it would be small spirited in me, wouldn't it, if I were to tell you that you are the exception that makes my general rule hold sound? I wouldn't, however, prescribe such a degree of perfection for any other man's daily diet. It would prove his destruction."

"Your own superiority, of course, rendering you immune?"

"Maybe." At least, whether she knew it or not, she loved his serenity. "Maybe—and maybe I'm an exception too."

He sat very still. She had turned away once more.

"You'll be back again in the spring?" he asked with that gentleness he saved for her alone.

"I hope—I think so." The smallness of her voice angered her. She feigned a short, carefree laugh. "Unless I am too busy. Getting married seems to become a more and come complicated problem of proper costuming, doesn't it, with every passing season!"

She couldn't have told why she said it; she was trying to think of something else to say which would be kinder by far. And then, half lifting her, he had swung her around to him. For a moment he held her, face close to that small, frightened face buried in its deep collar, while she struggled uselessly against those hard arms which tried not to hurt her. Her lips continued to rebel, long after her eyes had closed—long after body and brain were quiescent.

"You mustn't!" she gasped. "Oh, I can't let you ... the moon ... we—we're sure to be seen!"

His lips on hers silenced that last incoherent resistance. She sat, wavy brown head bowed, when he had set her free.

"I was going to ask you not to forget!" There was no weariness now in his voice. "I had planned to ask you just that, a little ago, and it would have been a weak and useless request, wouldn't it? Any man who has to beg to be remembered is not the sort to remain long in any woman's brain. So I have taught you to remember, instead. You aren't going to forget, ever, now! You're coming back in the spring, and you're coming to stay! And now *I'm* telling *you* good-bye. It's time you were asleep."

He helped her to her feet. Together they turned—and Archibald Wickersham, tall to gauntness in the moonlight, was coming across toward them from the direction of the cabin. The girl's slim body stiffened, but Steve saw her chin come up. His own body grew lazier still, it seemed, in length and limb.

Wickersham's approaching steps were crisply precise; he stopped an arm's length in front of them, and his words were an echo of that last sentence of Steve's.

"It's time you retired," he said, ignoring the other man's presence entirely. "It's cold, and you have a long, hard ride ahead of you to-morrow."

For a barely perceptible moment, with the eyes of both men upon her, Barbara kept her place. Neither of them saw that her teeth were tightly closed over one full lip; neither knew that she had closed her eyes, dizzily, for an instant. And then, without a word, she put her hand upon the arm which Wickersham offered her; but Steve, on the other side, walked with her that night, as far as the door of the storehouse shack. Miriam herself opened the door and snatched Barbara within, and then laughed with her consummate impudence into both men's faces.

"G'lang wid ye's now," she flung at them, "an' quit disturbin' dacint folks that likes to sleep o' nights!"

She slammed the door upon them.

They stood there a second or two, Wickersham an inch or more taller and inches narrower in shoulder and girth of chest. Perfunctorily they nodded, each to the other, and wheeled silently upon their heels.

Steve did not respond the next morning when Joe summoned the rest with a long spoon applied heartily to the flat of a huge tin basin; and over the breakfast table Joe explained to the assembled guests the reason for his absence. Before daybreak a rider had come from Morrison, bearing word from Hardwick Elliott that Ainnesley was on from Manhattan and wanted to talk with him; before the camp was fairly awake he had ridden away into the south. And returning two days later, travelling the lower, lesser trails that followed the river, in order to save time, Steve missed her party going out. So, in the last moment, after days and days of patient waiting, did Chance trick him sadly.

How much or how little Wickersham might have overseen the night before he betrayed not at all at breakfast the next morning, either by word or look. And throughout that day, and the day that followed, while she rode at his side, undetermined whether she should attempt an explanation, Barbara found his face inscrutable. It was a week later, the night preceding her departure from the hills, long after the girl had ceased to think of him at all in connection with the incident, before she learned how much he really knew.

Miss Sarah had found her brother most uncommunicative upon his return from Thirty-Mile. In response to her first question concerning Steve he had assured her, lifelessly, that the latter was looking very well indeed, and let it go at that. Because she was a very remarkable woman, Miss Sarah had been able to curb her curiosity for several days, but on that particular evening she found it impossible calmly to wait longer.

"You have not told me yet, Cal," she reproached him at dinner, in her slightly lisping voice, "how much progress Steve seems to have made. You know how interested I am, and you must realize how undignified a thirty-mile dash on horseback would be on my part, in order to find out, myself."

While up-river Caleb had found much time in which to talk with Garry Devereau—that is to say, quite a little time, in view of the fact that Miriam Burrell, in boots and mackinaw, had insisted upon following Garry wherever he went. And since his return to Morrison he had been spending a surprisingly large share of his days in conference with Hardwick Elliott and his partner, Ainnesley. Now his reply to his sister's query was startlingly fervid.

"Progress!" he exclaimed. "Progress! I tell you he's going to win out, in spite of all of them, damn 'em!"

Miss Sarah froze in her chair.

"Caleb!" she expostulated. "Caleb!"

And Caleb's face went hot.

"I am very sorry," he muttered contritely. "But I couldn't help it. When I think of the way that boy has plugged on alone, all his life, with no one to give him a lift, it—it angers me to think that the very man whom I have prized as a friend should be the one to make his problem harder."

"Would you mind explaining, lucidly?" Miss Sarah requested. "And if it is business to which you are referring, will you please try to make it as brief and non-technical as possible?"

Once he started to tell her, Caleb realized that it was just what he had needed to do all along, without knowing it. Briefly as she had requested, he sketched for her the facts which, so far as he was concerned, had made of his first sneaking suspicion an absolute certainty. And he waxed wroth in the recital.

"It's treachery," he snapped, "rank, contemptible treachery. And the worst part of it all is that, even now, when I am morally certain of his culpability, I—I can't bring myself to despise the man. He's been my friend for thirty years, Dexter has, and damn it— I beg your pardon, Sarah—but, damn it, I keep on thinking of him, in soft moments, as my friend now. I sit by the hour trying to foist the blame upon Archie Wickersham, and he's no more guilty than Dexter. Dexter's merely good-natured about his crookedness; wholesome about it, somehow. And Wickersham's a sneak!"

In all the years they had lived together Miss Sarah had never heard her brother talk so bitterly. Yet her voice remained soft.

"It's very unpleasant, no doubt," she sympathized, "although I can't quite see why they don't all join hands and try to make a success of the project between them. Surely it seems feasible. And, somehow, even after listening to you, I don't seem to find myself greatly perturbed about our boy, Steve. He's very big and strong, Cal, and—and I am very old-fashioned. I still believe in the might of right. It may sound very feminine to you, but I do not find myself worried at all over his lack of assistance in his work. And I must confess that I did not have it in mind, at all, when I asked in regard to his progress."

Caleb looked up, suspiciously.

"Well?" he said.

"I meant how—how did he and Barbara appear to—get on together?"

Caleb spilled a spoonful of soup.

"Her!" he exploded with no regard for his grammar. "Why, she is true to her blood! If she weren't she wouldn't be engaged to that thief who masquerades as a gentleman. She isn't blind, and she's going to marry him!"

"You are positively violent, Cal," reproved his sister. "And your reference to Barbara does not do you credit. If I were your wife I suppose I'd rise coldly now and sweep upstairs to leave you alone with your bad mood. But being merely your sister I remain to hear you apologize. Barbara is not yet married to Wickersham, I might add."

"I am exceedingly sorry," said Caleb.

"And, without any reason for it, save my womanly intuition, I feel very certain that she will never marry him," Miss Sarah went on. "But you spoke about Steve having no one upon whom he could depend for assistance, and it was really a helpful hint to me. Did I fail to hear you say how they seemed to get on together?"

"She didn't think he was good enough for her, ten years ago," growled Caleb. "She wouldn't think so, now. He cares for her, so she treats him like a dog, of course."

Miss Sarah had to smile.

"Then I think it is high time I did something about it," she stated thoughtfully. "For she is a lovable girl, and she hasn't any mother of her own. She's very pretty and little and finer than any girl I know. If she weren't, Steve would not be in love with her, I am sure. And Dexter Allison is no doubt an estimable man in many ways, even though, as you feel positive, he has a tendency to acquisitiveness which is deplorable. Your continued regard for him convinces me of that. I wish, however, that Steve was not so entirely dependent upon what he earns. There are many beautiful things—beautiful and intimate and feminine things—which no man can remain happy in seeing paid for by other money than his own, for the woman he loves."

Ten minutes after it was done Caleb could not have told what impulse was to blame for the deed, but he rose forthwith and went to his strong-box, to return with the legal-looking document and the bunch of tax-receipts which he had found among Old Tom's papers, years and years before.

"There's the deed to some thousands of acres of the finest timber in this country," he announced challengingly, "all ship-shape in the name of Stephen O'Mara, 2nd! Old Tom bought them for the boy he hid away with him, in the days when timber-lands were going for a song. He paid the taxes until he was drowned, and I—I've paid 'em since, my dear! Three or four hundred thousand dollars, or more, ought to buy quite an amount of—er—feminine necessities, it seems to me."

With delicately thin fingers Miss Sarah leafed the papers through.

"You have never told me of this matter before, Cal," she murmured.

"Never told anybody!" chirruped Caleb triumphantly. "I tried to find the boy—both of us did, that is—and we failed. And when he turned up of his own accord—well, I knew a half year more of ignorance concerning his legacy wouldn't see him starve. Sarah, I wanted to see how that boy of ours would behave, without any backing. I wanted to be sure of the stuff he is made of!"

They had finished a much interrupted meal, but Miss Sarah lingered a moment at table. With incredible calm she had listened to the secret which her brother had been keeping to himself so long.

"A very good reason," she agreed, "one that would seem to have many points to excuse it. And although it is not within the letter of the law I—I think, Cal, I shall become an accessory before the fact. Very shamelessly I am going to ask you to see that no one knows of this property of Steve's, for a little longer, at least. I have spoken with the utmost confidence concerning Barbara; your reference to all that she said to Steve in a childish burst of passion years ago does not affect my attitude at all. But I have not been blind to what might be her—opinion now, either, impossible and ignoble though it seems. You will not tell Stephen of this matter for a while, Cal, for it would please me to know, without room for doubt, just what stuff she is made of, too!"

She straightened her diminutive body and started upstairs.

"She will be over to bid us good-bye to-night," she added. "Will you see that she comes directly up to me?"

And once more, from the landing, she spoke over her shoulder:

"You said that she treated him like a dog, Cal," she managed to keep her features grave, "and being a woman I can understand exactly why that is so. The joy of a breathless pursuit, it is often said, is the only choice left for the female. But can you tell me why a man hunts out the deepest, most comfortable chair he can find and ensconces himself therein, once he had overtaken the idol of his fancy? They often do, you know, sometimes for the rest of their lives."

Caleb lighted his pipe and cast about for his paper. "Maybe it's only the natural consequence," he retorted, his face turned away, "of such a pursuit as you mention. Maybe he feels the need of a long, long rest!"

And then Miss Sarah laughed.

An hour later, when she ran upstairs, Barbara found Caleb's tiny spinster sister, in negligee and boudoir cap, sitting cross-legged like a girl in the middle of the floor. There was an orderly litter of papers around her, and a confusion of clothes; and Barbara hesitated on the threshold until Miss Sarah nodded her head.

"Come in, my dear," she invited. "I'm indulging in one of the few joys left to advanced, unmarried years, that is all. But even memories need prodding with more material things, at times, I find."

The dark-eyed girl crossed and found a clear spot and seated herself. Without seeming to look at her, Miss Sarah saw that those eyes were vaguely troubled.

"I'm leaving to-morrow," Barbara began after a minute. "I came over to say good-bye."

Miss Sarah went on with her sorting.

"We'll see you again soon," she suggested pleasantly.

There was trouble in the girl's voice, too.

"I—don't think so."

"It's a very pretty country—a hard country to forget." Miss Sarah very wisely gave no heed to the woebegone note. "Perhaps," archly, "perhaps you'll be returning as the new Mrs. Wickersham?"

Barbara flushed duskily. Miss Sarah, however, was gazing at a dog-eared picture—a very old-fashioned picture of a youth in brave and resplendent garb of a period long dead. No one but herself and her brother had seen that photograph for many years, and he only because he had rummaged in a pigeon-hole in which he had no licence to look. His sister's eyes, as well as her posture, were girlish when she laid it aside to hold up to view a battered black velvet suit with wide collars and cuffs.

"I wonder if you could ever guess who once wore this?" she laughed lightly.

Politely Barbara examined it.

"I'm sure I couldn't," she answered. And, very slowly:

"Miriam is going to marry Garry Devereau. She is disgracefully happy about it."

The older woman received this irrelevance with composure.

"How charming," she said. "And I am sure that they will continue to be as happy as I hope you will be soon. This suit was Steve's—little Steve's. Dear me, what a day that was!"

After a moment of hesitation Barbara leaned forward to examine the silver buttons.

"It—it doesn't seem possible," she faltered. "What sort of a—a day?"

And then, with smooth, serious face upturned, she listened to Miss Sarah's tale—her own story of how she had dressed a gloomy-faced boy in half-century-old finery and sent him townward for eggs. When it was finished and she had decided, abruptly, that she must be going, suddenly, wet-eyed, she wheeled in the doorway and went blindly back to the older woman's arms. Miss Sarah hugged her once; then stood her away at arm's length. She knew how few women weep, without hiding their heads.

"There, we mustn't be temperamental," she chided. "It's only for a winter, at most. Remember, I love you very dearly, Barbara; write to me whenever you are lonely. And be a very good girl."

It was a brave bit of comfort, but Caleb's tiny sister, whose face had never lost its pink-and-whiteness, looked suddenly tired and old when she was alone again. As blindly as Barbara had come into her arms, she reached for the dog-eared picture and held it to her flat breasts. There is no greatness of soul save there be simplicity. Very directly, very simply Miss Sarah stood there in the middle of her girlish room and spoke to her Creator.

"I do not mean to meddle, dear God," she whispered, with tears squeezing from beneath tight lids. "I only want to help a little, if I may. You see, I've never had a baby of my own."

The door of the ground floor room which served Dexter Allison as an office was ajar when Barbara re-entered the house beyond the hedge. There was a streak of light running out across the floor of the dim hall from within, and the girl lingered on her hurried way to her own room to bid her father good-night. But she found Wickersham alone when she pushed wider the door. The light was behind him and she could not see how distorted was his face, yet as she paused on the threshold and a thin and pungent odor crinkled her nostrils, she sensed, somehow, that he had not been long alone.

"Father gone to bed?" she called. "Well, that's wise. You'd better come, too; it's time you were asleep."

She did not remember, just then, that other night when he had addressed those same words to her. She only knew that his features became suffused with purple even before she had finished. And then she realized quickly that it was alcohol she smelled; knew, too, that it was not Wickersham who had been drinking, even though Wickersham had trouble with his tongue. And while she waited, puzzled and frowning, the man gave up an attempt at his usual nicety of phrase and blurted out all that which had been many days hidden behind his impassivity.

"We haven't yet set a certain date for our marriage, Barbara," his voice was strained. "Don't you think it is high time we did?"

The girl colored. It was, at least, very unexpected.

"Why, no, we haven't," she admitted. "But we can if you wish it. Have you thought of a day you'd prefer?"

"I have," he stated. "Would the first of May be too early for you?"

Often, afterward, she wondered at her humility of that night, for whatever the quick thought might have been which made her reach out one hand to touch the doorframe beside her, her words were merely mild.

"It is, rather. But I think I can manage it, if it will please you."

Wickersham had come to his feet, but he would not turn so that she might see his face. He spoke with eyes averted.

"It would," he answered with an effort, "and—and in the interim I am going to be very sure, now, that no thoughtlessness of yours will be derogatory, either to my profound respect for you or your own respect for yourself."

The small hand closed then until it was clutching whitely the woodwork beneath it. She understood at last how much Wickersham had seen; she was never to understand entirely her mood of that moment. For had she waited she would have left him with finger ringless. Instead she wheeled without a word and climbed, white-lipped, upstairs.

Miriam Burrell loomed in one window of her bedroom when she entered—a different Miriam than the one who had once sat in just such an attitude, gazing into the north. The older girl's gladness of heart throbbed in her voice.

"I don't want to leave it, Bobs," she sighed. "I love every brawling rapid and sulky, ragged old peak. Did you ever see a more perfect night?"

Through the gloom the younger girl's answer lashed back, reckless of what hurt she might do.

"I hate it!" she gasped vehemently. "I hate it—hate it! And I must ask you, please—I want to go to bed."

There is a poise which comes only with hard-bought knowledge of one's self. It was Miss Sarah's; Miriam had acquired it, too. Without a hint of resentment in her manner she rose and withdrew. But Barbara did not go to bed. She took that vacated seat at the window. And long after her breathing had ceased to be quick and sharp she was still wondering why the odor of stale alcohol should recall to her, with elusive vagueness, the threatening face of a red-haired riverman who found it hard to keep his feet.

CHAPTER XIX
SOME LETTERS AND A REPLY

Her letter came to him a week later, though she had posted it the morning she took the train from Morrison. It had lain for days in the post-office box of the East Coast Company, waiting the day when one of the teamsters should call and carry it in overland. Steve had never before seen her handwriting. It was his first letter from her; yet he recognized it the instant Big Louie put it in his hand. And he was glad that night that both Fat Joe and Garry were absent from the up-river camp—glad that he was to have the next hour alone. But when he broke the flap of it Big Louie, who lingered uneasily in the open doorway—even Big Louie, whose wits were not particularly keen—knew from the expression which passed over his superior's face that this heavy envelope which he had brought had not contained good news. The quick contraction of muscles which tightened his jaw was too much like a spasm of pain. For her first letter, so the sentence ran, was to be her last; she wrote "less kindly than she would have wished to write," that she and Mr. Wickersham had decided upon the first of May, and after the silence had become a throbbing thing Big Louie decided, instinctively, that he would let go until later the demand which he had planned to make for a raise to meet that raise which, so he had heard it gossiped in town, was being paid the men in the northern lumber-camps. He stumbled going out and lost his balance so that the door crashed to behind him, violently. But Steve stood as he had stood when his eye's sought the first line of her note, nor did the crash penetrate his ears.

Repeatedly, in the interval which had elapsed since she had bidden him good-bye, the latter had told himself that she would not write, but the repetition had been unconvincing. He knew that now. With the note which smelled faintly of her there in his hand he realized that he had gone beyond mere expectation of a letter; he had dared to hope concerning its contents. How was he to know that she, too, after mailing it, had suffered as keenly as he was suffering that moment, wishing that she had employed less abrupt phrases, rebelliously regretting that she had sent it at all?

That night his fingers closed until the monogrammed sheet was reduced to a crumpled ball. The edges of the paper took fire slowly, then it exploded softly into flame upon the bed of coals in the fireplace where he had tossed it. And at that he laughed aloud, a harsh taunt for his own high hopes, without thinking how much his mirth of that moment was like what Garry's once had been. He lowered himself into a chair, and he was still there, motionless before a dead fire, when morning dawned greyly. His face had become less hard; he even found it possible to smile a little when the cook-boy, starting at the sight of him fully dressed at that hour, advised with alarmed volubility that breakfast would be ready immediately. But the few men who still remained at Thirty-Mile, felling and hauling the piles which were to carry the track across the swamp, noticed a difference in their chief that morning which made them careful to hear him, the first time he spoke an order.

Barbara did not write again, and in this, at least, the man who loved her anticipated her correctly. The letters, however, which Garrett Devereau received each day from Miriam—bulky, extra-postage epistles—brought often news of her; and these fragments Garry, knowing without being told for whom they were meant duly delivered to Steve, in weekly or fortnightly instalments, whenever the latter's duties brought him to Morrison. For Garry and Fat Joe, who had been transferred to the lower end of the work, along with the bulk of the up-river force, had noticed that difference too.

"Miriam says for me to keep my feet dry this cold weather," he'd tell the other man, laughingly, "and Barbara sends her regards to all of us, and hopes that we are making splendid headway." Or again: "Barbara's looking a little pale, Miriam writes. She says she's—er—trying to do altogether too much for her endurance."

Whatever the bit of news was Garry passed it on religiously, a little guiltily, sometimes, because of his own great happiness. Once he had failed, signally, to read behind his friend's moody silences; his surmise concerning the reason for Steve's changed bearing was not so wide of the mark this time. Often, within himself, Garry's wrath seethed hot, but he was no longer as ready as he had once been with verbal, cynical criticism. Only to Fat Joe did he dare pour out his soul with that vivid incisiveness which always held Joe spellbound.

"He's eating his heart out over *her*," he'd explode, "over a girl who is proving every day that she isn't worth a minute's heart-ache of a man like him. I used to think she had brains, if any of them did; I used to think that Barbara Allison was something besides a fluffy little fool! Why can't he see for himself that she's just as worthless as most of the rest of them?"

And from there, without knowing how truly funny such argument sounded, coming from his lips, he would soar to wonderful heights of profanity. But save for the pleasure which he took in the pyrotechnics, his outbursts made little impression upon Fat Joe. The latter maintained a sort of placid superiority, perhaps because he had learned early that this attitude aggravated Garry's rages; perhaps because he was so very certain of his man.

"I wouldn't go to getting all stirred up like this, so early in the game," he'd reply with unvaried calm. "Shucks, it's too early to begin counting either man's pile of chips—" either man to both minds meaning Steve and Wickersham, without the naming of names. "You are too liable to premature enthusiasms or discouragements, Garry. That's why I mostly manage to beat you as easy as he beats me, whenever we throw a hand or two. Ain't you never going to learn that a man must gamble a bit on the cards still waiting to be dealt?"

And again, confidently:

"He's worried—of course he is! He ain't enjoyin' his meditations a little bit these days, but he's enjoyin' 'em more all by himself than he would be if we were up there with him, forcin' him to look everlastingly like four aces, when it's deuces at present he's holding. He's worried, and that's why I don't grow nervous myself. Because it is only the man who is too sure who is awful likely to finish broke. Don't you waste any pity on him yet, and I wouldn't let him hear me passing uncomplimentary words concerning his girl, either, if I was you. Lightning ain't particular where it strikes when it's been a long time cooped up. Every man to his own taste in such matters, says I—and shucks, man, can't you tell, just from seein' 'em together that they was made for each other? If a man quit every time a woman began to put him over the jumps we'd have a dangerous decrease in marriage licences staring us in the face. He's just learning to care more for her, that's all, and caring a lot about anybody never was a comfortable state to be in. It's entirely too uncertain and unsettling—but you wouldn't enjoy not caring about anybody at all, yourself, would you?"

Garry admitted that he wouldn't.

"Well, then, don't waste your time pitying him." A cold gleam flickered in those bleached blue eyes. "Don't you suppose I'd have taken apart long ago this animated ice-chest who is making all the trouble, just to see what makes him so cold, if I didn't know I'd be spoiling the big show? Couldn't you see, without my tellin' you, that I'd rise up some day and leave him looking like a premature blast, after all I've learned he's plannin' to slip us, if I wasn't sure that he's going to get it, worse than I could ever give it to him, from that girl herself? Well, I would. He makes me shiver, that man; makes me crawl and itch to take his head in one hand and his throat in the other and exert a little strength in opposite directions. Give our entry time! The game is running dead against him at present, I'll admit, but he's husbanding his chips. He ain't drawing wild and squandering his chances. And he's only *begun* to play."

Which, in part, was very, very true; in part not so close to the facts. Before snow came that fall Steve had recovered his outward confidence, at least; he had begun to hope again, while he waited and labored prodigiously against the coming of spring. But in his heart he was no longer sure; he could not summon back that serene self-surety which, toward the end, had shaken even the girl's certainty in herself. He could no longer argue convincingly with a vision of her, as he had often argued with Barbara herself, that his way would be her way in the end. For he had begun to realize the width of that gulf which he knew must seem to exist between them, if not to her then to the eyes of others of her world.

It was his memories which gave him consolation those long nights, but they also gave him doubt. Remembering the daintiness of her as she had come to him, the night of her party, recalling the things to which she had been accustomed since she had opened her eyes on the first light of day, he began to ask himself as every man like him has asked who ever loved a woman, how in any fairness he could expect her to accept the little which he could offer in return. To Steve and Fat Joe, to the men of his gang, his confidence was that of the old, old Steve who, ten years before, had cocked his head at one of Allison's switch engines and promised gravely, "I'll hev to be gittin' one of them for myself, some-day." But his heart ached. And when that ache became so leaden that he couldn't endure it any longer in silence, he carried it to the one person in his life who was best calculated to understand. Diffidently he broached the subject with Miss Sarah, approaching it in a roundabout fashion least likely to deceive that bright-eyed little lady.

"Garry is saving his money against the fatal day," he laughed one night. "He has become a rank miser! Joe says he goes for days at a time, borrowing his tobacco, and he won't play anything but penny-ante now, when he can be coaxed to play at all!"

Miss Sarah was too kind to look at him directly that evening.

"The regeneration of Garry is one of the things which had made my life most happy," she answered. And then, paving the way for what she knew was on his mind. "I suppose you will be surprising us yourself, one of these days. And no doubt you'll be just as happily positive as Garry is, that your choice is the only one in the world."

They were alone in the big living-room. Caleb was still in town, gossiping with Hardwick Elliott. And Steve's bruised smile clutched at Miss Sarah's heart.

"I!" he overdid his amusement. "I have lived too much alone, I'm afraid, ever to prove very attractive to any woman's fancy. Bachelors are not always born; they are sometimes the habits of loneliness."

"Stuff and nonsense!" the good woman ridiculed him. "Why—why, if it weren't for a suspicion that you might have your eye on some small person or other, I'd drop everything and hunt one up for you, myself. Why, Stephen, what a remark for me to hear from you!"

Both were silent for a moment.

"Marriage is a mighty—expensive proposition," he commented at length, profoundly.

"Is Garry such a plutocrat any more?"

"That is not a fair illustration for us to employ," he countered, and Barbara Allison was not the only woman who loved his lazily final statements. "Both Garry and Miriam have been taught that there are worse things than the hardship of making last year's limousine do for another season."

Miss Sarah laughed at this drollery. She was a better antagonist than most. She had practiced on Caleb.

"Can't one girl learn what another has been taught?" she wanted to know. "Stephen, do you mean to sit there and infer that you could continue to *care* for a girl who could not care for you, just for yourself?"

His reply told her how tired he had become in trying to stem the tide of doubt alone. It warned her, too, that she had gone too close, for he veered off sharply. Steve persisted in generalities, but he wanted to talk.

"I have been wondering if that is not an old-fashioned attitude," he said. "Women, they tell, us, have broadened since they usurped many places in the business world once held by men. They are looking mighty keen-eyed toward the vote now, and a share in the legislation of their growing affairs, or at least so they explain. You have heard many men say 'business is business.' Maybe you have watched quite a few charming brides walk to the altar, and wondered if that wasn't their sentiment, too."

She chose to be suddenly vexed with him.

"I do not like such humor, and of course you are joking. I have heard Garrett Devereau talk in just such a strain too often to be amused by it. And if you mean—"

"If I meant it, I was crying the baby," stated the man coldly, and Miss Sarah knew that he was rebuking himself. "I could care for such a girl—yes. But I doubt if I would marry a woman who had even the smallest doubt. There are too many sharp places to be smoothed over, without chancing that tragedy of discontent. It's merely habit that's to blame again, that's all." He cast about for a parallel. "One does not miss sugar so very much from a meal, until he knows he can't have it. And then—well, Miss Sarah, I have many times talked peevishly, for a man, because there was none to be had."

"We are talking of women. What about salt?" she inquired quickly.

"That is very indispensable, too, but—"

"Of the two which do you always take care shall not be missing from your pack, whenever you turn into the woods?"

"I see where you are heading, but—"

"I do not like dissemblance, Stephen," she warned. "You know without the salt of love the sugar of life can grow sickeningly cloying."

He did not win his argument, but defeat gave him far more happiness than could have come from victory. Leaving her that night, he closed his hand over her delicate fingers in a clasp which left her smiling in wonder after he had gone. She watched horse and rider disappear into the whiteness of the new winter till both were lost to her sight.

"Bless the boy," she murmured then. "Bless the boy!" And to Caleb, her brother, when he came stamping in: "I surely must take a hand with these children. They have been left to their own devices long enough."

Caleb had recovered his good-natured view of the whole affair; he was given to grinning those days at her flutterings. On more than one occasion he told her, none too flatteringly, that she made him think of an officious hen with a brood which a high rate of mortality and prowling night-raiders had left bereft of all save two of her hatch. But this particular witticism did not bother her in the least, perhaps because she realized how pat the comparison was. Instead of silencing him she showed him the letter which she constructed some days later—constructed most painstakingly, the second week in December. She deigned to read it aloud to him, before she dispatched it on its journey.

> "Barbara, dear child," she wrote, "this is the appeal of a lonesome spinster lady who finds that winter, still only a lusty infant here, is the season for younger, warmer pulses. I am very tired of Caleb's continued company; that is, with nothing to leaven it. The keenest of epigrammarians, my dear, becomes very commonplace, you know, to ears too long tuned to one voice. So I am writing you in dignified desperation to come to me this holiday season—Caleb is not always as epigrammatic as I could wish.
>
> "I am going to be positive that you will come, unless you have already made other plans. And, on second thought,

> if you have already done so, I am going to fall back upon the privileged tyranny of one who once carried you in her arms. You must come to me this Christmas!"

There was another whole paragraph of rambling, repeated arguments, and then a full page devoted to the beauties of the hills and season.

> "The days are diamond brilliant," she wrote, "and the nights as drily cold and crisp as Caleb's few last cherished bottles of champagne. We have a foot of snow, two feet in the ell of the house where the mint-bed lies, and that has afforded Caleb much peace of mind, too. The roots will live nicely under their warm blanket, you see—all of which must read frivolously to you, coming from staid Miss Sarah. I can only plead that already I must be less lonely for anticipation of your arrival. Are you well? You will find new roses for your cheeks in this climate. And you may telegraph your acceptance, this once, if you are too busy to write, although you know I deplore the lack of those punctillios which once made of all custom and etiquette a most charming thing."

It was signed, "Yours, my dear, Sarah Hunter."

There was a quaint twist to the letter S; sharp angles in the chirography which a newer decade of femininity might have found sadly lacking in a largeness of loops now indispensable as indication of "character." And there was a postscript, of course.

> "Stephen O'Mara has been several times to dinner, since your departure. He is working very hard, but most successfully, I am sure, for he appears to be very happy. He is thinner than he was, but who could have guessed that the boy he was would grow to be such a handsome man! Men with eyes like his and such voices used to break the hearts of susceptible maids, when I was sixteen. Do come! S. H."

She read it aloud from beginning to end, nor did she falter much when Caleb greeted the postscript with a shout of joy. Caleb was most high-spirited those days, for the line in regard to the progress of Steve's work was in truth an under-statement if anything, even though the assurance of his happiness might have been called a misconstruance of facts. Caleb had almost begun to think that he had done Dexter Allison, his friend, an injustice. He had begun to congratulate himself on having said nothing to him directly.

"What do you think of it?" his sister asked pleasantly, when she had finished reading. "Will it—do?"

"If you mean—will it fetch her, I can only say Heaven knows!" Indeed he was enjoying himself. "You feel positive that she cares for him, you say?... But I thought you were always inclined to believe Steve rather easy to look at, even as a boy?"

"I was!" maintained Miss Sarah. Her voice grew girlish. "Do you remember the night you gave him my old hunting coat, Cal, and he went to sleep with it in his arms?"

Some of the teasing note left her brother's voice.

"Then why do you tell Barbara—why do you seem to infer—" he foundered hopelessly.

"Stupid!" said Miss Sarah. "Will she come?"

"She won't!" he stated solidly.

When he spoke in that tone Miss Sarah always chose to believe the contrary, and events in this instance proved her right. Barbara did not wire. She wrote a long letter full of little twists and turns which led at last to the subject which Miss Sarah had mentioned so parenthetically.

> "I am delighted at the prospect of getting away from town for a week," she closed as she had opened her reply—"delighted at Mr. O'Mara's splendid success. Last night I overheard father telling some business associates that he would one day be the biggest power in the north country, unless something happened to check him soon. That was very flattering, wasn't it? It will make you very proud, I know. Tell Mr. O'Mara I wished to be recalled to him. As I have already warned you in this letter, father insists on coming with me. I think he must be a little tired of the city himself, for he is very restless. And remind Uncle Cal that I am to have the wish-bone, or I will not come at all!"

This reply Miss Sarah also read aloud to her brother, in a voice that was not quite Christian, however, for it was gloating in tone.

"There!" she breathed, "and, Cal, aren't you ashamed sometimes to have your judgment so often refuted by a mere woman?"

Caleb had been reading in the Morrison Standard that the East Coast Company had made unbelievable strides in its work, in spite of many conspiring hard-luck circumstances; he was frowning over that oddly veiled compliment of Allison's, which his daughter had so innocently repeated, but he was glad to hear that Dexter, too, planned to run up for the year-end. He was a bit bored himself. Now he grinned over another thought.

"She fails to mention whether she ever noticed the color of his eyes," he choked a little, "or—or the heart-breaking quality of his voice! Maybe she hasn't noticed 'em yet herself, eh?"

Miss Sarah scorned to answer. She went upstairs to her desk and she wrote two letters that night, before she retired. One went back to Barbara. The other had not so far to travel, but it was longer in reaching its destination.

CHAPTER XX
BLUE FLANNEL AND CORDUROY

The world was snow-bound—all that small world which lay between the hills in the valley at Thirty-Mile. For two days it had been snowing, great flakes so plume-like that they seemed almost artificial, making one think of the blizzards which originate high in theatre-flies under the sovereignty of a stage-hand who sweats at his task of controlling the elements. For two days it snowed so heavily that all work moved but intermittently at the up-river camp; and then, two days before Christmas, the mercury dropped sharply into the bulbs and the weather cleared.

Stephen O'Mara, standing at a window of his cabin late in the afternoon, peering out upon that cold white world, was wondering if she would have found it as wonderful as it seemed to him at that moment; he was wondering whether he would have to break a fresh trail himself, upon snow-shoes, if he were to join Fat Joe and Garry in town for the holiday, when a team of horses came toiling into view far across the snow. It was Big Louie, sitting huge and stolid upon his load of supplies, coming in a whole day late and cracking his long lash over the glossy backs of the bays which the lash was never allowed to touch. Behind him another sledge appeared in turn, with two figures on the seat, but even at that distance they looked neither so huge nor so stolidly reconciled to the bite of the wind. Fallon was driving; Shayne was beating his arms across his chest. And the second team was fagged and caked with frozen lather. Big Louie had been breaking trail for twelve bitterly hard hours, but his animals were still far from spent—not so tired in fact but what they could throw forward their heads and nicker at the sight of warm stables. Big Louie loved horses as he loved nothing else in his whole dull world. Sober he fed them bits of sugar, with strange throat-sounds which they must have understood, it seemed; drunk he threatened the life of any man who might chance to maltreat them. That was the reason Steve had made Big Louie his head-teamster only two weeks before.

From his window he watched the heavy loads crawl up to the store-house door; he watched the drivers throw tarpaulins over the boxes and knew that they were too weary to unload that night. And he was still there at the frosted pane when the three men, Big Louie still plowing ahead, hove into view again from the direction of the stables and came straight toward his own shack. He opened the door and bade them enter before they had had a chance to knock. The swagger in the shoulders of two of them told him what to expect. Big Louie was only clumsy, as usual.

"You did well to make it," he told the latter, kindly, as he always addressed him. His nod to the others, who reeked of white whiskey, was in part a question, in no wise a welcome. "Well?" he asked.

Apparently there had been a conference beforehand, for there was no hesitancy on the part of Fallon, who had been ordained spokesman.

"We've come for our time," he growled.

Steve nodded gravely.

"I see," he murmured. "May I ask what's your grievance, this time."

They were the satellites of Harrigan. Because of that he had kept them all where his eyes could find them at times. And even though their arch-leader in discontent had not crossed his path in many days he listened now to an echo of Harrigan's activities.

"They're offering three a day in the Reserve camps." Fallon should not have gloated. "Three a day and a bonus for the high week cut. We're going back to the river."

"I see," again observed Steve. "Are they guaranteeing this wage for as long as you want to work."

Apparently they had decided, too, that there should be no bargaining.

"We want our time," Fallon reiterated. "This is going to be a man's year on the river!"

"You, also?" Steve inquired of Shayne.

That worthy gloated too.

"Yes, me also," he came back, "an' a hundred others, before the ice goes out."

Big Louie he had given up for lost long before that, and yet it was with Big Louie that Steve made a sincere effort.

"I'd like to have you stay, Louie," he faced the third man. "I need you, for you can do more with horses than any man I know. You are worth three a day to me. Do you care to think it over?"

Big Louie's eyes had been mournful when he stumbled in out of the cold. They were that now. He started to turn toward the window for a look at the stables, and then thought better of it. Resolutely, for him, he shook his head.

"I am done—me," he muttered. "I work for no company that will leave honest men to starve."

It was hopeless from the start, yet Steve tried again.

"I can promise you work as long as you are able to hold a rein," he offered, but he moved nearer the door while he was speaking. "That is all I can promise."

Perhaps Fallon believed that Big Louie was weakening; perhaps he felt that the situation was too highly dramatic to be wasted, for he made a wide flourish with one hand.

"We want our time, and we want it now," he threatened. "We're going to show you who bosses this river, before we're done with you!"

Fallon shouldn't have gloated; he shouldn't have threatened. And Shayne shouldn't have smiled. Steve had slipped the latch loose. Now he swung open the door.

"Call for your time at the Morrison office," he said evenly, "and if you're going—why, go!"

By collar and belt he swung him back and drove him sprawling into a drift.

"Are you in a hurry, too, Shayne?" he asked pleasantly, and Shayne buried his head beside Fallon's in the snow. Then Steve closed the door carefully and turned again to Big Louie.

"Louie," he said, "I make it a rule to urge no man who does not wish to stay. If it needs persuasion to keep you, I do not want you here. But you are running with the wrong crowd, Louie; you'll learn it someday—but someday may be too late."

The big, dreamy-eyed man was hardly listening, but he gestured toward the door. And Steve treated his departure kindly, as he had always treated his presence. Outside where Shayne and Fallon had picked themselves up, Big Louie hesitated and fumbled in his pocket with a cold-cramped hand. He delivered the letter which had been entrusted to him, before he went down the hill. There are many men like Big Louie who are pitifully faithful until events outstrip their intellects. Steve was sorry for him; and a half hour later, after he had read Miss Sarah's prim note requesting his presence at dinner at seven-thirty, Christmas eve, he grew sorrier still while he watched the ill-assorted trio meet once more, blanket-packs upon their backs and snow-shoes on their feet. Big Louie had joined the other two from the direction of the stables. There were words between them, for Steve saw the huge man's arm lift to strike Shayne to the ground, and then drop harmlessly back to his side. And Steve knew what that bit of pantomime meant. Big Louie had been to bid his team good-bye. There was a smudge of brown sugar across his coat, though the watcher was too far away to see that. But he knew that Big Louie had been crying, knew that Shayne had smiled. It was the second time that Shayne had smiled that evening—his second bad mistake. Long after they had disappeared into the north toward the Reserve Company's camps, Steve wondered that it had not cost him his life.

Miss Sarah's note which had been almost a week on the way was very primly correct, but the inevitable postscript which under-ran it sounded a more intimate note.

"We are not excessively formal as a rule, Stephen," she wrote, "so a dinner jacket will be adequate. As I am expecting two other guests besides your friends, Mr. Morgan and Garrett Devereau, I must ask you to let no business matters interfere with your promptness."

Steve dared not let himself wonder who those other guests would prove to be, Miriam Burrell, he knew, had already written Garry that this was to be the saddest Christmas, and the merriest, that she had ever known, giving as respective reasons her inability to be with him, and the fact that she was so entirely his. Because he would not let himself hope this time he was not disappointed, or at least so he told himself, when he found only Dexter Allison with Caleb, the next afternoon near six. And on a sudden thought his eyes went roving around the room then, looking for Archibald Wickersham; but Miss Sarah gave him no time for a protracted scrutiny.

"Your room is ready, Stephen," she told him, and steered him toward the stairs. "You have an hour in which to dress—and you know already that I am old-maidenishly strict."

Surely Archibald Wickersham was the other guest whom they were expecting. Allison's very presence argued that. Yet Steve's nose played him a startling trick as he mounted upward. He could have sworn that he smelled that faint perfume which always made him remember, now, his first letter from her; had he not been afraid to hope he would have been positive that there was a flurry of skirts retreating above him. But he knew that she could not have come. He knew it! And then, three-quarters of an hour later, when he had dressed and turned again to the stairway, she was there at the foot of the flight, waiting for him to appear. In a little low pink satin gown that made rounded her slenderness—made her appear even smaller than she was—she gave him an elaborate courtesy from the main floor, and flung up at him her laughter.

"Merry Christmas, Sir Galahad," she called.

Just as he had paused there a half-score of years before, Stephen O'Mara paused now, with Caleb and Miss Sarah again gazing up at him. It was the first time Sarah Hunter had seen the grown-up Steve in conventional black and white; her emotions were much the same as they had been on that remoter day. But Steve did not even see her glowing face below him in that instant, nor Caleb's, nor that of Allison either, who watching Steve's eyes, had suddenly ceased to smile. Caleb knew what his sister's thoughts were, however, for he was recalling that black velvet suit with silver buttons himself. While Steve and Barbara were shaking hands he gained her ear in whispered admiration.

"Sarah," he commented, "Sarah, you are clever!"

Miss Sarah was on the point of taking Dexter Allison's arm to lead the way to table. Her reply was tuned to Caleb's ear alone.

"She had thought of him in terms of blue flannel and corduroy long enough," she said. "If you please, Dexter—Stephen, do you and Barbara want any dinner?"

Those two were still shaking hands. Steve, who was only dimly aware of the fact that Garry and Fat Joe had arrived, the latter guilty of his first dinner jacket and enormously proud of his guilt, stood looking at Barbara while she was chattering at him, without hearing distinctly a word she spoke. Miss Sarah's question helped to bring him back.

"You look as though I were a wraith," the girl accused him. "Am I so pale after a few weeks of sophisticated city air?"

But her man had taken command of himself again, by then.

"I thought you looked like—shall I tell you what I thought?"

"Most certainly," she was forced to insist. "Wasn't it a bald enough invitation for a pretty speech?"

"I thought you looked like a small pink bon-bon," responded Steve leisurely, and while the rest laughed at her discomfiture, Fat Joe leaned over and nudged Garry.

"What'd I tell you?" he demanded. "What'd I tell you? Say, ain't he working well to-night?"

But for once Joe had himself been misled into premature enthusiasm such as he had decried in Garry. For if Barbara had, in Miss Sarah's phrase, been thinking of Steve in terms of blue flannels and corduroy, until then, before the dinner ended she was aware of a difference in the attitude of this man who loved her, too great to be explained by the clothes he wore. The very light in his eyes, whenever she contrived to catch him gazing at her, convinced her of what was behind his new restraint; and then, immediately, perversely, she set herself to break it down by those very methods best calculated to strengthen it. More than once that evening Dexter Allison withdrew from the general conversation to watch the play of his daughter's glances upon O'Mara's tanned face; several times he fell to chewing his lip as was his custom when deeply perplexed. Complications scarcely ever troubled Dexter Allison. He was beginning to awake to one now which already worried him more than he cared to admit.

There was no keeping the girl within doors after dinner was over. She ran upstairs and changed into moccasins and white blanket coat, and skirt that barely met the moccasin tops half-way. And Steve, who had changed too and was waiting for her when she came down, had knotted a crimson scarf about the middle of his belted jacket to match the white one twisted about her throat. With much approval Miss Sarah noted, while she watched them away on snow shoes, the bit of color it added to his soberer garb; she promised herself to recall it to Caleb at some future date. Caleb had very pronounced views regarding the lack of vanity in men's dress. But for the time being she was content to go upstairs and be alone with her campaigning.

The man and girl climbed far that night in quite unbroken silence. They had reached the crest of the first hill and stopped with the higher ridges in front of them, black bulks filigreed with white, before Barbara decided that she would have to make him talk.

"Aren't you going to say anything at all?" she challenged then.

She needed no explanation of his mood. To a woman there is no subtler flattery than a man's dumb acknowledgement of her unattainability. He talked when she bade him talk, but she was not positive whether she was vexed or not because their conversation was of common-place things: The work he was doing, upon which he was aggravatingly reticent, or the severity of the last storm, or the amazing clarity of the night. Certainty, however, was hers that he was no longer sure of himself—that he was fighting silently against a growing conviction that she was beyond his reach.

It made her very happily sad, somehow, and when Steve told her about Big Louie and his horses, the sadness became a lump in her throat, and a blur in her eyes which the man could not help but see.

"It is too bad," he said slowly. "I have been sorrier for him myself, since his going, than I've been over anything for years. I do not know just why, but I'm afraid for him. The others—" He stopped there, catching himself before he had said too much. "I could always tell Big Louie how I wanted a thing done, and know without one little bit of doubt that he would stick to my orders. But that is the trouble with his kind. Because he has no initiative of his own, he has to depend upon the ideas which other men supply him. And there is no guarantee whether they will be good or bad ideas."

From the first he talked fitfully that night. On other occasions she had noticed how his mind seemed to veer, whimsically, from one topic to another with little apparent continuity of thought, only to swing back again, just when she was beginning to feel that she had lost the thread of inference, to point his argument with parallels that were new and delightful wisdoms to her ears. But to-night his grave-voiced divergences, oftener than not, left her thoughts behind his thoughts.

"It is a very easy country to get lost in," he next remarked, when he had had to insist that his sense of direction, and not hers, should be the one to be trusted. "He was never able to go fifty rods into the brush himself, without getting completely turned around, and he was born in these hills, at that."

Then he had to tell her that it was Big Louie to whom he was referring, before she understood quite what he meant. But he abandoned that trend, freakishly, the very next moment.

"It doesn't seem complicated," he pondered. "To a man who has come into the world with his sense of north and south and east and west all safely relegated to his backbone instead of having to depend upon the flighty functions of his brain for his guide, it's about the simplest thing there is. He finds his way without thinking about the lay of the land, or moss on the trees, or the sun or stars. But the other one—the one who has to stop and reason that he must travel so many miles to the west to reach home in the afternoon, because he came that many in the morning—why, he even gets to doubting his compass, until night catches him without a roof over his head and no wood collected for a camp-fire."

Long before then she had learned how sensitive a thing was his spirit—and she wanted him to go on.

"It must be a terrible thing to—to know that one is lost." Her hands were buried deep in her pockets; she found it hard to keep pace with his stride. "I am always afraid of the night noises in the woods."

It was the girl in her which had spoken at which he smiled, but his smile was absent-minded.

"That is very strange, too," he accepted her lead, after contemplating it for a time. "It is always the one who can't trust his compass who loses his head, once he knows he's mixed up. Big Louie was that way. He was lost once, for two days, before we found him; he was half mad with terror and pretty near dead with fatigue. He had been running in a big circle for hours, and we had to corner him before he would see that we were friends. He'd been listening to the night noises, you see; dwelling on the blackness and the silence and his lack of a fire, until his brain was no longer any use to him."

"What should one do?" she asked him faintly, when she knew that he was waiting for her to speak. Yet his answer persisted in adding to that word-image which his mind was molding.

"Quit letting yourself look back over your shoulder, to see if anything is following you!" He was suddenly gruff, and she knew that he was talking at himself. "Quit dwelling on the crackle in the brush, and the darkness, and the things you are afraid to fear. The wise man stops when he knows he's lost his bearings; he busies himself collecting wood for a fire, if not to keep the chill from his body by exercise, then because it keeps his mind off himself. And he sleeps if he can. Anyhow he lies quiet and rests. And when morning comes he uses his reason better for having rested, if his instincts still play him false. He has a look at the stars before daybreak; he watches the sun come up, and he holds a straight line by the height of land, or by the river flow, and he hits familiar country soon."

This time the girl did not interrupt him. She was watching his face.

"And that doesn't apply just to one little corner of the woods, or one little corner of life, either, does it?" he mused. "When a man's instinct fails him, he can stop and get his bearings back; when he's afraid he can kindle a fire within him, always, if he'll only rustle around before it gets too dark to search for fuel. But at that it isn't so very easy, in life, to get one's bearings straight again. It's stormy, some nights, maybe, and the stars don't shine; sometimes day dawns cloudy and the sun is not advertising its location too strongly. Instinct has always been strong in me, but there have been times, too, when I have had to hold my eyes mighty steady on some object far beyond me, to keep my line dead straight." He stopped short and faced her. "You would be afraid, yes," he told her, "but you would try hard to discipline yourself. You would never go rushing blindly into a worse tangle, spending your strength and breaking your sanity down. Big Louie is a child; discipline is wasted on him. And—and I have always been able to find my way myself."

She knew now toward what point he had been talking. Mentally he had been wandering, as Big Louie once wandered in the flesh, in a wide circle that fetched up again against that doubt in himself which was hurting her, even while it was making her happy. He had taken the example of Big Louie and applied it to his own life, and suddenly the girl realized how infinitely greater was his philosophy thereof than was hers.

"I shall try to remember that," she answered soberly. "If ever I am lost I—I shall try to wait confidently for daylight, and keep my eyes to the fore."

She was near to tears when he stooped and knelt in the snow to tighten a thong slipping from one webbed foot. Below them stretched a plain of shimmering frost-points, bounded by inscrutable walls of black timber. Somewhere within the warmer heart of a swamp a fox yapped hungrily; somewhere within her own heart his whimsical discourse had awakened a sense of the mystery of his wilderness—its friendship for those who love it—its implacable enmity for those who do not understand. And he looked up just when that emotion came flooding into her face.

"It is wonderful—wonderful—wonderful!" she breathed, throwing out both arms with that ecstatic impulsiveness which he knew so well. "Now I know why you said men always return to it, once they have felt its spell."

"You are lovelier than you know!" came back from him, almost gruffly again; and she could not parry with lightness so swift and strained a speech.

"You always tell me very pretty things," was all she could think of to say in reply.

But then, rising, he flung back his head and shook himself as if throwing off a burden too restraining and irksome. He laughed aloud, and from that minute until he loosed her feet from the snowshoes he was more like her "blue flannel and corduroy" lover again. But his attack no longer made her fear herself.

"If I cared for you, yes," he made her admit before he would let her go in that night. "If I cared for you, my engagement to no man could stand in the way. But that is the reason I know I do not care."

She had seen him grave with doubt that night; seen him fight to shake it off. There was doubt in his answer now.

"Because I am not—" But he could not force himself to ask it.

"Because I could never care as you would demand the woman should care who marries you."

She wanted to help him a little, she didn't know just why. Pity is a very dangerous emotion, when pity is not sought.

"You are loving me that way this minute," he said, but his words were dogged. "Loving me more than you know."

There was neither reference to her letter nor mention of that night at Thirty-Mile when she had stolen out to bid him good-bye. Other long tramps followed, on other pale and zero nights, but his attitude remained much the same. Whimsically at times he shared his innermost thoughts with her; always he told her that he cared, with a gentleness in the telling that made it hard for her to listen. Barbara least of all realized what those days were doing to her, but before that week had run its course even Caleb's eyes were opened to the change in Steve.

"I told you so," he said, but he took no delight in recommending it to his sister's attention. "If he didn't know it before, she's taught him this trip that he hasn't a chance."

"Your sensation is ancient history, Cal," was all she would reply.

And even though, so far as Steve's peace of mind was concerned, Miss Sarah's scheming had not helped at all, that tiny lady still chose to view her activities complacently the day Barbara took leave of her again.

"Write me every detail of your plans," Miss Sarah ordered her. "Proxy bridal preparations are better than none, my dear, and I am madly interested."

At the last minute Barbara bobbed her dark head in reply.

"I will," she promised meekly. And then, wide eyes vague with fear: "Aunt Sarah, I—I'm not sure that I want to be—married at all!"

"You will be coming back," he told her again the day he put her on the train. "You will be back in the spring?"

It was his old, hopeful challenge, with all the hope left out.

"I think so," she faltered in return. "I mean to come and see the completion of your work, if father will let me." She knew a moment of confusion. "I wonder, many nights, if you are safe, up here in the hills."

Indeed, Miss Sarah had made progress, though the surface indications were small. The girl would never think of him again simply in terms of blue flannel and corduroy. But that was not the most disturbingly vivid memory which she carried away with her.

"I love you," he framed the words silently as the train was pulling out, and although their positions were reversed, the moment was so reminiscent of that day when he had leaned out of her father's switch engine cab and asked if she wanted a ride, that it made her throat ache.

She waved a small gloved hand to him on the platform.

She did not want to go.

CHAPTER XXI
SETTING THE STAGE

There are two interviews which should be mentioned here, if for no other reason then merely because they were both so entirely the outcome of Miss Sarah's Christmas party. Neither of them were long; the last one which took place between Wickersham and the girl he was to marry was the briefer of the two. But her prettily serious argument that the first of May was too early a date for their wedding, in view of the work which he had to do and her own state of unpreparedness, left him so white of face that she felt guiltily sorry for him for many days to follow—felt guiltier still at the relief she experienced when she had established that reprieve. The other interview was longer, and took place days earlier, but it was no more of a delight to Archibald Wickersham.

Dexter Allison had returned home almost a week in advance of his daughter, pleading stress of business, but in spite of the demands upon his time and attention, he had found it impossible to forget the night of the dinner, when he had watched his daughter's eyes upon Stephen O'Mara's face.

Allison had never professed a knowledge of women. Like her mother, Barbara had been many, many times an enigma which he who had often taken men's souls apart had not dared even to try to solve. Partly because of that, partly because his observation in other quarters had taught him the dangerous futility of it, he had lifted his voice neither in encouragement nor protest of Archibald Wickersham. The two had grown up from childhood together—Barbara and the man whom she was engaged to marry—and more than once her father had assured himself that at least there was a long knowledge of each other's shortcomings to make for safety in the long run.

His own dislike for Wickersham he had never allowed to sway his middle course of non-interference. And he had never liked the boy; never learned to like the man he had grown to be. Underneath Dexter Allison's jovial exterior there was a cynicism which for hardness would have made Garry Devereau's worst moments seem mere childish fits of spleen. Men do not watch other men whimper and beg for mercy—little rascals who have been nipped in a greater schemer's trap—without beginning to wonder, soon or late, how much of man is warped and twisted; and he had been watching Archie Wickersham now for months. He believed that men's men were not women's men, the oft-repeated epigram to the contrary. He had eaten too many dinners at which the lion of the evening who sat on the charming hostess's right hand, was a man of rank and a thing of ranker repute. But after his first shock at the realization that his baby was a woman grown, he had promised himself that her engagement and Wickersham's should be a long one; promised that the man into whose keeping she was given should have earned the title in full.

Wickersham's code, in many respects, was above reproach. Allison had taken pains to ascertain that. But beyond that he did not let himself go; he neither allowed himself to wonder at, nor regret, her choice. He was too honest to decry in another much which he knew would not measure up to Golden Rule standards in himself. And he had a really great man's unshakable faith in his own flesh and blood.

Yet he had been troubled more than a little since his Christmas trip to Morrison. When he turned a page he turned it for all time, but in the last day or two he had caught himself surrepticiously trying to steal a glance at some which had only just rustled into place. Dexter Allison had left brilliant men of cross-examination panting impotently at the barrenness of their efforts; he had known it and enjoyed it to the full. But he knew, too, that he could never face, jauntily or otherwise, one reproach in the dusky eyes of the girl with whom he had more than once played truant, to breakfast with Caleb and Miss Sarah. And he was facing that thought, nearer to panic than he had ever been before, the night before New Year's, when Wickersham was announced at nine. He was thinking of Barbara's mother when he beckoned his guest to a chair, shook his head over his red cheeks, and offered a cigar.

"Devilish cold weather," he grunted, none too graciously, for he had not wanted to be disturbed just then.

The younger man admitted that it was. His mind, plainly, was not upon the weather, but he found difficulty in introducing a topic of his own choosing. Outspokenness had never been one of Archie Wickersham's boldest characteristics, so Allison assisted him now. Allison liked a man to be outspoken.

"Well," he demanded, "let's hear it. What's on your mind?"

There are times when hatred will betray 'most any man. Hatred now led Wickersham to speak not wisely but with venom.

"I want you to refuse to renew your name on the East Coast notes," he said. "They are due on the second."

Few men had ever said "I want you to" to Dexter Allison and, as he put it, "gotten away with it to any great extent." And of all nights this one in particular was the least likely to prove propitious for such an attempt. That was Wickersham's oversight.

"So!" said Dexter, "so! Well, now for your reason."

Wickersham had not learned until after Barbara's departure that she was spending the holidays in Morrison, for he had himself expected to be away. And it is only fair to the girl to say that she had honestly forgotten to apprise him of her plan, in her real excitement at going. But finding it out for himself had not made the fact any pleasanter to Wickersham.

"It should be clear enough without explanation," he enunciated each word nicely, "if you want that road they are building."

Allison glanced up, surprised at the tone employed.

"Meaning of course I do," he mused. "And yet—and yet, I don't know!"

Fear burned in the tall, thin man's eyes that night—fear that made his hatred for the absent man who was teaching him fear anything but a pretty thing to watch.

"I've tried to buy off their men." He was holding himself with an effort that made him tremble. "I've held up their supplies on every track that we control, but they've had the luck with them. They've made up lost time by working day and night. I've—"

"You've set a drunken fool to steal his plans," drawled the other with deadly sarcasm, "like a second-rate, one-night-stand villain. Don't forget to mention that, too!"

In many ways it resembled an earlier conference which they had shared together; in many points it differed from it. For if Allison had goaded the other man, on that former occasion, largely from a malicious delight in stirring him to verbal violence, such a thought was farthest from his mind now. Allison was talking from a new angle. If a turned page was a turned page to him, at least his memory was good. His lounging body shifted a little.

"Archie, do you remember what I told you about that woods-rat, as you called him once? Did I tell you that he would fight? Well, listen and listen closely while I repeat it for you. He hasn't even warmed to it yet!"

Wickersham went yellow at that, but his icy self-control held firm. He did not break into vituperation this night; he smiled, though his voice was only a whisper.

"Men have dropped out of sight before now, in those woods," he husked. "I'll win, or I'll see that he lies and rots in one of his own sink-holes."

A big voice is a wonderful weapon at times. Allison's booming bass made Wickersham's threat seem only mean and hollow when the heavy man leaped to his feet and shook a finger under that high-bridged nose.

"No you won't!" he snapped. "No you won't! And if I didn't know, after hearing you talk, that you haven't stuff enough in you to be dangerous, I'd fix you so you'd be in no condition to bushwhack anybody for the next six months. I'm in a bad mood to-night. Drop out of sight, eh? You'll play this fair—fair at least as I see it by my standards, and they are better standards than yours. You've come dictating to me, ordering me to slip a knife into their backs. Are you that kind of a sneak? Did you think I was? Now listen again, and listen well, for I mean what I say!

"I want that railroad, if the man who is building it is too weak to keep me from taking it away from him. But if I don't get it on such a basis, I'll know that there is a man at the head of it who is big enough to take care of my share of it. Have you got that? Very well. And now go back to your melodrama, if you want to. Steal his men, if he will let you; fight him every inch of his construction—that is your job—and I'll still insist that it is his fault if he is tardy on the first of May. But it's you and O'Mara from now on, Archie. I'll be a spectator now! And, by Gad, don't you ever come near me again with a request that I ... don't you ever let me hear you threaten that you—"

Allison's face was suffused before he finished, and Wickersham, astounded past utterance, slid from his chair away from that flourishing hand which had become a fist. It was no scene to take place between a man and his prospective son-in-law. Realizing that Allison tried to laugh, deprecatingly, at his temper.

"Go out and get him, Archie," he invited. "I'll be watching, don't doubt that. And I know how much you want to win. It's a bigger stake than most folks realize!"

Like Barbara he tried to make his side of the interview kindly at the end, but he sent the other man away wondering whether he had understood that last remark, and afraid to think that he had. And two other things Allison had done. For once he had started to pay hush money to his conscience. Once and for all, like Fat Joe, he had registered at last a refusal to interfere in any way that might spoil the climax of the "big show" for which Fate or Chance or Destiny, or whatever men may call it, was setting the stage, with an unhurried calm that contrasted, ironically, with the mad haste of her actors.

But he watched, as he had promised he would. The same day that more than half of O'Mara's men went on strike and deserted to the Reserve Company's payroll, the news reached him that a trainload of laborers had been shot in to take their places—those very types of laborers which Steve himself had warned Elliott would not last an hour, in the event of trouble. For a week Allison wondered that there was no clash between the displaced men who believed that the river was theirs alone and this new corps which Garry Devereau was handling at the lower end of construction, not by physical prowress, as Fat Joe had ruled, but just as surely and all because, as Joe himself put it, he could damn a man merely by bidding him good-morning.

"Honey crossed north to-day to have a look at his winter cut," Joe would observe to his chief at supper at Thirty-Mile; and before the night was many hours older Allison too, in Manhattan, would have learned by wire in less picturesque phraseology, that Archie Wickersham was missing no chances.

"They have now finished hauling their logs to the river," Joe told Steve one night after a prolonged scouting trip. "They are turning their attention to their float dams, now!"

And when that news was relayed to the big man who never ceased to watch he understood why there had been no violence when the rivermen went on strike.

With a clumsiness that shamed him Allison contrived to pass on to his daughter all such bits of gossip which dribbled down to him; that is, all which appertained strictly to Stephen O'Mara's race against time, and not to the opposition which he was meeting. Her excitement was a bubbling thing, innocent of suspicion or premonition, but he was like a war-worn veteran who stands watching column after column wheel into position, waiting the word to go in, and knows he cannot respond.

Many times Barbara tried to write to Steve in those days and each time destroyed the badly scored sheet, either in dismay at the wilful intimacy of her pen or disgusted with its stilted aloofness. She saw less and less of Wickersham that winter, partly because his affairs were monopolizing all his time, partly because she managed to spend most of her waking hours with Miriam Burrell or her father, who appeared doubly, humbly glad of her companionship. Always she insisted that Stephen O'Mara would win through; she made happy, petty wagers with both of them, in anticipation of their journey north, against the first of May. But there was one bit of news which her father had not been able to pass on to her. For Dexter Allison had had no way of learning of a night when the man who was most in their thoughts had finally lifted a bleak face from his arms, in his cabin up-river, and forced himself, hard-eyed, to acknowledge one defeat.

It was the bitterest January that the hill country had known in twenty years; but mile by mile that month the twin lines of steel crept steadily into the north under the urgings of Garry's smooth voice. The snowfall for

February broke all records for half that period; but Steve, with his handful of men at Thirty-Mile, put his piling down. And then it rained—it rained until small brooks ran torrents and the river tumbled white and thunderous its entire length.

The snow went off the last of March that spring and the gorges could not carry away the water. The sun turned summer hot; it burned the higher ridges dry while the valleys still lay hidden in flood. It was August temperature, the third Sunday in April, when Stephen O'Mara stood and watched, beneath the glare of kerosene torches, his bridge at Thirty-Mile go into position between dark and dawn.

There was no man among them that day who did not show upon his face the strain they had been under. They were few, they were unshaven and dirty and lean as hungry hounds; but they were the men whom Steve had once bidden Hardwick Elliott to watch, once they had begun to scent combat. Fat Joe was no longer plump. Steve was worn down to actual thinness. And it would have taken a careful eye to have selected the chief from their ranks that Sunday.

The huge timbers had dropped into place like bits of jig-sawed puzzle. At three in the afternoon, too tired both in body and soul for elation, Steve watched them drive home the last spike and heard their hoarse effort at a cheer. He had turned to start toward his shack, not like a man who knows that the end of a well-nigh hopeless task is in sight, but like a beaten man. The first of May meant more to Steve than any clause of the East Coast Company's contract could convey. He had not had even one letter since he put her upon her train. Wickersham's appearance on horseback, at the head of the valley, picking his way around the flooded meadow, halted him in his heavy-footed climb. A whistle shrilled, far to the south of them, down the completed track. And then, after ten years and more, they were face to face again.

"That bridge will have to go down!" Wickersham was breathing hard, for all that he had been riding. "I'm going through with my drive to-day!"

He had dismounted. Steve smiled at him.

"You're a whole week previous, Wickersham," he said, wearily. "I'll be signaling for your first load of logs in less than sixty hours."

Archibald Wickersham wished that he could have believed it impossible, for it would have given him courage and lent conviction to his stand. But he knew just how fast those few remaining miles of open roadbed would be spanned. His eyes were furtive; there was no body to his voice.

"My men are on the banks," he blustered. "My first head of logs has started down. It's too late to argue now—too late for your promises that none but fools ever believed!" The sure irrevocability of what he was saying blanched his cheeks. "I cannot wait for a miracle to be performed. My timber must come out on this flood."

Stephen O'Mara had whipped him once, but men had interfered. This day Chance or Destiny or Fate—whatever you may choose to call it—saved him from destruction. The lean and weary man who had not been out of his clothes for three days and three nights, save for a plunge in the icy river, had taken his first step forward, when the whistle screamed a nearer warning.

She had told him that she would come to see the finish of his race, but he had long since stopped believing that. And now when she stood and waved her hand at him from the brass-railed observation platform of Allison's private car which a switch engine, out of patience with the grade, was shunting across the lower end of the clearing, he could only stand and stare dully, no faith in his eyes.

The loud plaid of her father's garb flashed behind her in the doorway. Hardwick Elliott's fine face peered over his shoulder. And Wickersham, who had not seen his fiance in a month, had started toward them, stiffly erect in his immaculate whipcord habit. Wickersham was smiling; Wickersham was safe again. For Fate or Chance or Destiny who had been setting the stage was bringing on her principals. She would brook no *ad lib* now.

A low mutter in the north became an ominous murmur while Steve was following slowly in Wickersham's steps, and he realized what it meant. He stopped to stare at his handful of men, rearing their heads to listen, too. Steve had been all winter alone with the puzzle of his own inferiority which he could never understand. And a minute later, when he had reached out to help to the ground a little blue clad figure with fur at throat and wrists, she drew the be-furred edge of her skirt about her ankles and laughingly refused his assistance, and jumped to the ground unaided. She was far too excited to know what she was doing; she hardly saw him at all in that first moment, but the act spelled much to him. His hands were grimy, his face stubbly and streaked with sweat and mud, and he had been months alone with his too-sensitive spirit.

"You should not be here," was all he said to her. "This is no place for you."

He shook hands with the men, mechanically—Allison quizzical, Elliott concerned. He went back to his bridge. The water had come up a half foot in the last few minutes some one—Fat Joe, perhaps—told him; it was sucking greedily at the piles. And in the north the ominous murmur had become a rhythmic roar.

Wickersham's men were driving the river. They were singing "Harrigan, That's Me!"

CHAPTER XXII
IT HAPPENS IN BOOKS

It is said that men remember many things when death is imminent; and for days and days something had been dying hard in Stephen O'Mara's breast. His step was slow that afternoon when he drew apart to take up his position alone upon a bit of higher ground, his shoulders heavy and drooping; yet his brain was feverishly active. Recollection of many long gone days—thoughts of many things—came darting to his mind; but they were not thoughts of desperate, last-minute expedients which might stave off this present crisis. For if he had believed that force alone would win for him; if he had had faith that mere numbers could save his construction, he would not have left Garry Devereau with his scores of laborers, busy five miles to the south. Steve was not thinking of his construction now; it had become a dim and remote consideration. It had lost its importance in his scheme of things.

They came slowly at first—Wickersham's logs—thudding heavily, one by one, into the underpinnings of the bridge, sliding free or lodging cross-current as the case might be; then in a thicker and thicker tide that ground and up-ended and settled with the weight of the coffee-colored flood behind it. In the beginning the handful of men who had put those timbers into place set themselves, doggedly, to save their completed structure, until the man who had worked with them, shoulder to shoulder, through the night called them with a nod back to the bank. Obediently then they collected in a small knot behind him, murmurous, gutterally grumbling; waiting his further word they squatted on their haunches, staring hungrily at their chief who stood in seeming surrender, head bowed before them.

The coming of Wickersham's men was not a thing of degrees. They poured into view through the brush fringe at the north edge of the marsh and halted, but only for an instant.

"Who is your friend at the time when you need a friend?—Harrigan, that's me!"

The maudlin menace of that chorus rocketed from ridge to ridge. Then, a tight-ranked mass of humanity, they had formed and were sweeping forward again, stepping out to the beat of the ragtime which was their marching hymn. And still the man who stood apart from the rest gave no sign that he was aware of their approach. Once he did straighten; when separate faces began to be distinguishable in that reeling mob he turned and gazed, emptily, toward the group a few yards away—Wickersham putty-skinned before this storm which he had brewed; Allison himself pale; and the girl whose eyes were staring back at him with no clear understanding in their depths. He made no move toward action, not even when the singing pack surged up and spread out before him, until a jostling crescent, straggling at the points, half encircled him and swallowed up as well the little knot behind which had come bristling to its feet. Their onslaught had seemed an irresistible thing, bent upon instant violence; and yet little by little their syncopated defiance died away until they, too, were staring uncertainly at that worn and mud-stained figure which seemed to hang its head. His very inertia robbed them of their impetus.

"Harrigan, that's me!" they faltered now, and there came a lull in the valley at Thirty-Mile, broken only by heavy breathing and the crunch of logs jamming beneath the bridge, and the ugly swirl of backed-up water. It held quiet while Steve looked up, mildly, and scanned the ring in front of him and nodded in recognition to a sullen few; then oaths broke that silence, and a command for room to pass. An upheaval disrupted the crescent's centre. Steve saw Big Louie's face high above the heads of his shorter companions; he watched him plow heavily forward. Shayne he glimpsed, automatically, and Fallon, faithful henchmen. And then Harrigan stood forth.

Long arms dangling, palms back, almost to his knees, that red-headed one minced forward on the balls of his feet. Harrigan was redeeming a promise many weeks overdue. It was spring, and Harrigan had come back!

"I'm here," he spoke to that bowed head, "if you are afther carin' to welcome me!"

"I've been expecting you, Harrigan."

Again that startling mildness.

There is little wonder that it deceived the riverman. Listening, watching O'Mara's slack form even Fat Joe's face burned; even Archie Wickersham's dared flash in triumph. And Harrigan's went savagely exultant.

"You talked out loud to me, once," he taunted. "Is it so difficult you find it now to speak up so I can hear?"

"Would you promise to listen to argument, Harrigan?"

Vilification tore at the other's lips, until friend and enemy marveled at what Steve took in silence.

"You have begun many things in this counthry," the obscene tirade ended. "You came out of these woods with rags on your back and started at bein' a gentleman when we were only bhoys. You've made a gr-reat success av it with the ladies, we'll gr-rant you that; but you should have stuck to your soft and lily-white pastime. For when you aimed to turn this river into a gentleman's proposition you started something too big for you to finish. I'm taking it off your hands, now. Can't you even talk back like a man?"

There must be fire starting over in the north-east, Steve meditated with an irrelevance strange even to himself—and that reference to her surely was not needed! Yes, there was a smudge of smoke rising behind Twin-face; people should be more careful whore they dropped matches in an unseasonably hot spring like this—and Harrigan's sneer for the boy who had come, wonder-eyed, out of the wilderness and looked upon the picture-thing in kilted velvet which she had been was certainly squandered viciousness now. Past and present they trouped before him, thoughts that spanned years of time and covered leagues of country, yet long before Harrigan had finished with his question Steve knew how he was going to answer it. He didn't have to debate that, and deliberation only gave him the keener joy of anticipation.

All his life opposition had been a familiar of his. Days of hunger he had known and cold, and nights of black discouragement, but never so black until now but what he had been able to hold his vision clear. But that vision was not his any longer to contemplate.

Circumstance had been his handicap; Circumstance he had met and thought to bend to his will; and yet Circumstance had beaten him; in the end Custom was laughing in his face. Beside those intangible antagonists which had been his this personal enemy was only puny, only braggard and swaggering and cheap. But it was a bone and muscle antagonist; it was an entity—a thing upon which one might hurl oneself and spend one's bitter intoleration.

Steve had stopped thinking; he had had too much of thought. Suddenly that question which had been a riddle to him was a riddle no longer. He had the answer, and could see himself as others no doubt had seen him—a fool who had believed in the supremacy of fineness; a boy who had reached for the moon. But it left the issue clearer now. He, too, was a riverman; the degree was different, that was all. And rivermen did not vex their brains with abstract problems; they fought with their hands. His bowed head came back then, and the mass of men, catching sight of the mad, glad light that flared in his eyes, rolled back to give them room. He laughed at Harrigan. He was laughing at himself. They heard and marveled at the pleasantry of his answer.

"Maybe you are right, Harrigan," he said. "You may be—I do not know. I have started big things and left them unfinished. But you are wrong for the rest of it, Harrigan, for I am going—to—finish—you!"

Men tell of that encounter now; it is already epic on the river. One may listen to its details, and he chance into any of a half dozen places:— Mulcahy's, Laduc's, or Whitted's that once was Brown's. And always one will hear different details, but always one accord of verdict. They will tell you that no man ever went through worse vengeance and stayed a living man.

For like a blast of wrath O'Mara lifted and struck him. Harrigan's hands had not left his hips before he met the ground, and he was back on his feet like a bounding ball only to go down again before the smashing impact of those blows. Caution he tried to use in rising and they searched out his face, his chin, and drove him hither and yon. Open fighting was not the river style of fighting and he closed this time and wrapped his gorilla arms about this fury who fought with lightning strokes to keep him off. His greater weight o'erbore them both; he broke away and his hob-nailed boots, lashing out, bit the flesh of O'Mara's temple—they tore the turf where his face had been.

There was madness in Harrigan's hideous roarings of hate, madness in his blind rushes; but his bull-strength availed at first. He weathered destruction and managed to close again. This time the lighter man was ready for the scuff of those armed boots; he twisted and covered his face with his shoulder, and only his shirt ripped open to let blood stream from the rent. On their feet they rocked—to their knees! Faces grinding into the earth they strained and broke away. And always Harrigan came back and found him, blindly. Once his hairy hands searched O'Mara's face and O'Mara's forehead went wet with the agony of fingers tearing at his eye-sockets. Dropping he escaped that gouging grip, coming up he caught Harrigan's chin and turned him over backward.

Harrigan squandered his strength in drunken rushes, his breath in screams of hate. He tore forward when the other had already stepped aside, and Steve, shaking away the blood that was trickling rivulets into his eyes, met him returning. There came a time when Harrigan's enveloping arms found him less readily; came a change when Harrigan had to stand up and fight. And then, with deadly, insensate purpose which made the other's madness a wild and futile thing, Stephen O'Mara set himself to chop his face to pieces. Flail-like blows he side-stepped, and whipped to the other's eyes. That open guard he feinted wider and laid flesh open raw. Harrigan could no longer curse, for his lips were puffy things pulped between his own teeth and those merciless knuckles. He could only sob, great groaning gasps for breath—and then he couldn't see!

And now Steve was laughing aloud. He knew that *she* was watching; knew what loathing was in her eyes. And he—he was a riverman! Sobbing himself for air, dripping crimson from forehead and shoulder, he set himself and swung from the waist. Like a pole-axed ox, Harrigan stopped as he was lurching in. His mouth sagged; his eyes flew wide in a fixed and stupid stare. Then his legs folded under him and he swayed limply down. But that blast of wrath would not let him lie! It raised him and beat him down again; raised him and beat him down. By his throat Steve swung him up—by throat and buckled belt. High over his head he swung that bulk and lashed forward from his heels. And Harrigan went back to his panting followers; twisting and spinning, his body swept Shayne and Fallon to the ground.

Allison had not stirred, nor putty-faced Wickersham, nor the girl who stood with hands at breasts. And now toward them Stephen O'Mara wheeled. His legs would fail him, and he steadied them; blood blinded him, and he wiped it away. Swaying giddily, he managed, somehow, a smile.

"Wickersham, I have met the man whom you hired to fight for you," he called clearly, "and he has earned his wage! Are you man enough to step forward now and fight for yourself?"

Wickersham clucked drily in his throat, and lifted an elbow to shield his face. Shrinking back behind the first shelter that chance afforded him he put the girl between him and his fear. And then weakness seized upon that sick and swaying man, but he spoke to her—to the unspeakable horror in her eyes.

"Barbara," he called thickly, "Barbara!"

He groped toward her, and she cried out, and drew back from such hands as those. Then a black wall rose before him and shut her from his sight. Fat Joe caught him as he fell.

Like huddled sheep, O'Mara's men and Wickersham's watched Joe bear him up the hill. Shayne and Fallon were bending over Harrigan; by the others he lay ignored. It was a mob without a leader until, as is the way in all crises, a new leader arose. Big Louie, stolid face no longer stolid, strode between those two factions and achieved the unknown heights for which his eyes had always hungered.

"I work for no man but is a man," he boomed. "That bridge—she still is hold!"

Steve had bidden Hardwick Elliott watch these men if their big moment ever came. And Elliott and Allison watched now. They were sheep no longer, nor malcontents, nor misled tools of cunning. Like wolves they followed that nameless man who was out upon the jam. Wickersham's men were back on the river, but that bridge would continue to hold! And while they worked, while Elliott and her father watched spellbound, blindly Barbara Allison turned, with no thought of what she was doing, and walked blindly into the brush.

The river was running clear by dusk when they raised the first hue and cry for her. It was dark when a runner bore the news to the cabin on the hillside that she was missing. And when men had been beating the woods for her for twelve hours as best they could in the dark, and no word came that she was found, Fat Joe no longer dared let lie in sleep his friend whose body he had cleansed and bandaged. At daybreak Joe waked him and told him Barbara was lost. They tried to argue with him, for his knees were still unsteady; even Allison whose jovial body seemed to have shrunk during his hours of waiting tried to convince him that the men now looking for her would find her soon or had already found her, perhaps. But he brushed them away while he was dressing; he threw off the hands that tried to detain him. And it was Steve who found her, as he had known it would he, just before a second night of dread was closing in upon her.

In circles of ever increasing radius he traveled at a foxtrot which thoughts of Fallon and Shayne and Harrigan would not let him abandon; but he had to run her down when he caught sight of her, for she fled like a wild thing before him. Floundering in a cedar swamp, soaked to the knees, little blue be-furred suit heavy with black muck, he came up with her. She was kneeling, shaking with terror, face hidden by her loosened hair, when he bent over her and raised her to her feet.

"Please," she whimpered, "Oh, please—"

Yet when he spoke her name her head leaped back and she recognized him instantly.

"I tried to wait," she chattered with all the voice she had left. "I tried to sit still until someone came for me, but I thought I knew the way. I tried not to listen to the noises; I remembered about the stars; and I knew I shouldn't run. But I thought you were—I thought you were—"

Remembered terror choked her. Consciousness slipped away.

By the same trail which once had led him to the "city" of Morrison he carried her now to that cabin which stood on the balsam knoll in the crook of the west branch; nor was it far for she had traveled straight, though in the wrong direction. But it was long after dark when the river gleamed ahead of him through the trees, jet and glassy in the deep pools, streaked with blurred star-reflections in the riffles. A grown woman is a grown man's burden, even though she seem very small to him; and Steve had to travel slowly. His head was spinning from fatigue and the throb of the jagged tear above his temple when the log building, streaked white with clay chinking, loomed up ahead, and yet involuntarily he stopped there a moment with his burden.

He had pictured, many times, a night when he would bring her there, with both of them watching the moon in the rapids and listening to the waves lipping the banks. This was not that night; that night would never be. But the rebellion and bitterness was gone from his heart. After he had removed her wet shoes and stockings and brush-whipped suit and sheer black blouse, and she slept the sleep of exhaustion into which she had slipped from unconsciousness without even opening her eyes, he built a fire and sat before it until morning came. And when it dawned and she waked dazedly while he was preparing breakfast, he had finished reconstructing many things.

Her eyes went from wall to wall, frightened still and questioning at first, so he merely nodded and went outside and left her to remember alone. Returning with wood on his arm he found recollection of much in her gaze. She was looking at the thin heeled, buttoned boots before the fireplace; the stockings and furred garments cleaned of mud and dried on the backs of chairs. A cloud of color stole up from the blanket edge at her throat to the line of her hair.

"You were wet," he explained simply, "and you were too spent to help yourself. I could not let you sleep in them."

"I understand," her answer faltered a little. "I was just thinking.... I knew such things happened, but I thought it was only in books."

Drowsily she watched him bending over frying pan and coffee pot, content herself to lie and rest. But after a time, with fuller awakening, the bandage about his head claimed her attention. To her it seemed impossible that this smoothly shaven man in clean blue shirt could be the same one who had emerged from a struggle still sickeningly brutish to her. Involuntarily she shuddered a little without knowing that he watched.

"I am going to the spring for fresh water," he told her then. "There will be time for you to dress; and breakfast will be ready when I come back."

Submissive before his tone she replied that she was hungry; that she would be ready, too. She had donned blouse and skirt and stocking and shoes and finished braiding her hair when he re-entered. He showed her a tin basin outside filled with icy water for her face and hands. And then they sat down in silence to breakfast.

Once he had dreamed what their first meal together in that room would be like. This morning when she insisted upon pouring the coffee and scorched her hand in the attempt and chided him for careless housekeeping, pain showed in his smile. But she did not immediately understand. She only realized how sombre he was; how thin he looked and tired. Again her eyes went to the bandage around his head. It had a fascination for her, even though it filled her with repulsion for a decision which, she knew now, might have been hers, two days before. But eventually it was to that topic she turned.

"You have been very good to me," she said. "Far better than I was to you—the day before yesterday. I can never hope to thank you enough for coming to help me."

Wistful she had seen him, and grave and sober-eyed, but never sad until now.

"I should have helped you," she went on. "I would have, only I had come expecting … I thought to see—" Two days before when she alighted from her father's car, her heart a tumult in her ears, she could have told him perhaps. She could not tell him now. "I am not used to such things," she finished weakly.

"I know," was all he replied, but the words were final, somehow. They thrust her back, roughly, from any share in his thoughts. They ate again in silence.

"Miriam would have helped," she forgot herself and argued aloud once. "She would not have failed. But—blood sickens me, I think."

"It was neither a pretty nor prepossessing sight," he helped to excuse her, but excuse nor pardon was not what she wanted.

"I told you that you would find out someday," she murmured. "I warned you you would wake suddenly and see how shallow I am."

Until she had finished eating he would not talk. But she had finished now. He faced her with an abruptness that startled her.

"Waking has been no sudden thing with me! I finished with dreams a long time back, but you are what you have been always in my thoughts. It's conditions I've waked to, not you!"

With unwitting gruffness he had sometimes spoken to her, but never with constrained vehemence such as that.

"Why should I find fault in anything you have done, or failed to do?" he demanded of both her and himself. "Why should you be apologetic or regretful. Such a thing as I had to do two days ago has held no place in your world, and never could, but I can't find it in myself to be apologetic, either, because it is a part of mine. I meant to kill him—wanted to kill him—because I was certain of your scorn! That was vindictive; that was foolish for a man. But as for the rest of it—I know I may have it all to do over again, any day. It was a vulgar brawl to you; to me—"

"Not just a brawl," she contradicted quickly, anxious to be understood. "Just—oh, so needlessly brutal. At first it left me only dazed and nauseated, but after I had had time to think, I made myself see your side of it. You must crush insubordination. And still it seems as though there might have been a less horrible way."

"He had balked my work," he told her sternly. "He has fired upon me from cover, when he dared not come out into the open. He has been taking money for his work from a man who was bent on beating me at any cost. Could I ask him please not to spoil my bridge? Is that your idea of a man's way?"

She had given no thought to Wickersham until that moment, and now she thought of him only in connection with a night when she had found him alone in her father's office and wondered at the stale odor of alcohol.

"I do not know," she hesitated. "I am not sure, only—"

"You should know!" But he was less vehement now. Wearily he set himself to get at it in his own fashion. "Some men are only physical cowards," he went on. "But you have almost made a moral coward of me. Yes, you had nearly made me afraid to be the man I must be, if I am to do my work."

"There are other fields—"

He would not let her argue that.

"There is no other field for me at present. This is my work and while I continue in it men who oppose me with their brains I will fight with my brain. But men who force me to meet them with fists I must beat with like weapons. There is no alternative. I have no choice—unless I quit. And that is the reason I know that this is the end, for you and me!"

Sadness she had never known before in his voice, nor the edge which was cutting all it came against. Now it grew gentler, with that gentleness he saved for her alone.

"Once we argued whether I was 'good enough' for you, and we wasted many words that day, for 'good enough' can cover too many qualities to be a safe basis for general comparison. I have been arguing it with myself, blind to the vital question, but I am blind no longer. Combat which sickened you has cleared my eyes. What if I did believe that I was not good enough to touch your little finger? What if you believed that too? Would that have hindered us, in the end? You know it wouldn't; you have seen too many women give themselves to men whom they knew were unworthy in a hundred ways, because they could not help themselves. But that way would never have done for me."

"It isn't that," she cut in desperately. "I know you are big and fine and clean. It isn't that—"

But he knew better than she did what it was she could not phrase. He left her dry of lip now, for he had read her thoughts.

"My ways would have had to be your ways, and we have learned at last what I have feared for long and long. They lie too far apart for them ever to meet. My man's way is not your woman's way, but I could not stay a man in your eyes if I let it become secondary to yours; and I would have to do just that to earn you. Once I thought that there was no height I could not scale to gain your side. I worked for you, but that is no way for a man to work. He must work because he is a man and needs must win as big as he can to keep his own self-respect.

"I promised to teach you to love me, and I've failed. And knowing that my failure is not all my own fault is not going to make it any easier for me. You've taught me loneliness I'm never going to forget as long as I live, but I don't love you any the less for that. I dreamed big dreams for both of us." His voice was dreary of a sudden. "I promised I'd make those dreams come true, because I thought my life could be your life. I've not done so; that thing could never be. I've talked bigger than I could practice, and that is not going to help my self-confidence any, but as it stands now I can earn it back. I couldn't have done that if I had married you, and waked some day to find you shrinking from me. It would have killed it, and my self-respect too, to have learned too late that you believed still in your own greater fineness."

"I tell you it is not that," she cried out. "Can't I make you understand—"

"You have made me understand till I am sure," he stated. "I am no longer vexing myself with trivial things. Birth? My name means as much as yours. Education? You would not tell me, would you, that I am not wiser in most ways you'd think to mention. I'd break any man who gave to your ears many things I have learned." He was whimsical for a flash. "I could outspell you without an effort; books have been my partners when you had rather dance. Oh, you could not lose me, no matter where you strayed in fields like that. In any way you care to mention I have outstripped you, for I decided long ago that I must know more than you. Yet I have not forgotten how to play, either.

"You have been uncertain; I have seen that. You are certain now. And the fundamental thing remains unchanged. In me there is that man who once man-handled Harrigan—and you didn't want me to touch you! You don't have to tell me any more that you can't love me. When you drew away from me, that was enough."

His voice held a question, but the girl couldn't answer at first.

"Wasn't it?" he repeated very gently, for he would have it from her own lips.

Her face lifted. Her eyes were blurred with tears, but she nodded in affirmation.

So roughly that the dishes rattled he rose.

"I do not want your pity," he ended it. "I am the wrong sort of a man for you."

She sat and watched him put the room in order, and that hurt her more than anything else, for he would not let her help. He made her change her high-heeled boots for moccasins which he brought and laced upon her feet; but the remainder of the day it was the old Steve who helped her over the bad bits of going and talked disconnectedly of many things meanwhile. And yet no longer the old Steve, who had been so entirely her own. Hers was the sad face when they entered the clearing at Thirty-Mile and a hoarse shout saluted her return. In her father's embrace she clung and wondered that she did not cry. And two pages had turned for her that day, for she sent Wickersham back his ring the same night the private car rolled down to Morrison.

Harrigan was with Archibald Wickersham when the package, unaccompanied by explanation, reached the latter in his hotel room in town. Harrigan was waiting for a reply to a question which he had just asked, when Wickersham opened the box and sat fingering for a while the thin hoop of gold with its single brilliant stone. Once Fat Joe had spoken prophetically; this was the hour he had foreseen. And when Wickersham raised his head the riverman's battered face lighted shockingly with triumph.

"Go out and get him," said Wickersham. "And see that you get him—for good!"

CHAPTER XXIII
TO-MORROW&MDASH

For two days and two nights the girl fought on alone against the outcry of her own heart, and as on a former occasion she chose again the open roads for her battlefield. While she pounded Ragtime mercilessly over the little-traveled northern highways, she struggled rebelliously with stubborn arguments which only left her more and more bewildered, the more conclusive they became. She summoned parallels by the score to her support, but she lacked the trick of facile finality, somehow, which had always marked his usage of such argument. Hard moments she knew when she closed her teeth tight upon her decision and told herself that it was final, but the next moment, after she had laid whip across the black horse's flank and faced homeward, she was biting her lips in shaken, panic contemplation of another thought which would not be denied.

There were times without number when Barbara hated the one whose very gentleness toward her was making her position hardest to maintain; times when she hated the work which, absorbing him by day at least, must be making his suffering less difficult to endure. For she understood that there was still much for him to do, although the hill-country was already ringing with his victory. And throughout every hour she hated herself most of all for that spirit behind the doubt which was swinging her, pendulum-like, between brain's reason and heart's desire.

Barbara needed her mother in those days of wretchedness, for she came and went as blind to the helpless misery which followed her always from the eyes of her father as she was heedless of who might read the misery in her own. She turned a chill, set face to the one attempt to help made by Miriam Burrell, who, at the first inkling of violence on the river and possible danger to Garry Devereau, had come rushing overnight into the hills, purposed never to leave them again unless it was with him, as the wife of the man she loved. Barbara wanted her mother, and when that occurred to Miss Sarah, the latter could no longer continue in passive sympathy. Without compunction or loss of more time, she reversed a decision at which she had arrived herself only a short time before. For Miss Sarah had stopped campaigning. Caleb, with fire in his eye, had brought her the story of how "her boy" Steve had broken Harrigan with his bare hands. She had had little to say concerning that episode, but her brother, noting that she did not condemn it as regrettable, wondered too that he had never noticed before how hard his sister's eyes could be. The news that Barbara was lost had reached Miss Sarah hours before Allison's private car brought the girl and her father and Hardwick Elliott back to Morrison. Thereupon, with her first glimpse of Barbara's wanly mute and suffering face, she had pieced the details together; she had told herself, with sorrow and understanding in her heart, that she must no longer interfere. And now, though she did summon Barbara to her, the end of the second endless day, it was with no thought for evasion or finesse. Barbara obeyed that summons reluctantly. In the face of an almost sullen light in the girl's eyes when she entered on lagging feet, the older woman knew that she could not have persisted in such an attempt, even had she planned to employ it. Additional warning was not needed, but Barbara's first words told her that the hour was long past for such methods.

At first the girl refused to sit down. She wandered aimlessly around the room, switching nervously at her booted ankles with her riding-crop, to stop suddenly and raise a pale and stormy face.

"I know why you sent for me," she exclaimed, "and I know just what you think of me. But I must tell you, Miss Sarah, that there is nothing which can alter now, the least little bit, a decision which I know is wisest and best!"

So she had the first word, never dreaming that Miss Sarah had seen to that. Nor did the latter smile or seem to proffer argument at first. Oh, Miss Sarah had the true instincts of a big soul!

"Barbara," she answered quietly, after her formal firmness had prevailed and the girl had seated herself, "Barbara, when I sent for you it was not with a belief that I might influence you, for both of us know that this is your problem alone. I merely hoped to comfort, that was all. More than once I have been guilty of trying to manage you a little, but you will forgive me, I know, when I tell you that I have loved Stephen almost all his life, as though he were my own, and hoped as long for his great happiness. On more than one occasion I contrived situations which I thought might make your choice my happiness, too. I know now that I was no better than any other meddling old woman, whose efforts are well meant but dangerous for all that. And I will meddle no more. But—but my heart aches a little, too, to-day, Barbara. May I just talk to you?"

Barbara blinked in surprise at the subdued sadness in the older woman's voice. But her lips remained sullen.

"There is nothing more to be said," she reiterated uncompromisingly. "I tell you I am sure!"

And from that statement, minutes before she had thought to hear it, Miss Sarah learned, thankfully, just how deep was the girl's uncertainty.

"Then I need not fear that I may sway you one inch from your own way of reasoning." Her gentle voice might have held relief. "For you will not consider it argument when I agree with you that hard and fast reasoning is not always a dependable guide for a woman."

The girl was switching her ankles again.

"Why isn't it?" she demanded abruptly, hungry for it now that the other, ostensibly, did not want to argue. "If reason is no guide, what else is there left?"

"My dear, I do not know," acknowledged Miss Sarah. "Intuition is a much over-worked word. And yet, had hard and fast reason been your guide, you would not have refused Stephen, I am sure. For it would be difficult to name one particular in which he is not entirely a man."

The violet eyes grew quickly hostile. The girl was keen enough to argue, but she was in no mood for refutation.

"I am afraid that I do not follow you?" came coldly from her.

"There comes a day in every woman's life, of course," Miss Sarah ignored sweetly the interruption, "when she has to leave girlhood behind. And lest that sound bromidic and trite, I will add that I do not mean the trivial material things of immaturity, but rather the happy irresponsibility which has no place in a woman's life."

That statement offered a plain enough opening.

"Am I responsible for his unhappiness?" Barbara flashed out. "Is the fault entirely mine because—" She faltered, ashamed of her abruptness which had brought a hurt bit of color to Miss Sarah's cheeks. "I never gave him to understand—I told him always I could not care!"

"Please bear with me a little to-day." Miss Sarah's sweetness had become humble. "I seem vagarious, I know. And we are not considering Stephen, Barbara. If you had been doing so, all these hours while you have been wasting your nervous energy in tearing around the country-side, it would be different. But women never consider the man in such a situation, do they? Aren't they too entirely heedless for that? I was merely trying to tell you that the day has come when you must consider well your own happiness."

Instantly Barbara condemned such a doctrine.

"If that is true of others," she retorted, "they are even more despicable than I know myself to be."

Until that moment Caleb Hunter's tiny sister had kept her brave eyes clear. They clouded now. They went beyond that pale and sullen and stormily pretty visage.

"I was a woman like that," she said, with her quaint simplicity of accent. "Do you look upon me with any such degree of scorn? I was face to face with such a decision; and yet not the same either, for mine was far simpler than yours. But I considered neither his happiness nor my own, simply because I lost sight of the years and years to come, in the momentary joy I found in his—his importunity. He was very big and strong and cheerful, like Stephen, Barbara, and I was sure he would not grudge me my last moment of girl-vanity, when I did surrender—to-morrow."

There the quaint voice caught and broke. The girl's eyes flew wider and hotter shame for her sulkiness stained her cheeks. For suddenly Miss Sarah was fighting against tears.

"I did not know," Barbara breathed her contrition. "I never dreamed—"

"No one ever does," faltered Miss Sarah. "I—I am an old, faded, hopelessly unmarried woman to you, my dear—oh, child, you need not protest a kinder opinion! I am just 'Caleb Hunter's spinster sister' to the people of this village. But to—to myself, Barbara, I am at times the same girl who waited, roses in her hair and roses in her cheeks, for him to come, so that I might tell him that I was his, body and soul. And he never came! Oh, my dear, I do not mean to break down like this, for you have your own heart-ache. But I trusted to reason. I told myself that to-morrow would be soon enough. And when to-morrow came—they let me—go to him. He died very bravely, Barbara, to save the life of another.

"Since you are so sure, I can tell you this without seeming to warn you—without being accused of attempting to influence you. But now you know why I say that every woman, if heedlessness for which she is perhaps not to blame will not let her consider the happiness of the man she loves, should still take care that she does not barter for an hour of quickened pulses the happiness of her whole life. I was innocent enough. It was harmless play to me. But I have paid—and paid—and paid! I would not have you, whom I cherish, rise each morning and wonder why you had to be the only one to suffer out of thousands who played the same way. And now will you please forgive me this uncontrolled moment? I usually inflict them upon no one; I hide them in my room. But, Barbara, I was so proud of him—so sure—so positive that he was the only man in the world! And I lost my chance to tell him how much I cared."

The riding-crop lay neglected on the floor. It had slipped and clattered down while Barbara sat and stared at the tiny woman who was dabbing at her eyes with a very girlish square of linen. And then slowly Barbara rose and took an uncertain step or two. She sank to her knees and pillowed her head upon Miss Sarah's lap. Momentarily she had forgotten the struggle which was going on in her own heart. Now even pity for the other could not keep her from turning hack to it.

"But I do not know," she gasped. "I—sometimes I think I must care, and then I am afraid—" She lifted a face dry-eyed and tense. "I ought to be proud of him, too. If I loved him I would be, wouldn't I? If I cared I wouldn't ask anything more than just what he is. Don't you see I'm only petty and rotten with snobbishness?"

Miss Sarah sniffed, ever so delicately.

"What a sentimental old woman I am!" she exclaimed. "And, my dear, you talk as though you had just discovered a new and terribly perplexing complication. Don't you know that it is as old as the feminine mind itself?" Her handkerchief came down, then, disclosing eyes that were very bright and very tender. "Why, a woman never loves a man merely for what he is! She always reserves a few little things, at least, which she means—well, to rearrange. She loves him just a bit more for what she secretly promises herself he shall be."

Barbara's sullenness was gone.

"I know," she whispered. "I thought of that, too, long ago. But it isn't just a—little thing. A few days ago, Miss Sarah, when we took the train to go up north, I could scarcely wait for the engine to draw us there. I think I counted every click of the rails, I know I sang his name in my heart with every click. And then, when I wanted to walk straight off the steps of the car into his arms—when I ... Why do you sit there and listen and not say that you loathe me as I do myself? I know that he is all man, but his work and my world—oh, when that terrible thing happened, and he came lurching toward me, instead of helping him, do you know what I did? I was sick at the sight of him—sick at the reck and grime and blood of him! I just wanted to get away, and—and shudder at the thought of—"

Miss Sarah's composure had returned, but her face grew more sober still. This was a different, a graver thing, even than she had expected.

"Your world?" Deliberately now she dared to argue. "Barbara, didn't you know, from the beginning, that his world would have to be yours? Did you ever think that you could change him—that way?"

Barbara moved her head.

"I wanted both," she said. "I wanted all I have—and him, too. I learned that night he took care of me how much I cared; I know he'd be as careful of me, all his life. But I had thought that he might be able to do as father has done and let other men handle the— But he knows now! He understands me! I tell you I'm no good. I've no backbone. I'm just pink and white flesh without any spirit!"

The other woman sat and smoothed the bright head and wished she knew what to say. "It would please me to know just what stuff she is made of, too," Miss Sarah had once admitted to her brother. She wondered if at last she knew.

"I do not know what to tell you," she murmured slowly. "I thought if I talked with you I might be able to help you, but I am afraid now that I cannot. He is a better man than you are woman, Barbara; because he has builded with his hands, he has reared him a soul as well. He knows the depths, and the heights are far more wonderful for such knowledge. Oh, dear me, I wish I knew—"

She paused there, shaken by her own impotence. Doubt and aching regret were overwhelming her.

"I have told Mr. Wickersham that I will not marry him." The brown head burrowed lower and muffled the words. "I know that I could let no other man so—so much as touch me now. Is that—caring enough?"

But Miss Sarah only half heard the question. She was expecting no surrender now.

"—Nor how to advise you," she struggled on. "For you have lived as all girls like you live. You've lived for yourself; hoped for yourself; prayed for yourself—as all women pray, I suppose, directly or indirectly. And yet is merely a question of whether you could live with him in his world, day for day and night for night? Is it as simple as that? I have told you what difference one day made with me. Have you thought what it might mean to wake and realize that you must live *without* him, all the rest of your life?"

Miss Sarah had stopped hoping. And so there was sheer amazement in the triumph which rose and drove the regret from her faded pink-and-white face when the girl's dark-fringed eyes lifted.

Since Stephen O'Mara had brought her back to her father, Barbara had wondered why she did not cry. Great tears were sliding noiselessly down her cheeks when she raised her head.

"I've tried to think—I haven't dared," Barbara sobbed. "But he doesn't want me now. He doesn't want the kind of a girl I am any more!"

Thus in her moment of capitulation did the girl's heart cry aloud the one thought which, unknown to her, had been her unbearable pain. And straightway Miss Sarah's illuminated countenance became a glorification of her spirit. Silently she leaned over and folded the kneeling one round.

Later she found it possible to speak.

"You have convinced me forever of the futility of all snap judgments," said she, and she marveled at the shyness in her own voice, "but you could never convince me of that. You may go home now, Barbara, for you have worn yourself out. But to-morrow I would suggest that you—ask him for corroboration, if you still hold to such an opinion."

Instantly Barbara rose and bobbed her head. She had always been a slim creature of moods mercurial; she would always be that. And now her violet eyes radiated anticipation, perverse and impish and far, far different from the sullen dullness which had filled them an hour before. Miss Sarah had spoken with well-seasoned wisdom, as was her wont: there are sometimes big moments which are the bigger for lack of analysis. The girl did not know why, all in one breath, she no longer feared nor doubted—but she *knew*! And that was a world and all of joy. She bobbed her head.

"Ask him?" she echoed, demurely confused. "Ask—*him*! To-morrow I am going to dare him to ask *me*—again!"

But she did not obey Miss Sarah's suggestion that she return home and rest. On winged feet she flew back through the hedge-gap and ordered Ragtime saddled once more; yet when she touched that splendid beast with the crop and sent him at a gallop down the drive, there was no longer any sting in the lash. Even the groom, with critical eye, noticed the difference in the girl's seat that afternoon; for days and days to come he was the better contented with the companionship of horses, which was his lot, in dwelling upon the crazy moods of women. And Miriam Burrell, sighting Barbara's face as the latter wheeled toward the hills, flew from her window to scratch off a note to Garry—her third note that day, for she seemed always omitting most important things which needed saying.

"It's come," she scrawled in delighted haste, "and Miss Sarah is a visiting angel from Heaven!… When are we going to be married?"

Others knew of it almost as soon as she did herself, but knowledge of that did not mar Barbara's rosy contemplation of this new-found, totally unbelievable happiness. Once before she had ridden that road with him alone in her thoughts; now she realized that she had loved him then as she must have loved him always, and marveled at such blindness. Once, on that other day, she had told herself that all ignoble and unworthy comparisons of herself and him were done and gone. Now she did not need such reassurance, when her lips were tremulous.

Rest? Pressing steadily into the north that afternoon, first at a gallop, then more and more slowly until Ragtime was picking his own gait, the girl smiled in pity for Miss Sarah and her day which had never dawned. But there was scant room for sadness in her present mood. Tomorrow? She let herself be afraid for an instant, to tremble in delicious mock-terror, because there was nothing for her to fear now in the whole wide world.

She grew pensive at times; at times in an abandon of gaiety she chattered back at a quarrelsome squirrel in the thicket. She could rest later; and if she could not go to him immediately, at least every step the horse took was bringing them, for a little while, closer together. And her to-morrow was only one twilight and one dawn away; her to-morrow would be his, as utterly as was she herself. Dusk came, and regretfully she told herself that she must be turning back home. Two rifle shots, sharp and startlingly close, whipped through the quiet of that lazy afternoon, but they meant nothing to her. She had reached the height of land, where he had found her the day her roan mare strayed off while she sat mooning on a log; she was holding out both arms toward the spot where the valley of Thirty-Mile must lie, when a team of heavy horses broke around a turn in the road, slowed to a trot at the sight of her, and came to an abrupt standstill. When the girl rode nearer to them, merely surprised and curious at first, they snorted and showed the whites of their eyes and shied back nervously.

Something chill clutched at Barbara's heart while she spoke preemptorily to Ragtime, who was dancing in sympathetic panic. There was nothing to tell her, but she knew that these were Big Louie's horses. And Big Louie was a dreamy incompetent—he had left them for a moment, that was all, and they had become frightened and bolted. But Big Louie never neglected his team ... they were not wet ... they had not been running far. And their fright became less when she dismounted and approached them, soothing them with her voice until they let her touch their sleek sides, without rearing away.

Dusk had come and gone, for it was growing dark. Uncertain, more and more unnerved as she stood and gazed at the forbidding, black-shadowed ridges beyond her, the girl had to fight suddenly against an impulse to turn and race back to the lower country and Morrison and home. Even then the rifle shots meant nothing to her—and pride would not let her run. She remounted and rode on a rod or two, and stopped to look back at the team which was watching her; she pressed on and rounded the curve. Ragtime reared and snorted there, and she barely stifled the cry which his strange behavior brought to her lips. Because of her senseless panic she punished him the more severely, and sent him on. And then she saw what the horse had already seen.

A blue-shirted figure lay half in the road, half in the undergrowth that fringed it, one arm crooked under him and his face prone in the dust; a bulkier mass was stretched wholly within the trail—and she recognized him, too. Big Louie's face was upturned, and the explanation of the two rifle reports and the driverless team was here. For Big Louie's hand still clutched the handle of a canvas pail. They had stopped to water the horses; they had been shot down from behind. And first of all, unable to move, while horror parched her lips, the girl remembered words which the limp one, half in the road and half in the underbrush, had spoken to her in a moment of sternness.

"He has fired upon me from cover," the man who loved her had said. "He has been taking money from a man who was bent on beating me at any price!"

Giddiness rose and swayed her, and she beat Ragtime mercilessly for his fear. Instinct clamored flight, and she forced herself to wait, panting for that other shot which might leave her, too, lying in the road. But even in that first frozen moment she began to reason clearly. Back with the sleek team which welcomed her with questioning eyes she left Ragtime, for he would stand there, and retraced her way on foot. She could not do it, she sobbed drily—but she raced to him and knelt and searched with swift fingers before the words were past her lips. Her hand found moisture beneath his right shoulder; it was stained red when she held it up and stared at it. And then she was closest to fainting.

"Blood sickens me!" she whimpered aloud. "Blood sickens me!" But she managed to turn him over upon his back. With brown head against his heart, she listened—listened and would not believe that her to-morrow might come too late. And then she caught the slack pound of his pulse.

From there on she was less panic-stricken; she gained control of faculties shocked for a time into uselessness. Method marked her acts—deliberation mechanical but sure. She was horribly afraid of Big Louie, but she finally disentangled the handle of the pail from those loose fingers, and ran to the brook which babbled near at hand. Returning, she drenched Steve's face with icy water; she lifted his head and propped it, as comfortably as she might, upon one thigh, and opened his flannel shirt. The ball had passed through, for back and front the shirt became immediately wetter with fresh blood. Blood sickened her, but she whipped off the coat of her boyish riding-habit and wrenched the sleeves from her linen blouse. They were desperately scant, yet they provided pads with which to check that dreadful oozing. And when they were in place she turned again to bathing his forehead.

A folded sheet of paper came to view when she tried once to ease his heavy body from the position which was numbing her leg, and she seized upon it fiercely. It was only a brief line, bidding him come to her, but it bore her name. With instant, bodiless clarity which had marked all her mental processes so far, its purport was hers. She had not written—the hand that had traced her signature had been unstrung for once. She understood, though such knowledge seemed of little moment now.

She kept the pads cold and wet; she went for fresh water and stumbled and fell more than once, because of the treacherous footing in the deepening shadows. But she was no longer afraid of the dark; she had grown to fear Big Louie less, even though there was no help for Big Louie any more. It was the first time that Barbara had looked upon the face of a man who had died in violence. Big Louie's face was growing indistinct now, but she knew that he was smiling—knew that his eyes were dreamy and mild. Death, like Life, had been a quite incomprehensible puzzle to that slow-witted one who had no name. But he had smiled seldom in life. In death his smile was almost childish, almost sweet, and questioning beyond all else.

Alone with him who still lived, the pallid girl sat and waited and wondered how long—or how soon—it would be. But she wasn't afraid now. They were his hills; it was his wilderness. And could any harm come out of them equal to separation from him? This was only the beginning of one night of darkness, and Miss Sarah had endured with patience and bravery through a whole lifetime of days and nights as black. "Your face was the first ... it will be the last thing I'll see, as long as there is sight in my eyes!" had been his words to her. She waited and she prayed shamelessly for herself—for one more chance—as Miss Sarah had said women always prayed. But he was looking at her, when she opened her eyes after a long and incoherent appeal; at her first word he tried to rise and she had trouble in persuading him to lie back again. She heard herself scolding, while she rearranged the bandages so that they would cover both wounds, and he listened, hot-eyed, without recognizing her. Yet when she bade him wait, until she could bring the team, he nodded his comprehension; he was watching for her return. And he came to his feet with a readiness that made her heart leap with hope; but he fell twice before she lifted him, half with her hands, half with her voice, to the seat.

She crawled in beside him, and the next moment she had to struggle madly to prevent his returning to Big Louie.

"He will wait quiet until we come for him," she protested. "There isn't room for Big Louie—and he won't mind—"

Her logic made an impression upon him, for he smiled. There was no sequence in his acquiescence, however.

"I have always been afraid for him," he told her in reply, as studiously grave as though he had been conscious of what he was saying. "The others—they can take care of themselves. They are wrong ones together. But Big Louie is only a child—but he won't mind—he'll understand—"

She thought then that he had recognized her; she dared to hope that his brain was clearing. But when the team went forward, nervously unmanageable at first, then more decorous as they drew away from him who would never feed them brown sugar again, the man beside her only persisted vacantly with his topic.

"Big Louie never could find his way alone," he mused, "and that is strange, too, for he was born in these hills. He was always getting lost—" And with that he must not desert Louie! She had even more trouble with him this time. "He will lose his head," he expostulated mildly—his old, unfailing attitude of gentleness toward her. "He will lose his head and waste his strength in running from things which do not exist."

"Big Louie will find his way this time." She was whimpering again in her helplessness. "He is—already home."

There she learned that her voice could control him when her arms availed not at all against even his dead weight. And so she talked as steadily as she was able while she drove. Once he lurched against her; when he pulled himself together he was so sanely apologetic of a sudden that she searched his face with hungry eyes. But he was talking now to himself.

"I must not touch her!" he stated firmly. And then, drearily: "I am sick.... I have never been so sick—before."

With that he subsided, but his silence was far more dreadful than his wanderings had been; and as fast as she dared she pushed the heavy team on, with Ragtime following behind like a dog. He slipped back against her almost immediately, and this time he had not the strength with which to apologize nor lift himself erect. With his head heavy in the hollow of her arm, they came at length to the open pasture hills; they topped the rise and faced the loops on loops of highway that ran down to Morrison at the river-edge. And so she brought him home. At the sight of his "city" she sobbed aloud, but he, sunken and slack, was conscious neither of distance covered nor change of country. He climbed down from the seat, however, in response to her urgings, when the team halted before Caleb Hunter's white-columned house—he turned and started stubbornly back the way they had come.

She ran after him and clung to his arm.

"You promised that you would come back to me," she cried up at him. "Oh, you cannot leave me now!"

That halted him, momentarily.

"I must go back to my bridge," he explained, plainly nonplussed. "But then I'll surely come back to you."

She pleaded with him—raged at him.

"I must go back to my bridge," he reiterated gruffly now.

Her arms went around him in desperation, and then, with one swing, he had swept her yards away, reeling before his blazing wrath.

"Take your fingers from my eyes, Harrigan," he gasped in sudden agony. "I am going to kill you now—and *she* is looking on!"

The girl was afraid of him; she dared not try to hold him. She screamed wildly for help, and screamed again. And he had gone on, and wavered and crashed over upon his face, when Caleb Hunter and her father came running heavily across the lawn in answer to her shrieks.

Between them they lifted him and carried him into the house.

CHAPTER XXIV
AND TO-MORROW, AND TO-MORROW

They carried him into the house and bore him upstairs, and laid him, quiet now and almost pulseless, upon the bed. They stood there, dumfounded, at the bedside, until Miss Sarah, re-entering the room, coolly ordered them from underfoot and sent them back downstairs. And at that their unprotesting obedience was of greater assistance than their hands could have been; but when, after one glance at the girl's stricken face, she tried the next instant to dismiss Barbara, for once Miss Sarah's will alone proved insufficient. The girl refused, point-blank, to go.

"He half undressed me and put me to bed," Barbara flung back in reply to the spinster's final objection, "and if that did not shock you, surely my staying now need not!"

The refusal itself brought a glint to the older woman's eyes and the phrasing thereof a flush to her cheeks, but she wasted no more words in what she knew to be useless argument. And though the girl grew sick and sicker still while Miss Sarah cut away the sodden shirt and started, with competent skill, to cleanse the wound, the latter let her remain and hold a basin of antiseptic and replenish it when necessary.

Miss Sarah knew what to do; and she worked with unhurried thoroughness. They had sent for the doctor, and after ages had passed for the girl, maddeningly cool and unruffled, he arrived. But his first words, too, were an order that she leave the room, and unable to combat his professional bleakness, meekly she had to obey. Little and wholly hopeless she stole downstairs.

Caleb and her father were confronting each other before the fireplace when she reached the lower floor, but the queer note of restraint in their voices meant nothing to her, until she heard her father cry out in sudden anguish.

"Cal," he cried, "Cal, you don't think I was a party to this attempt at murder?"

Then, at Caleb's reply, which went hurtling back at him, the girl was crouching, white and still, and clutching at the stair-rail.

"Party! Attempt! Because you did not pull the trigger are you any the less guilty?"

"Do you believe that I would murder the man my girl loves?" Dexter Allison moaned now.

Barbara gasped at the deadly anger which crossed Caleb Hunter's face. Caleb had lifted a hand in righteous accusation.

"You have dealt in crookedness," he thundered. "You have thrived on cunning. And, being a law unto yourself in this country, you have gone unpunished until now. You aided and abetted a vicious and unscrupulous scoundrel in his villainy; and now you have looked upon the result of your works. Law has never touched you, sir—reprisal has passed you by. But, by God, sir, I warn you if that boy dies—if he dies—I shall see that you meet me at thirty paces the next morning. And I shall not miss—I shall be your law!"

They had been friends for close to forty years, yet they were worse than strangers now. Dexter Allison could not answer; he could not speak aloud. Caleb's finger had swung toward the door in a gesture unmistakable. Allison turned, and, ghastly of face, met the eyes of his daughter.

"Barbara," he appealed to her, frantically. "Baby—"

But she shrank, a huddled heap of misery, away from him.

"You—too?" she whispered. "You!" And then, dully: "And you're my father!"

The shoulders beneath the garish plaid rose and fell, pitifully. This, then, was the moment which he feared. He gulped aloud and hung his head, and turned his feet toward home. Barbara rose after he had gone and crept into a chair.

One after another they tried to persuade the girl to rest. Miriam came and talked to her, and Caleb; and even Miss Sarah, passing through the room, stopped to urge her again to go to bed. But she met them all with the same wordless refusal; she was waiting for him when the doctor, descending in the morning, tried to combine, diplomatically, praise for what she had done with disapproval of her obstinacy.

"My dear child, this insubordination will help no one," he said, "and it may end in your collapse at just the moment when you are needed most."

"Will he live?" was all she would say. "Will he live?"

And before such hopelessness the doctor could not lie.

"He is hard hit and very, very weak," he had to admit. "The shock is great and the tissue damage—unpromising. It is far worse than I expected, but he is still alive, and most men would have been already dead. And his vitality is a marvel, even to me."

He might have comforted her, but with no other statement could he have told the truth. He failed also in his effort to persuade her to go to bed; he had breakfast with Caleb, and she refused to eat. And she was still there in her chair, asking only to be let alone, when Garry Devereau and Fat Joe arrived. She rose and ran to meet the latter, but the doctor who knew how many such situations the pudgy riverman had weathered, summoned him immediately, and Barbara had to wait an hour before Joe came back downstairs. By the lapels of his coat she clung to him then.

"He's mighty sick," reluctantly Joe, too, told the truth.

"The doctor said that it was worse than he expected," she droned. "They sent me away, but if he isn't going to live I won't let them keep me from him!"

Joe's sympathy was unspoiled by professionalism.

"Sick is one thing,"—his confidence was almost convincing,—"and dyin' is another. And— Shucks! I ain't going to let no book-taught medico worry me yet! Men get well because they are bound to get well, or they die because it's their time to die—and he's got too much to live for now!"

Her hopeless face made deception impossible, but Joe comforted her, just the same. He persuaded her to eat with him, and when he found that his conversation made the waiting easier for her, he waxed quite garrulous.

"Why, he's been hurt almost as bad as this, once before," he rambled on, "but he's still alive, ain't he?"

The girl's eyes livened at that.

"Once, down on the island, he mixed in an affair in which most men would not have meddled. And he got it from behind that time, too, only it was with a knife."

"He never told me," murmured the girl.

"It ain't likely he would," the other stated with finality. "It was over a woman, and not a particularly pretty story, any way you look at it."

Her dark eyes widened. She bit her lip. It came to her how little of his life she had shared.

"Oh!" she barely breathed. And again, falteringly: "Oh!"

From that halting monosyllable Joe judged that something was amiss. Observation had never been a slow or painful process of concentration with him.

"He didn't even know who she was. He'd never even seen her before," quickly he put her right. "She was just a public dancer, that was all. But a man—mistreated her—and Steve, he just interfered—"

Indeed, Joe had found the way to comfort her and still tell the truth, even though he found it foolishly difficult to swallow food and watch at the same time the warmth which his words kindled. So for an hour he lingered at table and told her many things concerning the man she loved which she would never have learned from his own lips. And it was Joe's jocularity which in the end subdued her rebel spirit. She yielded at last and promised to go home and rest, but only after he had promised first in a fashion which could leave no doubt in her heart, that he would come for her if things grew worse.

Before she left him that morning she told Joe of Big Louie, whom she had had to leave in the road; but he interrupted her before she could finish. They had already found Big Louie. Then she gave him the note which she had discovered crushed beneath Steve's body. This Joe scanned ferociously; he flashed a strange glance at her from bleached blue eyes.

"Some one traced your name," he put into words the first thought that had been hers. "Some one who had your signature to copy."

She nodded, whitely, in horror. Joe folded the paper and tucked it into a pocket.

"We can touch nobody," he averred regretfully, "unless we catch Harrigan!"

Caleb himself took Barbara home, and on the way across the lawn she giggled suddenly at the funny way in which the distance seemed to increase and then lessen between her eyes and her feet. The ground persisted in rising to meet her, she said, until she had to cling to Caleb's arm. And the outer steps proved difficult to negotiate. But at the sight of her father, sunk in silence Upon his desk in the ground floor "office," she drew her hand from the crook of Caleb's arm and went swiftly across to him.

"Barbara," he beseeched her brokenly, the moment her cheek touched his. "You mustn't believe that I—"

She hushed him with gentle fingers laid upon his lips.

"I have been a very foolish and hysterical child," she said. "I'll try to behave more like a woman now. And you and Uncle Cal have been only—absurd!"

She had to laugh again at the behavior of her feet as she climbed upstairs; but her head seemed steady enough. It was only after she had reached her own room that she complained querrulously of the failing lights. Miriam had to help Cecile undress and put her to bed.

On the floor below, her father had turned again to his desk, his head bowed upon his arms. And total breakdown was imminent for Dexter Allison when a hand touched, awkwardly, his shoulder. He looked up heavily to meet this time the eyes of Caleb Hunter. Caleb stuttered furiously at first, for sentimentality shamed him. Then a happy thought showed the way.

"Dexter, I secured a few sprigs of very superior mint, yesterday," he made of it a ceremonial. "Do you think you would—care to join me, sir?"

They had been friends for close to forty years, not because of common tastes, but in spite of innate dissimilarity. Dexter came to his feet; he reached out and crushed the other man's hand within his soft, white fingers. Nor was his reply quite according to formula.

"I don't mind if I do, Cal," he accepted fervidly, "Thank God ... I don't mind if I do!"

Arm in arm, they recrossed to the white-columned house. And they kept close, each to the other, throughout the hours of suspense that followed, finding a potent though unconfessed reassurance in such companionship.

Delirium came again upon the sick man who lay in the room which Miss Sarah had always kept waiting for him. Fever strode upon him, while the girl who had brought him home slept in complete exhaustion. At times Steve lay quiescent, only muttering fitfully; the next moment he called crisply for Fat Joe—he feared for his bridge—and Joe had to exert every iron muscle to hold him down. And always he spoke Barbara's name, with a poignant gentleness that left Miss Sarah on the verge of collapse. But he continued to live, through that day and the next night, even when the doctor shook his head and Fat Joe rose to go for the girl, as he had promised he would, in the last extremity. He continued to live, and with the coming of the second dawn suddenly he was no longer delirious. Stephen O'Mara opened his eyes and gazed feebly but very understandingly into the eyes of Fat Joe, who was watching at that moment.

Joe tried to hush him, but he would talk a little.

"I know," he pronounced each word with calculated effort. "I have been very sick, and I must not waste my strength. But I have to be clear, first, on one point. Have I dreamed it, Joe, or—or did she bring me home?"

With his voice alone, when all else seemed failing, Joe had kept his friend alive. The doctor believed it; Miss Sarah knew it to be so. And first of all Joe had to voice his thankfulness, for it was an explosive thing.

"Didn't I tell her so?" he demanded in his whining tenor. "Didn't I say so, all along? And I let that doctor worry *me*, just because he's got a diploma in a frame, hanging on his wall!"

Then he answered Steve's question.

"She found you," he said. "She brought you home."

A long time the sick man lay and pondered. And finally he found it possible to smile.

"I have not cared whether I lived or died," he said in little more than a whisper. "All along I have seemed to know how near I was—to going across; and I have been near to quitting—at times. For I was happier than I'd ever dared let myself be, before—and then, with the first shot that dropped Big Louie, I knew—" He shook his head, still smiling vaguely. "I have not wanted to live, but I am looking at things—more like a man now.... You need not worry any longer, Joe. I'll sleep a little while, I think; and then I'll put my mind hard on getting well, when I awake."

That marked the end of delirium, and with sleep which came almost while he was talking, the fever began to abate. He "put his mind on getting well," when he awoke, twelve hours later. Strength was flowing in a steady tide back into his body long before Barbara's knees would again bear her weight. For she had squandered her endurance without counting the cost, and she paid the full penalty. She lay three days and three nights railing at her weakness before she could get up at all; and even then Cecile, her little maid, clucked discreetly at the dark circles beneath her eyes.

Joe was several days absent on that errand which had all but emptied the seething town of men; he returned the same day Barbara was about again, forced to admit that Harrigan and Fallon and Shayne had won clear. And there was nothing left to the disgruntled groups which straggled in behind him, save tall and heated conjecture. Some said that they must have managed to cross the border; others maintained that they had found sanctuary in the lumber-camps of the lake country to the west, but no matter which guess was right the net result stood unchanged. For it is upon the one who runs away that the blame is always laid, and Archibald Wickersham knew fully as well as did Caleb and Allison and Fat Joe that, without Harrigan, they could not hope to touch him. Harrigan had disappeared from the ken of men, and Wickersham delayed only until his departure could no longer be construed as flight. Then one evening modestly he boarded a train.

After she had rested Barbara proved almost humbly amenable to reason; until it was best for her to go to him, she would wait as patiently as she was able. And in the meantime, in a luxury of loneliness, wisely the girl spent her days out of doors, climbing oftenest to that hill-top where they had stood together, in the snow, the night of Miss Sarah's Christmas party. From that point she could see Morrison and the river basin, and even the steam that jetted ever and again from the whistles of the engines clattering over his railroad which lanced into the north.

But no discordant note of haste could reach her ears from so great a distance. That whole vast panorama, suggestive least of all of violence, lay blanketed in a sleepy silence that matched the subdued security of her mood.

Miss Sarah ordered a week of unbroken quiet and rest for her patient; and Steve, and not Barbara, proved the difficult one to manage during that period. For with returning strength there came to him recollection of many things which required his attention. He fretted over his work; he swore humorously at Fat Joe, who, coming to make daily reports as soon as Miss Sarah realized that the good in such visits far exceeded the benefits of sleep and solitude, assured his chief that they had accomplished much, unhampered as they were by carping authority.

But he lay and brooded, no humor in his eye, when he was left alone. Fat Joe had assured him that she had brought him home; but Fat Joe, who was ever averse to anti-climax, had told him no more than that. His efforts at entertainment were only the more spontaneous those days because of the soberness of his friend's face. And then, the same day that Joe raised him against the pillows so that he might watch a string of flat-cars, high piled with logs, roll into the yards, they let her go to him.

Steve was listening to the shrill salute of the whistle which he knew was McLean's paen of victory; he was smiling a little wistfully over the memory which, with McLean, always recurred to him, when he turned and saw her standing on the threshold. She had come on diffident, mouse-like feet. She was watching him. And before he believed it really was she, Barbara faltered his name.

"Steve!"

It was only a wisp of a sound—an aching, throbbing bit of tenderness lighter even than the breath that bore it.

"Steve!" she breathed again.

But thereupon, with a headlong little rush that scattered spools of bandage and rolls of lint, and set the bottles upon his table jingling dangerously, she flew to him and came, somehow, into his arms.

They had not told him—at first he could not speak. Dumbly he sat, his face bowed upon that brown head pillowed in his arms. She had told herself that she was a woman now—yet her first words were all girl.

"Tell me just once that I'm pretty," she quavered. "Say that I am still—half boy—to you!"

His tongue unsteadied with joy, he told her again, as he had told her on that other day; and watching the old, old wonder of her grow in his eyes, she listened as though she were taking the words, one by one, from his lips. But there was nothing boyish in the crooked little arch of her mouth—nothing boyish in the depths of her dark and brimming eyes. She remembered his wincing shoulder then; her arms crept higher about his neck. And now her face was uplifted and there was no more need for words.

Afterward, when they spoke of Big Louie, she loved him more for the sorrow which he did not try to hide. From Fat Joe he had already learned of Big Louie's last dereliction. Out of a deeper silence, Steve spoke gravely—an epitaph for the man to whom he had been unfailingly kind.

"Most any kind of a failure can live," he said, "but it takes a man—to smile and die."

He let himself marvel aloud at her littleness.

Their first hour together was only the happier for that moment of sadness they shared.

CHAPTER XXV
IN REAL LIFE TOO

There was no longer any objection raised by Miss Sarah; and Barbara spent every hour of her days with him. It grew warmer with aging spring—and almost immediately he was able to sit with her and watch the stream of logs coming in over the line from Thirty-Mile and beyond.

Miriam and Garry were married in that week which followed directly Steve's first days of convalescence. The former had returned with Garry to the northern valley, and already a note had come from her to the younger girl, in which she bewailed the servant question, as represented by the cook-boy whom her husband had inherited, along with the cabin at headquarters.

Over that particular paragraph Barbara allowed herself to show amusement. She tilted her nose, however, in vast disdain at the tenor of the rest of the letter.

"From the way Miriam raves on and on," she exclaimed, "one would think that Garry had saved the day."

They were at the window together on this occasion, Steve outwardly still a little pale and haggard, but for the rest his old serene self again. He managed not to smile at her small and serious face.

"It certainly has not strengthened my vanity a little bit, either," said he, "to learn how smoothly things can move along without me."

Day by day the girl was finding her way deeper into that innermost heart of him which he had never shared with other woman or man. Hour by hour she was learning to know him better, and yet his whimsical gravity still could deceive her—she was sometimes thoughts behind his thoughts. Hard upon his reply her eyes flashed with indignation.

"Pooh!" she scoffed, "Pooh! Most any old clock will run, after somebody's wound it up!"

It was a trick of speech that she had learned from him, but his employment of parallel, lazily amiable for the most part, had never been so hotly partisan as was hers at that moment. And suddenly self-conscious—suddenly confused and warmly disconcerted at the quality of his gaze—she had to hide her head. But she hid it upon a shoulder most conveniently at hand.

Spring gave way to early summer—and now Steve was able to be on his feet again, so absurdly uncertain of balance at first, however, that she ridiculed him unmercifully one moment, only to rush to him in a panic of solicitude the next. There came long walks, and longer trips in the saddle; came hours of silence that were the more wonderful for want of words—hours in which, in a hushed voice, she gave him shyly of her plans. But always, too, the interruptions grew more and more frequent and insistent. Fat Joe and McLean, and even Hardwick Elliott, made more and more pressing demands upon his time, until finally he insisted that he could no longer play, shamelessly, the invalid. He must look in upon the works up-river, if only for the moral effect which it would have upon the men. She assented, grudgingly; it would be but a day or two. And then—then he would come back to her.

The next morning, at the moment when Barbara and Steve were mounting their horses, for she wanted to ride with him a little way, Dexter Allison chose to disclose something which had been but lately in the process of preparation. He joined them at the edge of the lawn, before the white-columned house on the hill.

"Easing back into harness, I understand," he began, not quite comfortably, however, for he was aware of a gleam of disapproval in his daughter's eyes, at this interruption. "Well, there's no great rush, but it's wise, no doubt, to see that things don't lag." He hesitated, and shifted heavily to the other foot. "We'll want to start through to the border by fall, I suppose?"

"We'll be ready," Steve had to laugh at his lack of ease.

"No doubt—no doubt!" Again Dexter hesitated, momentarily. And then there came to the surface that proneness to accept men for what they were, in a man's world, which had long before convinced Caleb Hunter of Allison's inherent bigness.

"Elliott resigned the Presidency of the East Coast Company last night." The statement was brief to actual crispness. "I merely tell you this so that you can begin to lay tentative plans accordingly. Because, in view of the immediate need of filling that vacancy, I feel sure that there will be too many demands upon your time, here at the Morrison office, for you to plan on much field work for yourself in the future."

To Barbara, at the beginning, the speech seemed merely another of her father's rather involved, entirely labored attempts at the facetious. But when she saw the blood steal up and stain Stephen O'Mara's face, she realized that it was the very sort of a suggestion from which, on her lips, he had turned roughly away. Coming from the lips of her father, Steve accepted gravely, with a matching briefness that could not hide a surge of triumph. A month before Barbara would have been unable to understand why there was any difference, simply because the suggestion came from another. Now, when it could no longer make or mar her happiness, she understood very well indeed.

She rode with him that day until he told her that it was time for her to turn back. With Ragtime standing quiet, she laid her face against his, and complained that he had promised her she should never be allowed to go more than arms' length away from him, once she was his.

"This is the last time," he told her, in a voice vibrant and low. "This is the last time—for you and me."

He held her closer for a moment.

"You will be ready when I come back?"

She bobbed her head.

"Ready—and waiting," she said.

She sat and put up a hand to him, wistfully disconsolate, before he disappeared beyond a twist in the trail.

The next night, in the cabin up-river, after Miriam had left them alone to what she termed their complacent silence, Garry Devereau and Steve sat a long while before the former raised a face alight with his rare mirth.

"Remember Joe's one proposed journey into the realms of romance?" he asked suddenly.

Openly Steve grinned, and nodded.

"Remember how Joe threatened to close the last chapter?"

Steve nodded again.

"Well, here we are!" chuckled Garry. "I, poor but honest, already in the toils of matrimony; and you, a plutocrat in sudden danger of a government investigation, I'm told, and hovering on the brink!"

"Here we are!" echoed Steve.

And that was as close as either of them came to outspoken emotion. With a lightness somewhat self-conscious, Garry had alluded to the property which Caleb Hunter had turned over to Steve. There was a trace of like humor in the latter's reply.

"I certainly am oppressed with the cares of sudden wealth," said he.

They were silent again, and then they heard lifted at a distance a thin and reedy tenor. Joe was still humming his inevitable ballad, when he entered and closed the door behind him, with an alarming flourish.

"Evenin', folks," he saluted, but he did not seek a chair.

Before then they had seen him primed for a sensation; never until that moment had he failed to aggravate their curiosity. He circled the room but once, before he confronted them in a fashion that would have been challenging, had it not been for his fiery face.

"Well, you may as well congratulate me," he invited, "and have done with it. Because the suspense is over for me!"

Both men straightened in their chairs; both understood instantly. But Garry was the quicker in speech.

"Not Cecile?" he inquired, in feigned consternation.

"Why not?" Joe was quickly belligerent.

"Oh, dear!" mourned Garry. "Oh, dear! I wish you had consulted me—or some other married man first. Compatibility and common tastes, you know, Joe, and all that sort of thing. She's a little Parisienne, and you—well, you're only a riverman, like me!"

Joe condescended to draw up a chair. And his verbal condescension was large.

"Sometimes you're fair," he spoke with scornful superiority, "and sometimes you are so amateurish you make me homesick for Steve to come back."

She was waiting for him at the twist in the road. She was ready, two days later, as she had promised to be.

Only her father and Miss Sarah and Caleb were present when they were married. And then, and not alone because she knew he wished it, but because it was the dearest wish of her own heart, they turned their faces towards the cabin on the balsam knoll.

That day was theirs alone to be shared with no other living thing, save the lesser brethren of the wilderness. Noon found them far north of the foothills, deep in the hushed and higher ridges; twilight had come and gone and the first of the stars were already blurred points of light in the riffles, when they raised the river ahead. And there he checked his horse, to point out the cabin, white-streaked with clay chinking against a wall of green—he dismounted and lifted her to the ground, for suddenly she wanted to go the rest of the way on foot.

She let her weight lie against him, the top of her head scarce higher than his chin, and sighed a little.

"Tired?" he asked with that gentleness he saved for her alone.

The bright head shook.

"Happy?" he asked again, as gently.

She swung around and clung to him then.

"I'm so happy!" she whispered. "Do you suppose that anyone will ever be as happy again?"

There was ineffable content in her question. Whimsically her own phrase rose to his lips.

"Maybe," he said, "maybe sometime—in books!"

She lifted her face then. He had the dusky glory of her eyes.

"Maybe," she echoed, her voice tremulous,—"sometime. But this time in real life, too."